by
John B. Montville

A Transportation Series Book By:
AZTEX Corporation—Tucson, AZ

Library of Congress Catalog Card No: 78-18896
ISBN 0-89404-010-3

Designed by John M. Peckham

AZTEX Corporation
Tucson, Arizona 85703

Printed in the United States of America

Dedication

To the memory of the five Mack brothers: John M., Augustus F., William C., Joseph S., and Charles W.; whose determination and teamwork helped to create a famous manufacturing enterprise and a vital American industry.

Foreword

by
Don H. Berkebile

Shortly after 1900, while the Mack brothers were building their first commercial motor vehicle, America's intercity freight moved by rail, and intracity freight was carried on horse-drawn trucks. Automotive technology developed comparatively rapidly during the early years of the century, yet it was not entirely adequate to meet the needs of commercial carriers. Consequently, the faithful horse continued to be the principal mover in urban areas, traveling at a painfully slow pace, while spreading incredible amounts of disease-fostering pollution, a factor that is often overlooked by some of today's ecology-minded citizens.

Commercial houses and industry, blessed during the teens by substantial improvements in truck design and construction, abandoned some of their earlier conservatism and began to employ the now-reliable motor trucks, among them Mack's unforgettable AC Bulldog. The pneumatic tires and improved highways of the post-war years then gave rise to intercity truck shipments, following which the trucking industry enjoyed a relatively steady growth that accellerated rapidly after World War II. Today, over twenty million registered trucks and buses move on America's highways, and the trucking industry employs over ten million persons.

It is now becoming obvious to many Americans what a tremendous part the truck plays in the economy of the nation. Many of us are beginning to feel how our way of life is deeply dependent on the motor carrier, when we realize that nearly everything we use must move by truck for at least part of its journey to the consumer. Strikes and strike threats in the industry during the 1960's helped to remind us of this dependence.

As wagon freighting and railroading once influenced our music and literature, so too does trucking today, as the trucker and his life on the road become romanticized. Increasing numbers of popular songs and country-western tunes testify to the growing public interest in this romance of the road. The historian also turns his thoughts to this heretofore neglected benefactor, as evidenced by the several recent volumes that have begun to record and interpret the history of the trucking industry. The time is opportune for the onset of this task while many of the men who made this history still live. One can hope that each new volume will stimulate another author to add an additional chapter to the record.

Probably no truck-builder is better known to the layman than Mack, for the expression, "built like a Mack truck," has become a common analogy. The familiar French-style hood and the whirring chains of the sturdy Bulldog are remembered by middle-aged Americans, and even most of their children know which truck is being described by the word **Bulldog**. The famous Model AC, which first carried the Bulldog name, is as important to a truck exhibit as is the Model T Ford to an automobile display, or the piano-box buggy to a carriage exhibit, and thus was the first truck to be sought for exhibit in the Smithsonian collections. Still among the leaders of the industry, Mack in recent years has manifested an interest in the preservation of truck history, and has set aside a substantial amount of money for the construction of a truck museum. The acting officials of the proposed museum work in close cooperation with the American Truck Historical Society, each organization complementing the other's contribution to truck history. It would be immensely desirable if such efforts, assisted by the labors of comparable groups, could eventually result in the establishment of a national transportation museum.

John Montville, whose research into truck history dates from the early Forties, could scarcely have made a better choice for his first volume, for the Mack firm is one of the earliest and most significant pioneer truck manufacturers. His chronicle of the firm's growth has been thoughtfully developed, and the reader must be grateful to him for his careful elimination of statements based on hearsay evidence—the mark of a conscientious historian. The first edition of **Mack** was enthusiastically received, and the demand outlasted the supply. Now he offers this second edition, including an additional updating chapter dealing with trends in truck design, Mack's approach to the energy crisis, and its new manufacturing facilities.

Don H. Berkebile
Associate Curator

Division of Transportation
National Museum of History & Technology
Smithsonian Institution
Washington, D.C.

Contents

Preface

by
John B. Montville

This illustrated history of the Mack organization and product line is the outgrowth of a project started in 1971 for a series of books recording the development of trucks and trucking in the United States. The story of the Mack truck was selected due to Mack's pioneering role in the industry, and the almost universal public recognition of the name and Bulldog symbol. As originally intended, this history was to be only a part of a first volume covering the pioneer period of trucking, but with the uncovering of many facts heretofore unpublicized the story grew in size and depth, and a separate volume was decided upon.

It had been the author's intent to present a general survey of both the product line and corporate history of the Mack organization within the context of important external developments which helped to shape their growth. A conscious effort was made to include only those facts which could be verified so as to eliminate dubious information. It was thought that the sin of omission would be less severe than the perpetuating of unsubstantiated stories. The use of original public sources of information was deemed essential in developing the proper chronology of events, and the footnoting of many of these, it is hoped, will encourage others to do additional research on the many aspects of the Mack history.

The descriptions of the various motor vehicle models have been kept as non-technical as possible so as to hold the interest of those readers unfamiliar with the terms used. Where pertinent, the capacity range, horse-power, uses and length of production have been given for each vehicle, with the description of other features being added where they indicated an important improvement in product design. A table of domestic Mack vehicle production has been reproduced in the Appendix. Data for this table has been gathered mostly from production records, but also includes some sales figures. In addition, some prototype units have been listed where this information was made public. This table shows clearly the tremendous growth in truck models since the 1950's.

The reader should keep certain fundamental facts in mind concerning the manufacture of heavy-duty trucks and Mack trucks in particular. There being no annual model changes, new truck models are usually developed over a period of several years and, after thorough testing, produced for about five or more years with only minor changes. It is therefore common for many models to have been produced and demonstrated for several months before being formally announced to the trade. Also, it is possible that some units made for stock could have been sold as much as a year after their manufacture and may have then represented a discontinued model line. For the most part, commercial vehicle models are developed to meet the economic needs of certain specific markets and their success can be judged on their ultimate ability to perform the service for which they were designed.

Changes in the corporate structure of the organization have been detailed with a biographical sketch of each top official involved with the company since its start. With the use of anecdotes many of the interesting events which paced the company's early growth have been related, along with some of the personnel involved. Unfortunately, limitations restricted the story to only the most important events after the World War I period, and I apologize to all those Mack personnel whose names have not been mentioned, but whose contributions were vital to the progress of the organization.

It is the duty and pleasure of every author to indicate the help he has received from certain individuals and institutions, which provided his work with a degree of completeness and accuracy unattainable had he worked alone. These acknowledgements are stated in a general chronological order of association with the work, rather than their relative importance to it; which is really difficult to judge:

Henry Austin Clark, whose dedication to preserving automotive history prompted his saving many thousands of early Mack negatives and photos at the time of the move of the Mack Manufacturing Corporation from its Long Island City, New York facility. His generous offer of the use of this material and his research library was of incalculable help in completing this project.

The late Frank Pampinella, whose service in the Mack organization spanned 53 years; 1902 to 1955. He supplied important information on the first motor vehicles produced by the Mack Brothers in Brooklyn, New York, without which it would have been difficult to present an accurate picture surrounding the building of the first Mack bus.

Elbert A. Hanauer, former Mack engineer, whose personal knowledge of heavy-duty Mack models spans more than thirty years. His expertise in reviewing my later chapters and explaining both important and subtle changes in Mack engineering were of vital importance to the accuracy of this work.

Albert E. Meier, editor of **Motor Coach Age** magazine, publication of the Motor Bus Society, reviewed the text dealing with bus production and provided specific data on both Mack products and the transit industry in general. Information on the early rail cars was provided by the railroad historians, Henry Bender and Carl Skowronski.

Official contact with Mack Trucks, Inc. was made by the publisher only after the research project was nearly finished and most of the text had been written. Chairman of the Board, Zenon C.R. Hansen, gave strong backing to the objectivity of the history and assigned John C. Barry, Mack Engineering Dept., to read the drafts of the story. It has been a great pleasure in dealing with Mr. Barry in reconciling certain points in the story and to share in his great fund of knowledge, which personally spans fifty years of Mack history. He was capably assisted by A.L. Hulsted, who patiently dug out many photos to help illustrate parts of the chapters.

Joseph Mazzenga, manager of the New York City Mack branches; members of his staff, Loretta La Londe, Alf Rix and Joseph Hogan, helped in providing some of the illustrations used in the book.

A number of libraries, both public and private, and historical societies helped in supplying access to a great variety of publications and books, without which there would have been no story. The Research Divisions of the New York Public Library provided trade periodicals of endless variety and microfilm newspaper records which have been my basic source material. Also, the private libraries of Dun and Bradstreet, and **Forbes** magazine made certain publications available, helping to properly complete my last chapters. The Long Island Historical Society and the Lehigh County Historical Society provided early trade directories which have tied down most of the early corporate history in the first chapters. Also, James Waters, of the Kings County Clerk's Office, helped in providing and explaining early property records dealing with the Mack Brothers' early Brooklyn period.

Several former officials and employees of the Mack organization also contributed valuable reminiscences and insights into the early years of the company. Albert C. Fetzer, former Mack vice-president, whose personal knowledge of Mack history dates from 1911, and who is still active with Paterson Mack Distributors, Inc., supplied information on the pre-1920 period. Oscar Lear, former Allentown plant official, whose association with the Mack Brothers dates back to 1909, provided valuable insights into the company's formative years. The motor truck pioneer, John F. Winchester, former Mack and Hewitt engineering associate, and whose connection with the automotive industry dates back to the early 1900's, supplied valuable information on the early operations of the Hewitt Motor Company and International Motor Company.

The son of John M. Mack, Carroll Mack, was quite generous in giving time to discuss his famous father's business associations, and answered many questions which have helped to remove some of the uncertainties from the Mack story.

Several other people have contributed to the production of this history in various ways. Paul Guyer, public relations director of the Adolph Saurer Company, provided information concerning the early Saurer motor vehicles built in Switzerland, as well as pictures illustrating them.

And to all those not mentioned but who provided a small service, or good word to help the story along, a grateful "Thank You."

John B. Montville

October 1973

The House of Mack

After many months of arduous labor in hot and malaria-infested Central America, John M. Mack's arrival in the Port of New York, some time in the year 1890, must have been a pleasant change for him. His employment, upon arrival, with a local Brooklyn carriage and wagon manufacturer, where his younger brother Augustus was already working, would provide the challenges and opportunities he was always seeking. And, in a dozen years, the Mack Brothers, in business for themselves. would be on the road to producing commercial motor vehicles with a reputation for solid construction and dependability.

The Mack family has been traced back several centuries to a French Huguenot family which emigrated to Germany to escape religious persecution.(1) In May 1853, John Jacob Mack, with his wife and six children, landed in Philadelphia after their long ocean and land voyage from the Province of Wurtemberg, Germany. The Mack family had been in the teamster business in Germany, but settled on a farm near Mount Cobb, Lackawanna County, Pennsylvania, where they engaged in farming. It is believed that the advent of the early railroad lines in their native Germany forced the Macks out of the freight hauling business and thus prompted their move to America, the land of opportunity.(2)

One of the sons of John Jacob Mack was John Michael Mack, who was born in 1824 and worked as a teamster in his father's business before coming to America with him in 1853. John Mack took up farming and eventually succeeded to his father's farm where he died in 1880. He also served in the Civil War with the Pennsylvania drafted militia, between September 1864 and the close of the war in 1865.

In February 1855 John Mack was married to Christina Louise Laiblin, a native of Schoendorf, Wurtemberg, Germany. To them were born three daughters and six sons, but they lost one son and one daughter at early ages.(3) The remaining five sons of John Michael Mack were to play varying roles in the founding and early growth of a company which would be instrumental in fostering the start of the commercial motor vehicle industry in America.

The five sons in order of birth between 1859 and 1873 were: William C., Charles W., John M., Joseph S., and Augustus F.

John M. Mack was born near Mount Cobb on October 27, 1864. Quite early in life he displayed the independent spirit and love of challenging new ventures which, combined with his great interest in machinery, would propel him into the ranks of America's honored automotive pioneers.

Jack, as he was nicknamed, ran away from home at 14 and obtained his first job driving a mule cart for a construction gang building the Erie and Wyoming Valley Railroad in northeast Pennsylvania. His interest in machinery did not allow him to be a teamster very long, and in a couple of years he had become a fireman and then engineer of a hoisting engine which conveyed coal to canal barges in the Scranton, Pennsylvania, area. Hearing of a large construction project in the New York City area, where an improvement in the Croton Aqueduct system was being

(1) **Allentown Morning Call**, Aug. 26, 1911, p.10.

(2) **Ibid**.

(3) Charles R. Roberts, **History of Lehigh County Pennsylvania**, Vol. III, (Allentown, Pa., Lehigh Valley Publishing Co., 1914) p.847.

John M. Mack, the man of determination and inventive genius, who is credited with founding the truck manufacturing enterprise which later became Mack Trucks, Inc.; as he looked in the early 1900's.

Figure 1 shows how the upper ring "B" of the fifth wheel had a hinged section which opened to admit the insertion of the inner ring "A" to its seat. Figure 2 shows a vertical section of the installed fifth wheel.

The Fallesen wagon spring patent indicated the early application of torsion bar construction in vehicles. This design was considered especially adapted for wagons whose loads varied to a great degree in weight.

(No Model.)

C. FALLESEN & J. M. JENSEN.
FIFTH WHEEL FOR VEHICLES.
No. 278,786.   Patented June 5, 1883.

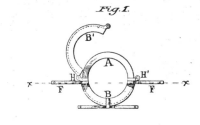

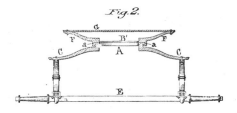

(No Model.)

C. FALLESEN.
WAGON SPRING.
No. 298,456.   Patented May 13, 1884.

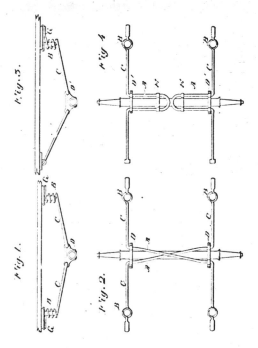

pushed, he left Pennsylvania and obtained a job supervising some of the machinery on the project. After this work was completed Jack became a second engineer on a ship traveling between the States and Central America, and spent at least a year at various jobs in the Caribbean area. It is believed that he worked for a short time on the ill-fated Panama Canal project started by the French in 1879, and contracted malaria which almost brought his career to an untimely conclusion.(4)

(4) **Allentown Morning Call**, Aug. 26, 1911, p.10.

The Christian Fallesen wagon factory

Augustus F. Mack, the youngest of the five Mack brothers, was born on July 14, 1873, in Mount Cobb, Pennsylvania. Gus, as he was commonly called, attended rural schools and a business school in nearby Scranton. After a short job in a Pennsylvania Flour mill he came to New York City in 1889 and obtained a clerical job in the office of Fallesen and Berry, a carriage and wagon manufacturer located near Brooklyn's busy waterfront. It was here that his business acumen and interests in science and invention would come to the fore in the founding of the Mack brothers' first enterprise.

Brooklyn was still a separate city in the year 1890, not being absorbed as a borough into New York City until 1898. Founded as a Dutch settlement about the year 1636, and following a basically open door policy, it grew at a fantastic rate after 1840. The population in 1840 was about 30,000, but grew to nearly 800,000 by 1890, representing mostly foreign born people who had emigrated from North, Central, and Southern Europe. Busy would be the best description for the Brooklyn of 1890, for this huge multilingual community supported a multitude of light manufacturing and mercantile industries, and 13 miles of waterfront provided Brooklyn commerce with a window on the world.

The carriage and wagon firm of Fallesen and Berry dated back to 1853, when it was founded by Christian Fallesen. Born in Denmark in 1825, and being of an extremely industrious nature, Chris Fallesen had opened a local carriage and wheelwright business at 3rd Avenue and 22nd Street in the City of Brooklyn soon after arriving in the United States about 1850. During the early Civil War period Isaac Hand, a Brooklyn carriage maker, whose experience dated back to the 1840's, joined Mr. Fallesen, thus forming the partnership of Hand & Fallesen. This arrangement continued until 1884, when Mr. Hand dropped out and was succeeded by Mr. Immig, until 1887, when we was in turn replaced by Mr. Berry. A description of the business in 1886 will provide some measure of its size and reputation.

Fallesen carriages and wagons were highly esteemed for their strenght, lightness, and durability, which created a steady demand for them from various parts of the United States as well as Cuba, Australia and other foreign countries. Adding to the quality of the product were several patented features, the most important of which was a fifth wheel that was designed so it could be used with or without king bolts. The fifth wheel on a wagon allowed the front axle to pivot when corners were turned, and served a similar purpose as the fifth wheel currently used as a flexible connection between a tractor and semi-trailer.

The factory was located on the northeast corner of Third Avenue and 22nd Street, a block from the Brooklyn waterfront, and was a three story brick structure with basement. The width of the building was 30 feet, which faced on Third Avenue, and the length of 100 feet ran adjacent to 22nd Street. A 75 horsepower steam engine powered the machinery, and steady employment was provided for 32 skilled workmen.(5) It was as stationary steam engineer that Jack Mack successfully sought work at the carriage factory of Fallesen and Berry in 1890.

(5) **Half-Century's Progress of the City of Brooklyn - 1887**, (New York International Publishing Co., 1886) p. 219.

Considering Jack Mack's vast experience in handling various types of steam powered construction equipment, the stationary steam engine powering the woodworking machinery in the carriage factory must have been but a small challenge to him. Also, Jack's predilection for machinery must have brought him to a full mastery of every machine in the building before more than several months had passed. Taking an interest in the actual production and construction of the carriages and wagons was a logical next step for Jack, and before a year or two had passed it must have been obvious that if a partnership situation were not offered, Jack could move on to a better job in another firm.

As it turned out, by 1893, Christian Fallesen was 68 and getting ready to retire. Mr. Berry was evidently only a limited partner involved with running the office and not in a position to take over the operation himself. It therefore was a natural situation for the brothers Jack and Gus to start their own partnership. In the three years that Gus had been with Fallesen and Berry, he had learned the office routine thoroughly and had, studying after hours, also increased his academic knowledge. Gus was now ready to be office manager and perform other functions in the Mack Brothers venture.

A partnership becomes a corporation

It must have been with considerable pride, and possibly some trepidation that the two young Mack brothers, Jack and Gus, took over the Fallesen factory on July 1, 1893. Jack was not quite 29 years old and Gus was just two weeks shy of his 20th birthday. They evidently had planned to capitalize on the previous owners' good will by calling their firm the Fallesen Carriage and Wagon Manufacturing Company,(6) however, severe economic forces restricted their original plans and the Mack Brothers remained basically a partnership up to 1901.

(6) **History and Commerce of Brooklyn, N.Y.**, (New York, A.F. Parson Publishing Co., 1893) p. 296.

In 1893 the United States was in the throes of a financial panic which lead to the depression of 1894. Simply stated, the panic was a liquidity crisis with the payment of debts demanded in gold. With the calling in of loans and great restrictions on credit, many new companies failed, and few new ventures were started during this period. It was reported that the money Jack Mack had made in the carriage business was lost about 1894 due to a bank failure.(7) Although it was not a very favorable time to begin a new business venture, the difficult economic conditions would help to shape the character of their trade and have another interesting ramification for their business ten years later.

(7) Mack Brothers Motor Car Co., **Mack's Messenger**, October 1911, p. 2.

A reorganization was quickly undertaken with another brother being prevailed upon to add his talents to the venture in 1894.(8) William C. Mack was the eldest of the brothers, having been born in 1859. Willie, as he was nicknamed, was well seasoned in the business, having previously conducted a wagon building plant at Scranton, Pennsylvania.(9) With both Jack and Willie preferring to build wagons, the carriage end of the business was gradually phased out. Also, with the business depression through 1894 and into 1895 resulting in a continuing scarcity of orders for new vehicles, the Mack Brothers built up a considerable repair business. They quickly established an enviable reputation for the quality of their work, which included painting, trimming, and general blacksmithing. During this period the building of milk wagons became a staple part of the business, with other types of brewery and contractors wagons also being built later. The multistory carriage factory was not suitable for the Mack wagon building and vehicle repair business; a large one story structure would be more adaptable for their activities.

(8) **Ibid.**

(9) **Ibid.**

In 1897 the Mack Brothers moved their operation to 532-540 Atlantic Avenue, which was near the corner of Third Avenue, and while not adjacent to the waterfront, its location nearer to the heart of the main Brooklyn business area was considered better for their trade. Also, Atlantic Avenue had many businesses located directly on it, or adjacent to it, for many miles of its length to the city line. The avenue was quite wide and the Long Island Rail Road had run steam trains right to its foot at South Ferry, the boat to Manhattan Island, prior to the Civil War period. Because of indignant protests by local property owners to the noise and air pollution, Long Island steam trains were barred from their route to the Manhattan Ferry, and a horsecar line was set up which was run by the Atlantic Avenue Railroad Company of Brooklyn. This company had constructed a car barn and shop facilities at the intersection of Atlantic and Third Avenues, which then became surplus

when electrification came in the early 1890's and larger facilities were built else-

(10) **New York Times**, April 21, 1916, p. 11.

where. The Mack Brothers found a large brick stable and foundry, formerly part of the horse car property, quite suitable for their wagon business and they quickly rented the buildings from Alexander Campbell, the new owner.

The owner of the Mack Brothers plant on Atlantic Avenue was a highly successful businessman in his own right, having started Brooklyn's largest dairy, the Alexander Campbell Milk Company. Mr. Campbell was credited with being a pioneer in the retail dairy business, having started the first creamery for bottled cream in the United States and building up a large retail milk trade from a single route begun in 1862.(10) A lasting association was built up between Mr. Campbell and the Mack Brothers through his purchase of their milk wagons, and later, in 1907, his company was one of the first dairies to adapt the motor truck for the bulk delivery of milk from the railroad to the bottling plant.

By 1898, the year Brooklyn became a borough in a greater New York City, the fame of the Mack product had spread, with many dairies in both Brooklyn and Manhattan ordering milk wagons from the Mack Brothers. With the dairy trade being such a large part of their business, the Macks were in a position to see the problems involved with the delivery of milk products and offer solutions. One problem that Gus Mack helped to solve was the loss of bottled milk in transit due to the breakage of the wooden cases under rough handling. He designed, and patented in the early 1900's, several types of angle iron reinforced milk cases and a rack in which bottles nested in cells constructed of metal with an elastic bearing which contacted the bottles.

With the steady growth of their business, the brothers decided to incorporate and filed a Certificate of Incorporation of the Mack Brothers Company, with the Secretary of State at Albany, on July 26, 1901. The capital of the new corporation was $35,000, with $30,000 of this made up of common stock and $5,000 preferred stock. The three directors at the time of incorporation were: John M. Mack, Augustus F. Mack, and William C. Mack. Each had signified that they would take 75 shares of stock with a par value of $100 a share in the new corporation, but it is not known how much each eventually wound up with. The purpose of the corporation as stated in the certificate was: "the manufacture of carriages, wagons, and harness, and to deal in all carriage, wagon, harness and blacksmith materials and for the purpose of doing a general wheelwright and blacksmith's business." It is interesting to note that although the term **motor vehicles** was not included as part of the purpose, the Macks had already become interested in self-propelled vehicles and would soon be working on a project that would mark them as pioneers in the commercial vehicle industry.

Brooklyn meets the auto age

The concept of self-propelled road locomotion had intrigued many people since the discovery of steam power in the 1700's. By the early 1800's a few efforts had received a moderate degree of success in both the United States and Europe, but the construction of the first railroad lines, starting in the 1830's, over shadowed their further development for many years. By the Civil War period a few inventors had produced several steam propelled vehicles in the cities of New York and Brooklyn. Their size and weight in combination with the cobble-stoned streets over which they had to run tended to cause leaks to develop in their piping and excessive repairs negated their intended utility.

After the production of a fairly reliable compact gasoline engine in the 1880's, renewed interest in perfecting self-propelled vehicles developed rapidly in Europe and America. The new vehicles looked more like buggies or wagons, and now steam had strong competition in gasoline and electric power. A Chicago newspaper-sponsored race in 1895 placed heavy emphasis on the general practicality of the horseless vehicles entered in their 54 mile endurance contest. It was really the publicity following this 1895 event that gave inventors and promoters the courage to push forward with their plans to build motor vehicles for sale to the public.

The New York City area, being an important center of international commerce and domestic industry, was one of the focal points of important developments during the birth of the automotive industry. By the mid-1890's a number of New York and Brooklyn inventors had constructed experimental motor vehicles using various forms of motive power. Gasoline power seemed to hold the most promise for future development as it was a gas-powered Duryea motor wagon which won the Chicago race in 1895. Also, most of the automobiles imported from Europe were gas powered and considered to be ahead of American engineering for many years. In Long Island City, the Steinway Piano people had set up under license the Daimler Manufacturing Company to build gasoline engines for various stationary and marine uses, and by 1901 this firm was producing motor delivery wagons for several New York department stores.

A small French car, the DeDion-Bouton, was assembled in Brooklyn from imported parts, starting about 1900. Also in Brooklyn, the Riker Electric Motor Company had built electric delivery vehicles in 1898 and 1899 for a couple of New York stores, and a small fleet of battery powered cabs were also operating in New York City by this time. However, their slow speed, coupled with the heavy weight of their batteries and low mileage per charge, tended to hold back public enthusiasm for the electric vehicle. Battery powered vehicles found their field in city delivery and intra-plant use where speed and mileage were not important factors in the economy of their operation.

Ironically, the self-propelled steam vehicle at which many had tried their hand, finally became popular only after the sale of the original Stanley Brothers patents to a syndicate in 1899. The syndicate broke into two companies which in turn built lightweight steam cars called the Mobile and Locomobile. The Mobile was built in North Tarrytown, New York, by the publisher of **Cosmopolitan** magazine. The Locomobile steamer, built in Bridgeport, Connecticut, was probably the most popular car of its day, reaching a total production of over 6,000 by November 1901.(11) However, their early success with the steam car did not stop the Locomobile Company from switching, in 1903, to gasoline cars designed by Andrew L. Riker, who had himself switched from electric vehicles in 1902. Heavy steam trucks were experimented with in New York by the Adams Express Company, starting about 1900. Later, the firm had a group of these built in Brooklyn under the direction of their mechanical engineer, Arthur Herschmann.

(11) **Horseless Age**, Vol. 8, No. 33, (Nov. 13, 1901) p. 709.

Public reaction to the increasing presence of the automobile tended to be mixed. Many people objected to the danger of runaway horses which had been frightened by the sight and sounds of the new contraption. Parks were quickly barred to the automobile and then reopened, first to electric vehicles which, because of their silence and lack of smoke, were considered less objectionable. In 1900 the Long Island and Brooklyn Auto Clubs were formed to help protect the interests of local automobile owners; and such groups helped to defeat punitive legislation which was aimed mainly at a minority of auto owners who operated their vehicles at unsafe speeds. By the spring of 1902 autos were allowed to use all public roads in Prospect Park, Brooklyn, the issue being won by the local automobile club.(12) Also by 1902, the importance of automobiles was being more seriously considered because of their use by doctors, lawyers, and other professional people. The aspect of automobile racing, however, still tended to have automobiles assailed as a rich man's hobby, and to back this attitude up, news of interest to automobilists was reported on the sports page of nearly all newspapers.

(12) **Brooklyn Eagle**, May 8, 1902, p.3.

The dawn of the motor age had shone quite brightly on the city of Brooklyn and its portent was not lost on the mechanically minded Jack Mack. Legend has it that the Mack Brothers constructed a steam car in 1894 and an electric one in 1896, neither one of which was very satisfactory.(13) The Macks had a wagon building, general carriage and wagon repair business to operate and it was not likely that they would waste time with a venture once it proved impractical. And the light cars which ran around the vicinity of the Mack shop on Atlantic Avenue, in the late 1890's, had little to recommend them to the builders of heavy wagons.

(13) **Allentown Morning Call**, Aug. 26, 1911, p.10.

(14) Mack Trucks, Inc., **The Mack Bulldog**, First Series, Vol. 4, No. 7, (1925) p.2.

(15) **Horseless Age**, Vol. 8, No. 32, (Nov. 6, 1901) p.686.

The actual inspiration for building a large commercial motor vehicle is reported to have occurred when Jack Mack was invited for a ride in a neighbor's new 2-cylinder Winton automobile.(14) The neighbor was Theodore Heilbron, Captain of William Randolph Hearst's private yacht, who lived at 33 Third Avenue, a block from the Mack shop on Atlantic Avenue. The ride most likely took place in the late fall of 1901, when the new 1902 Winton touring car was introduced.(15)

While rated at only 16-horsepower, the new tourer, with rear entrance tonneau body, was still twice as powerful as its companion one-cylinder runabout model. It had a huge cast iron flywheel attached to an engine having its two cylinders set in a horizontally opposed position parallel with the sides of the chassis frame. To carry the larger touring body and to support the more powerful and heavier mechanism, a new frame design was made up from flat steel and angle iron, neatly riveted together to form a very substantial unit.

The superior performance of the new Winton, together with the invigorating cool air, soon had the two automobilists in an enthusiastic mood. And it was not long before their conversation centered on the future developments of gasoline engines and motor vehicles. Captain Heilbron suggested to Jack Mack that the adaptation of a large gasoline engine to a truck or sightseeing bus would be a great idea.

The Mack bus hits the road

The concept and success of the first Mack gasoline vehicle has often been credited to Gus Mack, who it is believed made the original contact for its sale. While Gus was officially the Secretary of the Mack Brothers Company, handling most of the important office work, he also maintained direct contact with the customers, suggesting solutions to their problems as well as seeking new accounts. He was the one man sales force for the Mack Brothers and promoted the business in every way he could. In 1900 he had a discussion with Isaac Harris, who had recently been granted a concession to run horse drawn sightseeing stages in Prospect Park, on the idea of using large motor vehicles for his service.

It was not likely that the Mack brothers would undertake any new projects unless all agreed to the feasibility of the undertaking. But with Jack Mack, president of the Mack Brothers Company, now inspired by his ride in his friend's Winton, work on the bus chassis was soon started. Gus Mack made drawings of a beautiful touring body with a rear entrance tonneau, which was similar to the more expensive automobile styles then in vogue. And, with Mr. Harris agreeing to purchase the vehicle after a satisfactory trial, it was full speed ahead for the first Mack bus.

Construction of the chassis frame was started first and its general design was quite similar to that of the Winton touring car that Jack had ridden in, but of course on a greater scale. The side rails of the frame were built up from flat steel to which angle irons were riveted along the edges, at the top and bottom, to form an extremely rigid structural unit. The wheels selected were of the wooden artillery type, 36 inches in diameter and shod with 4-inch Turner solid tires. Axles were made of nickel steel for exceptional strength, and long semi-eliptic springs were used for a smoother ride.(16) The chassis was so well constructed that as a truck, it would have had at least a 2,000 pounds capacity.

(16) **Cycle & Automobile Trade Journal**, Vol. 8, No. 7, (Jan. 1, 1904) p.84.

Originally the Macks decided upon using a 4-cylinder opposed engine purchased from an engine manufacturer, but a year or so later this was changed to a 4-cylinder vertical type of their own construction. The original opposed engine was rated at 24 horsepower while the Mack engine used later had 36 horsepower. Also, on the original bus a simple coil-pipe radiator was set just behind the front chassis cross-member, under the leading edge of a sheet metal hood having beveled sides. This arrangement was also changed, for with the larger 4-cylinder vertical engine the radiator was moved ahead of the frame and a hood with rounded sides was designed. The normal speed of the bus was given as 12 miles per hour, but a speed of 20 miles was possible, if desired.

FRONT VIEW OF SAME MACHINE SEEN IN LAST ISSUE.   COMFORT AND STYLE EVERYWHERE.

Headquarters for GOODRICH CLINCHER TIRES.

We have rebuilt many 1902 cars and in every case are giving perfect satisfaction. We design and build all kinds of wheels, bodies, springs and canopy tops. Do all machine work, such as rebore cylinders, put in new pistons, springs, pins, and connecting rods making your engine like new. New gears and sundry repairs. As the time is near when you will lay up your machine why not let us repair and paint it and put it in thorough order? Our business has been established since 1853. Our experience is thorough and our workmen are of the best.

THE MACK BROTHERS COMPANY, 532-540 Atlantic Avenue, BROOKLYN, N. Y.

A 1902 Wintor touring car was featured in a series of advertisements taken out by the Mack Brothers Company to announce their automobile rebuilding service in September 1903.

ONE OF OUR PRODUCTIONS.

The above cut represents our 15 passenger car, built expressly for public and private use. Its construction is the best and is mechanically perfect; is handsome in appearance.

It is equipped with a 24 horse power horizontal motor, four cylinders double opposed, sliding gear transmission, three speeds forward and reverse. Double chain drive, bearings on countershaft, thrust bearings and axles are roller bearing; double band brake on countershaft, and emergency brake direct to rear hubs. Turner Solid Tires and Springs of special design, which make the car ride easy.

This car will ascend a 12 per cent. grade, fully loaded on the high gear with ease; normal speed 12 miles per hour, but can be run 20 miles if desired. Average gasoline consumption, one gallon to every seven miles.

Price $5,500, complete, f. o. b. New York; to order only.

Will design and build cars to carry from 10 to 30 passengers, and guarantee them to do the work.

We do all kinds of machine repairs, rebuild bodies, make canopy tops, wheels, springs, etc.; in fact, everything pertaining to an automobile. Our prices are low, consistent with good work. Correspondence solicited.

THE MACK BROTHERS CO., 532-540 Atlantic Avenue, BROOKLYN, N. Y.

The first successful version of the Mack Brothers sightseeing bus was advertised in November 1903. Note the similarity of riveted frame and front spring horn construction to that of the Winton auto in the first Mack ad.

This highly retouched 1904 view of the second version of the Mack Brothers bus indicates that the radiator was moved forward to allow the larger 4-cylinder vertical engine and a rounded hood was substituted for the bevel sided one.

After several months of planning and building the Mack Brothers were ready to test their still uncompleted motor vehicle, which was lacking a body and some other components. The engine had to be cranked by hand and all the employees gathered to watch the strongest man in the shop try to start it up. After several fast turns of the crank, the engine back-fired, spraining the strongest man's arm. A break for lunch was then called so that the Mack workers could fortify themselves before another encounter with the balky engine was tried. A coin was tossed to see who the lucky engine starter would be, but this time the new man was luckier and the engine started with a roar. However, just as the employees finished congratulating themselves, the flywheel suddenly loosened and, dropping to the floor, dashed out through a hole it tore in the sidewall of the shop.

Following several weeks of work, the finished chassis, still minus a body, was ready for its trial run. Another volunteer was called from the ranks of the Mack workers and he was soon seated behind the wheel ready for action. The engine performed smoothly and the driver was soon on his way out of the Mack shop clinging to the wheel of a monster which seemed to want its own way. After several near misses and an encounter with a steel fence the chassis was driven around the neighborhood on its first shakedown run. It was not long before the cobbled streets had shaken something loose to create further excitement. A gasoline line had worked loose or snapped, causing a fire which soon attracted a crowd and the fire department. The firemen had the fire out in short order, before any real damage had been done, and the chassis was then hauled back to the shop.

Later a beautiful body was constructed from the designs that Gus Mack had submitted to Mr. Harris. The nominal capacity of the tonneau body was 15, considering that only three would sit on the three cross seats in the front part of the body. Actually, these seats were wide enough to hold four people each and the rear tonneau could also seat more than six, so the capacity of this body was also referred to as 18 and 20 passengers.

All the feverish automotive activity at the wagon shop on Atlantic Avenue soon set the stage for new business opportunities and vital people to come to the attention of the Mack Brothers. As word spread through the neighborhood of their invention, the pioneer motorists of the area were soon dropping by their shop and it was not long before the Macks were offering a complete automobile rebuilding service. This, of course, necessitated an enlargement of their machine shop and mechanical department, but by this time Jack Mack had become a licensed stationary engineer, and was also well versed in mechanics and able to train the needed apprentices. One important person attracted to the organization at this time was Frank Mueller, a tool and die maker for the American Tobacco Company, who had constructed his own successful automobile between 1901 and 1902. Jack Mack and Frank Mueller were to become very good friends, with Mr. Mueller remaining with the Mack Brothers for many years as their chief experimental engineer.

The successful operation of the Mack bus in Prospect Park led to a second order in 1903 from the same customer and many inquiries from other potential users. Up to 1903 the sightseeing buses in New York City were, with few exceptions, battery powered. The battery propelled buses, while generally dependable, were quite slow and averaged two or three round trips between recharging of the batteries. Also, they lacked the thrill of riding in a gasoline propelled machine with its higher speed and sounds of life. It followed that other businessmen saw an opportunity in using the Mack-built buses in Manhattan, and for trips to Coney Island and other major attractions.

An advertising campaign was launched, at the end of the summer of 1903, in **Horseless Age** magazine to acquaint the readers with the Mack Brothers automobile rebuilding service. In November the same magazine carried an advertisement showing the first Mack Brothers bus and describing its original chassis components. And in January 1904 the same bus was shown with the title, The Manhattan, and stating that it would be shown at Exhibition Hall, which was attached to the annual Madison Square Garden automobile show. The use of the

name "Manhattan" as the trade name for Mack motor vehicles most likely stemmed from a desire to avoid any misidentification of the firm's new motor vehicle line with their old horse-drawn products. The name Manhattan was familiar to every tourist who visited New York and took a tour of the island that New York County was situated on - Manhattan.

During 1903 a very good growth rate had been recorded by the automobile industry and the 1904 auto show continued to indicate this surge with many exhibitors booking orders for most of their expected production for the year. The Manhattan, which was exhibited for the first time, drew good reviews from the automotive press which alluded to its beautiful body and substantial construction. More sales and a number of important business contacts were made at the show. The Motor Tally-Ho Company was incorporated in New Jersey, in the spring of 1904, and it operated two Manhattan sightseeing buses in the Asbury Park area of that state later in the summer. Other Tally-Ho companies were set up during 1904 and 1905 with the purpose of operating sightseeing buses in such cities as Boston, New Orleans, and Havana, Cuba.

Production methods employed in putting together these early Mack buses were quite simple, but not really adaptable to mass production. The length and width of the proposed frame was marked out on the shop floor, using the accepted horse drawn vehicle standards of the day. After the frame was fabricated it was placed on wooden horses and the motor and other components were blocked up in their relative positions. The pattern maker was then called in to design adequate support brackets.(17) Using these methods of construction, and with the constant experimenting that was taking place, it is not likely that any two of the buses built in the Atlantic Avenue shop were exactly alike. However, the Mack Brothers and their staff were quick to adopt sound automotive principles and no Mack-built motor vehicles ever had friction-drive or other component designs which were tried and found inadequate by other manufacturers.

As the orders for Manhattan motor buses grew during the spring and summer of 1904, it became quite obvious that larger quarters would have to be found for the

(17) Mack Trucks, Inc., **The Mack Bulldog**, First Series, Vol. 4, No. 7, (1925) p.3.

(18) Interview with Frank Pampinella. Sept. 1954.

automotive phase of the business. Jack and Gus had some very definite opinions on the subject of component design, and it was their feeling that their company should design and build their own motors, transmissions, and axles. They had already started to make their own four cylinder vertical engines, late in 1903, and by late 1904 were experimenting with a 90 horsepower six cylinder engine.(18) It must have been obvious to those in the business by 1904, that every advance in automotive design kept taking it further away from the art of the blacksmith and wagon builder.

Another brother, Joseph S. Mack, who had stayed in Pennsylvania, where he had entered the silk business, had learned of the problems facing his other brothers. Joseph suggested to Jack that he come to Allentown, Pennsylvania, and look over a large foundry, which was located not far from his own silk mill, and recently put up for sale. Jack and Joe drove down to Allentown, late in the fall of 1904; the trip, in a small French car owned by Joe, took 14 hours. As Jack liked what he saw, arrangements were soon made with his brother Joe and some other financial backers to incorporate a new company for manufacturing a line of standardized commercial motor vehicles and their component parts.

By late 1904 the buses turned out by the Mack Brothers shop had grown in size. This 20 passenger model, posed in front of the Grand Army Plaza monument at the entrance to Brooklyn's Prospect Park, had top and side curtains for inclement weather.

William C. Mack is shown in the center of this view of the Mack Brother's Atlantic Avenue plant force taken about 1906. Mr. Mack has his hands on the shoulders of the apprentice in front of him, and "Big Ed" Turgeon is standing just to the left.

Getting organized in Pennsylvania

The city of Allentown, Pennsylvania, turned out to be a very fortunate choice for the home of the main manufacturing operations of the new Mack Brothers Motor Car Company. Situated in the extreme easterly part of Pennsylvania, Allentown is about 15 miles from the New Jersey border, and, in 1905, a two hour train trip from New York City. In Pennsylvania, Allentown could be described as being located along the longest side of a triangle whose points were: Philadelphia, 55 miles to the south; Reading, 35 miles to the southwest and the Wilkes-Barre and Scranton area, from 60 to 75 miles to the north. These nearby industrial and commercial centers provided easy access to both the human and material resources, as well as potential markets, that would help to sustain the continued growth of the manufacturing enterprise conceived by the Mack brothers.

Equally important to its general geographic location was Allentown's specific location in the Lehigh Valley area of Pennsylvania. This area was settled during colonial days by farmers who prospered as a result of hard work and the richness of the land, on which a wide variety of crops could be raised. The discovery of coal to the north and northwest, and the coming of the Civil War period, created a period of growth and prosperity for Lehigh Valley industry, which tended to be heavily metallurgical in nature. While the panic of 1873 caused the immediate collapse of Allentown's one-industry economy, metals (1), the way was actually opened for the development of a diversified industrial economy which would compliment the surrounding agricultural community. By 1900, besides a few foundries and machine companies, Allentown had attracted a number of concerns each in the cement, cigar, and textile industries.

Joseph S. Mack, Jack's younger brother, who was born in 1871, had come to Allentown in 1900 to enter the silk business. In 1901, along with a partner, Leo E. Schimpff, he had incorporated the Joseph S. Mack Silk Company, and then taken over the mill of the West End Silk Company. Silk manufacture, at that time, was one of America's growth industries, with a product valued at over $107 million in 1900.(2) While Paterson, New Jersey, had already been called the Silk City, many new silk mills were being opened at this time in the Scranton and Allentown areas.

Not too far from the Joseph S. Mack silk mill were located the buildings of the Weaver-Hirsh Company, in what was then South Allentown, across the Little Lehigh Creek from the City of Allentown. The Weaver-Hirsh Company's plant had consisted of several large foundry and machine shop buildings, totaling 58,000 square feet of floor space, which were in disuse during 1904, due to the company's failure. The buildings occupied both sides of South Tenth Street, part way up the side of the small valley in which the Little Lehigh ran. The large brick buildings, with their high ceilings, were perfect for the manufacture of large vehicles, and after preliminary agreements were worked out, in December 1904, arrangements were quickly made to transfer the work-in-process, part of the skilled work crew, and some machines from the Brooklyn shop.

Incorporation papers for the Mack Brothers Motor Car Company were filed in the Lehigh County Court House on January 2, 1905, and approved at the state capitol, Harrisburg, on February 1, 1905. With an eye to the future the new corporation's stated purpose was given a broad base: "Said corporation is formed for the purpose of manufacturing motors, cars, vehicles, boats, locomotives, automobiles and machine and hardware specialties of every description." The Mack brothers, Jack, Joe, Willie, and Gus, made up four of the

(1) **History of the Allentown-Lehigh County Chamber of Commerce**, (Allentown, Chamber of Commerce, 1972) p.1.

(2) **Brooklyn Eagle**, May 18, 1902, Sec. II, p.14.

eight stockholders listed in the incorporation certificate, having 50 to 100 shares of stock each. Jack Mack was the first president, with Joe Mack as Treasurer, and Leo Schimpff named as secretary of the new organization.

The need for additional working capital was evidenced by the calling of a special board meeting on February 7, 1905, at which time a resolution was unanimously approved to increase the indebtedness of the company from nothing to $100,000. Later in the year, the Allentown National Bank and Shoemaker & Company, bankers, helped to float a first mortgage, 5%, 20 year, bond issue for the Mack Brothers Motor Car Company.(3) In addition to the sale of stocks and bonds to raise capital, it was decided to sell a large brick foundry building, on the west side of 10th Street, which was considered excess at the time. The Traylor Manufacturing and Construction Company purchased this property when they began to set up operations in Allentown, late in 1905.

With Jack Mack's attention devoted to the manufacturing operations at Allentown, the need for another individual who could promote the commercial and financial interests of the company in New York and other large cities was soon apparent to the board of directors. On April 29, 1905, Otto E. Mears was elected president of the Mack Brothers Motor Car Company, with Jack Mack remaining as a director of the company and manager of the Allentown plant. Mr. Mears was a man of many accomplishments who had become interested in the Mack Brothers venture back in New York, most likely because of a similarity in his and Jack Mack's backgrounds, and their common interest in commercial transportation.

Otto E. Mears was born in the old Baltic province of Courland, in European Russia, and emigrated to America in 1854 at the age of 13.(4) Legend has it that an uncle was supposed to meet him when he left the ship at San Francisco, but never showed up, putting Otto on his own at an early age. After working at a number of trades, he enlisted during the Civil War in the California Volunteers, and served at various frontier posts in the Southwest, part of the time under Kit Carson. After his discharge from the army, in 1864, Otto settled in the south-western part of the Colorado Territory. His endeavors at farming in this rugged country prompted his attention to the nearly impassable roads of the area, which deprived him of access to several potential markets. With the determination which marked all his undertakings, Otto decided to improve the roads near his home, and before long found himself in the toll-road and commercial haulage businesses. The discovery of silver and gold deposits in his area, San Juan County, Colorado, further encouraged his road building, and by the mid-1880's he had converted parts of these to narrow-gauge railroads. Otto had just completed his most outstanding engineering and construction achievement, the Rio Grande Southern Railroad, when the panic of 1893 struck, and set in motion the chain of events that would bring him in contact with the Mack Brothers enterprise.

The panic of 1893, with the resulting depression which followed, had severe economic effects on the silver mining areas of the western states. Adding to the usual restrictions on credit, which put Otto Mears' new Rio Grande Southern into receivership, was the Federal government's discontinuance of its silver purchase and coinage programs. The resulting sharp drop in the price of silver caused many mines to close, which, in turn, effected the earning power of the other small railroads owned by Otto Mears. Seeing little improvement in this situation by 1897, he decided to visit Washington, D.C., and while there he built and operated the Chesapeake Beach Railway, until 1902. Between short trips back to Colorado, to observe his properties, he spent considerable time in the east, and, no doubt, was attracted to the commercial possibilities of the Mack Brothers buses, which were displayed at the New York Automobile Show in Januay 1904.

In addition to serving as president of the Mack Brothers Motor Car Company, between April 29, 1905 and January 9, 1906, Otto Mears was also a director and president of the Mack Brothers Manufacturing Company, from February 2, 1906 to November 30, 1906. This latter company was set up in New York to continue the

(3) **Allentown Morning Call**, Sept. 14,1905, p.10.

(4) **New York Times**, June 26, 1931, p.21.

13

An advertisement in the *Horseless Age* for August 16, 1905 featured the improved version of their Manhattan tonneau sightseeing bus, first built at the Allentown plant. Note the coil pipe radiator has been partially enclosed in a neat brass shell.

Another August 1905 ad shows the direct front view of an enclosed 12 passenger hotel bus with an unusual radiator design.

This combination passenger and express vehicle was built in 1905 for service on a route serving a few outlying towns near Lexington, Kentucky. The radiator has been retouched to show the style introduced later in 1905 as well as the rounded front frame design.

operation of the Brooklyn plant, on Atlantic Avenue, which, while still manufacturing a few wagons, was the main Mack storage and repair depot for the New York city area. Mr. Mears was very generous with his financial help to the Mack enterprises, and only resigned when the pressing need to look after his own businesses forced his return to Colorado at the end of 1906.

Developing an expanded product line

When the Mack Brothers started building their first commercial motor vehicles, the automotive industry was still in its infancy, with many construction concepts to be sorted out, along with various sales possibilities to be tried and tested. The motor vehicles built for hauling groups of sight-seers around Prospect Park, and in New York and other cities, were often referred to as observation cars, and, in essence simply considered to be large automobiles with touring bodies. Although the Macks were interested in commercial vehicles, their first Manhattan buses were generically called motor cars, hence the name of their enterprise: The Mack Brothers Motor Car Company.

The substantial construction, along with the beauty and luxury of their bodies, suggested a promising field for the Manhattan bus wherever the comfort of the passengers was of prime importance. In resort areas the Manhattan buses could perform the dual purpose of bringing the vacationers from the local train station to their hotel, and, later, taking them on tours of the area. Another possible use, that was soon conceived, was in suburban transit service, where local street car service had not as yet reached. However, it should be noted that the decade prior to 1910 witnessed a tremendous growth in local traction companies, which built trolley lines to every conceivable point within their reach and means. Because of an actual over-building of these lines, there would be little need for motor buses in general transit service for a number of years, even though a few notable exceptions came about.

During 1905, the Allentown plant had orders for buses from many parts of the country, and completed its first bus in April for the New England Motor Tally-Ho Company,[5] a firm set up to operate a sightseeing service in the Boston area. While sightseeing buses were their main product, the Mack plant also received orders for hotel buses and a combination express and passenger vehicle, which took special bodies. By July, a 12 passenger enclosed body hotel bus had been completed, and in November a combination baggage and enclosed bus, ordered by a Kentucky interurban motor line, was ready for its trial run.[6] Ten buses had been ordered by two Cuban companies, and most of these were shipped during 1905. By October, it was reported that the Mack Brothers had built 51 large buses, 34 in the last 12 months.[7] This would indicate that a total of 17 buses had been built in Brooklyn, and company records show a total Brooklyn production of 15 vehicles.

In late 1904, just prior to the move to Allentown, the Brooklyn shop had started the construction of a rail car for two of the narrow gauge railroads, owned by Otto Mears, which ran out of Silverton, Colorado. This unusual car had one of the first Mack 6-cylinder engines, which would provide the power to pull a trailer that was being adapted from a former Brooklyn horsecar. The rail car "Mary M," which had been named for Mrs. Mears, was shipped to Denver on August 22, 1905.[8] The trailer was still reported to be under construction at the Allentown plant early in September.[9] A mystery seems to surround the Mary M, as while a number of stories were published heralding its coming, no information has been found to indicate that it ever reached Silverton, or operated in the area.

The construction of motor trucks had been contemplated during 1904, but the actual work of building the pilot models did not take place until the spring and summer of 1905. Besides the interest that Jack Mack took in the truck project, his brother Gus helped with certain component designs, and Frank Mueller, whose main job later involved running the experimental department, also contributed his knowledge and energy to the success of the first Mack built trucks. During the late summer and early fall several trucks were finished, then thoroughly tested

(5) **Allentown Morning Call**, April 21, 1905, p.3.

(6) Ibid. Nov. 28, 1905, p.1.

(7) **Motor Age**, Vol. 8, No. 15, (Oct. 12, 1905) p.14.

(8) **Allentown Morning Call**, Aug. 23, 1905, p.7.

(9) Ibid., Sept. 7, 1905, p.6.

A group of tourists waiting for a 1906 Manhattan 20 passenger sightseeing bus to drive them around parts of New York City. Photo taken on Broadway looking north, with 42nd Street crossing behind subway kiosk to right of bus.

A Mack rail car used by the Uintah Railway between Mack, Colorado and Utah, circa 1910. This railway was owned by the General Asphalt Company, whose president was also a John M. Mack, but of no known relation to the commercial vehicle builder.

The prototype 5-ton Manhattan truck demonstrating its ability to haul a heavy load of flour for a local Allentown bakery in 1905.

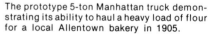

(10) Mack Trucks, Inc., **The Mack Bulldog**, First Series, Vol. 8, No. 1, (Feb. 1929) p.12.

(11) International Motor Co., **The Mack Bulldog**, First Series, Vol. 4, No. 4, (Sept. 1924) pp. 8 & 9.

(12) **Allentown Morning Call**, Sept. 7, 1905, p.6.

and demonstrated before any sales were made. The motor trucks, like the buses, were given the trade name "Manhattan," but it was also made clear that they were built by the Mack Brothers Motor Car Company.

Two delivery trucks of a nominal 1-1/2 to 2 tons capacity, following the basic chassis construction of the smaller 12 to 15 passenger buses, were built during 1905. The first Manhattan truck to be sold is believed to be one of the delivery models, which was purchased by a local Brooklyn provisions merchant in 1905. However, a 5-ton truck built in 1905 had the driver's seat over the engine. The 5-ton truck was designed for hauling heavy commodities such as coal, building material, beer and food stuffs. Its first demonstration load was five tons of flour, which was delivered to a local Allentown bakery.(10) Both 3 and 4-ton cab-over-engine truck models were then produced, and demonstrated quite extensively in the Paterson, New Jersey, and New York City areas, during 1906.(11) A heavy-duty winch truck, for the delivery of safes in New York City, was reported under construction towards the end of 1905.(12)

The foundry, forge, machine shop, and drafting room at the Allentown plant gave the Mack Brothers the necessary facilities to implement important improvements in chassis design. The first year in their new plant proved to be a highly formative one for the Mack product, with most of the major component innovations retained as standard designs through 1912.

The most basic chassis component to be improved was the frame, which had previously been built up from riveted pieces of flat and angle iron stock. At Allentown, two symetrical pieces of heavy rolled channel steel with their ends bent at right angles to each other, so that each formed half the front and rear cross members, were riveted together at each end to form a simple, but substantial unit. At first, both the front and rear ends of the frame were straight across, but by late 1905 the front end had been curved outward to form a protective bumper for the radiator.

Radiator design was also refined during 1905, with an improved coil pipe construction being used first. This type had a greater number of copper tubes of a smaller diameter with added fins to help radiate the heat faster, and brass shells to dress up their basic utilitarian design. Several different radiator shapes were used during 1905, until the new cellular type of construction became standard, late in 1905. The cellular, or honey comb radiator did not use continuous tubes through which the water flowed. Instead, there were hundreds of small horizontal tubes placed so that the air went through and the water around them. The cellular radiators used by Mack had a distinctive rounded design on top, and were made by the W.J. Kells Manufacturing Company of Jersey City, New Jersey.

At the heart of every motor vehicle is the engine, and Jack Mack was determined to produce the most powerful and durable gasoline engines. The first 4-cylinder engines produced at the Atlantic Avenue shop had what is called an F-head, wherein the inlet valve was located at the side of the combustion chamber and the exhaust valve on top. The exhaust valves were operated by rocker arms, which tended to be very noisy. Lack of an adequate means to lubricate the exhaust valves made them sound even noisier, and so a new, more powerful, engine was designed for production at Allentown.

Work on another ill-fated engine had been started at Brooklyn in 1904, and was continued, in a limited way, at the Allentown plant up to 1906. This engine had six cylinders and, when first completed, would not run. It was reported that the crankshaft of this engine had all its throws made in one plane, making it impossible for all cylinders to deliver their power strokes. At Allentown this particular problem was worked out.

(13) Interview with Frank Pampinella, Sept. 1954.

The bore and stroke of the 6-cylinder engine were quite large, being 6 x 7 inches, and the head was of the T design, having the inlet and exhaust valves on opposite sides of the combustion chamber. Very few of the 6-cylinder Mack engines were built. One was used in a fishing boat plying from a Brooklyn pier, and another went into the Silverton Northern's rail car Mary M.(13) The 6-cylinder engine was rated at 90 horsepower, which was really in excess of that power which could actually be used by heavy-duty trucks, whose speed was restricted

The first 4-ton Manhattan truck was completed in the fall of 1905 and equipped with the Mack built coil pipe radiator.

The first 3-ton truck built by the Mack Brothers Motor Car Company being demonstrated in Passaic, New Jersey, in 1906 by Edward Turgeon.

The famous Mack gasoline engine of 50-60 horsepower, which was built at the Allentown factory with little change from 1905 to 1916.

by their solid tires over the poor roads of the day. Two other engines of four cylinder design, and rated at 30 and 70 horsepower, were developed during 1906. However, these engines were soon dropped, along with the 6-cylinder model, with production concentrated on a 4-cylinder engine rated at 50-60 horsepower.

A brief description of the basic Mack engine, designed in 1905, and produced with little change until about 1915, will indicate the basis for the Mack reputation for building durable and adequately powered heavy-duty motor trucks. A bore and stroke of 5-1/2 x 6 inches produced a nominal 50 brake horsepower at 1,000 revolutions per minute. Crankshafts, connecting rods, and valves, were made from drop forgings, with nickel steel used in the most critical engine parts. Large bearing surfaces, and case-hardening of certain parts, contributed to a long, trouble-free, service life of the Mack engine.(14)   The crankcase was cast aluminum, and was, along with most of the other engine parts, except the pistons, made at the Mack plant.

(14) **Cycle and Automobile Trade Journal**, Vol. II, No. 7, (Jan. 1907) p.339.

Another key to the success of early Mack commercial motor vehicles was the use of a patented, constant-mesh, selective gear ratio transmission. The constant-mesh feature was designed by Gus Mack, with his patent application filed in February 1905. This concept relied upon separate jaw clutches to lock the gears in place on the transmission shaft when a change in gear ratios was made. This protected the gears themselves from being damaged or stripped by inexperienced drivers, who did not use care in manipulating the gear shift lever and clutch pedal when "shifting gears."

The selective feature of the transmission was patented by Jack Mack, and this concept allowed the driver to immediately shift from high to low, or vice versa, without going through any intermediate speeds, as with the progressive transmissions in common use at the time. The Mack Brothers Motor Car Company collected royalties from other manufacturers using these patented transmission features for a number of years.

Although frames, springs, and wheels varied to some extent, the same basic engines and transmissions were used in 2, 3, 4, and 5-ton Manhattan trucks. This lead to the 1907 motto of the Mack Brothers: "Simplicity, Strength, Durability and Plenty of Reserve Horsepower."

The early sales campaigns

The early day motor truck tended to be an unknown quantity, as well as quality, to the businessman who was its basic potential user. What, in effect, the Mack Brothers, and other pioneer commercial motor vehicle producers, were trying to do was introduce a completely new system of merchandise delivery to the business world. To dislodge the horse from his traditional role as the world's beast of burden would be a slow process for a number of reasons. Owners of simple horse drawn delivery equipment were not about to invest thousands of dollars in any form of complicated machinery, as a substitute, unless they could see an adequate savings on their investment. Added to this was the problem of the training of truck drivers and mechanics to run and service the vehicles properly. These obstacles, and others, tested the determination of the Mack Brothers, but their success is a testimony to the inherent economic value of the early commerical motor vehicles, and the exhaustive missionary work which sold their merits.

A natural first step in introducing a businessman to the wonders of the motor truck was a practical demonstration. One of the early truck demonstrators for the Mack Brothers was Edward V. Turgeon, who helped to introduce some of the first Manhattan trucks starting late in 1905. Big Ed, as he was called, was almost seven feet tall, and was well qualified in his job, having driven horseless vehicles since 1899. He was also able to handle any sticky situations which might arise from the objections to his machine's presence among horse drawn wagons, whose motive power tended to shy from the noise and sight of the gasoline propelled monsters.

The Mack transmission had patented designs which had been worked out by the brothers Jack and Gus Mack. The constant-mesh gears and quality materials provided a long service life for the Mack-built tramsmission.

Wagon drivers disliked the early motor trucks, which tended to pass their slower moving vehicles, and sometimes frighten their horses. Some of these drivers resorted to guerilla warfare tactics on the streets and at loading docks, where radiator tubes became dislodged by a wagon being "accidently" backed into the front of a motor truck. Fist fights between motor truck and wagon drivers were not uncommon occurances in the early days, and truck drivers had to be rugged to survive.

As the sales of motor trucks gradually increased, the need for competent drivers grew. In order to properly train the new drivers, a special truck with dual controls was constructed for the purpose of actual road instruction. This special truck was operated mainly in the New York City area, where it is believed close to 1,000 men received their basic training in the "Mack School."(15) A driver was also considered to need a knowledge of basic mechanics, in order to provide the daily care for his truck, and also to get it back to the garage in case of a minor breakdown on the road.

In the early days of the automotive industry it was quite common for manufacturers to contract with one or two agents to handle the entire output of their factories on a yearly basis. In this way, management could concentrate on producing the vehicles without getting involved with the setting up of a dealer organization, with agents that, most likely, had to be trained from the ground up. As the Mack Brothers Motor Car Company went into high gear in motor bus production, and also began to produce their first motor trucks, the one agent sales route must have appealed to the desire to establish a dealer organization as soon as possible. In January 1906, the Mack Brothers Motor Car Company signed an exclusive sales agency agreement with Miller Reese Hutchison,(16) who was president and manager of the Universal Motor Car Company, of 1 Madison Avenue, New York.

The backers of the Universal Motor Car Company were also involved with the various related Motor Tally-Ho companies, which had contracted to purchase many of the Manhattan buses in 1904 and 1905. It was the objective of the new sales company, after contracting for the entire Mack output, to take over the maintenance and also possible operation of many of these vehicles. Great things must have been expected from this agent, as its president, Miller Reese

(15) International Motor Co., **The Mack Bulldog**, First Series, Vol. 4, No. 4, (Sept. 1924) pp. 8 & 9.

(16) **Horseless Age**, Vol. 17, No. 3, (Jan. 17, 1906) p.149.

A Manhattan 3-ton conventional type truck dating from the 1908-1909 period used to haul produce from the Harlem Market to Mount Vernon, New York. Note that a brace has been added to the frame so that heavier loads could be carried without bending the frame.

(17) **New York Times**, Feb. 18, 1944, p.17.

(18) Interview with Frank Pampinella, Sept. 1954.

(19) Don Russell, **The Lives and Legends of Buffalo Bill**, (Norman, University of Oklahoma Press, 1960) p.445.

Hutchison, was an electrical engineer with a doctorate and several other degrees from different universities. However, he became best known for his electrical inventions, which included the Klaxon horn and the Acousticon hearing aid.(17)

During 1906 the Universal Motor Car Company contracted for the building of a highly unusual vehicle for Buffalo Bill's Wild West Show, which had recently returned from a long European tour, and was being reconstituted with new acts. A train hold-up scene was to be depicted through the use of a powerful motor vehicle, which would have a sheet metal superstructure designed to look like a Union Pacific steam locomotive, and would pull several replica railroad passenger cars without the use of tracks. The Mack Brothers constructed a chassis in which one of their 6-cylinder engines was installed(18), and special effects, such as puffings of the engine, black smoke, and an electric headlight, were engineered by Mr. Hutchison.(19) The Mack Brothers "locomotive" was used with Buffalo Bill's show during its 1907 season, but it seems to have disappeared soon after.

After 1906, it was decided to push the establishment of local agents, starting first in various East Coast cities, which the Mack factory could keep in close contact with. Even though the commercial motor vehicle industry was coming into its own by 1907, with several trade publications to boost its claims, on-the-spot demonstrations were still the only sure-fire method of selling for many years. A very modest advertising budget was directed to a few individual trades, such as the brewing industry, and testimonial letters were also circulated to sales prospects. A minor amount of advertising was also used to attract new agents, but the major effort to build a strong dealer organization was undertaken by Gus Mack, who handled this important job until 1911. The addition of the line of Manhattan trucks, in 1905 and 1906, came to over-shadow the bus models in a short time, and as production at the Allentonw plant grew, so did the problems involved with sustaining the company's growth.

Growing pains during the formative years

The importance of having a stable and alert management was never so critical to the Mack organization then during its first years in Allentown. After Otto Mears resigned from the presidency of the Mack Brothers Motor Car Company, in January 1906, he was succeeded by Jacob Sulzback. Mr. Sulzbach was a dyer of textiles with a business located at 70 Wooster Street, in New York City. In additon to his activity in the textile industry he was also a director of the Universal Motor Car Company during 1906.[20] Mr. Sulzbach remained as president of the Mack organization only one year, being replaced by Thomas E. Rush, on January 8, 1907.

(20) **Directory of Directors in the City of New York**, 1906 Edition, (N.Y., Audit Co. of N.Y., 1906) p.748.

Mr. Rush was a Wall Street lawyer who remained as president of the Mack Brothers Motor Car Company until December 1908. No doubt, he played an important role in steering the company through the financial complications of the panic of 1907, which, while of short duration, saw many banks and established firms go under. The panic of 1907, although starting for reasons differing from previous financial crises, had the same basic effects: the hoarding of cash, calling in of loans, and the restrictions placed on business by the severe limitations on credit.

After the resignation of Thomas E. Rush, in December 1908, John M. Mack, although holding the office of vice president, acted as president until he was actually elected to that post in March 1910. The Mack management in Allentown was learning to handle all the financial and production problems, of which there were many during the formative years.

Early in 1906, it was announced that an addition would be made to the machine shop. This was about the time that Mack disposed of the huge foundry building, which was acquired with the original Weaver-Hirsh property, and no doubt the sale of one was advantageous to the building of the other. This expansion, which was necessitated by the addition of the truck models, in turn led to other problems.

Since gasoline propelled motor trucks were so new, especially the sizes built by the Mack Brothers, sample models had to be produced for demonstration, with the hoped for sale to take place soon thereafter. However, many sales were conditioned on trial periods, during which time the Mack organization saw very little money for its efforts. In fact, money had to be spent by Mack for labor and materials while the organization waited patiently for its return with a hoped for profit for reinvestment and dividends to stockholders.

Many types of trades were employed in the building of commercial motor vehicles, with machinists and mechanics being much in demand. There were also draftsmen, foundry workers, blacksmiths, pattern makers, wheelwrights, and the body makers, who were skilled in the arts of woodworking, painting, and trimming. A first class man in most of these trades did not usually have a hard time finding another job, should he be laid off. It therefore behooved the Mack organization to try to carry as many workers as possible during slow periods, or lose their skills and training to another company.

With all these pressing needs for money, it was not long before the working capital was strained, and new sources of funds had to be found. It has been stated that Jack Mack personally sought out the leading citizens of Allentown to interest them in the Mack Brothers Motor Car Company. He also did much searching for skilled labor during the first years. Joe Mack also helped in keeping the Mack organization on the road to financial solvency, as he was treasurer, and had many business contacts through his interests in the silk industry. After 1907, Martin E. Kern became very important to the company, arranging many loans through his contacts in the banking industry. He was later made vice president and a director of the Mack Brothers Motor Car Company.

During those first years at Allentown it was not unusal for Jack Mack to lead the workers in a small celebration on pay day. The sale of a new model, especially when the customer paid cash, was the cause to celebrate. And it is told that Jack lead more than one group of employees to the pretzel "foundry," which was part

The traditional annual Clam Bake was held every summer between 1906 and 1911. This group most likely represents the 1909 Allentown force and includes Joseph Mack 1, Jack Mack 2, and Gus Mack 3.

The 1908 5-ton dump truck was the first of a series of successful dump models developed later on the engine-in-front, or type one chassis.

(21) Mack Brothers Motor Car Company, **Mack's Messenger**, Oct. 1911, p.8.

way up 10th Street, where a respectable "Lehigh Valley thirst" was acquired. From there, it was on to the brewery for a quick one, which was then followed by Jack treating the party to dinner uptown.

The shop force reciprocated Jack's kindness by inviting him, and the other Mack officials, to their first annual clam bake, which was held in the summer of 1906. Company officials had such a good time at the first one, that they contributed to the next two, and starting in 1909, the annual clam bake was completely paid for by the Mack organization. Only 60 people had attended the first one, but 1,500 employees, relatives, and customers came to the Mack clam bake that was held on August 26, 1911.(21)

The official clam bakes were a sign that the Mack organization was both growing and keeping its head above water. While the panic of 1907 had been rough, it was of short duration, and the end of 1908 saw the renewed growth in truck sales. A line of dump trucks with an under-body hoist was introduced during 1908. The 5-ton dump model was of the cab-over-engine style, and the 3-ton had the engine in front. It was also during this period that a line of

23

This 1910 1-ton Mack was the smallest model in what was referred to as the Mack, Jr. line.

When this Wagon stops at your door, what it leaves is paid for.

BERNHEIMER BROS.
BIG HOME STORES.
FAYETTE ST. near LEXINGTON.

The 1½ ton Mack, Jr. was popular with department stores and other merchants who needed the speedy delivery of their goods in moderate quantities.

engine-in-front truck models up to five tons capacity, which paralleled the cab-over-engine models, was developed. Later, the dump models were offered only in the engine-in-front design.

The fact that Manhattan trucks were of basically heavy duty design, with structural steel frames, 50 to 60 horsepower engines, and nominal capacities of from 2 to 5 tons, tended to limit sales to those customers whose product tended to not only have a dead weight, but be economically shipped in large lots. The manufacture and use of standardized engines and transmissions, with only slight variations in frame, axle, spring, wheel, and sprocket sizes, to conform to the structural needs of the various truck models, helped to keep production costs down, but it also meant that Mack was missing out on a large market for models of under two tons capacity.

To remedy this situation a new line of trucks having pressed steel frames and a smaller motor, rated at 32 horsepower, was introduced in 1909. These new models were built in 1, 1-1/2, and 2 tons capacity, and all had the motor in front. Also, they all had chain-drive and the same cellular type radiator as the larger

Manhattan trucks. Later, the Mack Sales Department, in order to distinguish between the two lines, referred to the heavy duty models, those above two tons capacity, as the Senior line, those below three tons, as the Junior line.

The creation of the Junior line, and the adding of the dump truck models, required an expansion of the Allentown factory in 1909. The plant of the Liberty Silk Dyeing Company was acquired then, and after raising the roof of the main dye house, an adequate assembly shop was obtained. The engines for the Junior line were purchased from a small Newark, New Jersey, firm, the F.A. Seitz Company, which sold their engines under the Excelsior trade name. In 1910 the Mack Brothers Motor Car Company purchased the Seitz operation in order to assure a steady supply of engines. Two heavy duty truck models were also added during this period: a 7-1/2 ton in 1909, and a 6-ton in 1910.

Early in 1910, Charles W. Mack, the second born of the five surviving Mack brothers, came down from the family farm in the Scranton area, to work at the Allentown plant. He was nominally in charge of company real estate, but he is remembered best driving some of the company trucks to and from the railroad freight station, and at other hard tasks around the plant.

(22) Interview with Frank Pampin-ella, Sept. 1954.

(23) **Brooklyn Eagle**, Aug. 9, 1907, p.12.

The Brooklyn plant remained the headquarters of the New York City operations, with some wagons still being built there, up to 1906 (22), but a switch about that time to the heavy wooden truck bodies of the period was an easy transition. A fire was reported to have wiped out the Brooklyn plant, in August 1907, destroying many vehicles which were being repaired or stored there.(23) However, the fire was not as serious as first reported, and the plant was soon back in operation, remaining at the same Atlantic Avenue location for several more years. In June 1910, the Mack Brothers Motor Car Company of New York was incorporated, with William C. Mack as vice president in charge of the Brooklyn operation.

About the middle of 1910, the trade name "Manhattan" was dropped and all motor vehicles leaving the Allentown plant now carried a neat script sign on the sides of their cabs: MACK.

Many new agents, in various parts of the country, were added during 1909 and 1910, with the New England and Middle Atlantic states showing an especially

The cab-over-engine models were particularly popular with many brewers. This 5-ton Manhattan produced in 1909 was part of a large fleet of early Mack trucks owned by a New Jersey brewer in 1920.

strong sales growth. The Manhattan Motor Truck Company was incorporated in Massachusetts on January 20, 1910, to operate several dealerships in that state. This company became the Mack Motor Truck Company by 1914, and continued for many years afterwards to run all the Mack branches in the New England area. The branch system was just getting under way at Mack during 1910, and by mid-1911 the company controlled its own outlets in Washington, D.C., Philadelphia, Pittsburgh, Baltimore, and Brooklyn, New York.(24)

The steadily rising demand for motor trucks was starting to attract more companies to the field and with the industrial growth potential also becoming apparent at this time, it would not be long before Wall Street capital would influence the fortunes of some of the truck manufacturers.

(24) **Allentown Morning Call**, Aug. 26,1911, p.11.

The largest truck model was the 7½ ton introduced in 1909. Note the sectional block tires on the rear wheels.

The petroleum industry began motorizing their delivery fleets about 1908, with this 1910 4-ton Mack tanker being one of the largest oil trucks of its day.

Mergers and Macks

The automotive industry had the fate of being born at the height of "merger fever" with the popularity of the all-pervading trust company concept, and the anti-monopolistic agitation which it tended to arouse. Around the turn of the century large combines had been formed in many industries, which usually saw some of the largest companies in a specific industry merge to form a super-corporation, or "trust" as they were called. Congress had enacted laws to fight the monopolistic practices of the larger business combines, which, it was proved, tended to wield their economic influences unfairly.

In general, the automotive industry remained too fragmented in the first decade after 1900 for any large combines to have much influence on the industry. However, one large corporation, formed to operate electric cabs and build motor vehicles, tried to wield the monopolistic power of its ownership of a broadly based patent on the gasoline propelled automobile. The ensuing struggle between the group of automobile and motor truck manufacturers recognizing the patent, and those that did not, produced many interesting ramifications in the still emerging automotive industry.

In January 1897, two Philadelphia inventors, Henry G. Morris and Pedro G. Salom, had succeeded in placing several electric taxicabs upon the streets of New York City. The cabs produced by the Philadelphians were built by their own firm, the Electric Carriage and Wagon Company. The early success of this enterprise attracted another Philadelphian, Isaac L. Rice, who owned the Electric Storage Battery Company. He then purchased the Electric Carriage and Wagon Company, and formed a new firm, the Electric Vehicle Company, in September 1897. Less than six months passed before a group of New York financiers led by William C. Whitney, who were heavily involved with promoting the electric street railway industry, became interested in the possibilities of forming a chain of electric cab companies to operate in all the principal cities in the United States.

The Whitney group quickly came to terms with Isaac Rice, and started to promote their venture on a grand scale, reporting that they would place 12,000 electric cabs in service in various cities. In order to acquire the needed vehicles in the shortest possible time, the Whitney group approached the largest electric vehicle manufacturer of that time, the Pope Manufacturing Company, which in turn led to another merger, in 1899, and a further expansion in the horizons of the Electric Vehicle Company.(1)

However, by 1900 the Electric Vehicle Company was highly over capitalized. The operation of its electric cabs not bringing it the revenue it had projected, and only the timely acquisition of the Selden patent injected new life into a rapidly sinking promotional scheme.

The United States Patent Office in 1895 had granted a broadly based patent on the invention of a self-propelled road vehicle, using liquid hydrocarbons as fuel. The inventor was George B. Selden, a Rochester, New York, patent lawyer, and his patent meant that any manufacturer producing automobiles or motor trucks using an internal combustion engine and a petroleum product for fuel could owe Mr. Selden a royalty, or be sued for patent infringement. In actuality, the patent design was based on a very outmoded type of engine, but the general concept, and wording of the patent was so all-encompassing that the courts quickly upheld its validity in the first minor test case. The Electric Vehicle Company then pressed its case against the Winton Motor Carriage Company, the largest maker of gasoline automobiles in 1900, which fought until 1902 in an effort to see the Selden patent invalidated.

(1) John B. Rae, **American Automobile Manufacturers**, (Philadelphia, Chilton Co., 1959) p.68.

However, just as Winton was giving up the costly court battle, a group of mid-western and eastern auto manufacturers decided to effect a compromise with the patent holders. An agreement was reached in 1903, which set up the Association of Licensed Automobile Manufacturers, and very modest royalty fees, based on the sale prices of the members' motor vehicles, were to be split between the A.L.A.M., the Electric Vehicle Company, and the inventor, George B. Selden.(2) But, it was not the intent of the A.L.A.M. to take just any auto manufacturer into their association, and the exclusionary nature of the group soon started further litigation.

(2) William Greenleaf, **Monopoly On Wheels**, (Detroit, Wayne State University Press, 1961) p.98.

One very constructive thing was accomplished by the A.L.A.M. A Mechanical Branch was set up to establish standards; such as sizes of spark plugs, tire rims, and bolts used in the construction of all the members' motor vehicles. The industry, as a whole, was soon to adopt these conventions, which brought efficiency and lower cost to the manufacture and repair of motor vehicles. In 1909 the Mechanical Branch turned over its equipment and records to the Society of Automobile Engineers, which continued this vital work. The S.A.E. had been formed in 1905 and grew very quickly after 1910, eventually taking in aeronautical engineers and then changing its name to the Society of Automotive Engineers.

It is not clear if the Mack Brothers tried to join the A.L.A.M. as they got into series production in 1904. By the time the Mack Brothers Motor Car Company was formed in 1905, and their Allentown plant had reached a full production basis, another automotive pioneer had decided to fight the patent holders, and offered protection to any independents who remained out of the A.L.A.M. The Pioneer was Henry Ford, who formed the American Motor Car Manufacturers Association, an anti-Selden trade group, which the Mack Brothers joined by 1908.(3)

(3) **Ibid**., p.171.

Actually, Ford gained considerable publicity and sympathy from his fight against the A.L.A.M., with its implication of being a monopolistic trust, and the production of Ford automobiles rarely kept up with the demand, as the lawsuit dragged on for several more years.

Combinations of several manufactuers had been talked about prior to 1908, but little had been accomplished in the formation of a large automotive holding corporation until William C. Durant created the General Motors Company. Using his control of the Buick Motor Company as a base, Durant, in quick succession, acquired the Cadillac Motor Car Company, the Olds Motor Works, and several other prominent and not so prominent automobile manufacturers of the day. By 1909, General Motors even owned several established truck manufacturers, including the Rapid Motor Vehicle Company, of Pontiac, Michigan, and the Reliance Motor Truck Company, of Owosso, Michigan. These two firms were merged during 1912, at Pontiac, Michigan, and a new trade name, G.M.C., was adopted for the combined line of trucks being produced then by the General Motors Truck Company. This and other mergers in the rapidly expanding automotive industry, especially since the court defeat of the Selden patent in 1911, did not escape the Wall Street financiers.

By the summer of 1911, as the Mack Brothers enjoyed the sixth annual clam bake, they could not help but look back at the tremendous strides their enterprise, the Mack Brothers Motor Car Company, had made in the six years of its existance. Employment at the Mack Allentown plant had gone from about 100 in 1905, to almost 700 in 1911. In addition there were 50 employed at the Brooklyn plant, and another 75 at the newly acquired Newark, New Jersey, engine plant, for a total of about 825 employees.(4) Annual production, although increasing each year, had remained below 100 vehicles until 1910, and then had shot up to about 600 in 1911.

(4) **Allentown Morning Call**, Aug. 26, 1911, p.10.

Mack, by 1911, was acknowledged as being one of the largest, if not the largest producer of heavy-duty motor trucks, of over three ton in capacities. Their slogan, "The Leading Gasoline Truck of America," indicated the pride that the Mack organization took in the production and acceptance of its product.

Expansion of the Mack firm did not happen at a carefree pace, as there were many management problems involved which required outside help. The chief one was the need for the financing of plant expansion, as well as the purchase of larger quantities of materials. The Mack Brothers became increasingly involved in the complications of obtaining these funds from the local financial institutions, which, in turn, most likely also had problems in fulfilling the larger capital requirements.

Another problem loomed just on the horizon in 1911, when several prominent automobile manufacturers announced plans to produce heavy-duty motor trucks. These included Pierce-Arrow, Peerless, and Locomobile. The Packard Motor Car Company had already been marketing gasoline trucks since 1905, and the White Company since about 1909, but the addition of more well-known auto makers, with established sales organizations, spelled severe competition ahead for the Mack Brothers.

Wall Street money had evidently backed the expansion of another truck manufacturer, the Saurer Motor Company, which with a plant at Plainfield, New Jersey, had a license to build the Swiss-designed Saurer motor truck in America. In October, 1911, only a few months after the announcement of the incorporation of the Saurer Motor Company, came the news of the formation of the International Motor Company, to act as a holding corporation for both the Mack Brothers Motor Car Company and the Saurer Motor Company. It was stated that the International Motor Company was capitalized at $10,000,000 and that the two truck manufacturing companies would continue as distinct organizations, but with the selling and servicing of Mack and Saurer trucks to be combined as a distinct function of the holding company.(5) In March 1912, the combine was enlarged further by the addition of the Hewitt Motor Company, a New York City based builder of highly engineered motor trucks.

(5) **Commercial Vehicle**, Vol. 6, No. 11, (Nov. 1911) p.568.

An indication that the heavy-duty motor truck had finally arrived was the exclusive truck show held in New York City in January 1911.

The Mack exhibit included the four trucks located on the left hand side of the isle starting in the lower right of the picture.

A Mack advertisement which appeared in *Scientific American* in September 1911, just a month before the merger with the Saurer Motor Company.

An illustrator's composite view of the various buildings comprising the Mack Allentown factory in 1912.

The precise action which led the Mack Brothers to become involved in the International Motor Company was never made public knowledge, although it has been said that their need for additional capital prompted the bankers backing the Saurer Motor Company to suggest a merger. The fact that the new Saurer Motor Company set up its headquarters at 30 Church Street, New York,(6) in which building the General Eastern Sales Agent for the Mack Brothers Motor Car Company, Arthur C. Brady, had his sales office, may have actually been the simple circumstance which introduced the possibilities of a merger of the two companies.

A description of the backgrounds of the Saurer and Hewitt organizations will be helpful to an understanding of the combined operations of the International Motor Company in 1912.

(6) *Commercial Car Journal*, Vol. 1, No. 2, (April 15, 1911) p. 61.

By the dawn of the gasoline motor age, in the 1890's, the Swiss had already acquired a reputation for the meticulous quality of their clocks, embroidery, and other products. So when about 1894, a Swiss manufacturer of embroidery machinery put his hand to automobile building, it was not surprising that his automotive products were winning gold medals just a few years after their perfection.

The firm was Adolph Saurer, originally founded in 1853 by Mr. Franz Saurer and expanded by his son Adolph. Mr. Hippolyt Saurer, a grandson of the founder, was a mechanical genius whose engineering concepts were responsible for a number of the inventions and designs which made the Saurer motor truck a technically superior product.

The first Saurer automobiles are reported to have been completed in 1896, and those models built prior to 1900 had a single cylinder engine mounted under the back seat.[7] However, by 1900 the Saurer organization had turned its attention to designing a large motor truck for use in delivering its delicate embroidery machinery to nearby textile mills or the local railway freight station.

(7) Information supplied by Adolph Saurer, Ltd., May 18, 1973.

(8) Ibid.

The first heavy-duty, 5-ton, Saurer truck, produced in 1903,[8] contained a number of design elements which characterized Saurer trucks for many years: fish-belly frame, four cylinder motor, rear mounted gasoline tank, and enlarged rear wheels. By 1905 the Saurer truck had a patented motor brake, which retarded the vehicle's downhill speed, by causing the motor to act as an air compressor. This brake was considered a great safety feature, and the Swiss Post Office, which had many mountainous routes to cover, was quick to standardize on Saurers. Another patented feature was the air starter, which used compressed air under 50 pounds of pressure to start the engine revolving under compression, until normal ignition could take hold.

The superior Saurer won 11 first prizes and 42 other awards at various European industrial exhibitions and fairs, between 1900 and 1909. Licenses to build the Saurer truck, or trucks using the other trade names having the Saurer patented features, went to firms in England, Austria, Germany, France, and even Switzerland. The other Swiss-built truck based on the Saurer designs was called the Safir, and one truck transportation expert made plans to introduce this truck to the American market in 1907. However, the Safir truck was only produced in limited numbers, and few, if any, reached the United States.

It remained for Albert T Otto, a pioneer American automobile producer and sales agent, to introduce the Saurer truck to the U.S. market in 1908. Mr. Otto exhibited an imported Saurer chassis, with a stated capacity of 3 to 4 tons, at the New York Automobile Show in January 1909. Later in the year Mr. Otto also received a smaller, 2-ton model,[9] but it was the larger, heavy-duty Saurers which really found a market, with many New York City area brewers buying them.

(9) Horseless Age, Vol. 24, No. 8, (Aug. 25, 1909) pp.211/213.

The importation from Europe of the heavy-duty Saurers could have only been accomplished in an economic manner if the chasses were shipped "knocked down," which meant that the wheels and other protruding parts were detached and packed so that each chassis presented a compact object for crating. However, an even lower cost method of importation was the shipping of only the major components to America, and having an assembly plant put the parts together. With that idea in mind, the Saurer Motor Truck Company was formed in the late summer of 1909 and its president, Albert T. Otto, later arranged with the Q.M.S. Company, of Plainfield, New Jersey, to do the assembly work.[10]

(10) Ibid, Vol. 24, No. 16, (Oct. 20, 1909) p.438.

(11) Ibid., Vol. 24, No. 25, (Dec. 22, 1909) p. 748.

The Quincy, Manchester, Sargent Company had developed a line of automobile parts and speciality items, such as step brackets and wrenches, by 1909,[11] which fitted the company's role as assembler of the major Saurer truck components, as well as manufacturers of the minor chassis parts. William D. Sargent, president of the Q.M.S. Company, was also president of the Reading Steel Casting Company, and a director of the American Steel Foundries and the American Brake Shoe and Foundry Company.[12] Mr. Sargent's prominence in the heavy industrial field may have played an important part in the sponsorship

(12) New York Times, Feb. 16, 1940, p.19.

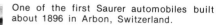
One of the first Saurer automobiles built about 1896 in Arbon, Switzerland.

The first heavy-duty Saurer truck was built in 1903 and had a number of the design elements which characterized Saurer trucks for many years. Note rear mounted gasoline tanks and fish-belly frame.

that the Morgan banking interests were about to lend to the Saurer truck project.

A new corporation was created in March 1911, with the expressed intention of building Saurer trucks, under license in the United States. The Saurer Motor Company was capitalized at $1,600,000, which was eight times greater than the amount of capital stock its predecessor, the Saurer Motor Truck Company, had intended to issue in 1909. The headquarters of the Saurer Motor Company, at 30 Church Street, was not far from the financial district in lower Manhattan.

Charles P. Coleman became president of the new company, leaving his post of secretary and treasurer of the Singer Sewing Machine Company. Mr. Coleman was an engineering graduate of Lehigh University, and after beginning his career with the Lehigh Valley Railroad, he became purchasing agent and assistant to the president of the Bethlehem Steel Company. In 1903 he joined the Singer organization and supervised the construction of its New York office building,(13) which remained a landmark on lower Broadway for over 60 years. He was also, by 1911, prominently identified with the banking firm of J.P. Morgan & Company.(14)

On March 1, 1911, a 4-1/2-ton Saurer truck with a crew of three, and loaded with over 3 tons of oak planking and camping equipment, left Denver for its first destination of San Francisco. A large sign was attached to the front of the truck's canvas cover, up over the driver's seat, proclaiming the goal of the expedition: Ocean to Ocean. The final destination of the Saurer "Pioneer Freighter" was New

(13) **Ibid.**, April 14, 1929, p.29.

(14) **Allentown Morning Call**, Oct. 18, 1911, pp. 5 & 8.

A Saurer motor truck, called the "Pioneer Freighter," made the first transcontinental truck trip in 1911. It is shown here crossing a railroad line in one of the western states.

Taking to the railroad ties in order to make a few miles where roads do not exist.

(15) Commercial Vehicle, Vol. 6, No. 5, (May 1911) p.273.

York, but that city would not be reached until August 2nd, five months later. However, the speed of the journey was not part of the announced goal. Rather, the main object was "to demonstrate to mine and ranch owners along the route the practicability of the motor truck for the transportation of freight where no railroads or means of transportation exist other than mules and horses."(15)

A brief analysis of the trip will indicate the problems encountered and the actual good showing made by the Saurer Pioneer Freighter. The most difficult leg of the trip was the first, 1,483 miles from Colorado to California, which consisted of many long miles through snow drifts, heavy sand, arroyos, boulder-strewn canyons, and mud holes. The load of oak planks came in handy when most of the bridges and culverts on the route had to be strengthened. There was also a winch attached to the truck which was used on more than one occassion to pull the truck out of a bad spot. Over three months were spent in the western states, with the Saurer spending 27 days to cross New Mexico.

After finally reaching San Francisco, the truck was shipped by rail back to Pueblo, Colorado, for the second leg of the trip to Chicago, and then the third to New York. The entire trip covered 5,263 miles, 500 of which represented

The Saurer Pioneer Freighter entering New York City along upper Broadway on August 2, 1911, after its cross-country journey of over 5,000 miles.

The Pioneer Freighter with its final crew, A.C. Thompson and George McLean, who drove the Saurer into New York City.

demonstrations at various stops. Total retail cost of repair parts needed for the Saurer during the entire trip was $40.64, and the average speed for direct route miles was 7.84 miles per hour.(16)

(16) **Ibid**., Vol. 6, No. 10, (Oct. 1911) pp. 512/513.

The Hewitt Motor Company

The introduction of a single cylinder, ten horsepower automobile of moderate size marked the start of the Hewitt-Motor Company in the spring of 1905. This not too auspicious offering to a sophisticated Eastern motoring public, which had already accepted the much more powerful four cylinder automobile, actually belied the creative talents of its builder, Edward R. Hewitt. In one decade Mr. Hewitt and his engineering staff would have proven their ability to design some of the biggest, as well as efficient, commercial motor vehicles of their day, and also put a faltering manufacturer on the road to success with a superior line of motor trucks.

Edward Ringwood Hewitt was born on June 20, 1866, the son of Abram S. Hewitt, who became Mayor of New York in 1888, and Amelia Cooper Hewitt, daughter of Peter Cooper, the famous American inventor, industralist and philanthropist.

Peter Cooper is credited with building the first American steam locomotive, "Tom Thumb," and is honored for his creation of the famous school of design in New York City known as Cooper Union. Edward Hewitt had the good fortune of being exposed to the ideals of his famous grandfather and being instructed in mechanics by some of his associates.

In 1889 and 1890 Edward Hewitt assisted Sir Hiram Maxim with his basic research into aerodynamics, and the engineering data obtained from their experiments was later passed on to the Wright brothers.(17) In 1891 and 1892 Mr. Hewitt took post-graduate courses at two German universities to help prepare him in his job as plant chemist at the Peter Cooper Glue Factory in Brooklyn, New York.

Although Mr. Hewitt was a highly qualified chemical engineer, his first loves were mechanical inventions and the great outdoors, which his work in the family glue factory tended to stifle. However, indications are that he did start his own serious automotive experiments by 1902, and his father's death in 1903 left an inheritance which helped him get started in his chosed field - automobiles.

Forsaking the glue factory in 1905, he got together with another inventor, Charles O. Snyder, and incorporated the Hewitt-Motor Company on April 20th of that year. They purchased an old three-story livery stable at 6-10 East 31st Street, just off fashionable Fifth Avenue in New York, and quickly rebuilt the structure into a combined factory and garage. The first, or ground floor, was set up for chassis assembly and automobile storage and repair work. The second floor was reserved as the machine shop and engine test area; the top floor was to serve as the radiator manufacturing plant and paint shop.

Edward Hewitt's long association with inventors and inventions had taught him the importance of patents to protect both the exclusiveness of a product and the hard work which had gone into its development. Besides the patents that Hewitt and Snyder had taken out, several others were obtained, the biggest group of which were on a new light-weight cellular type radiator, invented by D. McRa Livingston.

The Livingston Radiator Company soon found its home on the top floor of the Hewitt automobile factory, and its product was sold commercially as well as used in Hewitt motor vehicles. Hewitt also became the New York agent for the Timken Roller Bearing Axle Company, shortly after it was formed. And rather than wait for a license to build gasoline automobiles from the Association of Licensed Automobile Manufacturers, with the possibility of being turned down and sued, Hewitt took over the Standard Motor Construction Company, of Jersey City, New Jersey, which already had an A.L.A.M. license.(18)

The Standard Motor Construction Company was an outgrowth, in 1904, of the U.S. Long Distance Automobile Company, builders of Long Distance gasoline automobiles and Standard marine engines. The Standard Company seems to have gone on producing marine engines, up to the World War I period, after providing Hewitt with the A.L.A.M. license. However, there may have been a brief tie between the two companies after 1905, as the first 4-ton Hewitt truck demonstrated in New York, in June 1906, used a four cylinder engine of a design very similar to those marine engines without the usual cast iron crankcase. Instead, the cylinders were supported on steel columns rising from a steel bed-plate, in marine fashion, with diagonal braces adding stiffness to the cylinder supporting system.(19) Easily removable cover plates kept dust from getting into the engine, and provided ready access to check bearings or remove pistons, if need be. Although later 4-cylinder Hewitt engines followed standard automotive construction more closely, the large inspection ports remained a Hewitt design characteristic.

By 1905, an agreement had been reached between Mr. Hewitt and the Adams Manufacturing Company, Ltd., of Bedford, England, for the production in that

(17) Edward R. Hewitt, **Those Were The Days**, (N.Y., Duell, Sloan & Pearce, 1943) p.126.

(18) **Horseless Age**, Vol. 15, No. 25, (June 21, 1905) p.693.

(19) **Commercial Vehicle**, Vol. 1, No. 5, (July 1906) p.174.

country of Adams-Hewitt single cylinder automobiles. The agreement also allowed the Hewitt firm to acquire its motors and gear boxes from the Adams Company at extremely low prices, which could not be matched by any American parts makers in the small quantities needed.(20) This was especially true because there was little demand for the Hewitt single cylinder automobile, even though several pleasing body styles were provided, including a small delivery type. To make up for his apparent miscalculation in the trend of pleasure car design, Hewitt exhibited a V-8 engined car at the 1907 New York Automobile Show. However, the V-8 model stimulated few sales, and Mr. Hewitt's evaluation of the overall problem of design was "that it was just as bad to be in advance of the trend of business as behind the procession."(21) The Hewitt-Motor Company built few automobiles after that point, concentrating on the design of a wide variety of distinctive motor trucks.

Just as the years 1905 to 1910 were the formative ones for the Mack Brothers' enterprise at Allentown, Edward R. Hewitt, in New York City, received a liberal business education from the successes and failures he encountered during this period. In 1906, his first partner, Charles O. Snyder, decided to leave automobiles and the Hewitt-Motor Company for another field. And early the following year, Hewitt's vice president, Leonidas Preston, who was an incorporator of and business manager for the Timken Roller Bearing Axle Company of New York, decided to commit suicide, after being wiped out in some "speculations." Unfortunately, he had also involved the accounts of those businesses he managed, and could not face Messrs. Timken and Hewitt when they came to confront him at his hotel.(22) The missing funds crippled Hewitt's business for some time, but with the assistance of his family, the firm was able to survive.(23)

In July 1907, the Hewitt Motor Truck Company was formed with Alfred Fellows Masury as one of the incorporators, beginning his long and invaluable association with the Hewitt enterprises. Mr. Masury was born in Danvers, Massachusetts, in 1882, and received a degree in mechanical engineering from Brown University in 1904. His first full-time job was with the General Electric Company, as junior engineer at their Lynn, Massachusetts, plant between 1904 and 1906.(24) He was next employed by the Corwin Manufacturing Company, the successor to the Vaughan Machine Company of Peabody, Massachusetts. The Vaughan Company was highly experienced in the design and manufacture of machinery for the leather, textile, and printing industries, and had also built some early automobiles. In 1905, the Vaughan Machine Company started construction of a lot of 25 6-ton Coulthard steam trucks, which Mr. Masury later became involved with, as his specialty had become the design of heavy equipment and custom machinery. As with other early day steam trucks built in America, the Coulthard was not a success and Masury decided to accept work as designer and factory manager at Hewitt's New York City factory.

Besides the 4-ton truck model that was demonstrated in New York during 1906, a 3-ton Hewitt was evidently designed for introduction the same year. However, a 5-ton truck, with similar design concepts to the 4-ton model, was finally decided on for production and the first of these was sold to the Valvoline Oil Company of New York in September 1906. Besides the readily accessible 4-cylinder, 36 horsepower engine, placed between the cab seats, the truck had a "fool proof" planetary transmission with two speeds forward and reverse which was operated by three pedals, so connected that the engagement of one pedal released the other. This type of transmission was later used on the Model T Ford for many years.

During 1907 a line of 2 and 3-ton trucks with 2-cylinder opposed engines, and using the same basic planetary transmissions, was developed. Except for their planetary transmissions and chain-drive rear ends, these Hewitt models were very similar to the famous 2-cylinder, seat-over-engine Autocar truck, which was also designed about 1907, and made without basic changes until the mid-1920's. The Hewitt 2-cylinder engine was rated at 24 horsepower, and had the characteristic large cover plate which greatly facilitated inspections and

36 adjustments.

(20) Hewitt, **op.cit.**, p.216.

(21) **Ibid**.

(22) **New York Times**, March 9, 1907, p.1.

(23) Hewitt, **op.cit.**, pp.218/220.

(24) John F. Winchester, **American Society of Civil Engineers - Memoirs**, No. 327, 1933, p.1.

the Hewitt single cylinder delivery car used the same basic chassis as the early Hewitt cars introduced in 1905.

The success of the Hewitt 5-ton coal truck, introduced in 1908, soon led to the development of the 10-ton model introduced the following year.

This 1908 Hewitt five-ton model is loaded with over six tons of newsprint.

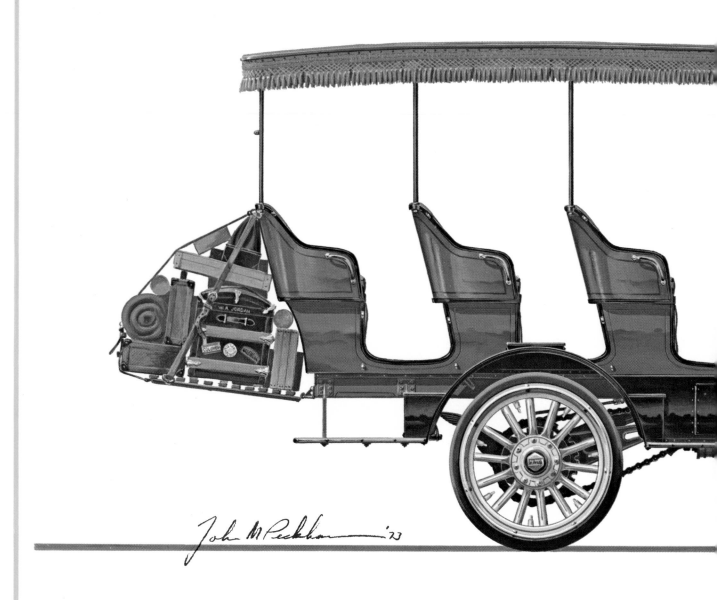

John M Peckham '23

1912 MACK - 20-2

Jackson's Mountain House

2

WILLIAM S. JACKSON, PROR.

Passenger Stage

A lineup of five 2-cylinder Hewitt trucks owned by a New York soap manufacturer in 1909.

While the Hewitt ten-ton truck was developed for the delivery of coal, a number of brewers in New York also purchased this model.

The Hewitt light delivery unit was redesigned in 1910 and received the Everitt 4-cylinder automobile engine.

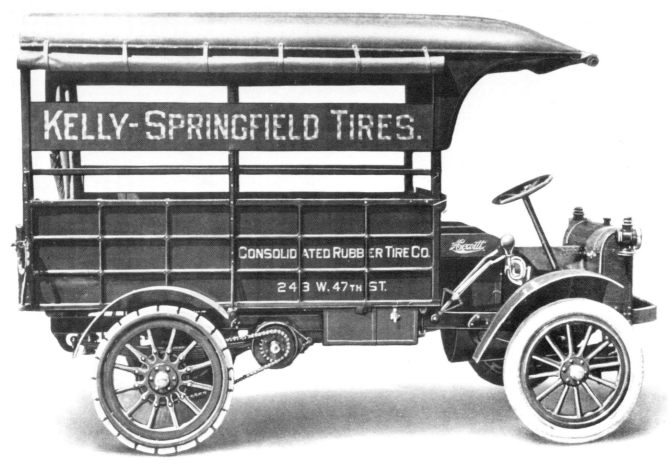

(25) **Horseless Age**, Vol. 23, No. 4, (Jan. 27, 1909) p.143.

In January 1909, the largest and most famous of the Hewitt truck models was introduced. This was the 10-ton model which used the basic frame and power plant of the 5-ton Hewitt, but with larger springs and wheels to support the extra weight.(25) The use of the same size engines and frames on various models was very common among truck producers at this time, as the builders invarably planned for at least a 100% over-load factor in many of their models. Even though the huge Hewitt trucks looked very ponderous, and were restricted to a speed of between 6 and 8 miles per hour, their pressed steel frames and cast aluminum crankcases did save considerable weight.

Because of the lack of space in the New York City plant, the Hewitt 10-ton models were built at the Peabody, Massachusetts, factory of the Machine Sales Company, during 1908 and 1909; and by the Brooklyn, New York, millwright concern of Phillip H. Gill and Sons, during 1910 and 1911.(26) A 7-ton model was also added in 1909.

(26) Information supplied by John F. Winchester, March 28 & June 6, 1973.

A merger was effected in January 1910, between the Hewitt-Motor Company and the Metzger Motor Car Company, which had been organized by William E. Metzger, in September 1909, to manufacture the Everitt automobile in Detroit. Mr. Metzger had been the first sales manager for the Cadillac Motor Car Company, and had earned an enviable reputation as one of Detroit's top automobile salesmen and promoters. The reason given for the joining of the Metzger and Hewitt organizations was Metzger's need for the A.L.A.M. license,(27) and it may have been Hewitt's need for another supplier of certain components, at low cost, which prompted his agreement to the merger.

(27) **Horseless Age**, Vol. 25, No. 1, (Jan. 5, 1910) p.44.

During 1910 and 1911, the Hewitt factory in New York was operated as the truck department of the Metzger Motor Car Company, although plans were announced to build a large Detroit factory for the production of Hewitt trucks in 1911. In 1910, the single cylinder Hewitt light delivery truck was replaced with a new 4-cylinder, 1-ton model, using the Everitt 17 horsepower engine, which was placed between the cab seats, in similar fashion to the larger 5, 7, and 10-ton models. However, the new 1-ton Hewitt used a conventional 3-speed sliding gear transmission, and this type of gear-set was also used on several new heavy-duty truck models in the 3-1/2 to 5-1/2 ton capacity range. Also, a slightly larger 4-cylinder, 40 horsepower engine, built by P.H. Gill Company, was used in all the Hewitt truck models above three tons capacity.

The opportunity to refinance the Hewitt truck building venture took place late in 1911, when Ambrose Monell, a friend of Mr. Hewitt's, offered to raise funds among his business associates to start a new Hewitt Motor Company. Mr. Monell was president of the International Nickel Company, as well as a director of several other large industrial corporations. During a lunch hour he was able to raise $600,000 of new capital,(28) with which to buy back the old Hewitt factory for its machinery, and to move to a larger and more substantial building at West End Avenue and 64th Street, in New York City.

(28) Hewitt, **op.cit.**, p.220.

Another important backer of the new Hewitt project was Edmund C. Converse, who was considered a power in the financial world. Like Mr. Monell, he was a director of the International Nickel Company as well as a number of other big corporations. However, with all this important backing Edward R. Hewitt did not have control of the new firm bearing his name, and he had scarcely started operations on West End Avenue when the news came, in March 1912, that the new Hewitt Motor Company had joined the International Motor Company.

The combined operations of 1912

As already indicated, the International Motor Company was created with strong backing from the J.P. Morgan & Company banking interests, which had also backed the establishment of the Saurer Motor Company. A breakdown of the 18 directors of the International Motor Company, reported in November 1911, shows that 8 were important officials of various banking and financial institutions, 7 were leaders of industrial corporations, and 3 were lawyers.(29) Of the 7 directors who are classified as industrial leaders, only 2, Jack and Joe Mack, had any long-term connection with motor trucks, and they had left the International Motor Company by the summer of 1912. The first president of the International Motor Company was C.P. Coleman, and the first chairman of the board of directors was W.D. Sargent, both of whom had also been officials of the Saurer Motor Company.

The first effort to coordinate the activities of the Mack and Saurer subsidiaries was made shortly after the merger, when it was announced that a combined sales office and general headquarters was to be set up at 30 Church Street. But by February 1912 the New York headquarters had been moved to Broadway and 57th Street, in the heart of the city's automobile district, and on March 1, 1912, the Hewitt executive and sales offices were also amalgamated at this location.(30)

Soon after the acquisition of the Hewitt Motor Company, their building on West End Avenue was greatly enlarged, and had become, by 1914, the combined New York headquarters and service station.

A healthy increase in sales was forecast for 1912, with a total projected production of over 2,000 Mack, Saurer, and Hewitt trucks. In order to meet the increased production schedules, the Mack plant was enlarged by the purchase of the Unity Silk Company, early in 1912. The Saurer plant in Plainfield also underwent enlargement in 1912, which was stated to double its capacity. Continuing the Mack policy of establishing company owned branches, the International Motor Company set up many new sales and service centers in eastern and mid-western states, during 1912 and 1913. The branches set up in St. Louis and Kansas City used the name of the Saurer Motor Company, perhaps to capitalize on the Pioneer Freighter's extensive demonstrations in the western states during its trip across the continent in 1911.

Advertising of the combined truck line commenced in December 1911, with space taken in a number of national magazines, such as the **Literary Digest** and **Saturday Evening Post**, during 1912 and 1913. Saurer trucks were featured prominently in most of these ads, which was to make up for the fact that little, if any, advertising of the Saurer trucks had been done before the formation of the International Motor Company. On the other hand, the Hewitt was rarely shown in the advertisements, and by March 1913 all three names; Mack, Saurer, Hewitt, appeared under the heading, "International Motor Trucks."

In August 1911, just a couple of months prior to joining the International Motor Company, the Mack Brothers Motor Car Company had begun the publication of **Mack's Messenger.** The format for this house organ set the pattern for other future Mack periodicals, with illustrated articles of interest to truck owners and drivers in general, and to Mack owners and employees specifically. After Jack Mack's departure from the firm in the summer of 1912, the name of the publication was changed to the **Mack Messenger**, and was discontinued in 1913 during a cutback in general advertising.

Under International Motor Company management the Mack Jr. and Mack Sr. truck lines were continued basically unchanged through 1912. The Mack Brothers had enlarged their dump truck line in 1911 by adding 4, 6, and 7-1/2 ton models, which were built for a few years. Two smaller dump models added in 1912 were soon dropped. However, the trend toward special equipment and modified chasses for certain types of special equipment had become very strong by 1912. In that year the Mack experimental department, after suggestions by the Bell Telephone Company of Pennsylvania, developed a truck mounted post-hole digger, which could plant a large telephone pole in 15 minutes.

Mack had also received their first fire apparatus orders by 1911, and late that year constructed the first Mack pumper chassis for Cynwyd, Pennsylvania. Orders for Mack chemical and hose wagons grew at an increasing pace as most American fire departments started to motorize in 1912 and 1913. There was renewed interest in Mack buses as extensions or feeders to railroad and trolley lines in suburban areas, and a special catalog showing the Mack and Saurer bus models was published in 1913.

(29) **Commercial Vehicle**, Vol. 6, No. 11, (Nov. 1911) p.568.

(30) **Horseless Age**, Vol. 29, No. 10, (March 6, 1912) p.481.

Many additional dealers were signed up for the International Motor Company's line of Mack, Saurer and Hewitt trucks. This garage in Floral Park, Long Island housed the agent for parts of Queens and Nassau Counties in New York. Photo taken in 1915.

Better Your Business

The right motor-truck — the right one — enlarges the scope of business and makes it more effective.

Henry Hanlein & Sons, well known contractors of New York, have displaced six double teams with one of our 5-ton trucks.

In this connection we offer:

Mack   Saurer   Hewitt

Proved by 12 years of real use   Proved by 18 years of real use   Proved by 10 years of real use

"Leading gasoline trucks of the world"

1. A truck for every need of every industry.

Capacities of 1, 1½, 2, 3, 4, 4½, 5, 6½, 7½ and 10 tons, with every method of load distribution and bodies adapted to all kinds of business.

2. Trucks that have already earned their owners more than the investment.

3. Accurate data covering every need of every business.

4. Unbiased advice from a competent Engineering and Traffic Department.

Inform yourself what motor-transportation with International trucks means to your business.

International Motor Company

General Offices: Broadway and 57th St New York   Works: Allentown Pa; Plainfield N J
Sales and Service Stations: New York, Chicago, Philadelphia, Boston, Cleveland, Cincinnati Buffalo, Baltimore, Newark, Pittsburgh, St Louis, Atlanta, Kansas City, Denver San Francisco, Los Angeles and other large cities
Canadian Sales Agents: The Canadian Fairbanks-Morse Company, Ltd, Montreal

Besides trade publications, advertisements for the Mack, Saurer and Hewitt trucks were placed in many popular magazines during 1912 and 1913. This one, featuring a 5-ton Saurer, appeared in *The World's Work* for November 1912.

This 1913 photo provides a good comparison of the Mack, Sr. line, a 4-ton model on the left, with the Mack, Jr. line, a 1½ or 2 ton model on the right. Note the similar radiators, but the pressed steel frame showing at the spring horns on the Jr. model.

The Mack 5 and 7½ ton automatic power dump truck models proved popular with coal dealers and contractors after their introduction in 1911. In this 1913 scene asphalt is being delivered outside the establishment of a "Practical Horse Shoer."

The first Mack fire department pumping engine was build in 1911 for the Union Fire Association of Lower Merion, Pennsylvania where it served the Philadelphia suburb of Cynwyd, now known as Bala-Cynwyd.

Mack fire apparatus proved very popular with the New York Fire Department with the first units being delivered in 1912. This combination chemical wagon and squad car is shown being tested on the steep Lexington Avenue hill in the Yorkville section of New York in 1913.

Saurer trucks were built only in the 5 and 6-1/2 ton models, the smaller 2-1/2 ton unit that had been imported by the Saurer Motor Truck Company was dropped. The 5-ton model proved to have good sales appeal, and many were soon hauling building materials, coal, food stuffs, and general merchandise in the larger eastern and mid-western cities. In order to facilitate the building of the Saurer truck in America, steps had been taken to convert all the metric standards to inch dimensions, and the first truck built using the domestic standards rolled out of the Plainfield plant early in 1911. A Swiss engineer named Gotfried Wirrer had come to America about 1910 to help in the changes being made to the drawings and patterns, and he stayed to become a research engineer with the International Motor Company, designing some special production machinery and truck components.

Four Hewitt trucks, ranging in size from 1-ton to 10-ton capacity, were displayed at the special truck section of the New York Automobile Show in January 1912. At this time few other truck manufacturers offered such a wide range of models, and no other company was building a commercial vehicle with a ten ton capacity. That the Hewitt Motor Company was able to achieve this distinction, in spite of its limited operations, was a credit to the ingenuity of its founder, Edward R. Hewitt, and his enthusiasm for tough problems and hard work, which was also shared by his associates.

After the merger with the International Motor Company, the small Hewitt models were soon dropped, and only the larger trucks, of 5-ton capacity and up, were built. Also, the old Livingston radiator operation was reincorporated as the El Arco Radiator Company, in 1912, with its new plant in the West End Avenue factory building.

(31) **Commercial Car Journal**, Vol. 3, No. 2, (April 15,1912) p.6.

The first change in management of the International Motor Company came in April 1912 when it was announced that Ambrose Monell and Edmund C. Converse had been elected to the board of directors, and W.D. Sargent had been replaced as chairman by Mr. Converse.(31) These changes reflected the acquisition of the Hewitt Motor Company and its importance to the merged operations. Also, by the summer of 1912, Jack Mack had resigned his position of first vice president, to try his hand at some new truck building ventures in Allentown. However, the announcement of a $1,500,000 loan which was secured from stockholders in December 1912, was the harbinger of many more changes in the organization of the International Motor Company to come in 1913.

Financial crisis of 1913

A shortage of working capital, which became evident at the end of 1912, was due to a number of reasons, but the main one given was the existence of an excessive inventory at the time of consolidation and that working capital could not be stretched to cover the merchandise claims.(32) The article giving this reason for the need for more funds also indicated that during the first ten months of 1912 orders for 1,150 trucks had been received, resulting in a gross of $4,500,000.

(32) **Commercial Vehicle**, Vol. 8, No. 1, (Jan. 1913) p.75.

Projecting the ten months figures for the complete year would indicate total sales of about 1,400 trucks and gross income of over $5,000,000. Since the sales forecasts earlier in the year had called for plant expansion to cover the total production of at least 2,000 trucks, it is likely that an inventory problem existed by the end of 1912, especially when it was not a basic policy at that time to make many chasses for stock. The "net earnings" for 1912 were given as $590,149, but this amount was stated to be before deductions for interest, preferred dividends, and special charges, which then reduced the net to $196,637,(33) for an approximate return on sales of 4%.

(33) **Horseless Age**, Vol. 31, No. 11, (March 12, 1913) p.487.

The fact that sales reached only 70% of the projection for the year did not necessarily indicate a lessened growth in the popularity of trucks in general and Mack trucks in particular. It did, however, indicate a more severely competitive market for heavy-duty trucks, with a number of the quality automobile producers

This winter scene with the American flag raised over the Saurer truck chassis most likely shows the first vehicle to be built to American standards after the converting of the metric scale drawings in 1911.

The factory of the Saurer Motor Company as it appeared in 1912.

having good marketing setups publicizing their new truck lines. Many dealers for these automobile companies found themselves under pressure to sell a certain quota of trucks, and many extravagant deals were offered, such as demonstrations that lasted months at a time. Prospective owners were encouraged by over anxious salesmen to consider overloading a normal operating procedure. In short, the truck market almost became demoralized during the hectic selling pressures of 1912 and 1913.

A loan of $1,500,000 was finally secured by the International Motor Company, but its price was high. In addition to 6% interest payable on the loan, stockholders were requested to surrender 55% of their shares to provide a bonus to the financial interests advancing the money.(34) Cash dividends were to be suspended for two years and William C. Dickerman, vice-president of the American Car and Foundry Company, was appointed to make a detailed inspection of the company's properties. A number of new officials joined the organization and several realignments were made in both the executive area and board of directors during late 1912 and early 1913.

The resignation of Jack and Joe Mack, and two other representatives of the Mack organization, from the board of directors of the International Motor Company created vacancies, which were filled early in 1913 by three important backers of the Hewitt Motor Company. Among the three were William E. Corey, president of United States Steel Corporation, and T.L. Chadbourne, Jr., who later became chief counsel for the International Motor Company.

(34) **Commercial Vehicle**. Vol. 8, No. 1, (Jan. 1913) p.75.

One of the new officials brought into the company during this period was John Calder, a mechanical engineer who had just spent a few months in 1912 with the Cadillac Motor Car Company as associate manager, involved with production and general organizational work. Mr. Calder was made first vice-president, and then also succeeded Mr. Dickerman in his duties as chairman of the executive committee; he resigned from the board of directors in May 1913. Also at this time, Ambrose Monell succeeded Edmund C. Converse as chairman of the board of directors.(35) In June 1913, John Calder succeeded to the presidency after C.P. Coleman resigned to become vice-president of the International Pump Company.

Reductions of Mack truck prices from 10 to 25 per cent marked a liberal new sales policy instituted in September 1913. It was stated that the lowered prices were made possible by the steadily increasing business of the company, but it was also indicated that lower prices and the easing of credit to purchasers were considered the key factors in converting many operators of horse-drawn vehicles to motor trucks, and thus increasing production to the extent that much lower unit costs could be obtained. However, this policy was taken by some people in the trade as an indication of the sluggish condition of the motor truck market.(36)

When the officials tried to get stockholder permission to pledge $1,200,000 of the company's assets for an additional loan, in October 1913, a court battle

(35) **Horseless Age**, Vol. 31, No. 20, (May 14, 1913) p.885.

(36) **Ibid**., Vol. 32, No. 12, (Sept. 17,1913) p.450.

The big price-reductions announced in this 1913 advertisement was considered by many in the trade to be symptomatic of the sluggish condition of the motor truck market at that time.

This 1913 model S 3/4 to 1-ton delivery truck was the first truck produced by the International Motor Company to have the I.M.C. monogram. It also had a newly designed monobloc motor and was supposed to be followed by other heavier models having a unified design.

ensued. A group of minority stockholders, many from the eastern part of Pennsylvania and represented by a Scranton lawyer, seemed angered that estimates had proven so different from actual results, causing their stock dividends to be passed and their stock to fall in value from $97.00 to $11.00 bid.(37) A temporary injunction to bar the company from any further action on the loan was obtained by the stockholder group when its representatives were barred from an important company meeting.

At the height of the controversy, in October 1913, John Calder resigned his position as president, reportedly because of a dispute over the loan. Vernon Munroe was then made the new president of the International Motor Company, shifting from his former job of secretary. In November, a Supreme Court judge, acting in Brooklyn, New York, allowed the company to proceed with its borrowing plans, but with specific limitations, meant to indemnify the stockholders for any losses, until the case was finally settled.(38) A week later the court settled most of the case and directed the company to proceed with its basic refinancing plans.

Some of the additional funds were needed to develop new truck models during 1914. Plans had already been developed by Mr. Stratford, the chief engineer during 1912, for light, medium, and heavy-duty truck models, which were designated the S, T, and W. Only the model S, a 3/4 to 1-ton truck, with the IM monogram on the side of the lower dashboard, and International spelled out in raised letters across the back of its chassis, ever got into produciton. This was evidently an attempt to build a standardized series of new trucks and its failure to get off the ground has been attributed to the excessive expense of producing the larger models, although a prototype of the model T, the 3-ton unit, was built in 1913.

(37) **Ibid.**, Vol. 32, No. 16, (Oct. 15, 1913) p.605.

(38) **Ibid.**, Vol. 32, No. 21, (Nov. 19, 1913) p.855.

Mack Brothers epilogue

The exact terms of the sale of the Mack Brothers Motor Car Company do not seem to have been made public, although it is obvious that the Macks, along with other stockholders, received either cash, preferred stock in the new International

(39) **Fortune**, Vol. 3, No. 3, (March 1931) p.67.

Motor Company, or a combination of both. It has been reported that Jack Mack had received as much as $1,000,000 for his share of the company,(39) and that a couple of other brothers also received fairly large sums. What the Mack brothers did after the sale is explained briefly for the record.

Gus Mack, who had travelled extensively in the western states while he was setting up Mack agencies, decided to settle in the San Diego area, where he purchased an ostrich farm. Prior to World War I ostrich feathers were decorative items used in women's hats and commanded a good price. However, a switch in fashions put the ostrich out of style and Gus then went into the real estate business. Charlie Mack went to San Diego also, and is believed to have been involved with some of the Gus Mack enterprises.

Joe Mack remained in the textile business in Allentown and New York, but evidently suffered a severe setback in his businesses after 1912. Joe also joined his brother Gus in San Diego, during World War I, when part of the Mack property was taken for Camp Kearny by the United States Government.

Willie Mack remained with the International Motor Company until about the time he retired, during the 1920's, although he did try his hand at building an assembled truck during World War I. His truck building venture was called Metropolitan Motors, Inc., and aside from a few pilot models being built in a small Bronx, New York, factory during 1916 and 1917, little activity was evidenced by this company.

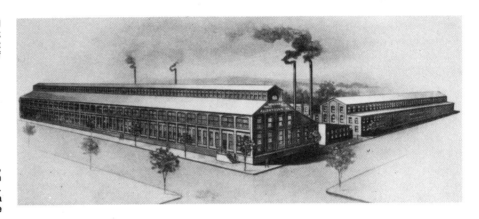

Former factory of the Allentown Foundry and Machine Company purchased by Jack Mack and his backers in 1912. It became the first home of the Maccarr truck and last home of Webb fire apparatus.

By the early World War I period the Maccar, spelled with only one "r" now, had been firmly established in Scranton, Pennsylvania. This 1916 1-ton delivery model was sold to a Brookyn, New York customer, where the Mack name was already a legend.

Even though Jack Mack had retained his title as president of the Mack Brothers Motor Car Company, and was also first vice-president of the parent organization, the International Motor Company, in 1912, it was not like the old days at the Allentown plant. Corporate headquarters for the International Motor Company had been quickly set up in New York City, and it was there, not in Allentown, where most of the final decisions were now made. Jack, of course, was used to making the important decisions, and so, gathering together some of his close associates, he left the International Motor Company in June 1912 to run his own group of truck manufacturing companies in Allentown.

Along with a man named Roland Carr, Jack Mack organized the Mac-Carr Company, in 1912, to make a line of 1,500 to 3,000 pound capacity Maccarr delivery trucks. Jack and his associates also acquired the Webb Motor Fire Apparatus Company, St. Louis, Missouri, which was renamed the Webb Company and moved, in the fall of 1912,(40) to the former plant of the Allentown Foundry and Machine Company. This factory was also the home of the Maccarr truck, and for a brief period in the summer of 1913, the Lansden electric truck, which Jack had acquired in 1912, and had moved from its Newark, New Jersey, factory.

(40) **Fire & Water Engineering**, Vol. 52, No. 5, (July 31,1912) p.75.

The same financial problems which affected the International Motor Company, in 1913, also struck Jack Mack's truck building empire, but without the same financial resources his collapsed. The Maccarr Company was reorganized as the Maccar Truck Company and moved to Scranton, where it remained in business until about 1935, when its struggles with the depression finally ended. The Webb Company disappeared, but the Lansden Company was reorganized, and had a factory in Brooklyn during the First World War period.

Jack remained in Allentown, where, after another unsuccessful try at building trucks, he formed the J.M. Mack Corporation, and became an agent for the Republic truck. Besides his successful truck agency, Jack remained active in the consulting field during the early 1920's, and was participating in the reorganization of the Northway Motor Corporation of Natick, Massachuestts, when tragedy struck.

Jack was driving north to Weatherly, Pennsylvania, on a business trip in his Chandler coupe, early on the afternoon of March 14, 1924, when his car became involved in an accident with a trolley car of the Lehigh Valley Transit Company, which was crossing the road diagonally.(41) He was killed almost instantly when his light car, being pushed off the road ahead of the trolley, was caught against a heavy pole and crushed like an egg shell. His body was interred in Fairview Cemetery, just above the Mack plant on 10th Street, with the inscription on his grave marker:

(41) **Allentown Morning Call**, March 15,1924, pp.5 & 7.

FOUNDER OF MACK TRUCK

1865   Jack M.   1924

Jack Mack's grave marker, in an Allentown cemetery overlooking the original Mack Brother's plant, pays a unique tribute to his founding role in the truck industry. Although the year 1865 is given for his birth, other sources state the year 1864.

The AB Mack - first of a new breed

That cataclysm of blood and steel, which a couple of generations knew as the Great War, was responsible for many profound changes in both the personal and business lives of nearly all Americans.

Most observers of the conflict, which started in August 1914, predicted a short war, but as more nations joined the fray it soon became obvious that several years might pass before a settlement would come. It took only two months for the Allied nations, England and France first, to start placing orders with the larger American truck producers. Such orders, while not too large at first, were welcome news for the motor truck industry, which was still feeling the effects of a sluggish economy and severe competition.

As the European conflict continued into 1915 orders started flooding into American manufacturers for all kinds of products, which greatly stimulated the American economy into one of its strongest growth periods. Truck sales, which had only grown from 22,000 to 25,000 in the 1912 to 1914 period, shot up astronomically to over 227,000 by 1918.(1) It is generally agreed that the First World War demonstrated the value of the motor truck in such a dramatic manner, that a solid base was laid for the continued growth in its use.

Even prior to the war-born economic boom, the International Motor Company had been making progress in the effort to improve its financial situation and consolidate its product line. In May 1914, a supreme court judge, acting in New York, threw out a legal action, which had been instituted by a group of stockholders to bar the company's plan to refinance its various loans.(2) A moderate retrenchment plan had already been underway since the fall of 1913, with a number of changes being made to improve the efficiency of the over-all operations.

In New York City the greatly enlarged facilities, at West End Avenue and 64th Street, were opened by the summer of 1913. This building had a floor area of over 200,000 square feet, and was set up as a service station with a garage capacity of

(1) Automobile Manufacturers Association, **Automobiles of America**, (Detroit, 1961) p.104.

(2) **Horseless Age**, Vol. 33, No. 20, (May 20, 1914) p.777.

A Saurer truck being demonstrated at a U.S. Army encampment in Southern California during 1915. Over 1,000 American-built Saurers joined the Allied cause during 1916 and 1917.

350 trucks,(3) and also had a plant area for the manufacture of Hewitt trucks and El Arco radiators. In the fall of 1914 an agreement was made with the American Locomotive Company to supply repair parts to owners of Alco trucks, manufacture of which has been discontinued during 1913.(4)

Corporate headquarters were set up in the new building, along with enlarged engineering and experimental departments. Edward R. Hewitt was made chief engineer in 1914, and given the assignment to come up with plans for a new medium-duty truck line to replace the Mack Junior models. The engineering staff, which had at its core most of Hewitt's former assistants from his previous business venture, had plans for the new truck drawn up in record time.

A brief description of some of the interesting features found in the new model AB Mack, will indicate the strong influence of E.R. Hewitt, its basic designer. The four cylinder engine had two large inspection ports which could be quickly opened for checking the crankshaft and connecting rod bearings, which were of generous size for an extra long service life. The engine was rated at a little over 30 horsepower, and a centrifugal type governor, mounted inside the camshaft timing gear, controlled the truck's speed at 16 miles per hour. A cross-shaft at the front of the engine drove the magneto, this design being popular on certain cars and trucks of European manufacture. An El Arco radiator was used and a rounded gasoline tank was installed under the driver's seat.

The most striking thing about the new AB Mack was the sheet metal work used for fenders, hood, cowl, and cab, to create a smooth but businesslike design. The styling was said to indicate a strong British influence, as did the use of a worm-drive rear axle, which was just becoming popular in the United States since its perfection in England by the David Brown organization. A 3-speed transmission was bolted directly to the flywheel housing behind the engine, and a well braced pressed steel frame was used with a curved channel bumper in front of the radiator.

Since the board of directors had not authorized the expenditure of funds to design chassis components other than the engine, the first series of the AB

(3) Commercial Car Journal, Vol. 5, No. 6, (Aug. 15, 1913) p.13.

(4) Horseless Age, Vol. 34, No. 16, (Oct. 14, 1914) p.542.

The Hewitt factory, acquired in 1912, was greatly enlarged during 1913, then served as both the main New York service station and executive office of the International Motor Company through the World War I period.

The AB chassis, originally built in 1, 1½ and 2 ton capacity models, was adaptable to a wide variety of uses. Here is a worm-drive open express model hauling coal for the owner of a stock farm in 1917.

models relied upon vendor built parts, such as Timken axles, Brown-Lipe transmissions, and Gemmer steering gears. But with the quick popularity of the AB in 1915, funds were soon approved to design and produce the needed components. Also, while worm-drive was first featured when the AB was introduced, late in 1914, chain-drive soon became a standard design, and customers then had a choice of two types of rear axles.

A first step in the consolidation of the product line of the International Motor Company was the gradual discontinuation of the Hewitt truck line, with the last heavy-duty models being produced before the end of 1914. The introduction of the Mack AB in 1, 1-1/2, and 2-ton models, that same year, marked the beginning of the phase-out of the Junior line, with the last 2-ton Mack Juniors being built in 1916. Production of the small model S, 3/4 to 1-ton truck, continued up to 1917, but demand was very low and a total of only 98 of these were built.

Most likely with the desire to spend more time on specific projects that intrigued his inquisitive and inventive mind, and to avoid the routine office duties of chief engineer, Edward R. Hewitt had resigned that position by the fall of 1914. He did, however, retain his seat on the board of directors of the International Motor Company for several years, and also remained as a consulting engineer for the Mack organization, contributing his valuable talents to a number of important projects over a period of thirty years.

Mr. Hewitt's successor as chief engineer in 1914 was Alfred F. Masury, who had been appointed service manager at the recently enlarged West End Avenue facility in the summer of 1913. Other former Hewitt Motor Company employees on the engineering staff at this time were August H. Leipert and Maximilian Frins. The next project for the staff to tackle, after the plans for the AB had been approved, was a basic heavy-duty truck, and work on this vehicle was well under way by November 1914.(5)

(5) Letter dated Nov. 27, 1914, to J. Winchester from A.F. Masury.

The Mack "Bulldog" truck is born

The improved financial prospects of the company during 1915 favored further product development, and the board of directors quickly approved plans for the production of a new heavy-duty truck model to be built in 3-1/2, 5-1/2, and 7-1/2-ton sizes. This new Mack model was called the AC and embodied several patented designs as well as construction features that were new to American practice. The AC Mack with its highly distinctive hood and a very apt nickname would help to place the name "Mack" in the lexicon of the American public: "Built like a Mack truck."

Some of the preliminary design work for the AC was done while Mr. Hewitt was still chief engineer, but he still must have followed this project closely after becoming a consultant, and therefore has been given credit for its finished design.(6) The engine of four cylinders had a bore and stroke of 5 x 6 inches, similar in size to the Mack Senior engine, which had a 5-1/2 x 6 bore and stroke. However, the new AC engine was rated at 74 brake horsepower, which was higher than the Senior's 50 to 60 horsepower rating. Inspection ports in the crankcase, governor built into the camshaft timing gear, and the cross-shaft at the front of the engine, were similar to design to those features found in the AB engine.

(6) **Commercial Car Journal**, Vol. 11, No. 2, (April 15, 1916) p.29.

Left hand side of the AC engine showing the large inspection ports which were characteristic of both the AB and AC power plants.

A basic designing concept of the "Hewitt School of Engineering" was the stress placed on balancing lightness of weight with adequate strength, so that dead weight, which contributed nothing to the efficiency of component parts, was eliminated as much as possible. Being a chemical engineer by early training, E.R. Hewitt achieved the weight efficiency by the use of various alloy metals and heat treatment processes to create parts which proved the value of their extra cost.

The Hewitt-endorsed metallurgical and heat treatment formulas were used extensively in making the AC engines, which seemed to have an endless service life, under normal care. The frames used in the AC were of pressed steel, heat treated to give them added resiliency, and were a decided improvement over the heavier structural steel frames used in the Mack Senior models.

Another important Hewitt concept was the striving for simplicity in mechanical design in order to avoid using complicated parts, which not only raised the cost of the product, but could also create a servicing problem. An example of the Hewitt's simplified designing was the casting of the oil piping as an integral part of the upper and lower sections of the aluminum crankcase and the front cylinder block, thus doing away with external piping that was subject to leaky connections. Also, the large curved front cross member of the frame acted as a bumper, and could be easily removed in case of major work to the front of the engine.

The AC had a simple, but very substantial, 3-speed selective transmission without the constant-mesh feature so famous in the Mack Brothers built trucks. A clutch-brake was provided in the AC, "to prevent the driven member from spinning when the clutch is released for shifting gears." This simple device prevented the clashing of gears to a great extent, and therefore eliminated the need for the constant-mesh feature to protect the gears from careless shifting.

Chain-drive was also a feature of the AC because of its claimed superior pulling capability over other types of final drive. The fully accessible drive sprockets could be easily changed to obtain a different gear ratio, and the high ground clearance provided by the solid rear axle was considered highly desirable by many dump truck operators. But the chain-drive was a subject of great dispute among rival truck producers, who claimed that enclosed drives, such as worm or bevel gear, were superior because they were quiter and not subject to dust or dirt. However, chain-drive was a standard feature of the AC for over 20 years, and contractors, whose equipment literally lived in the dirt of building excavations, were especially loyal users of the AC Mack.

The placing of the radiator behind the engine, and the development of a very distinctive hood design led to the public's easy recognition of the model AC truck. The radiator core was made of copper tubing in two semi-circular sections, each placed just in front of the dashboard, and shrouded by a steel screen. In the center of the two-piece radiator was placed a blower-type fan, which was driven from a V-belt running in a groove in the flywheel. Air drawn from under the hood and from inside the cab was forced out through the radiator and then out through the screening located at the front of the cowl.

At first, a sloping, rounded off hood was described as being of the Renault type, which referred to the French cars and trucks which had made this type of radiator placement and hood design famous. However, after production of the first prototype models, the edges of the hood were squared off, resulting in a

One of two prototype Model AC's built in 1915. The E-2 is shown here as it joined a military convoy leaving New York City for Plattsburg, New York, in August of that year. Note Chief Engineer Masury standing on the E-2's tailgate to observe the operations.

more rugged design, and leading later to a legendary nickname being given to the model AC.

It should be pointed out that both the AC and AB had all-steel cabs which came with an optional metal roof. These models were really the first American production trucks to be so equipped, as nearly all trucks at that time were delivered with cabs which were little more than wooden seat boxes, unprotected from wind and weather.

The first AC prototype, the E-2 test truck, was loaned to the Federal Government and driven up to the army camp at Plattsburg, New York, in August 1915. Other sample models were built and sold on a demonstration basis, before the AC was finally announced early in 1916. As acceptance of the new model quickly grew, the Mack Senior line was gradually phased out, with some of the last of these being sold as fire apparatus in both conventional and cab-over-engine styles during 1916.

In the spring of 1917 the British government ordered 150 of the 5-1/2-ton AC chasses for quick delivery to their military forces. An article regarding this purchase, in a trade publication, gives the following information about a very famous nickname: "In appearance these Macks, with their pugnacious front and resolute lines, suggest the tenacious quality of the British Bull Dog. In fact, these trucks have been dubbed "Bull Dog Macks" by the British engineers in charge."(7) The Mack "Bull Dog" was soon to prove its performance did not belie its looks, and thousands more were ordered for military service in the Allied cause in World War I.

(7) **Ibid**., Vol. 13, No. 3, (May 15, 1917) p.21.

Motor trucks help build America

With the quickening pace of business activity following the European conflict, the need for faster transport of merchandise and equipment became evident. Everyday motor trucks were being called upon to tackle new and unusual assignments to help speed commerce and industry in the United States. A building boom, starting about 1913, started to create a stronger market for heavy-duty trucks, which were used on some important, but difficult construction projects around the country.

The continued influx of emigrants into the various boroughs of New York City had created a transportation problem that necessitated the building of additional rapid transit subway lines after 1910. The Brooklyn Manhattan Transit Company, known locally as the B.M.T., was organized about this time to build a main line from Brooklyn to City Hall, in Manhattan, and then up Broadway to the Times Square area. Thousands of tons of excavated materials, from beneath the streets, had to be hauled away in the quickest method available so that traffic would not be tied up. Haulage contractors, who had been using horses and wagons, found that motor trucks were the fastest for this service, and one such contractor had 25 heavy-duty Macks transporting the earth and stone to piers, where it was dumped into scows for deposit in the waters outside New York Harbor.(8)

(8) **Motor Truck**, Vol. 7, No. 9, (Sept. 1916) pp.359/364.

The World War I era saw a strong public backing emerge for the "good roads" movement, with the Federal Government helping to sponsor America's first transcontinental road, the Lincoln Highway. Motor trucks played an important part in the building of the needed roads, with many contractors in the East and Midwest using heavy-duty Mack and Saurer trucks to haul crushed rock and asphalt used in highway construction.

Engineers of the International Motor Company, following the developments of E.R. Hewitt and some petroleum engineers, helped to develop what was called a "hot penetration" road oiler, which sprayed a hot bituminous binder on crushed rock to form a solid road surface. These units were first mounted on Hewitt chasses, and later AC Macks carried this heavy equipment, which contributed materially to the building of many of America's first modern automobile highways.

A highly dramatic undertaking in Southern California was participated in by

Mack and Saurer trucks, during the 1915 to 1917 period. The building of the Mt.

During 1916 and early 1917 the model AC hoods had screening for engine compartment ventilation. This photo, taken in 1917, shows a typical hood design for this period.

Building of New York City's additional subway lines in mid-town Manhattan during the First World War period necessitated the quick removal of thousands of tons of material. A 7½ ton Mack automatic power dump Senior model doing the job in 1915.

One of the last Hewitt's built fittingly received this special road oiling equipment, which was first developed by representatives of an oil company in conjunction with Hewitt engineers.

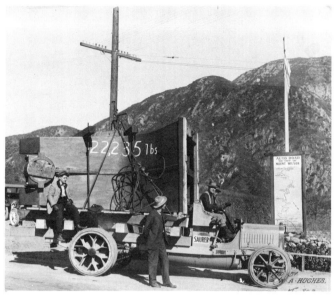

Saurer 6½ ton model ready to start its nine mile haul of a steel casting for the Mt. Wilson observatory telescope, representing a 100% over-load.

Only at this point on Mt. Wilson, the Devil's Elbow, where the road both climbed and doubled back on itself, did the Saurer need some assistance from the smaller Mack's which accompanied the move.

Grades as stiff as 19% had to be overcome by the Saurer, as indicated by this picture which shows the rugged beauty of the Mt. Wilson area.

Because of the extreme width of the load carried by the AC Mack up Mt. Wilson in 1916, the whole truck and its cargo almost went crashing down the mountain side.

The Mack AC not only survived the ordeal of its perilous ascent of Mt. Wilson, but bragged about its accomplishments.

Wilson Solar Observatory, at the summit of the 6,000 foot peak, three miles east of Pasadena, necessitated the movement of various materials up a winding mountain road, nine miles in length.

John A. "Jack" Stoner, the local agent for Mack and Saurer trucks, had sold two 2-ton Mack Junior models, early in 1915, to help the builders of the observatory in their task. However, the need to move a large prefabricated section for the base of the telescope, weighing 11 tons, prompted the builders to seek Stoner's help, late the same year.(9)

(9) **Commercial Car Journal**, Vol. 10, No. 5, (Jan. 15, 1916) pp.55/56.

A 6-1/2-ton Saurer was taken from stock and with only the addition of an overload spring and the removal of the muffler, the truck was ready to take on an almost 100% over-load. Jack Stoner decided to drive the Saurer himself on its dangerous journey up the side of Mt. Wilson, and agreed to make no charge for his services. The road was basically a dirt and gravel trail that had been hewn from the mountain side, and its course was a series of zigzags which averaged 12%, with short pitches as steep as 19%. The Saurer made the ascent in an unflagging manner, although it did need some help from one of the smaller Macks to negotiate one tight switch back, called the Devil's Elbow.

The biggest problem that had confronted Jack Stoner was that the tread of the Saurer was 16 inches wider than the road, forcing the truck to hug the inside of the trail, and more or less break some new ground as it went. There had been many tight spots on the trip up the mountain, and the successful demonstration was a great tribute to both the product and the man representing it.

A corporate and product realignment

One year later, Jack Stoner was again approached by the builders of the observatory, and he willingly agreed to transport another large section of the telescope; this one weighing 10 tons. A 3-1/2-ton Mack AC chassis was selected, resulting in a huge overload factor. And this time the load was 13 feet wide, presenting a clearance problem because of the narrow sections in the road. The AC had gone 8-3/4 miles with its tremendous load, and was nearly to the top, when the outer wheels broke away the edge of the road, almost pitching the Mack and its contents down the mountain side.

Luckily the AC with its load came to rest when the rear axle struck the ground, and seven hours were then required to right the Mack from its tilted position, and the load was safely deposited at the observatory.(10) A final trip to bring up the giant 100 inch mirror for the telescope was made without incident by Jack Stoner with another AC Mack, in June 1917, thus successfully completing an epic undertaking.

(10) **Ibid.**, Vol. 12, No. 4, (Dec. 15, 1916) p.7.

By 1916 the unprecedented domestic and foreign demand for motor trucks had soon used up all models and parts in stock, and caused many plants to work on a two shift basis to keep up with the orders flooding in. Under such conditions, new models, which were on the drawing boards in 1914 and 1915, were well into production by 1916, with their initial developmental costs being written off very quickly. With the plants of the International Motor Company sharing, to a great extent in the huge demand, a reorganization in both the corporate structure and product line of the company was deemed necessary for greater efficiency by the end of 1916.

A new holding company, the International Motor Truck Corporation, was formed on November 8, 1916, to assume the notes payable obligations of the International Motor Company. Additional funds were also obtained at this time to help finance plant expansions. With the International Motor Truck Corporation also owning 98% of the stock of the International Motor Company, the latter firm, through its ownership of the Mack Brothers Motor Car Company, Saurer Motor Company, and Hewitt Motor Company, now became the operating organization with its main plant at Allentown.

The International Motor Company also owned the International Mack Motor Corporation, which had been set up in December 1915 to run most of the company owned branches. However, by the end of World War I, the title of this company was changed to the Mack-International Motor Truck Corporation, which continued to operate most of the Mack branches for many years.

Production of the new AC engine by the Saurer plant at Plainfield, New Jersey, put continued pressure on those facilities with the steadily rising demand for both Saurer and Mack AC trucks. During 1915 the Saurer Motor Company had received several large orders for military trucks from England, France, Belgium, and Russia. However, for the sake of efficiency, it was decided not to accept any more large orders for Saurer trucks, since the Mack AC had been proven a worthy successor, and the Saurer plant could then specialize in engine manufacture. The last Saurer trucks were produced by the Plainfield plant during 1918, and the title of the Saurer Motor Company was changed to the International-Plainfield Motor Company in 1920.

With the discontinuance of the Hewitt truck in 1914 and the Saurer in 1918, only trucks bearing the Mack name plate were then built. This fact bothered E.R. Hewitt, who felt that since it was his work coupled with that of the engineering staff picked by him that had developed the new AB and AC models, the Hewitt name should have been used.(11) However, the Mack name was much better known, and the AB and AC truck models were being built at the Mack factory at Allentown, so with great regrets E. R. Hewitt agreed to the absence of his name from the product he felt so responsible for. And it has been said that the name Mack, with its short sharp ring, gives an indication of what a heavy-duty truck is all about: Business!

A very important part of the corporate realignment was the selection in May 1917 of Alfred J. Brosseau as the new president of the International Motor Truck Corporation. Vernon Munroe had resigned at that time and later became an associate of the banking house of J.P. Morgan & Company.(12)

(11) Edward R. Hewitt, **Those Were The Days**, (N.Y., Duell, Sloan & Pearce, 1943) p.221.

(12) **New York Times**, July 16, 1957, p.26.

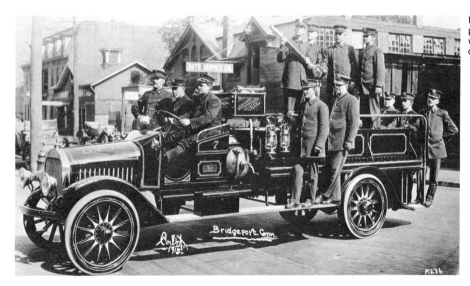

Mack fire apparatus continued to grow in popularity during the First World War period, with the AB chassis particularly suited for chemical and hose wagon service.

An increased use of motor buses became evident by 1916, with the production of faster truck chasses and the inability of many local tractor lines to serve growing suburban communities. An AB truck chassis fitted with pneumatic tires and special bus body, used in Los Angeles in 1916.

This 1917 AC hose wagon rigged up with a snow plow so it could respond to the call of duty in spite of the rugged winters around Wallace, Idaho.

Mr. Brosseau had had his basic business training in farm equipment and had held several important posts with implement manufacturers. Before accepting the top post at the International Motor Truck Corporation, Mr. Brosseau had been vice president of the Federal Motor Truck Company of Detroit, Michigan. He was later also made chairman of the board of the International Motor Truck Corporation, after the resignation of Ambrose Monell, who had joined the American Aviation Forces in France in 1917.

Trucks meet a transportation crisis

The growing burden being placed on the railroad network was evidenced by freight car shortages which were felt by automobile and truck producers by the end of 1916. Special railroad box cars had been developed for the shipment of autos and trucks, but with these in short supply other methods of delivery had to be found. At first, flat cars were obtained with the motor trucks being crated after being firmly secured to the cars. But with even flat cars becoming scarce, the motor vehicle manufacturers resorted to mass drive-away programs, with dealers and customers providing the drivers for the overland trips.

A growing shortage of freight cars had become so severe by 1917, that Federal action was taken to set up the United States Railroad Administration to coordinate the operation of the country's railroad lines. Even the continued shift of short-haul freight from rails to motor trucks provided little relief, for the unimproved roads outside most American cities still prohibited the economical use of heavy-duty trucks in intercity freight service.

Up to 1916 solid tires had been standard equipment on nearly all trucks of one or more tons capacity, and such vehicles rarely exceeded a speed of 20 miles per hour; and over rough country roads a speed of more than 10 or 15 miles per hour might be unsafe for the truck and its contents. But American commerce could not wait for better roads, and sought a solution in better transportation equipment. The development of the large pneumatic truck tire was one answer to the need for greater commercial vehicle speeds, and by 1919 most trucks of up to 2 tons capacity were offered with pneumatic tires as optional equipment.

The railroad freight car shortage and the need to conserve manpower also led to the popular use of semi and full trailers. One truck was said to be able to haul a double load through the use of a full trailer that tagged along behind it, but only in a few sections of the country did this system catch on. On the other hand, semi-trailers pulled by truck-tractors could haul a lot more than a straight truck of the same horsepower, and conserve time too; as the driver after dropping off a loaded trailer could then proceed to hitch up another fully loaded one, without having to wait for a trailer to be loaded or unloaded.

A continuing reliance on motor transport during the World War I period promoted the growth of many private and common carrier truck fleets, although **61**

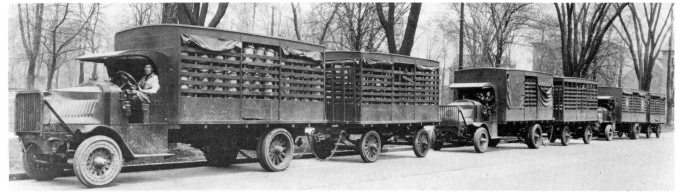

The use of full trailers caught on in some mid-western and far-western states during the World War I period. A Detroit dairy using full trailers with their heavy-duty Mack Bulldogs in 1920.

their impact on the transportation of freight was considered to be mainly a stop gap at the time.

Mack participated in developing speedier pneumatic tired trucks during the 1917 to 1918 period, and some of these were used by the Goodyear Tire and Rubber Company to deliver their products overland to Boston, New York, and other distant cities, from their plant at Akron, Ohio. By 1918 Mack AC tractors were being offered in 7, 11, and 15 ton capacities, and these were mostly used with the heavy-duty wagon type trailer having steel tired wheels. But with America's entry into the war, production and engineering facilities of the International Motor Company became heavily devoted to war work, although a supply of stock AB and AC Macks were also produced for the civilian market.

In order to raise production, large extensions were built at the Allentown and Plainfield plants during the 1917 to 1918 period. At Allentown, in addition to the construction of a large factoy building, a warehouse was built on newly acquired land about a mile from the 10th Street factory complex.

Sales of trucks zoomed in this period, going from 2,986 in 1917, to 3,834 in 1918. Financial results were also very promising, with net earnings of $1,245,771 on sales of $19,234,338 in 1918, for a return of over 6% on sales.(13)

(13) International Motor Truck Corp., **Annual Report**, 1920.

The Macks are coming

After the torpedoing of the British steamship Lusitania off the Irish Coast, in May 1915, with the loss of a number of prominent Americans, preparedness became a big issue in America. Sympathy for the Allied cause was commonly felt, and United States Army forces were gradually built up, especially after the Mexican border incident of 1916. Many patriotic Americans volunteered for an enlarged army and national guard, but the acquisition of motor transport for the various branches of the armed forces met some resistance from the traditionalists in charge.

Early in 1916, the New York City plant on West End Avenue turned out several armored cars for use by the New York State National Guard at their Plattsburg, New York, encampment, later in the year. Two standard 2-ton AB chasses were used, which were rebuilt with the control mechanism relocated in a lower position so that guns inside the vehicle could be fired over the driver's head.(14) The International Motor Company plant also fitted the armor plate to two other makes of chasses, with all the work being in the nature of an experiment.

(14) **Commercial Car Journal**, Vol 11, No. 2, (April 15, 1916) p.12.

America's entry into the European War, in April 1917, marked the beginning of a huge purchase program for motor trucks to be used by all branches of the armed forces. In fact, the projected number of trucks needed prompted government officials to gather a task force of engineers to design two standardized military trucks, which could be built in large quantities by a number of truck manufacturers. The Class B "Liberty" truck, with a nominal capacity of 3 tons and a maximum of 5 tons, was first produced in October 1917. However, many orders for non-standardized army trucks were placed with the manufacturers before this, as the first doughboys had already reached France in June 1917.

To prove the reliability of pneumatic truck tires, one rubber company equipped their fleet of heavy trucks with the new tires and then sent them overland for hundreds of miles. An AB Mack equipped with pneumatic tires in 1920.

This 1916 heavy-duty AC tractor was used in the New York City area. Note the sectional block tires on the front wheels and the large steel tired wagon wheels on the trailer.

This composite view of the Allentown plant shows the large additions, upper left and lower right, which were needed to keep output from falling far behind the huge demand for Mack products at the end of 1918.

It is believed that over 4,000 Mack AC trucks were ordered for the American armed forces, during 1917 and 1918, with most of these being the 3-1/2-ton models used for general cargo service. However, there was also a large group of 5-1/2 and 7-1/2 ton AC "Bull Dog" models which were used by the Army Corps of Engineers serving with the American Expeditionary Forces in France.

The big Bull Dogs carried forward all kinds of heavy equipment for Engineers, such as bridge timbers, pontoons, portable power plants, and construction machinery. The AC's earned a solid reputation for their hauling and pulling capabilities, among the doughboys in the A.E.F., which helped to immortalize the name "Mack Bulldog". In fact, the army declared the Bulldog to be their only standard truck in capacities of 5 tons or over; a unique acknowledgement of their superiority.

The International Motor Company developed a number of other products during the late World War I period, most of which were for military service. A special Bull Dog model with an electric generator, mounted at the front of the truck, just ahead of the engine, and equipped with a double radiator, was developed for aircraft searchlight service. There was also a patented gun carriage for anti-aircraft use.

Another project, at this time, involved the development of a welded sheet metal engine, with several engineers contributing patents on its features. A couple of these engines were later placed in experimental Mack truck models for further study, but continued testing evidently did not bring the desired results.

Many employees of the organization served in the armed forces, some of them making the supreme sacrifice. Mr. Monell, who had resigned from his active business posts in 1917 to become a colonel on the staff of the Commander of the American Aviation Forces in France, died in the spring of 1921. The report of his death indicated it happened as a result of a breakdown due to his work overseas; he never returned to an active business life after the war.(15)

(15) **New York Times**, May 3, 1921, p.17.

Just a fraction of the more than 4,000 Bulldog Macks ordered by the Federal Government for military service during World War I.

The tank was a British invention, but the armored car, in the right hand side of this 1916 photo, was built on an AB Mack truck chassis.

The AB armored car was developed in 1916 as an experiment sponsored by a private citizen for use by the New York State National Guard.

Engineers of the International Motor Company developed this special mobile gun carriage, which is believed to have been intended for anti-aircraft use.

This unusual looking 1918 Bulldog aircraft searchlight truck was constructed with dual radiator and specially designed generator and light projection equipment.

The 1919 experimental Mack shown here was used as a test vehicle for the welded sheet metal engine developed by company engineers at the end of World War I.

5 | 1919 - 1927
The heyday of the Mack Bulldog truck

A government demonstration

When the four million plus doughboys started returning home in 1919 they found the factories humming and America eager to turn warborn prosperity to satisfying peace time needs. The 1914 to 1918 period had made profound changes in public thinking, speed, efficiency, and being up to date had become a part of the American mentality. This advanced way of thinking was possibly an extension of what had been called the pioneer spirit. World War I provided the stimulus which sharpened this mood to the fast, competitive period we have come to call the roaring twenties. This new spirit powered the Good Roads movement that helped turn the mud ruts that still abounded in America into the smooth ribbons of concrete that replaced them by the mid-1920's.

To demonstrate the importance of motor trucks and other motor vehicles in national defense and also as a comparative test of vehicle operation, the War Department sponsored, in 1919, what was billed as The First Transcontinental Army Convoy. There were 72 army vehicles of almost all types in line, with motor trucks predominating. The convoy left Washington, D.C., on July 7, with orders to follow the route of the nascent Lincoln Highway, and finally arrived in San Francisco on September 6, two months later! There were numerous incidents on the way, most of which, caused by the poor roads and weak bridges encountered, kept the daily pace of the convoy almost to a crawl.

The Transcontinental Army Convoy traveling the Lincoln Highway somewhere in Pennsylvania, about three days after leaving Washington, D.C.

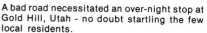

A bad road necessitated an over-night stop at Gold Hill, Utah - no doubt startling the few local residents.

(1) Dwight D. Eisenhower, **At Ease: Stories I Tell To Friends** (Garden City, New York, Doubleday & Co., 1967) pp. 157-166.

In one of his memoirs, Dwight D. Eisenhower described this trip and some of the events which happened along route.(1) The convoy had not even gotten out of Maryland on the second day when trouble developed with some of the trucks being stuck in mud along side of the road. Crawler type tractors had to be unloaded and called to the aid of the stricken vehicles which had wandered off the road for night bivouac and could not make it back in the morning. Also, the mud roads in Pennsylvania and Ohio caused many of the trucks to slide into ditches where they were helpless until rescued by either the crawler tractors or larger trucks.

Among the Mack Bulldog trucks belonging to the Army Corps of Engineers on the trip, five were effectively used to carry essential equipment needed for shoring up weak bridges and making major repairs in the field. One Mack was set up as a portable machine shop and another, a mobile blacksmith shop.(2) The trip focused attention on the strategic importance of motor trucks and the need for continued improvements in the nation's road network. President Eisenhower evidently never forgot the lesson of that 1919 trip, as he sponsored the now famous 1954 legislation which provided federal funds for the Interstate highway system.

(2) Mack Trucks, Inc., **The Mack Bulldog**, Fifth Series, Vol. 1, No. 1 & 2, (April-May 1970) p.18.

With the postwar business boom and the ever-great demand for the movement of goods, the market for motor trucks was at an all time high. The excellent publicity gained by the Mack Bulldog model while serving with the A.E.F. only heightened the good reputation which Mack had already earned in prior years. The Mack plants were run at capacity during 1919 and 1920, and a general expansion program was instituted in late 1919 to provide adequate manufacturing and servicing facilities for the future.

With the big AC Bulldogs in the lead, the Army Convoy heads up Market Street in San Francisco, after its grueling trip across the continent.

The Mack expansion program

The first major step in the postwar expansion program came on December 17, 1919, with the acquisition of approximately $8,000,000 in assets of the Wright-Martin Aircraft Corporation, including their main engine plant located at New Brunswick, New Jersey.(3) Later, Wright Aeronautical Corporation was reorganized at Paterson, New Jersey, and today (1973) as Curtiss-Wright Corporation operates facilities in various New Jersey locations.

(3) International Motor Truck Corp., **Annual Report**, 1919

The New Brunswick plant was ideal for making precision parts as it was originally the main plant of the Simplex Automobile Company, which had been building a custom automobile chassis selling, without body, in the $6,000 to $7,000 price range. Wright-Martin had purchased the Simplex plant during the war to provide manufacturing facilities for the building of Hispano-Suiza aircraft engines for which they had a large military contract. With the sudden ending of hostilities in November 1918, and the subsequent cancellation of large government contracts, most of the airplane manufacturers found themselves without a product that could be readily absorbed in large quantities by a peace-time economy.

The New Brunswick, New Jersey plant was acquired in 1919 and was then operated as the International-Brunswick Motor Company, a subsidiary of the International Motor Company.

The iron, bronze, and aluminum castings sorely needed by the Allentown and Plainfield plants, could easily be produced, in quantity, by the New Brunswick plant. With the new plant, vital space taken for foundry and machine shop work at the two others could be freed for concentration on the speciality of each plant. Thus, to New Brunswick was assigned the job of making, to Mack's exacting standards, all the geared components: steering gears, transmissions, jack shafts and dual reduction drives; New Brunswick had a very fine chemical laboratory used for metalurgical analysis and the precision testing equipment needed for the accurate matching of gears.(4)

During the years 1924 through 1926, extensions were made to both the Allentown and Plainfield plants.(5) While almost all industrial production sagged during the recession years of 1921 and 1922, the economic recovery which started in late 1922 brought record production to Mack. Sales more than doubled between 1922 and 1925, being $31,070,289 in the former year, and $68,912,183 in the latter. The broadening in the Mack product line also mandated the addition of new and expanded production facilities. The International Motor Company had complete facilities to produce, except for tires and electrical equipment, all the component parts needed for their line of medium and heavy-duty commercial vehicles.

The policy of product sales and service through company owned branches was continued and enlarged upon during the 1920's. By 1927 Mack Trucks, Inc. had completed a major building program, through a subsidiary, Mack Trucks Real Estate, Inc., which saw 99 branches operating in the major commercial centers across America.(6) Rather than leasing local garages, it was decided that buying the land and constructing service facilities on a model plan developed out of its experience would prove more effective in the long run.(7) Mack, as a local land owner and tax payer, was in closer touch with the communities in which the bulk of its product was distributed and this contact benefited the growing business in fire apparatus, buses and other public service vehicles.

In the New England area the sales and service facilities were operated by a subsidiary, Mack Motor Truck Company, and in the rest of the country, the Mack-International Motor Truck Corp. had charge. However, up to the mid-1920's, the New York City area branches were operated by the International Motor Company. The Canadian branch operation was under the aegis of Mack Trucks of Canada, Ltd., and starting in 1925, the Mack Acceptance Corporation began handling the financing of some customer credit.(8)

The largest local sales and service facility was the building in Long Island City, Queens County, New York, just over the Queensboro Bridge from Manhattan Island. The Long Island City branch was built in 1925, and, with its parking lot, took up an entire city block. The old Mack service center and main office building, at West End Avenue and 64th Street, in Manhattan, was phased out by the early 1930's. The Mack corporate headquarters had been located in the 64th Street building until 1921, when they were moved downtown to the Cunard Building on lower Broadway.

Until World War I, the storage and distribution of repair parts was handled by the Mack and Saurer plants. However, with the production of only the Mack AB and AC trucks, it became apparant that a separate department would have to be

(4) International Motor Co., **The Mack Bulldog**, First Series, Vol. 2, No. 4, (April 1, 1921) pp. 8 & 9.

(5) Mack Trucks, Inc., **Annual Report**, 1924 and 1925.

(6) **Motor Age**, Vol. 51, No. 13, (March 31, 1927) p.35.

(7) **Ibid**.

(8) Mack Trucks, Inc., **Annual Report**, 1925.

(9) Mack Trucks, Inc., **The Mack Bulldog**, Fifth Series, Vol. 1, No. 1 & 2, (April-May 1970) p.16.

(10) **Motor Age**, Vol. 51, No. 13, (March 31, 1927) p.35.

(11) International Motor Co., **The Mack Bulldog**, First Series, Vol.1, No. 11, (Dec. 1, 1920) p.14.

(12) International Motor Co., **Model AC Motor Trucks**, (Catalogs: 32, 33, 34, & 35, dated: 3-24, 10-24, 5-26, & 8-27)

set up to act as a central warehouse to supply parts for both the old and new models.(9) Also, parts were needed for the discontinued Saurer and Hewitt truck models, many of which were still in daily service in the larger cities. It was not practical for every branch to try to stock all the possible repair parts that might be needed at any one time and so a central parts depot was set up at the New York City headquarters building on 64th Street. However, by 1920 larger quarters were found for the fast growing department in the former Wasson Piston Ring plant, on New Jersey Avenue, in New Brunswick, New Jersey. In turn, the move to Wasson plant turned out to be a temporary one, as the large Pond plant, of the Niles-Bement-Pond Company in Plainfield, was purchased in 1926 and made into the General Service Parts Depot in 1927.(10)

What may have been the first delivery of a service part by airplane was made late in 1920 by the Richards Motor Company, Mack distributor for the state of Utah. A.B. House, the Mack territory manager, used a plane to fly a mechanic and an oil gauge to a Bulldog truck which was out of service and vitally needed on a local road building project.(11)

The Bulldog and the Baby Mack

The unparalleled success of the Mack model AC as a heavy hauler was due to a number of factors, chief among them being the balance of design. The chassis, while having adequate safety factors designed in, was not, at the same time, over-built, and therefore did not have the burden of unnecessary weight. Strength in components was achieved by a combination of good, generally simplified design, the use of alloy metals, and the heat treatment of critical parts. The rugged beauty in the outer appearance, especially the determined looking hood design, made the "Bull Dog" - as it was officially spelled at the time(12) - easily recognizable.

Another, and probably the most important reason for the Bulldog's success following World War I, was the returning servicemen who had seen it in action. Many of the Bulldogs had been inducted into the Corps of Engineers and many of the servicemen in the "Engineers" went back to civilian jobs in the contracting field where big trucks were a necessity. There is no doubt that a good many initial sales of the AC were made to ex-servicemen who wanted a Bulldog of their own. In some parts of the country the Bulldog had a virtual monopoly of sales to the general contractors and dump truck operators for many years.

In the latter part of 1922 an improved cooling system was devised for the model AC. The two-section radiator was redesigned so that the sections on each side of the cowl, in front of the cab, projected slightly and were no longer screened. Also, the belt driven fan was replaced by a squirrel cage blower attached to the flywheel through the clutch housing. Another change introduced late in 1922 was the complete redesign of the transmission from a three speeder with sliding gears to one having four speeds and a patented type of gear arrangement. Both the old and new transmissions had one reverse speed, but the main gear shaft in the new transmission was called an Interrupted Spline Shaft and had gears which revolved freely until moved, or shifted, to the splined section of the main shaft.

Late in 1925 the Long Island City plant became, upon completion, the major truck rebuilding facility in New York as well as housing the body shop and the Engineering Department.

Many big city buildings owe their deep foundations to the Mack AC dump trucks which hauled away excavated materials from far below street level.

The Mack Bulldog was not just a big city truck, as many could be found in the mining and lumbering industries. This 1921 Bulldog was used by a Wisconsin logger.

A popular sight along the New York waterfront up to the 1950's was the faithful Mack Bulldogs doing their bit for international commerce; long past the average truck's retirement age. This 1927 Bulldog is almost brand new.

The massive front axle and rugged suspension and steering components offer a fair indication as to the AC's solid construction and stamina which made it the favorite of the building industry.

(13) **The Commercial Vehicle**, Vol. 23, No. 9, (Dec. 1, 1920) p.303.

(14) International Motor Co., **Mack Dual Reduction**, (Sales folder, circa Jan. 1921) p.1.

(15) **Motor Transport**, Vol. 29, No. 9, (Dec. 1, 1923) p.318.

As a heavy duty truck the big city Bulldog was usually found hauling fuel, foodstuffs, structural steel, and rubble from excavations. The country Bulldog was most often found in lumber camps, rock quarries and mines where the going was rough.

The first major change in the design of the Model AB, or Baby Mack, as it was nicknamed, came late in 1920, with the introduction of a Mack designed double reduction drive. The Dual Reduction, as the new Mack axle was named, was not a substitute for the chain drive offered on the AB, but replaced the worm-drive which had been optional with the introduction of this truck in 1914.(13) Mack engineers considered the dual reduction drive more efficient than the worm, whose efficiency was said to fall off at slow speeds and under heavy pulling.(14) The frame of the new dual reduction axle housing, or "banjo" as it was called, was inclined to face the greatest angle of road shocks, which in turn also provided additional ground clearance for the differential housing.

The next major change in the AB occurred in 1923 with the substitution of a larger radiator of fin and tube design for one of smaller capacity of ribbon-cellular construction.(15) The new radiator not only had increased cooling capabilities, it also changed the design of the truck somewhat, as the radiator's brass upper tank extended a couple of inches above the top of the engine hood.

With the perfecting of motor-propelled fire apparatus in the decade preceding 1920, the few major American cities having horse-drawn fire apparatus retired them by 1924. The fire chiefs, being a very individualistic group, specified various combinations of fire fighting equipment to be installed on their apparatus and manufacturers rarely entertained the thought of a really standardized fire engine which could be produced in quantity at lower cost.

Up to 1926 modified AB and AC truck chasses, with a combination of Mack made and vendor supplied fire fighting equipment, were built at the Allentown plant. The Mack AB was fitted to medium duty service, where speed and not pumping capacity was needed. The AC, Bulldog, served principally as a tractor for aerial ladders and pumper with capacities up to 600 gallons per minute.

By the mid-1920's fire chiefs wanted greater power in their apparatus for increased speed and pumping capacity. Mack introduced in 1926 the type 15 fire engine having the 150 h.p. model AP engine with six cylinders and a 1,000 gallon per minute pump. The model AL bus chassis, also having a six cylinder engine, provided a speedy and powerful unit for fire fighting service. The model AP, types

15 and 19, had a longer hood to cover its six cylinders, but otherwise was similar in outer appearance to the famous Bulldog. The AL had its radiator mounted in front, hidden by perpendicular louvers, but the sloping hood had the determined Bulldog look.

A model AB "Baby Mack" taking on a load of gasoline from a newly built refinery in Southern California, about 1923.

This photo, taken in 1926, shows an AB dump truck with pump being driven by a power-take-off on the transmission.

Mack AB used to haul milk wagons to the central repair shop from various local depots. These wagons are similar to the ones built by the Mack Brothers in the late 1890's.

Mack fire apparatus took a big step forward in 1919 with the introduction of an improved rotary pump, which was designed by Mack engineers and built by the Northern Fire Apparatus Company. The prototype Bulldog fire engine with the new pump.

View of driver's controls on prototype Bulldog pumper. Note screened air intake for the radiator's cooling fan.

Another view of driver's controls on Bulldog pumper.

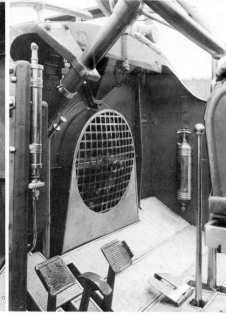

Pump and controls on prototype pumper show clearly in this view.

A Bulldog fire engine, built about 1920, with the rotary pump.

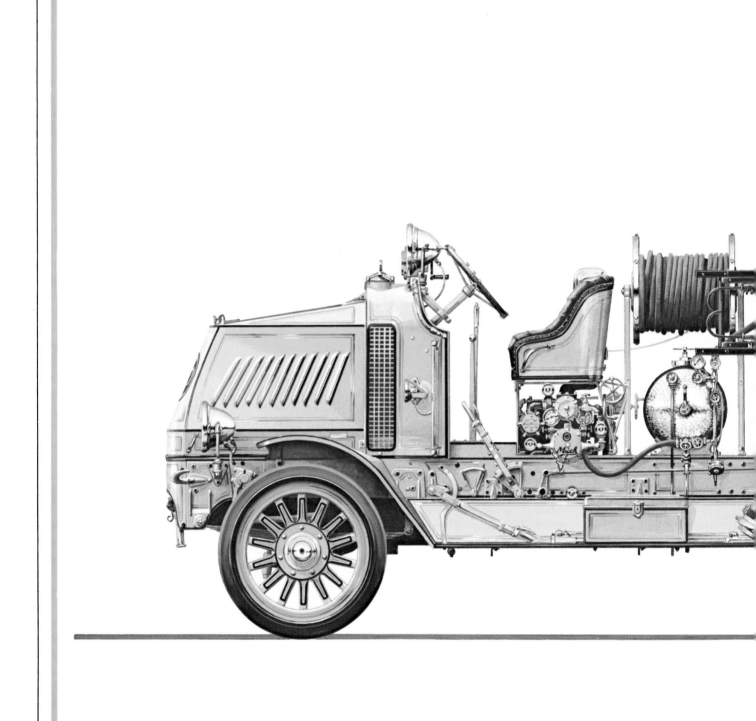

1919 MACK - A

Rotary Pumper

The motor of the 1919 AC fire engine was modified for fire service. Note extra water piping, with valve, near front of motor to allow additional water into cooling system while unit is pumping at a fire.

A Mack Bulldog hook and ladder built in late 1923. The Bulldog served mainly as a tractor for aerial ladders, and as a pumper with capacities of up to 600 gallons per minute.

The type 15, 1,000 gallon per minute pumper with the 150 horsepower model AP engine, marked a breakthrough for big Mack fire apparatus in 1927. This unit was delivered to Seattle, Washington the same year.

Without its radiator and protective metal skin, this 1925 Bulldog shows its rugged power plant and simple control mechanism. Note the air cleaner on top of the rear of the engine.

The 1926 model AB dashboard and controls were the epitome of simplicity. Spark and throttle were still located on the steering wheel, but the air cleaner was mounted on the lower right side of the dashboard.

(16) International Motor Co., **The Mack Bulldog**, First Series, Vol. 2, No. 11, (Nov. 1, 1921) pp. 8 & 9.

(17) Mack Trucks, Inc., **The Mack Bulldog**, First Series, Vol. 5, No. 7, (Circa fall 1926) pp. 8 & 9.

The motor bus and rail car

The development of the motor bus, in the early 1920's, as a specialized vehicle customed to the needs of the riders and operators was the natural answer to the increased need for flexible mass transportation in growing urban and suburban areas. Prior to the first World War, there were few common carrier bus operations in the country, due mainly to the tremendous expansion of the steam and electric rail networks in the score of years prior to 1910, which, in turn, helped to retard the building of good roads. However, with the tremendous population growth in the suburban areas and the building of many new roads following the first World War, local traction companies were hard put to serve the new communities and many motor bus operations sprang up as feeders to the local city car lines.

A standard or slightly modified truck chassis with a body built by a street car manufacturer passed as a motor bus during the teens and early twenties. It was quite obvious to riders and operators that comfort was lacking as well as ease of access and egress to the vehicle itself. The development of the Mack Shock Insulated bus in 1921, using the patented rubber Shock Insulator, was an important step in taking the jar out of solid tires, which were still being specified on some buses.(16) The next step was the universal use of pneumatic tires and the introduction, in 1924, of the special model AB bus chassis of low slung or drop-frame construction. Bodies for the new bus chassis were built in two basic styles: the City Body for local urban and suburban transit routes, and the Sedan Body for inter-city and charter uses.

The success of many motor bus operations, with longer routes and stiffer grades coming into use, led to the need for a larger, more powerful bus chassis. Several different experimental Mack bus models were developed, between 1924 and 1926, before a satisfactory six cylinder bus chassis, known as the AL, was placed on the market in late 1926.(17) Both the AB and AL bus models had, as an option, electric drive, which was a substitute for the mechanical, or geared transmission, normally supplied. With electric drive, the gasoline engine drove an electric generator which, in turn, supplied current in varying amounts, depending upon the speed desired, to an electric motor attached to the drive shaft. The AL bus was just the forerunner of a whole new generation of Mack six cylinder vehicles which were to follow in a couple of years.

The same conditions which led to the creation of the six cylinder AL bus chassis - the demand for a more powerful, faster, smoother riding vehicle - led to the use of both the AL and AB bus chasses by highway freight carriers. The Good Roads Movement of the early 1920's had been chiefly responsible for the decent

The 1921 Mack Shock Insulated Bus was an important step in the design of a modern low-slung smooth riding bus chassis. Note the use of rulers to indicate lowered body height.

The Mack Great Coach, developed during 1924, was one of a number of experimental six cylinder bus designs worked out by Mack during the 1924 to 1926 period.

A model AB bus of the mid-1920's with the deluxe sedan body used basically for intercity or charter service. City type AB buses were also offered with more utilitatian type bodies.

The AL bus, introduced in 1927, marked a major effort by Mack to market a larger and more powerful intercity coach which could also serve the longer local routes then being set up in some cities.

It took only a year after its introduction in 1924 for truck operators to discover the speed and hauling capabilities of the AB bus chassis. A 1925 Mack AB Bus-Commercial used in New Jersey.

inter-city roads which existed in many parts of the country by the mid-1920's. These roads were now being used by freight haulers, who, since their speed was no longer restricted by poor roads, needed faster trucks to accomplish a quicker delivery and faster turnaround. Moving van operators and other deliverers of expensive but bulky loads were quick to appreciate the value of the Bus Commercial to their businesses.

The roaring twenties was an age of speed, and businessmen had become aware of the importance attached to a swift and efficient distribution system employing the latest type of motor vehicle equipment. The solid tire was quick to disappear from highway equipment and found its last refuge, by the late 1920's, in heavy duty trucks, whose use was basically restricted to local city haulage work.

The use of self-propelled, gasoline powered, railroad cars for carrying passengers and baggage was not new, they having first appeared in the early 1900's on a few American railroads. However, with the greater use of automobiles following the first World War period, and the concomitant decline in branch line rail traffic, many railroads were hard put to provide adequate service at a breakeven point, much less at a profit.

There seemed little gain in a railroad using a steam locomotive and tender with full crew to pull only one or two partially filled cars on a branch line a dozen or so miles long. Therefore, the Rail Motor Car, as they were officially designated, or Rail Car, as they were commonly called, was taken up by a number of railroads during the 1920's as a means for cutting the losses on their branch lines. Most of

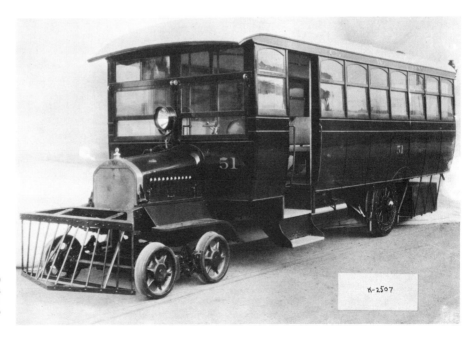

The first AB rail car was built in the fall of 1920 for the Chesapeake Western Railway. It was equipped with a body built by the J. G. Brill Company, as were all other AB rail cars built up to 1922.

79

the rail cars built during the early 1920's were basically adaptations of automotive designs, being, for the most part, medium and heavy duty models of such trucks as Service, Kelly-Springfield, White, and Mack.

Except for its two AC engines, one in each of its two railway trucks, the ACP rail car was far removed from automotive design concepts.

The first post-World War I Mack rail car was an extremely modified AB chassis with a bus body which went into service on the Chesapeake Western Railway, running between Elkton and Stokesville, Virginia, early in 1921.(18) The model AC was also adapted for rail car operation and three of these went into service on various branches of the New York, New Haven and Hartford Railroad early in 1922.(19) About 28 of the AB and AC rail cars went into service on various railroads in North America and Cuba between 1921 and 1924.(20) During 1923 an improved Bulldog type rail car, named the model ACX, was designed and approximately a dozen of these were sold during the years 1923 through 1925.

Interest in a larger rail car of standard railroad coach construction was shown by some rail officials in 1922 and a 55 foot prototype car, model AH, was assembled from a standard railroad car body with a Mack propulsion unit installed in the forward rail truck. After rigorous testing the AH was scrapped and a new dual engine rail car, model ACP, was developed at a cost in excess of one million dollars.(21) Three of the ACP rail cars were assembled at the Allentown plant during 1925 using bodies built by the Pullman Company and Mack model AC engines. After satisfactory testing of the ACP, the railroads indicated a strong preference for a rail car having a combination gas-electric propulsion system, instead of the direct mechanical drive employed in the Mack design.(22)

(18) **Automobile Topics**, Vol. 65, No. 3, (March 4, 1922) p.213.

(19) **Ibid**.

(20) Randolph L. Kulp, Edit., **History of Mack Rail Motor Cars and Locomotives** (Allentown, Pa., Lehigh Valley Chap., Natl. Ry. Hist. Soc., Inc., 1959) pp. 23-27.

(21) **Ibid**. p.33.

(22) **Ibid**. p.35.

Mack engineering achievements

The most outstanding developments during the Heyday of the Mack Bulldog were the sharp engineering advances made as a result of experiments conducted by the engineering staff of the International Motor Company. The Chief Engineer, A.F. Masury, along with Consulting Engineer, E.R. Hewitt, and a group of highly competent staff engineers, conducted a series of original engineering studies, which led to the assigning of numerous basic patents to the International Motor Company.

Early in 1920 an elaborate experiment was set up to gauge the relative effects on the tires and suspension systems of both pneumatic and solid tired trucks when run at speed off an inclined plane.(23) Five Mack truck models, ranging in capacities of 1-1/2 to 5 tons, were driven at speeds, from 15 to 18 m.p.h., along a straight-away and then up and over a sharp incline running to a height of 1-1/2

(23) **Automotive Industries**, Vol. 42, No. 8, (Feb. 19, 1920) p.514.

The importance of live rubber as a shock insulator in chassis construction, proven by the 1920 jump tests, led the Mack engineering staff to design and patent many chassis parts using rubber as a cushion connection.

These Mack trucks lined up from the 1920 "jump tests," are starting at the left after the World War I dreadnaught which did not participate in the test: AF-experimental, AB, two AC's and an AB.

(24) **Ibid.** pp. 514-515.

(25) International Motor Co., **The Mack Bulldog**, First Series, Vol. 3, No. 2, (Circa spring 1922) p.7.

(26) Mack Trucks, Inc., **The Mack Bulldog**, First Series, Vol. 6, No. 7, (Feb. 1928) pp. 16 & 17.

(27) International Motor Co., **The Mack Bulldog**, First Series, Vol. 3, No. 6, (July 1923) p.10.

feet in a six foot distance. As the trucks sailed off the end of the ramp to an abrupt drop back to the ground, the effects on the spring suspensions and wheels were recorded by two motion picture cameras. One of the cameras was a new type, called a Novograph, which took pictures at the rate of 144 frames per second. When played back at normal projector speed, the Novograph film resulted in a slow-motion view of the test and these views were shown in sequence with films taken at normal speed to help analyze the effects.(24)

Actually, the Jump Test had its origin, in part, in the investigation of the Belflex, composition rubber, spring shackle, recently on the market. The studies showed that the new spring shackle was not practical as then designed, but that the use of live rubber in the suspension system held promise. Consequently, the Mack Rubber Shock Insulator was developed and patented in 1921 and first used on the model AB as a cushion connection between the springs ends and chassis frame in place of the regular spring shackles then in vogue. The principle of using live rubber as a cushion in mounting chassis components was developed in the years 1921 through 1927 and used on all Mack products wherever practical. Such components as engines, transmissions, radiators, steering gears, and cabs, were all mounted with the patented Shock Insulator in one form or another. There was even a patented flexible rubber steering wheel, made up of soft rubber on the outside and fabric and wire reinforcements on the inside, which lessened driver fatigue by damping road vibration.(25)

Because solid tires were not very effective in absorbing shocks before they reached the chassis, solid tired trucks were not usually warranted for speeds over 15 m.p.h. It must be realized that pneumatic tires for medium and heavy duty trucks were still in the developmental stages, tended to be quite expensive, and did not give the mileage of solids. The use of the Mack Rubber Shock Insulator principle on motor vehicles prolonged the life of various components by damping out the destructive vibration normally transmitted through the chassis by the pounding effects that even pneumatic tires developed, at certain speeds, over the uneven roads of the day. The potential for use in automobiles was so great that the Rubber Shock Insulator Company was set up to exploit this market through licensing agreements with other automotive firms. Such autos as Chrysler(26), Peerless, and the Yellow Cab(27), were licensed to use the Shock Insulator with various components for a number of years.

During the years 1919 through 1927 more than 270 patents were granted to various Mack engineers and assigned to the International Motor Company.(28) These patents ranged from accessory designs, such as bumpers and trailer hitches, through components, such as engines and transmissions, to industrial processes. Examples of the last named patent category were special processes for the heat treatment of metal and special machinery for accuracy in gear-grinding. The International Motor Company also used exclusive processes for case hardening and burnishing of vital engine parts which extended their life. To name all the engineers and describe their inventions would take at least one book, but the overall result was quite clear. The Engineering Department of the International Motor Company, led by A.F. Masury, was responsible for making the Mack truck original in both mechanical design and process of manufacture, more so, than any other commercial vehicle of its day!

(28) U.S. Patent Office, **Index of Patents**, 1919 to 1927, (Washington, D.C., Gov. Printing Office, 1920-1928)

Mack in the Roaring Twenties

It was decided in 1921 to change the title of the parent company, from the International Motor Truck Corporation, to Mack Trucks, Incoporated, and this was accomplished at a board meeting held on March 22, 1922.(29) The change in title was basically made to identify the corporate name more closely with the company's product, but it also lessened any misidentification of Mack products with those of a competitor, the International Harvester Company. The International Motor Company continued as the manufacturing subsidiary of Mack Trucks, Inc. until 1936.

(29) **The Commercial Vehicle**, Vol. 26, No. 4, (March 15, 1922) p. 36.

The national advertising campaign in **Literary Digest** magazine started during the war to spotlight the model AC, was continued into 1920. This same year, during February, the house organ, **The Mack Bulldog**, made its first appearance. For the first couple of years the publication was issued on a monthly basis and contained a wide range of articles relating to the rapidly changing motor transport industry. While new Mack products were often high-lighted, the main thrust of **The Mack Bulldog** centered on how Mack owners were effectively using their vehicles. These articles served to underscore the Mack slogan: Performance Counts.

Starting in 1923 **The Mack Bulldog** appeared on a bi-monthly basis and the format was reduced from 9 x 12 inches to pocket size during 1927. The main advertising effort during this period was through trade publications and direct mailings to potential customers.

Mack products during the mid-1920's also included a line of truck equipment, such as winches, dump bodies, full trailers, and an aluminum container unit used with less-than-car-load railroad freight. In short, Mack had an exclusive line of

By the late 1920's Mack products also included truck equipment such as dump bodies, hoists, winches, and this aluminum container for the economical shipment of less-than-car-load railroad freight pictured in 1926.

tools for commercial land transportation as well as the correct selling methods to insure their proper application. The Mack salesmen were taught in the early twenties, by Merrill C. Horine, to analyze the potential customer's needs and talk of the economic efficiency involved with selecting the correct equipment. The world traveler, writer, and soldier of fortune, Negley Farson, writing of his days as a Mack salesman in the 1920's stated: "Horine, and those transport engineers of the Mack company showed American genius at its best."(30)

Production and financial figures relfected the high quality and teamwork that had brought wide spread public recognition to the Mack product line during the 1920's. Total Mack chassis output went from about 5,000 in 1919, to over 7,500 in 1927. Sales in 1919 were reported as $22,143,699, which resulted in a profit of $1,983,469.(31) But by 1927 sales had more than doubled to $55,270,295, resulting in a net profit of $5,844,307, which was before payments on preferred stock of about $1 million.(32)

(30) Negley Farson, **The Way of a Transgressor** (New York, Harcourt, Brace, 1936) p.342.

(31) International Motor Truck Corp., **Annual Report**, 1919

(32) Mack Trucks, Inc., **Annual Report**, 1927

1928 - 1935 | 6
A transition in transportation

Power and speed in highway haulage

The boom and bust economic conditions of the late 1920's and early 1930's had a profound impact on most American industry. The fast-developing highway transportation industry, along with its suppliers, occupying a strategic position in the commercial life of the country, was quick to feel the change in the national economy. Nearly all industries were riding the crest of a wave of general economic expansion during the late 1920's, only to see that crest crash with the stock market in October 1929.

The resulting financial reaction in the national economy created an ambivalent attitude in industry toward the purchase of new equipment. While industry tried to hold down capital spending due to severely restricted profit margins, the need for added efficiency in operations demanded new investment in improved processing and distribution equipment. The trend of the 1920's toward high speed, special purpose, highway haulage equipment, was actually accelerated during the depression of the 1930's. Power and speed were the hallmarks of the new commercial vehicles and their savings were measured in the efficiency of hauling the most for the lowest cost in the least amount of time.

The Chicago Century of Progress in 1933 and 1934 helped to generate interest in new industrial and consumer products. The "Mack Highway" exhibit at the 1934 edition of the fair is shown here.

The successful use of Mack model AB and AL Bus Commercials in the trucking industry during 1926 and 1927, led to the introduction of a complete line of high speed six cylinder Mack trucks. The first of the new six cylinder trucks was the model BJ, introduced in the summer of 1928. Its basic features included: a power plant similar to the model AL bus engine, having 126 brake horsepower; four speed transmission; dual reduction rear axle and four-wheel brakes.(1) The nominal capacity of the BJ when introduced was 3-4 tons, but this was increased to 5-8 tons by 1931. The lower frame height of the BJ was a direct result of favorable results achieved with the lower slung bus chasses when used in trucking.

In late 1928 the light duty Mack model BB, of 1-1/2 tons capacity, was introduced. The model BB was said to be the first motor truck to be equipped with hypoid gear drive. The new hypoid rear axle was a single reduction type of exclusive Mack design and manufacture.(2) The BB used the standard AB engine of 60 horsepower and was phased out by 1932, after the introduction of the BG model in late 1929.

The new BG had the same nominal tonnage rating as the BB, but was speedier, having the more powerful BG engine, which developed 75 horsepower at 2,200 r.p.m., and four wheel brakes with vacuum booster.(3) This model was quite popular, being manufactured until the mid-1930's.

A new light delivery truck of one ton nominal capacity, called the BL, was introduced in March 1930.(4) The BL featured four-wheel, Lockheed hydraulic brakes, and was also built up to the mid-1930's. This was the first one-ton Mack built since 1918, when the lightest capacity AB was dropped.

As the depression deepened during the 1930's, revolutionary changes took place in medium and heavy duty truck design and use. The slow moving four cylinder, 60 horsepower, solid tired, urban work-horse of the 1920's, gave way to the high speed, six cylinder, 100 plus horsepower, pneumatic tired, over-the-road truck and tractor-semi-trailer combination of the 1930's. Also, the perfecting of six wheel trucks and the re-introduction of the cab-over-engine design, gave new dimensions to highway haulage.

The model BC, of 2-1/2 to 3 tons nominal capacity, was introduced late in 1929. This truck had a 100 brake horsepower BC engine and with a relatively fast rear axle gear ratio, was considered a speedy truck.(5) The BC with chain-drive was the first of the new Mack six cylinder trucks to be offered as a dumper unit and its rating was later raised to 4-5 tons capacity. With the introduction of the BM and BX models in 1932, the BC was phased out during 1933.

With the new lower capacity B models, the AB had lost its claim, by 1930, to the nickname, Baby Mack. Also, by 1930, the AB was available with the BG six cylinder engine, in addition to its own four cylinder power plant, and by 1933 even

(1) **Commercial Car Journal**, Vol. 35, No. 5, (July 15, 1928) p.24.

(2) Mack Trucks, Inc., **The Mack Bulldog**, First Series, Vol. 7, No. 3, (June 1929) p.24.

(3) **Commercial Car Journal**, Vol. 38, No. 4, (Dec. 1929) p.38.

(4) **Ibid**., Vol. 39, No. 1, (March 1930) p.36.

(5) **Ibid**., Vol. 38, No. 3, (Nov. 1929) pp. 38 & 39.

The use of four wheel trailers grew in certain sections of the country as local state laws limited the maximum weight that could be carried on each motor vehicle axle. A BJ tractor with trailers serving a Missouri dairy in 1934.

The model BB was introduced in 1928, and with the lightest rating of the new B series Macks was referred to as the "Baby Brother."

The popular BG model as a soft drink delivery truck serving the Louisville, Kentucky area in 1934.

A model BC tractor pulling a Mack open top aluminum bodied trailer, pictured at the Allentown plant in 1932, and destined for a New York haulage firm.

(6) Mack Trucks, Inc., **Mack Model AB**, (Sales folder, dated 8-34.)

(7) **Commercial Car Journal**, Vol. 43, No. 5 (July 1932) p.38.

the sheet metal on the AB resembled the other B model Macks.(6) The AB had lost its traditional brass radiator, but was still available with the standard AB four cylinder engine and dual reduction rear axle.

In 1931 Mack started production on the medium duty BF, of 2-1/2 to 4 tons capacity. The BF was originally offered with the BG engine and dual reduction drive. However, by 1935 it had been assigned the more powerful CU engine of 100 brake horsepower and the option of single reduction rear axle.

The year 1932 saw the introduction of the Mack BM, BX, and BQ(7) which were the last models in the B series. The BM had a nominal capacity of 3-5 tons and was first offered with the BC engine, but after a couple of years the new CE engine, of 108 brake horsepower, was substituted. This model also had the dual reduction axle and found favor in the general trucking field.

The BX chassis was a larger and more powerful unit than the BM, having a BX engine of 104 horsepower when first introduced and a nominal rating of 4-6 tons. It also had the option of dual reduction or chain drive and was an immediate success in the construction industry as a dumper. The BX was, in a sense, the

The AB model was restyled during 1933 and continued to serve the medium-duty delivery field for several more years. This handsome delivery unit was finished in 1934.

The Mack Statotherm refrigerated body mounted on the BM 3 to 5 ton chassis, pictured here in 1934.

The repeal of prohibition in 1933 created a good market for trucks of various capacities. Here is a heavy-duty BX model delivered in August 1933.

The BQ Mack marked the heaviest model in the B series, with a six cylinder engine of 128 horsepower and a capacity of at least 6 to 8 tons. This gasoline tanker was delivered early in 1934.

first real substitute for the model AC, Bulldog truck. After a couple of years, the new CF engine of 117 horsepower replaced the original BX power plant.

The largest of the B series models was the BQ, which had a nominal rating of 6-8 tons capacity. When introduced in 1932, the BQ was offered with dual reduction, four speed amidships transmission, and the BQ engine of 128 brake horsepower. This model was described as a : "heavy-duty highway freighter and long-distance, high-safe-speed-schedule-clipper, with a speed of 40 miles per hour with capacity load."(8) However, the BQ met with a limited degree of success as a highway freight carrier due to the increased use of tractor-semi-trailer combinations, which could legally haul heavier loads than a straight truck with the same horsepower.

While not a new concept, the tractor-semi-trailer combination had been used in short haul operations since the first World War period; its usefulness as a tonnage mover in highway service was finally realized in the early 1930's. The direct factory to warehouse delivery of many manufactured products became a reality during the early 1930's and meant direct savings in time and reduced damage claims over other indirect methods of shipping. To the railroads, as the main tonnage losser to trucking, it was a double blow, as they were already suffering from the wide spread effects of the depression.

The general results of trucking's success of the early 1930's were the extending of punitive laws enacted by many states to restrict the size and weight of commercial motor vehicles. To comply with the laws and to meet this challange to the trucking industry, new truck designs and modifications of old ones had to be conceived and tried out.

The Mack line of tractors for semi-trailers during the 1928-1930 period was restricted to the shortened AB and AC chasses. These models were not the basic type of tractors best suited for over-the-road haulage and it was not until 1930, with the development of six cylinder truck models, that Mack produced a complete line of highway tractors. These were adaptations of the medium and heavy duty truck line and included by 1932 the AB, AC, AK, AP, BG, BF, BC, BM, BX, and BQ models.

The six wheeler had received its growing popularity in certain states during the 1920's, with truck owners attempting to adapt their vehicles to local laws limiting the maximum weight that could be carried by each truck axle. At first, many of the older trucks in use were converted to six wheels by the application of third axle attachments of local manufacture. It was obvious that new six wheel trucks had to be made with a unified and balanced design so that chassis life and operating efficiency would not be adversely effected by improper distribution of weight on, and power to, the rear wheels. The first Mack six wheeler was announced in 1927 and had a Krohn Compensator for proportioning the power between the two rear axles, or bogie, as the unit grouping of the four rear wheels was called.(9) Later, Mack patented their own Power-Divider, which was used on all the Mack six wheelers having drive to both rear axles and which were variations of the AC, AK, AP, BX, and BQ models.

The restrictive local limitations on rear axle loading, gross vehicle weight, and the overall length of trucks or truck and trailer combinations were basically behind the re-introduction in 1933 and 1934 of a modernized version of the cab-over-engine type truck that was popular in the United States prior to World War I. The c.o.e. design and its close-coupled variations were, in essence, the best method of obtaining the 1/3-2/3 distribution of weight on the front and rear axles, while at the same time maximizing the loading space and overall length of the chassis.(10) Any greater proportion of the vehicle's weight on the front axle would have made steering difficult on the heavy duty trucks and both manufacturers and operators wanted to avoid the additional cost of power steering.

The close-coupled, Traffic Type, model CH and CJ Macks, were introduced in late 1933 and nominally rated at 3-5 and 3-1/2 to 6 tons capacity, respectively.(11) These trucks were snub-nosed in appearance, having the radiator and hood protruding about two feet in front of the cab, and in the cab, the top of the engine

(8) Mack Trucks, Inc., **Mack Model BQ**, (Sales folder, dated 9-32)

(9) Mack Trucks, Inc. **The Mack Bulldog**, First Series, Vol. 6, No. 3, (Aug. 1927) p.18.

(10) **Commercial Car Journal**, Vol. 47, No. 2, (April 1934) p.16.

(11) **Ibid.**, Vol. 47, No. 1 (March 1934) p.34.

A revival of interest in the cab-over-engine truck in the early 1930's prompted the production of this Mack model CH in 1934 for a Baltimore warehousing firm.

A group of heavy-duty CJ Macks which joined the circus, pictured on a mid-western lot in 1935.

compartment had a special fume-tight covering between the driver's and helper's seats. The model CH had the CE engine and was comparable to the model BM of conventional truck design. The CJ used the CF engine and was comparable to the model BX. The close-coupled design of the Mack Traffic Type trucks suited them for the crowded and narrow street conditions of urban delivery work and in many cities the CH and CJ won immediate acceptance in the field of fuel delivery.

The Bulldog and his relatives

The great popularity of the model AC Bulldog truck, led in late 1927 to the introduction of the model AK, having the same general hood and radiator design as the Bulldog, but with certain basic engineering differences.(12) The AK had a specially designed engine with detachable aluminum heads, which produced slightly less horsepower than the AC engine. The turning radius was much sharper than on the AC, an important feature for city operation.

The AK also had four wheel brakes and its own specifically designed front and rear axles and purchasers had the choice of either chain drive or dual reduction. The AK cab was similar to the one on the AC, with the gasoline tank under the seat, but it had the gas filler cap with tank gauge on the outside, while the AC gas tank could not be filled without lifting a seat cushion in the cab first.

When introduced the AK had a nominal capacity of 3-1/2 to 5 tons, but after modifications this was raised to 5 to 8 tons in about 1931. The original AK four cylinder engine was replaced by the AC engine in 1929. The AK six cylinder truck used the BK engine when introduced in 1930, but the BQ engine was substituted in 1932. Its popularity for various kinds of haulage kept it in production into 1936.

The advent of the Mack AP, six cylinder engine of approximately 150 horsepower in 1926 led to the introduction of the chain-drive AP truck in

(12) Mack Trucks, Inc., **The Mack Bulldog**, First Series, Vol. 6, No. 5, (Dec. 1927) pp.16 & 17.

When introduced in 1927, the AK represented an adaptation of certain design characteristics of the famous Mack Bulldog. However, note the shaft drive which was never a regular feature of the Bulldog truck.

(13) **Ibid**., Vol. 7, No. 4 (Aug. 1929) p.18.

(14) **Commercial Car Journal**, Vol. 38, No. 4, (Dec. 1929) p.77.

(15) Mack Trucks, Inc., **Mack at Hoover Dam**, (Sales folder, dated 3-32)

mid-1929.(13) This model had the same style hood and radiator arrangement as the Bulldog, but of larger proportions due to its huge six cylinder engine. The AP, which was offered in both four and six wheel versions, along with the AC six wheeler, were christened: Super-duty Trucks. The AP had a nominal rating of 7-1/2 tons capacity in the four wheel version, 10 tons as a six wheeler, and 15 tons in highway tractor service.(14)

As a highway freighter, the AP achieved limited success, due to the restrictive motor vehicle weight laws enacted at the time. The AP found acceptance in the heavy construction industry, and about a dozen four wheel AP's were built for the gigantic Hoover Dam project in 1931 and 1932.(15) These huge trucks had 14 yard rock bodies and really qualify as the first Mack off-highway trucks built. In fire apparatus, the types 15 and 19, using the AP engine, found good acceptance due to their large reserve of power for speed and pumping performance.

The AC truck model became available with the six cylinder, BK engine, as a separate version in 1930, and in 1932 this engine was replaced with the BQ of 128 horsepower. Also in 1932, the AC was redesigned, and although retaining the general outer appearance of the old Bulldog, certain important chassis modifications were made. The new model AC had the jack shaft, brakes, and springs redesigned to accomodate dual pneumatic tires without excessively increasing its overall width. The front axle was replaced with one similar to the one used on the AK model, and a new tubular type rear axle replaced the former I-beam type.

By 1931 the AK was increased in capacity and a large six cylinder, six wheel version became popular for hauling heavy loads of building materials.

A large super-duty AP model Mack, produced in 1934, represents a refinement of the off-highway dump trucks developed for the Hoover Dam project in 1931.

Two six cylinder AC model dumpers with heavy-duty rock bodies at work on a Pennsylvania construction project in 1934.

The traditional chain-drive was retained in the new Bulldog due to its preference in the construction industry, where the AC now received the bulk of its sales. The AC was designed to take abuse from sudden loads, uneven ground, and steep grades, found in construction work, and contractors preferred the chain-drive for its strength, efficiency, and dependability. Private as well as government sponsored building projects of the early and mid-1930's helped to keep up the demand for the Bulldog, even after its heyday had passed.

Transition in urban transit

With the improved roads and competition from autos during the later 1920's, many small city trolley lines gradually switched to motor buses, or abandoned operations altogether. Even in large cities where the convenience of public transit was generally realized, some of the less patronized car lines were abandoned. The depression years of the early 1930's witnessed the additional failure and scrapping of many city and inter-urban traction lines, which, in turn, gave impetus to continued development of the motor bus. In addition, during the early 1930's, many cities converted some car lines to trolley-bus operation and this type of vehicle became an important mode in urban transit for many years.

(16) Mack Trucks, Inc., **The Mack Bulldog**, First Series, Vol. 7, No. 2, (April 1929) p.22.

(17) **Ibid.**, Vol. 7, No. 5, (Oct. 1929) pp. 16 & 17.

(18) Mack Trucks, Inc., **Model BG 6 Cylinder Bus**, (Sales folder, dated 5-31)

To meet the increased demand for modern motor buses, Mack introduced in 1929 the model BK bus with 110 brake horsepower, six cylinder, BK engine.(16) The BK bus was of conventional design and replaced the AL model, which was dropped the same year. Late in 1929, the improved AB, four cylinder, and the BC, six cylinder, buses made their appearance.(17) The new AB bus was basically for city service and was discontinued by 1934. The BK and BC buses were offered in different body styles for city route service or inter-city operation. A smaller conventional bus model, the BG, was introduced in 1931, and this was offered as a 21 passenger city bus or 17 passenger parlor car.(18)

In the late 1920's a new generation of motor bus for city operations, looking not too unlike its railed counterpart, was born. The "street car" or transit type bus, with box-like shape and engine recessed in or under the body became, by 1932, the new standard type of motor bus for urban operation. The Mack BT, 42 passenger, transit type bus, received good reception in 1931, with the Brooklyn

Mack developed the BK model specifically for long distance interstate bus service and produced this 33 passenger version of the BK in 1931.

This BT transit type bus, seating 42 passengers, was one of 50 sold to a New York operator in 1931. However, smaller Mack transit buses proved to be more popular than the BT, and less than 100 BT's were produced by 1934.

The 30 passenger Mack CL transit type bus, introduced in 1932, became a popular model for city use. Pictured here in 1934 is one of a fleet of CL Macks used to motorize New York's Grand Street car line.

Bus Corp. of New York ordering 50 of this model.(19) Special features of the model BT included: power steering, for ease of handling in heavy traffic; extra wide entrance, aisle, and exit, for faster passenger flow; rubber shock insulation in the spring suspension and chassis component mountings, for smoother, quieter ride.(20)

As the transit type bus proved its worth on city routes, additional models were added and the conventional style was continued for inter-city service. The CL Mack, 30 passenger, transit type bus was introduced in 1932 and both the BT and CL had a roll-out engine mounting for quick power plant removal and servicing.(21) In 1933, the 20 passenger, CG, transit type model, with BG engine, was introduced to round out the line of Mack city route buses. The conventional style, model BK, inter-city bus, was dropped by 1933, and continued Mack bus development was centered on the transit type.

A further improvement in transit type bus design took place in 1934 with the introduction of rear engine design. The Mack 30 passenger CQ, rear engine, transit type bus, introduced in the fall of 1934, was soon followed by other models of modern styling. By the fall of 1935, Mack was offering five basic modern transit type buses, three with rear mounted engines and two with engines in front. The rear engines models with general seating capacitites were: CW, 21 passengers; CQ, 31 passengers; CT, 35 passengers. Mack buses with engines still in front were: CG, 21 passengers and the CX for 29 to 31 passengers.(22)

Changes in urban transit modes took place at a quickening pace during the 1930's and Mack products marked this progress with quality built vehicles. In the summer of 1934 the Community Traction Company of Toledo, Ohio, ordered seven 40 passenger Mack trolley buses, which went into service on the Dorr Street line, early in 1935. These CR model trolley buses had electrical equipment made by Westinghouse and used the BQ dual reduction axle in an inverted position for low floor clearance.(23) Mack also built one bus called an All Service Vehicle, in 1935, which was essentially a gas-electric bus capable of operating as either a trolley bus or motor bus, as conditions warranted.

(19) Mack Trucks, Inc., **The Mack Bulldog**, First Series, Vol. 7, No. 11, (Dec. 1931) p.13.

(20) **Transit Journal**, Vol. 76, No. 11, (Oct. 15, 1932) p.119.

(21) **Transit Journal**, Vol. 76, No. 11, (Oct. 15. 1932) p.121.

(22) **Ibid.**, Vol. 79, No. 10, (Sept. 14, 1935) p.360.

(23) **Ibid.**, Vol. 79, No. 3, (March 1935) pp. 86 & 87.

The CQ Mack, with a seating capacity of 30 passengers, had modern streamlining and its engine placed at the rear. Note the fan and circular intake at the back of this 1935 CQ bus.

The Dorr Street line in Toledo, Ohio received the first Mack model CR, 40 passenger trolley buses early in 1935.

Other Mack products

With the shift of interest, by railroad operating officials, to the gas-electric type of rail motor car, the Mack rail car program was moved from Allentown to the Plainfield plant in 1926. At a recently acquired factory buiding in Plainfield, a whole new series of gas-electric rail cars, using the new AP engine, either singly, or in multiples, was developed by the fall of 1927. Market potential was considered much greater for a larger type car which conformed more to the traffic needs of the Class I railroads.

The first gas-electric rail car produced at Plainfield was the dual engine AQ and after satisfactory testing was sold to the New York Central Railroad for service in the Adirondack Moutain region.(24) Both the AQ and its more powerful companion model AR, having three AP engines, had car bodies of slightly over 76 feet in length, which were supplied by regular railroad pasenger equipment manufacturers. Three model AS cars, of 52 feet overall length, and having one AP engine each, were produced in 1928.

Before the gas-electric rail car program was phased out at the end of 1929, with a production of about 20 total units, plans for the production of gas-electric industrial locomotives, in various sizes, had been set. The Allentown plant had built, in 1921, a 33 ton, chain drive, switch engine, for shunting railroad freight cars on the factory sidings. This locomotive had two AC engines, one at each end, with Bulldog hood arrangement, and was used for many years at Allentown. The Plainfield plant produced about 20 locomotives in five sizes of from 12 to 60 tons, between 1929 and the mid-1930's.(25) A few truck and bus rail conversions were made at Allentown and Plainfield during the early 1930's, but the depression effectively dried up the market for new Mack rail equipment.

(24) Randolph L. Kulp, Edit., **History of Mack Rail Motor Cars and Locomotives** (Allentown, Pa., Lehigh Valley Chap., Natl. Ry. Hist. Soc., Inc., 1959) pp. 37 & 47.

(25) **Ibid**., pp. 51, 63, & 65.

The first of a series of large rail cars produced between 1927 and 1929 at the Plainfield plant was this model AQ, having two AP engines and seats for 77 passengers.

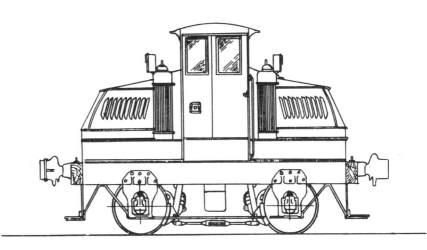

The first production model locomotive built at the Plainfield plant, in 1928, was this model BR which was patterned after the original Mack switch engine built at the Allentown plant in 1921.

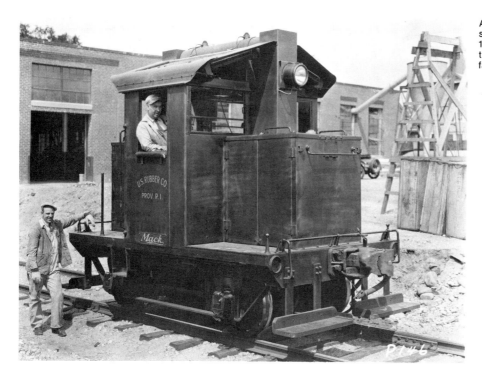

About 10 of these 15-ton Mack gas-electric switching locomotives were produced by 1930, with most being purchased by industrial companies for use around their manufacturing facilities.

Mack fire apparatus took on added importance with the continued development of the six cylinder engine during the late 1920's and early 1930's. As regular commercial and bus models, with more powerful engines, were introduced, the adaptation of these chassis to fire service became the basis for a wider variety of fire apparatus models.

The largest Mack fire engines were the type 19 and 90, having power plants of 150 and 120 brake horsepower respectively.(26) The AP engine was used in the type 19 and the 90 had an engine similar to the AL. Both were capable of utilizing the larger fire pumps of 1,000 g.p.m. The last Mack fire apparatus using the Bulldog type hood with AP engine was built in 1930 for delivery to the New York Fire Department.

The type 75, with a power plant of 110 horsepower, was produced with a 750 g.p.m. fire pump, and the types 60 and 55 had 600 g.p.m. pumps. There were also smaller Mack models having smaller pump capacities, which were mainly used in towns and rural areas. Fire department needs vary with the size and type of district served, and Mack designed equipment to meet the most divergent requirements.

In 1928, Mack developed an engine-driven mechanical hoist for aerial ladders,(27) which was the first of this type put into production. Most aerial ladders at this time were either spring assisted or operated by compressed air. The Mack engine-driven power hoist used a power take-off, from the transmission on the tractor, to drive a vertical shaft, which passed directly through the center line of both the fifth wheel and ladder turntable. The Mack aerial ladders came in 65, 75, and 85 foot lengths and were extremely strong, being fully trussed.

Other fire equipment improvements instituted by Mack during the 1928 to 1935 period included pressure-volume, series parallel centrifugal pumps and improved rotary types. The centrifugal pump, while not a new development, realized its potential after the introduction of the high speed six cylinder engine in commercial vehicles and eventually became the standard pump for heavy duty fire service.

Booster tanks, as a means of hauling a limited amount of water to a fire, were often specified by fire departments in rural areas or new developments lacking fire hydrants. Mack fire engines, because of their substantial construction, were often chosen to be equipped with booster tanks, and one Mack having a 2,500 gallon tank, on a six wheel chassis, was built in 1935.(28) Mack introduced the first enclosed body, or sedan type, fire engine in America during 1935, and the

(26) Mack Trucks, Inc., **Aerial Ladder Truck** (Sales folder, dated 11-31)

(27) Mack Trucks, Inc., **The Mack Bulldog**, First Series, Vol. 6, No. 11, (Dec. 1928) p. 12.

(28) **Fire Engineering**, Vol. 88, No. 7, (July 1935) p. 301.

slogan: There's a Mack For Every Fire Fighting Need, were not idle words.

The Mack line of truck equipment was expanded in the late 1920's to include four wheel trailers of 5 and 10 tons capacity using the model AB and AC truck components. There was also a six wheel trailer of 12 to 15 tons capacity, and all trailers had some form of powered brakes. With the rapid development of highway trucking, Mack expanded the line, by 1932, to include semi-trailers with capacitites ranging from 5 to 18 tons in four model sizes.(29) Mack also offered a variety of custom built trailers, and all semi-trailer hitches were later protected by the patented Mack Coincidental Safety Lock.

The manufacture of Mack dump bodies was continued into the 1930's and much progress was made in the development of specially designed refrigerated bodies. The Mack Statotherm refrigeration control equipment was capable of maintaining enclosed truck body temperatures within a variation of one degree Fahrenheit.(30 The building of truck bodies was, for the most part, a custom area, not lending itself to quantity production methods, but Mack continued much of this work at their Long Island City plant.

Mack duels the Depression

With the deepening depression, Mack, along with many other builders of medium and heavy duty commercial vehicles, suffered from a reduction in domestic sales of over 75% by 1932. Mack's new domestic truck registrations for 1932 equaled 1,425 units, as compared with 6,890 in 1928.(31) The resulting loss in 1932 was $1,479,598 on sales of $13,217,992(32) as compared with a net profit of $5,915,301 on sales of $55,850,861 in 1928.(33) The problem of slackening demand for heavier trucks during the early 1930's was compounded by the builders of light trucks who invaded the medium duty market and truck equipment firms who offered third axle conversion units to beef up the capacities of light duty trucks already on the road.

(29) Mack Trucks, Inc., **Mack Semi-trailers**, (Sales booklet, dated 6-32)

(30) Mack Trucks, Inc., **Mack in the Dairy Industries**, (Sales booklet, dated 10-34)

(31) **Commercial Car Journal**, Vol. 57, No. 2, (April 1939) p. 21.

(32) Mack Trucks, Inc., **Annual Report**, 1932.

(33) Mack Trucks, Inc., **Annual Report**, 1928.

A powerful type 19, 750 gallon per minute centrifugal pumper, pictured just before its delivery in 1931 to the community of Mountain Lakes, New Jersey.

Mack is credited with building the first enclosed body fire engine in the United States during 1935. This type 19 had seats for 10 fire fighters and was delivered to Charlotte, North Carolina.

Mack's chief engineer between 1914 and 1933 was Alfred Fellows Masury. His tragic death in 1933 deprived the organization as well as the industry of a great inventive genius.

Obviously, the basic reason for losses during the early 1930's was that low manufacturing profit margins had to cover many fixed operating costs. Also, the increasing number of different truck models, with lower production runs per model, created a problem for the write-off of developmental costs. The interchangeability of parts between certain trucks helped to ease the problem associated with introducing new models, but lower overall sales still could not justify the continuation of an extensive branch network, which numbered 105(34) in the United States and Canada by 1931.

(34) Mack Trucks, Inc., **Mack in Public Works**, (Sales catalog, dated 6-31)

A human tragedy which had a profound effect on the Mack organization, came with the crash of the huge U.S. Navy airship Akron, off the coast of New Jersey, in April 1933. Among the 73 victims of the disaster was Lt. Col. Alfred Fellows Masury, U.S. Army Reserve Corp.(35), who as Chief Engineer and a Vice President, had assigned over 115 patents to the company, in addition to many others which he co-invented with various staff engineers. Col. Masury had supervised a large engineering department which was responsible for keeping Mack commercial vehicles at the peak of technical excellence.

(35) **New York Times**, April 5, 1933, p.16.

A.F. Masury was an active member of the Society of Automotive Engineers, contributing many papers on important technical matters. He had also spent his entire business career in the motor truck industry and his loss was a serious one to both the Mack organization and the automotive industry. The famous Bulldog radiator mascot that Masury designed and patented in 1932(36), has appeared on Mack trucks since then, serving as a memorial to this man's genius.

(36) U.S. Patent Office, **Index of Patents 1932**, (Washington, D.C., Gov. Printing Office, 1933) Pat. No. Des. 87,931.

The major thrust of Mack engineering, starting in the late 1920's, was in the development of six cylinder engines and improved chassis components needed for an increasing line of diversified commercial vehicles. Patents assigned to Mack during the four year period, 1928 to 1931, totaled 224, while the total received for the eight years ended in December 1935 was 352. Development had begun in 1928 of a diesel engine, but encounted severe technical problems relating to reducing the Diesel's weight to horsepower ratio. The tremendous pressures built up as part of a Diesel's normal working cycle required heavier engine block castings and other related parts. But in various trials the Diesel had proved its basic economy and so the engineers worked long hours to overcome metalurgical and combustion chamber problems.

In order to survive the depression and get back on a profitable operating basis, two basic courses of action were apparently open to Mack management. First of all, they could have saved money by reducing the quality of the product, introducing much cheaper models, and cut their branch operations drastically, using dealers on a much wider scale than before. Or, they could keep faith with company tradition and loyal customers by keeping quality in the Mack product, but sell a non-competing line of lighter duty trucks through their branches, in order to cut overhead losses. Mack chose the latter course.

Late in 1933 negotiations had been reported between Mack and Ford for the sale of the Ford line of light trucks through Mack branches.(37) However, a year later, in October 1934, an agreement was made with the Reo Motor Car Company to sell Reo trucks through a limited number of Mack branches.(38) Reo had made the famous Speedwagon light delivery model and Reo trucks had a good reputation for dependability.

Also, by 1934 the business picture looked brighter, with confidence returning to many sectors of the economy. This same year Mack Trucks, Inc. reported a net profit of $17,134 on sales of $18,346,222.(39) By 1936 Mack was operating on a profitable basis, but had pared their branches to 76,(40) the smaller ones having been sold to dealers. Mack had dueled the depression without impairing its reputation for quality built products and had kept its organization essentially intact.

(37) **New York Times**, Dec. 13, 1933, p.37.

(38) **Commercial Car Journal**, Vol. 48, No. 3, (Nov. 1934) p.50.

(39) Mack Trucks, Inc., **Annual Report**, 1934

(40) Mack Trucks, Inc., **Model EH**, (Sales folder, dated 6-36)

1936 - 1940 | 7
Last days of the Bulldog - first days of the Diesel

The modern Macks multiply

The generally improved business conditions of the mid-1930's helped to further stimulate the flow of technological improvements begun during the early 1930's. With the changing technology and shifting economic conditions, some industries gained at the expense of others. There were still a number of depressed areas in the economy and many firms still suffered from the effects of the prolonged depression. But by 1936, the changes had provided opportunities for many new businesses and created conditions which would bring still further expansion in industry and the economy.

One of the most dramatic changes of this period, was the tremendous growth of the inter-city and inter-state trucking business. An example of this growth was the movement of milk into the New York Metropolitan area, which was only 6% by truck in 1930, but shot up to 62% by 1940.(1) The movement of perishable products always required short lines of distribution, and any mode of transportation which could speed up the shipping of such products would also tend to cut losses due to spoilage.

(1) Athel F. Denham, **20 Years' Progress in Commercial Motor Vehicles**, (Detroit, Automotive Council for War Production, 1943) p.XX.

The tight financial conditions also prompted many local merchants to purchase manufactured goods in smaller quantities, which could be financed and stored with less difficulty than larger carload lots. Smaller shipments previously meant higher less-than-carload freight rates and certainly less speed in delivery. Modern merchants now wanted faster delivery of such merchandise to take advantage of favorable local sales conditions while they lasted. The combination of demand for smaller and yet faster shipments provided the opportunity for the trucking industry to grow and eventually to show its capability of moving tonnage freight as well.

Improvements in truck design and construction continued apace in the mid and late 1930's, with streamlining being one of the most obvious influences on new models. Light and medium duty trucks were the first to be streamlined, but truck bodies and trailers also received attention from the stylists. Less obvious, but more important to operators, were the changes being effected in power plant, transmission, and other component design to help the operators with specific haulage problems. Truck fleet owners, who measured efficiency in the speed and cost of ton miles hauled, needed more power in their vehicles for the longer and varied routes their expansion now covered.

With improved gasoline engines and a practical automotive Diesel now becoming available, new transmissions and rear axles were also developed to apply power at the most effective gear ratios possible for maximizing operating efficiency over extended routes. Truck operators of all types soon saw the potential economy of using vehicles designed for their particular operations. This prompted manufacturers to offer many new models and component options to satisfy the growing demand from sophisticated fleet owners. Mack, which had offered about 24 different truck models in 1935(2), was offering a total of 64 by 1940.(3)

The agreement with the Reo Motor Car Company to sell Reo trucks through some of the Mack branches during 1935 led to the introduction of Mack, Jr. trucks and buses, which were built at the Reo plant in Lansing, Michigan. The Mack, Jr. line for 1936 consisted of four basic chassis sizes with capacities from 1/2 to 3 tons.(4) These trucks were well built, but of lighter construction than regular Mack models and comparatively less expensive. During 1936 the Mack, Jr. models and capacities were designated as: 1M, 1/2 ton; 10M, 1-1/2 tons; 20M, 1-1/2 to 2 tons and 30M, 2 to 3 tons. There was also a variation of the 30M, called the 30MT, which was a Traffic Type and had the engine between the seats.

The Mack Traffic Type line was broadened, in the spring of 1936, to include two new models in the medium capacity range.(5) These were the model EC, with the BG engine, and a nominal capacity of 1-1/2 to 3 tons, and the EB, with the CU engine and a capacity of 2-1/2 to 4 tons. The EC and EB were of the engine between seats design and were equipped with a modern deluxe cab, similar to the ones used on the recently restyled CH and CJ models. The EC and EB had a saving of three feet in length over corresponding conventional models and found immediate acceptance as city delivery units and tractors for semi-trailers.

The year 1936 also marked the introduction of the Mack model EH, the first of a new streamlined conventional E series put into production prior to World War II. Modern styling of the EH included full bodied fenders with shrouding between the fenders and engine hood, and sloping chromium plated radiator grill.(6) The cab was of modern design with sloping windshield, and chromium plating was extensively used to give a bright, highlighted appearance. The BG engine of 79 brake horsepower was used and a five speed, unit transmission, with overdrive on fifth speed, could be had as an extra.

The combination of a broadened truck line with new styling on light and medium duty models, and the general business resurgence resulted in a tremendous jump in Mack sales during 1936. New Mack truck registrations for 1936 were 4,226, the best year since 1930, when 4,943 were licensed.(7) The model EH along with the Mack, Jr., line received excellent reception, filling a wide variety of hauling needs. The Mack, Jr. series was continued only one more year and the 1937 model designations were: 2M, 1/2 to 3/4 ton, with 4 or 6 cylinder engines; 10MF, 1-1/2 tons route delivery; 11M, 1-1/2 tons; 21M, 1-1/2 to 2 tons; and 31M of 2 to 3 tons capacity. There were also two Traffic Type models: the 21MT and the 31MT, and a transit type bus, the 91MT.

(2) **Commercial Car Journal**, Vol. 49, No. 6, (July 1935) p.56.

(3) Mack Trucks, Inc., **The Mack Bulldog**, Second Series, Vol. 1, No. 6, (Jan. 1940) p.6.

(4) **Commercial Car Journal**, Vol. 50, No. 6, (Feb. 1936) pp. 32 & 33.

(5) **Ibid.**, Vol. 51, No. 1, (March 1936) p. 31.

(6) **Ibid.**, Vol. 51, No. 4, (June 1936) p.28.

(7) **Ibid.**, Vol. 55, No. 2, (April 1938) p.22.

A study in contrasts is provided by this view of the model 20M Mack, Jr., a 1 1/2 to 2 ton unit introduced in 1936, and the huge six cylinder Mack Bulldog dumper.

The smallest model in the 1936 Mack, Jr. series was the 1M, shown here as a handy pickup.

The moderately priced Mack, Jr. line proved to be a popular delivery unit and could be found hauling a wide variety of products. The 1936 10M model, with a capacity of 1½ tons, is shown here.

The Mack models EC and EB were additions, in 1936, to the Traffic Type series in the moderate tonage range. This model EC had a capacity of 1½ to 3 tons.

A restyled CJ model shown here, in 1937, hauling a capacity load of newsprint weighing in excess of 12 tons.

The year 1936 saw the first of the popular E series introduced. This EH Mack was the lead model in the new series, and with a moderate capacity range served a wide variety of uses.

The Mack, Jr. trucks during 1937 were equipped with an improved cab having a V-type windshield. This model 21M was delivered early in 1937.

This ER chain-drive dump model had a gross vehicle weight, including chassis, body and payload, of 10 tons. It is shown in use by a Canadian operator, early in 1937.

Stating the capacities of truck models in terms of nominal tons efficiently carried became unrealistic with the growth of interstate trucking and conflicting state laws concerning gross vehicle weight. State laws restricted the weight of a motor vehicle by limiting the pounds that could be carried by each axle and new operators were soon made aware of these restrictions by state operated weighing stations and the fines which were imposed for overloading. By 1937 some truck manufacturers published only the maximum gross vehicle weight as a general rating for their models. The g.v.w. rating was basically the sum total of the chassis, body allowance and payload that the manufacturer considered reasonable before an over-loaded condition was reached and the truck's warrantee was voided.

The expansion of the E series with three new models in the 16,000 to 23,000 lbs. g.v.w. range, by the spring of 1937, allowed for the replacement of the famous model AB. In its final form, the AB was rated at 20,000 lbs. g.v.w., and was still being offered with dual reduction or chain-drive. The ER model, with chain-drive and a 20,000 lbs. g.v.w., and the model EM with spiral beval drive and a similar g.v.w., were more than adequate substitutes for the old AB. The AB, or Baby Mack, as it was once called, had served the trucking industry since 1914, and its long production record is substantial testimony for the customer satisfaction and loyalty this truck engendered. Other new E models in production by the spring of 1937 were: EJ of 16,000 lbs. g.v.w. and the EQ of 23,000 lbs.

With the dropping of the Mack, Jr. line during 1938, a new series of lower capacity E models having Continental engines was introduced. The three smaller models were: EE of 12,000; EF of 14,000, and EG of 16,000 lbs. g.v.w. The models BG and BF were dropped before the end of 1938, being substituted by the models EM and EQ, respectively. The ES, of a similar rating as the EQ, but

The largest E series model was the EQ with a 23,000 lbs. gross vehicle weight rating. Here we see an EQ tractor hauling an ST-30 semi-trailer with a special wooden vinegar tank, in 1939.

An unusual body, used to advertise one firm's product, was placed on an ED model in 1939. The ED was the smallest model in the E series, and was at times referred to as the "Baby Mack."

101

A model MR, also known as the Mack Retailer, was placed in production in 1939. This MR model was delivered to a large New York department store in May 1940.

having chain-drive, was introduced by the end of 1938. A new "Baby Mack" called the ED, having a chassis list price of $675, was first produced in 1938, and most of the E models were made available with a version of the Traffic Type cab the same year.

To completely round out the line of lower capacity trucks, the Mack Retailer, model MR, was placed in production in 1939. The Retailer had a specially designed chassis with forward control and gear shift lever mounted on the steering column. The body was built in the body shop located in Mack's Long Island City plant(8) and was designed for easy access and had a large payload carrying space.

(8) Ibid., Vol. 58, No. 3, (Nov. 1939) pp. 44 & 71.

The Bulldog bows out as the Diesel drives in

By the year 1936, the models BQ, AK, AC, and AP were the largest Mack models, and represented the Custom Line, produced only on special order. Their heavy-duty components had made these trucks essential to firms in the construction and heavy haulage fields, but after 1936 no AK and few AP Macks were produced, being replaced by other models. There was no longer a specific need for the AK model as the BX and BQ Macks had similar components and capacity ratings, and had proven themselves in the heavy haulage field.

The AC had established an enviable reputation with many contractors and their suppliers, a reputation which lasted long after faster Mack models had taken over other types of hauling duties from the Bulldog. There were some special off-highway AC's built in 1936 and 1937, but the last ones for city use were manufactured in December of 1938. The Bulldog was built to the end of its production with both 4- and 6-cylinder gasoline engines available, and starting in about 1936, Buda and Cummins Diesels had been optional. Even with the discontinuance of the AC in 1938, many of the old Bulldogs could be seen in daily service in the larger cities, especially in New York, up to the mid-50's, with a few still serving until the mid-60's—an unexcelled record for motor truck longevity, proving over and over the old Mack slogan, Performance Counts.

A new F series of Super-Duty Macks was started on during 1936 to replace the last of the AC and AP models, and to expand the truck line into higher capacity ratings. New heavy-duty components were engineered for a unified model series which would be compatible with the new Diesel and gasoline engines being developed. The economy of larger units hauling huge payloads per man-hour was still applicable to off-highway mining and construction operations, even though state highway regulations continued to restrict the use of such motor vehicles on public roads.

This AC-6 hauling the crane on a low-bed trailer was an impressive sight as it stopped long enough to have its picture taken in the summer of 1937.

(9) **Ibid**., Vol. 54, No. 6, (Feb. 1938) p.19.

This FCSW was the largest in a new series of chain-drive models, introduced in 1937 to replace the AC and AP models which were phased out soon after.

Two model FC, six wheelers, said to be the world's largest trucks, were sold to the Sunlight Coal Company for strip mining in southwestern Indiana in 1937.(9) The FC had chain-drive, like the other F models, and the six wheel version was rated at 100,000 lbs. g.v.w., while the four wheeled FC had a rating of 60,000 lbs.

To satisfy demand from the construction industry for faster, more powerful trucks, the models FG, FH, FJ, and FK, of 35,000 to 50,000 lbs. g.v.w., were put into production during 1937 and 1938. Although these models were comparatively lighter than the FC, they were, for the most part, special permit vehicles, being over the maximum legal axle capacities for state highways and used mostly in big cities. With the building boom in the New York City area, fueled in part by the construction of the 1939 - 1940 World's Fair, a couple of large fleets of F model Macks were sold in 1938. In the summer of that year the Colonial Sand and Stone Company ordered over 60 FH, FK, and FKSW models, with Cummins Diesel engines, for use as dump and concrete mixer units.

The Bulldog model, with either 4 or 6 cylinder engines, had been built in its last years with gross ratings of from 35,000 to 50,000 lbs., depending upon the tire sizes used with each truck. In effect, the new F series, excepting the FC, constituted a breakdown in the g.v.w. range of the Bulldog into roughly 5,000 lb. steps: FG, 35,000, FH and FJ, 45,000; FK, 50,000. One of the basic differences of each model therefore was the tire sizes, which had different weight or capacity ratings. And while components also differed to some degree, being of heavier

This huge off-highway FCSW model was completed in 1940 and represents one of the first Mack trucks equipped with an off-set cab.

construction on the larger models, all were available with a five speed main transmission and two speed auxiliary box, for a combination of 10 speeds. The ER and ES chain-drive models were phased out by 1941, being replaced with the larger FP model, which had a 26,000 lb. g.v.w., rating, and was produced between 1940 and 1942.

To a great extent the development and subsequent success of the automotive type Diesel was the result of the depression. Its comparatively lower operating cost over gasoline engines of a similar horsepower more than compensated for its higher initial cost. The vast majority of Diesels produced during the 1930's were purchased by fleet owners as replacement engines, and it was not until 1939 that new truck installations surpassed replacement sales.(10) Fleet owners in particular, having high fuel costs, were in a position to benefit from the fact that the cost of Diesel fuel was half that of gasoline. However, the long term economy of the Diesel was more the product of its fundamental design characteristics than the current cost of the fuel that it used.

The thermal efficiency of the Diesel engine is based on its extremely high compression ratio, which provides for a higher air to fuel ratio for better combustion of the fuel charge and therefore the release of more energy. The Diesel compression ratio, roughly three times that of comparative gasoline engines, also meant that a charge having three times more potential energy resulted with each power stroke in the Diesel. Naturally, there are off-setting losses due to friction, but it has been estimated that the thermal efficiency of the Diesel is 40 per cent greater than the gasoline engine, and the negligible amount of carbon monoxide traces in Diesel exhaust is the proof of almost complete combustion. Also, Diesel fuel by its very nature has greater caloric content by volume than gasoline and therefore contains more potential horsepower.

The major hurtle that faced the engineers working on development of the automotive type Diesel was in controling the rate of combustion and subsequent power stroke, so that the flexibility needed in an automotive power plant could be achieved. The large industrial Diesel engine had been used for many years, but it

(10) Denham, **op.cit.**, pp. 72 & 73

This model FJ concrete mixer truck came equipped with the new Mack Diesel engine when it was delivered in spring of 1939.

was slow, with an average maximum speed of about 1,000 revolutions per minute. In order to maximize the power, while at the same time reducing its size, the speed of the automotive Diesel had to be at least between 1,600 and 2,000 r.p.m.

Being a compression ignition engine, the method of introducing the fuel into the cylinders for the proper rate of combustion was different from the gasoline engine was very critical, involving coordination in design of both the fuel injector and combustion chamber. If the fuel injected mixed too slowly with the air, the mixture tended to detonate with sledgehammer like blows on the pistons, resulting in a rough running engine with a shortened life expectancy. In order to produce and maintain high peak pressures during the power stroke, without an inordinate increase in the rate of pressure rise, many combustion chamber and fuel injector designs were tried out by various manufacturers.

After testing many experimental designs, as well as stock engines, the Mack Diesel was introduced in 1938, using the Lanova combustion chamber design. Initial research into the feasibility and development of an automotive type Diesel by Mack had been undertaken about 1928, with the travel to Europe of several key engineers; during the early thirties both Mercedes-Benz and Cummins Diesel engines were installed in Mack chasses and tested over long periods. Many experimental engines were built having both six cylinders and single cylinders, sleeve-valves and poppet-valves, two-stroke and four-stroke cycles, open

Installation of a Mack-Lanova Diesel engine in a large FH truck chassis. The FH model Mack used the 131 horsepower ED519 Diesel engine as optional equipment.

chamber, air-cell and ante-chamber combustion chamber designs. There was no simple formula on which to base the design of the combustion chamber system, and therefore what seemed like an endless series of experiments was pursued before a satisfactory design was adopted.

The selection of the Lanova combustion system was based on its efficiency in providing the highest practical power per cubic inch of displacement with minimum peak pressures, bearing loads, fuel pressures, and compression.(11) The Lanova principle, invented by Franz Lang, was based on a combination energy cell and figure eight turbulence chamber, which, in effect, provided for a controlled mixing and ignition of the fuel. Mack had offered the Buda Diesel, which also used the Lanova design, as an optional engine in some heavy duty models, starting about 1936.

After the introduction of the Mack Diesel of 519 cubic inches displacement and 131 brake horsepower, Buda Diesels were still optional in Mack trucks in sizes from 212 to 468 cubic inches. Other makes of Diesel engines were also available and a few of the first fleets of Diesel propelled Macks were powered by Cummins. However, Mack was the first independent truck manufacturer to produce its own Diesel engines, incorporating a number of patented improvements resulting from their years of extensive experimentation.

The BM and BX truck models were replaced by the new heavy-duty L series in the fall of 1940. First of the L models were the LF, LJ, and LM, and were powered with the new Thermodyne engines of 124 to 160 brake horsepower. The L series achieved instant success as highway tractors and were quickly adapted to many other heavy hauling functions.

Buses, fire apparatus, and other products

The transition in urban transit modes continued through the mid and late 1930's with many small as well as medium sized cities converting to an all bus operation. However, many cities converted some street railway lines to trolley bus operation and the change over to rubber tired transit vehicles provided the needed impetus to bus manufacturers for expanding their production as well as introducing improved models.

During this period most manufacturers adopted unitized, or integral, bus body construction, which cut overall vehicle weight by doing away with a separate frame for both chassis and body. The integral construction, combined with the transit type design of rear mounted engine and other improvements, resulted in a well balanced vehicle of greatly increased performance and lowered maintenance costs. In addition, the integral transit type design was fully adapted to inter-city buses by 1937, with only school buses using the old engine in front, separate chassis and body construction.

As an indication of the improved bus business, Mack, in January 1936, recorded the largest orders for any corresponding month since 1931.(12) One of the orders, from the Portland (Oregon) Traction Company, was for 120 trolley coaches and 28 gasoline buses. The success of the CR model Mack trolley coach led to the introduction of a smaller version, the FR, having seats for 33 passengers.(13) However, orders for the FR came only from Greenville, South Carolina, for the trolley coach was basically a big city transit vehicle, whose best efficiency was in moving large crowds at low cost. By the fall of 1936, Mack bus models having rear mounted engines were: CT, 35 passengers; CQ, 31 passengers; CW, 25 passengers. The Mack, Jr. bus model was offered with a front mounted engine and a seating capacity of 25.(14)

Mack bus sales during 1937 reached nearly 1,000,(15) and by 1939 there were over 800 Mack buses in operation in the New York Territory alone.(16) The New York World's Fair of 1939-1940 was the spur to many local bus operators to add new vehicles to their fleets in anticipation of the huge crowds which would be descending upon the fair grounds.

The Mack Diesel bus was introduced in the fall of 1938 with the first two CT-4D, Diesel-Electric models going to Boston in November. Over 200 CM-4D, 41

(11) **Transit Journal**, Vol. 82, No. 13, (Dec. 1938) pp. 492 & 493.

(12) **Ibid.**, Vol. 80, No. 3, (March 1936) p.108.

(13) **Ibid.**, Vol. 80, No. 11, (Oct. 1936) p.426.

(14) **Ibid.**, Vol. 80, No. 10, (Sept. 15, 1936) pp. 358, 360, 362, & 365.

(15) **Ibid.**, Vol. 82, No. 2, (Feb. 1938) pp. 31-34.

(16) Mack Trucks, Inc., **The Mack Bulldog**, Second Series, Vol. 1, No. 3, (Feb. 1939) p.1.

Over 1,300 of the small model CW buses were built between 1935 and 1941. This CW was delivered in 1936.

This CM model Mack bus having a seating capacity of 40 was delivered in June 1939, just in time to serve people bound for the New York World's Fair of 1939 and 1940.

passenger models were ordered by New York's Third Avenue Transit System between 1939 and 1941. As more and more bus operators turned to the Diesel as an economic necessity, Mack offered a full line of transit type buses to meet this demand. On buses with mechanical transmissions, Mack offered a new automatic air actuated clutch, which worked through the shift lever, thus doing away with the clutch pedal.

The need for modern, high-speed, fire apparatus for urban, suburban, and rural communities across the nation grew with the expanding population and the necessity to replace out-dated apparatus still being used by many budget conscious communities. Purchases of new apparatus revived during the late 1930's, and the many innovations of the early 1930's plus the streamlining concepts of the mid-1930's resulted in an almost over-night transformation in equipment design.

The most striking change in apparatus design in the late 1930's, besides the obvious streamlining, was the adaptation of the sedan cab for protecting the firemen while riding to and from the scene of the alarm. Having the firemen ride inside the apparatus was a revolutionary change, as the traditional place was usually a perch at the rear of the apparatus, and many men had been killed or injured when thrown off in accidents. Mack had pioneered this type of body for fire apparatus in 1935, with the delivery of a sedan pumper to Charlotte, N.C., and by 1940 many communities specified some form of sedan cab or body.

Mack apparatus was broadened in the lower capacity types with the additions to the E series commercial truck line from 1936 to 1939. The Mack District Fire Apparatus, introduced in 1939, was designed for the use of small communities whose requirements and limited budgets precluded the purchase of larger and more expensive units. The District pumpers were types 25, 30, 40, and 45, having pumping capacities ranging from 100 to 500 g.p.m. The larger types 19 and 21 pumpers continued in popularity with New York City purchasing 20 of the 1,000

A large type 80LS pumper having sedan type cab for transporting the firemen to and from the scene of the alarm with speed and safety.

The type 45 District Pumper had a pump capacity of 500 gallons per minute and represented the lower range of Mack fire apparatus built during the 1940's.

The picture at the bottom of the page shows a group of 20 type 21 fire engines undergoing acceptance tests in New York, spring of 1937. These engines had pump capacities of 1,000 gallons per minute.

g.p.m. type 21's in 1936.(17) By 1940 there were over 600 cities using one or more Mack fire units and the Mack line consisted of 14 distinct and specialized fire apparatus models.(18)

In 1938 the new type 80, 750 g.p.m. pumper was introduced with the first of a new type of gasoline engine trade marked Thermodyne. The Mack Thermodyne engine of 611 cubic inches displacement developed 168 brake horsepower at 2300 r.p.m., used overhead valves, and had a one piece crankcase and cylinder block casting.

Overhead valve configuration, although more expensive, has been for many years considered superior to the standard L-head design for engine combustion chambers. The name Thermodyne was coined for the new line of Mack gasoline engines to reflect the superior thermodynamic qualities achieved in the arrangement of the combustion chamber, valve and porting, which resulted in a more powerful, even running engine.(19) The new Thermodyne engines were a result of basic Diesel and gasoline engine research, and were adapted with

(17) **Fire Engineering**, Vol. 89, No. 3, (March 1936) pp. 98 & 99.

(18) **Ibid**., Vol. 93, No. 5, (May 1940) pp. 214 & 215.

(19) **Ibid**., Vol. 91, No. 9, (Sept. 1938) p.438.

The adaptation of the Mack-Lanova Diesel for marine use was announced in 1940. This model ENDM405Y Mariner Diesel was produced in 1941 for yacht installation.

A 125 horsepower Mack Mariner Diesel engine powered the 45-foot party fishing boat "Americana," which is seen cruising the waters around Key West, Florida in the fall of 1940.

(20) Mack Trucks, Inc., **The Mack Bulldog**, Second Series, Vol. 1, No. 6, (Jan. 1940) pp. 1 & 2.

certain modifications to both fire engine and regular commercial vehicle use. In fact, the same basic engine block casting was used for both the new Thermodyne gasoline engines and the Mack-Lanova Diesels of the same or similar displacement.

Another spin-off of Mack Diesel engine development was the introduction in 1940 of the Mariner line of marine Diesel engines. The Mack Diesels were produced in two types, the Y for yachts and the W for work boats.(20)

During the mid-1930's Mack semi-trailers were built at Allentown in three basic models, with capacities ranging from 3 to 18 tons. In 1937, the lower priced models ST-20, 3 to 5 tons, and ST-30, 5 to 8 tons capacity semi-trailers were introduced.

Mack bodies were still built at the Long Island City service plant, where extensive machine, sheet metal, wood working, and paint shops were maintained. Large custom-made panel and flat bed bodies were a specialty, although many other types were made too.

Mack on the eve of Pearl Harbor

Mack management underwent a series of important personnel changes during the 1936 - 1940 period, due to the loss of several key officials, some of whom had been with the International Motor Company since its founding in 1911. And the name of the International Motor Company itself was changed at the end of 1936 to the Mack Manufacturing Corporation, a more accurate description of the company's chief function. Also in 1936, the New York home office was moved **109**

The Mack BULLDOG

Vol. III
No. 6

REG. US. PAT. OFF.

10 Cents the Copy

PORTER

(Above) First series of the Mack house organ *The Mack Bulldog*, was published during the 1920 to 1932 period. Most issues featured a colorful cover.

(Right) The longevity of Mack trucks was illustrated in this ad showing the famous Bulldog in a big city scene. Art work by Peter Helck. Appeared in *Saturday Evening Post*, May 5, 1945.

How long should a good Truck last?...

Did you know that Mack trucks you see today with the famous, slanting Mack "bulldog nose" shown below — *are between 13 and 29 years old?*...

Did you know that Mack case-hardened timing gears — to name just one of many points of special Mack mechanical quality — are so durably constructed *that not one has ever worn out?*...

The very first Mack built in 1900 served its owners faithfully for 17 years — and ever since *extra* durability, stamina, dependability and long life have been built-in "features" of every Mack truck.

That's what "Built like a Mack truck" means... and it saves Mack owners money. It means *more work per dollar spent* when Macks are on the job!

How long should a good truck last you?...The answer, of course, depends on the type of work you have. But it ought to last as long as a Mack... and *unless* it's a Mack it's not apt to!

from lower Broadway to the Long Island City plant, where it remained for seven years.

An important loss to the organization was the early retirement, in 1935, and subsequent death in April 1938, of Robert E. Fulton. Mr. Fulton was considered one of the pioneers in the automobile business, having started about 1905 as a salesman for Pope-Toledo automobiles. He later took on the American agency of the German made Mercedes automobile and during this time became acquainted with the importer of the Swiss made Saurer truck. Sensing an opportunity in the future of the motor truck, he joined a group of industrialists who formed the Saurer Motor Company, in 1910, to build the Saurer truck under license in America. He was with the Saurer Motor Company when it merged with the Mack Brothers Motor Car Company, in 1911, and was made First Vice President in charge of sales of the International Motor Company in 1913.[21] Mr. Fulton was president of the sales organization, the Mack-International Motor Truck Corporation, at the time of his retirement in 1935.

(21) **Horseless Age**, Vol. 31, No. 26, (June 25, 1913) p.1133.

Robert E. Fulton's successor as sales manager, in 1935, was William R. Edson, who had been with the Mack organization since 1911. His grandfather, Franklin Edson, had been mayor of New York in 1883 and 1884, and founded the New York Produce Exchange. Unfortunately, William Edson died in April 1938 after a brief illness, and was, in turn, succeeded by F.F. Staniford, who had many years' experience in managing various Mack branches.

The most serious loss to the Company during this period was the death, in September 1936, of Alfred J. Brosseau, who had headed the Mack organization since 1917. Mr. Brosseau had provided the clear eye and steady hand which guided the progress of the organization through two boom and bust economic cycles. The steady expansion of the 1920's and the insistence upon engineering excellence of all Mack products were, to a great degree, the result of his understanding and faith in the future of the highway transportation industry, and Mack's place in it.

After seeing Mack launched on a steady expansion program, Mr. Brosseau devoted some time to problems affecting the automotive industry. He was at various times vice president of the Commercial Car Division of the Automobile Manufacturers Association, and represented the A.M.A., and its predecessor the N.A.C.C., on the board of directors of the United States Chamber of Commerce. He wrote many papers and articles on highway and transportation matters, and had frequently testified before official and non-official bodies representing the automotive industry.[22]

(22) **New York Times**, Sept. 25, 1936, p.23.

After the loss of Mr. Brosseau, Charles Hayden, senior partner and co-founder of the investment banking house of Hayden, Stone & Co., was elected chairman of the board and temporary president. Again, misfortune struck, as Mr. Hayden died in January 1937, only three months after taking the top Mack posts. While well known in the financial community at the time of his death, Mr. Hayden is best remembered for some of his philanthropies, such as his generous help in establishing the planetarium, named in his honor, at the American Museum of Natural History in New York City.[23]

(23) **Ibid.**, Jan. 9, 1937, p.17.

Shortly after the passing of Charles Hayden, Emil C. Fink was elected President of Mack Trucks, Inc. He had started with the International Motor Company shortly after its formation, and had an extensive background in the machine tool business in Cincinnati, Ohio. In April 1913 Mr. Fink was named Third Vice President[24] and supervised production until being made head of the parent organization in 1937.

(24) **Horseless Age**, Vol. 31, No. 16, (April 16, 1913) p. 680.

The spector of international conflict had been rising since the beginning of the Spanish Civil War in 1936, and the involvement therein of France, Germany, Italy, and Russia. Although American public opinion had favored a generally isolationist role in world politics since the early 1920's, the rising tide of violence and subjugation in Europe and Asia had increased concern for a better national defense posture. Also, sympathy for traditional European allies, in addition to satisfying domestic needs, led to an active rearmament program by early 1940.

In late 1939, the U.S. Army ordered 535 Mack military trucks for troop transport and towing heavy equipment. These vehicles were developed from civilian truck models with various modifications for military service. The largest group was 368 model NB's with six wheels, which were used for transporting searchlight and sound locators for the Army's anti-aircraft defenses. These trucks were basically EEU, cab-over-engine models fitted out with special five man cabs for the searchlight crews. There were 87 model NM-1, six wheel prime movers having all wheel drive, with axles supplied by Timken, and Mack EY Thermodyne engines. Also included in this order were 80 EE models with dump bodies for use in administrative service at various army posts.(25)

After the involvement of Great Britain and France with Germany in active warfare starting in the fall of 1939, the production of military equipment for shipment to England went into high gear. The Mack EXBX, a modified version of the civilian BX six wheeler, was developed for a French contract in 1939, but the bulk of these tank transporters went to the British campaign against Rommel's Afrika Korps in North Africa.(26) From this model was developed the NR-4, 6 x 4, 13 ton g.v.w., tank transporter, which was also supplied to the British army, starting in 1940.

(25) Mack Trucks, Inc., **The Mack Bulldog**, Second Series, Vol. 1, No. 6, (Jan. 1940) p.1.

(26) Bart H. Vanderveen, **Fighting Vehicles Directory, W.W.II**, (London, Fred Warne & Co., Ltd., 1969) p. 85.

The U. S. Army received a total of 700 of these Mack NJU 4 x 4 tractors during 1941. They were basically used to pull pontoon trailers, and had collapsible ballast boxes mounted behind the cabs.

The NR-4 military six-wheeler was developed in 1940 as a tank transporter for the British Army for its North African Campaign. Note the heat shield on the roof of the cab, and large air cleaner, for the 134 hp Diesel engine, located on the right hand side.

Toward the end of 1940 the U.S. Army ordered 700 NJU, 4 x 4, 5 to 6 ton, c.o.e. tractors, which were based on the civilian CH and CJ models. Also ordered at this time were a group of NO model, six wheel, prime movers, with Mack built EY engines and front drive axles. Although irregular, defense orders placed with Mack and other manufacturers took on increased importance on the eve of open American involvement in World War II.

By 1940 net profit had soared to $1,805,821 on sales of $44,052,346(27) from a net loss of $395,616 on sales of $20,210,885 in 1935.(28) Domestic sales had risen from 1,515 in 1935 to 7,754 in 1940.(29) Mack had achieved a sound operating basis and the 1940 product line was the most comprehensive of any manufacturer of commercial vehicles, starting from the smallest multi-stop delivery trucks to the largest off-highway dump units, buses of various sizes and custom built fire apparatus of every type. In short, Mack was geared to respond to the needs of all who used commercial vehicles, including national defense commitments, which foreshadowed their future scope by 1940.

(27) Mack Trucks, Inc., **Annual Report**, 1940

(28) Mack Trucks, Inc., **Annual Report**, 1935

(29) **Commercial Car Journal**, Vol. 61, No. 2, (April 1941) p.19.

8 | 1941 - 1946
Wheels for war and peace

Mack at the Front

Mack's contribution to the survival of the western democracies was a vital one, as their production of specialized military vehicles had started in 1939, just prior to the crucial first days of World War II, and was greatly expanded by the time the United States became involved in the conflict in late 1941.

The events leading up to the start of World War II are rather complex, and, for the most part, involve what is commonly referred to as power politics. Suffice it to say that most of the origins of World War II can be traced back to the world conflict of 1914 to 1918, and from the strictly military view point, there are some interesting comparisons in the tactics and equipment used in both wars.

The German use of the fast flanking attack in their effort to capture Paris at the start of World War I, in August 1914, had been blunted by the quick arrival of English forces, and by the rushing of French reinforcements from Paris to the critical battle of the Marne by commandeered taxis and buses. Allied forces used motor transport afterwards to supply many parts of their front lines, while the Germans depended more on their unhampered internal rail network, which was vital for shipping forces from one front to another during the entire war period. This, of course, was in the days before strategic bombing, and before the Germans had built their magnificent system of inter-regional superhighways called the **Autobahn.**

The stalemate that developed on the western front in France, at the end of 1914, was characterized by the extensive use of trenches and permanent fortifications. In order to break the impasse, the British developed a secret assault weapon, which was sprung on the enemy lines in 1915. This new weapon was the tank, which achieved only limited success until better tactics were developed for its use towards the end of the war. The use of massed tanks in World War II was so extensive that many battles were fought between armored divisions on most of the fronts in Europe. The motor truck was heavily relied on by both the Axis and Allied nations for supplying most of their campaigns, although the Germans still used railways as much as possible because of the length of their supply lines and their lack of an adequate source of petroleum to power their motor vehicles. Also, the Axis motor transport was a conglomeration of German, Italian, and captured English and French vehicles picked up in 1940, which made parts supply a real problem.

Mack received several government orders at the beginning of the war for administrative vehicles, which were regular commercial models for use around military bases. Here is a Mack EE dumper delivered in 1940.

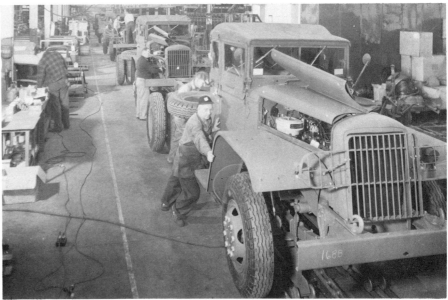

Mack plants were completely geared for the production of military vehicles for the Allied cause by 1943. EH army cargo trucks are seen here coming off an Allentown assembly line.

The German high command profited from their losses to the British secret weapon, the tank, during World War I, and also from the desire to avoid being caught in the quagmire of trench warfare. Their answer was the **Blitzkreig**, or lightning war, to be waged by highly mobile forces able to launch a fast, decisive, attack capable of piercing the enemy's lines of defense and overwhelming all resistance through fast enveloping movements. New mobile weapons, such as tanks, personnel carriers, amphibious vehicles, and even planes and ships, were developed with the improved military tactics in mind. Hard-skin attack vehicles with tanks weighing as much as 60 tons, were formed into **Panzer**, or armored divisions.

After the defeat of Poland in the fall of 1939 and the surrender of France in the spring of 1940, all of Europe was either under Axis domination or effectively neutralized. England was in a tough spot, for not since Napoleon had she been so isolated, and much of her survival depended upon fast action to save her access to vital Middle East oil. British positions in Egypt and other Middle East areas were quickly beefed up with the arrival of Commonwealth forces and additional military equipment from England and the United States.

British North-African forces were the recipients, in 1940, of the Mack model EXBX tank transporters, which had been ordered by the French government in 1939. Mack engineers, working closely with a British military staff, then

115

developed the model NR, 6 x 4, series, with the object of overcoming specific problems found in the Middle East. The bogie axles were placed futher apart than normal, to accomodate 14.00-20 tires, an extra large size needed for flotation on the desert sands found in many parts of the Middle East.

Many NR-4 tank transporters and LMSW heavy breakdown (wrecker) trucks were supplied to the British and their Commonwealth forces, under Lend-Lease, during 1941 and 1942.(1) Also, the British received hundreds of commercial type EH, EHT, EHU, EHUT, trucks, and ST-20 semi-trailers, for general supply and troop transport service.

Some of the most famous and, for that matter, crucial battles of the Second World War were fought on the Libyan Desert. The British and Axis forces, operating out of their respective bases in Egypt and Libya, fought a series of armored engagements between 1940 and 1942, with neither side being able to achieve a decisive victory. Specially trained **Panzer** divisions, under General Rommel, proved a serious threat to British command of the vital Suez Canal area, and it was not until American forces landed in Algeria that a decisive Allied victory was achieved. American armored divisions opened a second front on the western border of Axis held Tunisia, and the British, advancing through Libya from the east, met the Americans and together squeezed the Axis armored forces into a small coastal area for a final battle. With the Middle East life line secured for the Allies and the southern flank of what was referred to as Fortress Europe exposed to an Allied Attack, the whole course of the war swung in favor of the western democracies.

Although Sicily was quickly overrun in the summer of 1943, the Nazi armies retired in orderly fashion to the Italian peninsula, where they contested nearly every mountain and valley. Progress was slow and Allied armies had to bring up long range guns to blast the entrenched Nazi positions. Huge Mack NO model

(1) Bart H. Vanderveen, **Fighting Vehicles Directory, W.W.II**, (London, Fred Warne & Co., Ltd., 1969) pp. 84 & 85.

A composite view of the Allentown factory on the eve of World War II. The huge one-story building at the top left is assembly plant 5C, which was requisitioned by the Navy during World War II.

Field Artillery officers being instructed in proper maintenance methods on huge model NO prime movers, by Mack service experts and engineers.

Although originally designed for desert service in the Middle East, later versions of the NR, like this 1943 NR9, were modified for use in the European theatre of the war.

The NO model with six wheel drive was built basically as a prime mover rather than cargo carrier, and its major function was to pull the Army's long-tom field gun.

(2) **Ibid.**, p.72.

prime movers were used extensively in Italy to pull the 155-mm. Long Tom field guns from position to position. The 7-1/2 ton, NO model had six wheel drive, and Mack was the major builder of this type of vehicle for the U.S. Army and for Allied forces.(2)

Although planned for a number of years, the Allied invasion of Europe across the English Channel finally occured in June 1944 along the coast of Normandy, France. Tremendous stock piles of all kinds of military supplies had been built up in England, and these were quickly transferred to the beach heads as they were secured. As General Patton's armored columns rushed inland, a road network and truck convoys were quickly set up to supply the fast moving front. Medium and heavy-duty army transport trucks were used in the top priority **Red Ball Express**, which kept expanding its main route as various Channel ports were taken and cleared of obstructions. On the return trip to the coast some of these trucks carried prisoners and wounded soldiers. Many of the Mack NR series general cargo trucks built during 1944 were used in this operation.

Mack-built transmissions were used in many of the medium tanks built after 1941, and supplied to United Nations forces. Great numbers of medium tanks took part in the North African campaign and Normandy invasion, which actions helped to turn the tide of the war and bring it to a victorious conclusion.

After some desperate battles in late 1944, German territory was finally reached, and the last of the Nazi armies surrendered after Hitler's suicide, in the spring of 1945. The Japanese surrendered a few months later, but only after almost four years of island hopping encirclement by U.S. amphibious forces and the dropping of two atomic bombs.

The Axis started this war of machines...but Uncle Sam's Army is coming up fast with the weapons to finish it! One of the newest and most effective is this giant Mack Army Prime Mover.

Made-to-Order for the World's Toughest Customer...

The Army's newest and biggest prime mover is probably the best single job in truck history. Most of its details can't be made public . . . but you can see for yourself that it's *big*. And we can tell you that it hooks up to a whale of a big gun, takes on a terrific load and goes almost anywhere except straight up. We're proud of it, at Mack, and with good reason. Proud that the Army called on Mack men and facilities to develop and build it. Proud, as Americans, that our fighting men are getting fighting equipment so fine. And proud that this, too, is "built like a Mack truck". . . with all that phrase has stood for in ruggedness and reliability for forty-two years! *Mack Trucks, Inc., New York, N. Y. Factory branches and dealers in all principal cities for service and parts.*

IF YOU'VE GOT A MACK, YOU'RE LUCKY...IF YOU PLAN TO GET ONE, YOU'RE WISE!

Mack
TRUCKS
ONE TON TO FORTY-FIVE TONS; BUSES,
FIRE APPARATUS AND MARINE ENGINES

BUY U. S. WAR BONDS

118 The war-time scene in this ad, with illustration by Peter Helck, shows a huge Mack prime mover pulling the Long Tom field gun somewhere in Europe. It appeared in the **Saturday Evening Post** issue of November 21, 1942.

War time production achievements

After the Japanese attacked Pearl Harbor on December 7, 1941, Mack, as well as all other manufacturers, came under the close supervision of various governmental agencies, which were set up to administer priorities for, and the rationing of, all essential goods and services. The Office of Production Management was to give priority ratings to all materials used by industries and the War Production Board was to supervise the effective use of all manufacturing facilities.

Production of civilian trucks was severely curtailed and many of the undelivered new truck chasses were put into a pool from which allocations were made to both the military and essential civilian users. The Office of Defense Transportation monitored all motor vehicle fleets, advising the owners in vital maintenance programs. The O.D.T. also advised the War Production Board on the number and size of new replacement vehicles and parts that would be needed for the essential home front fleets. Chrome plating for the exterior use on motor vehicles was banned for the duration, due to its greater need as an alloy for steel that was used in the manufacture of ball bearings, tools, and dies.

"Keep 'em rolling," was the war cry of all those who watched over the home front fleets. With new trucks being stringently rationed from the national motor vehicle pool, extensive preventive maintenance programs were set up by Mack in co-operation with the O.D.T. Representatives of both large and small fleet operators were invited to the Mack branches where they were instructed in the methods of proper maintenance, which would help preserve their vehicles and also result in considerable savings in money and lost man-hours.

As part of America's national defense program, the construction of a third lock for the Panama Canal was started in 1941, with a cost of $275,000,000. Two of the important contractors on the project ordered about 80 huge Mack, model FC and NW off-highway dump trucks. Wunderlich-Okes Construction Company pur-

Mack trucks, such as this model EMUT, with sleeper cab for long over-night hauls, served the vital home front during World War II.

This veteran 1933 Mack BG tractor had over 1,000,000 miles on it by 1943 and was still going strong at that time delivering essential materials in the southwest.

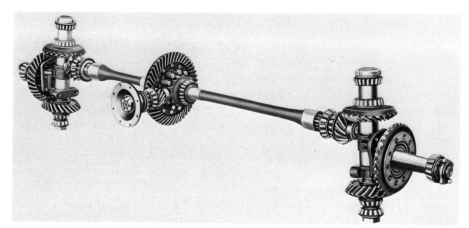

A highly unusual front drive axle was designed and built by Mack for use with the huge NO military truck. Note that the drive is transferred to the wheels through kingpin shafts, eliminating the need for universal joints.

chased 26 Mack NW, 30 ton g.v.w. dumpers, which were specially designed to operate in what was considered to be bottomless mud.(3)

The model NW had drive to all six wheels, and utilized an unusual Mack designed front wheel drive axle, which used an ingenious gearing arrangement in the king pins so that no universal joints were needed and the axle had a higher ground clearance than any other front axle. The Mack NO prime mover used a similar front axle, but having been designed mainly for pulling, it had a lighter frame and consequently a smaller carrying capacity.

The job of the W.P.B. was essentially to direct the manufacturers in their efforts to produce the vital defense equipment, almost as if they were a single huge organization, and some products were switched from their original industries in order to meet production quotas. The automotive industry produced huge quantities of planes, and the government even built new plants for their manufacture, but the elimination of so many civilian products allowed most factories engaged in work to do so without the need for expansion.

The War Department's program of medium tank production during 1941 required the making of heavy-duty transmissions, and Mack, having the essential experience with producing large truck transmissions, was given the main order. Mack Manufacturing Corporation's New Brunswick, New Jersey, gear plant was enlarged in December 1941 through the purchase of the Empire Chemical Company factory so that production of the vital tank components could be expedited.(4) A total of 4,600 power trains were produced by Mack during the war for the M-3 and M-4 medium tanks.

In December 1942, the Mack bus plant at Allentown was requisitioned by the Navy for Vultee Aircraft, Inc., which firm had a large contract for Navy torpedo bombers. It was estimated by Charles E. Wilson, production vice chairman of the W.P.B., that six months could be saved in starting production of the planes if the Mack plant could be used.(5) Mack was still building some essential motor buses and trolley coaches when the order came, and phased out their production early in 1943.

While Mack resumed production of motor buses right after the war, 1943 marked the end of the line for the Mack trolley coach. About 300 Trolley buses had been built between 1935 and 1943, with transit properties in a dozen American and Canadian cities operating them.

During the early part of the war, in order to fully utilize plant facilities, Mack fire apparatus manufacture was transferred from Allentown to Long Island City. The chasses were still built at Allentown and then driven to the Long Island City plant, where the large body shop and other facilities were ideally suited for what was essentially a custom operation. And while some civilian apparatus was still produced, a number of orders were received for special types of military fire engines. Mack produced for the Army Air Force many of the bodies for the class 155, high pressure fog foam, crash trucks, which were mounted on Brockway C-666 and Kenworth 572 military wrecker chasses.(6)

(3) Mack Trucks, Inc., **The Mack Bulldog**, Second Series, Vol. 2, No. 2, (Dec. 1941) p.7.

(4) **New York Times**, Dec. 13, 1941, p.34.

(5) **Ibid**., Dec. 16, 1942, p.16.

(6) Vanderveen, **op.cit**., p.96.

During 1944 and 1945 Mack fabricated bodies for many of the Class 155 high pressure fog foam crash trucks, whose chasses such as this model C-666 Brockway, were supplied by other contractors.

Mack also supplied many pieces of fire fighting equipment to defense contractors who maintained their own plant fire fighting departments. This Type 75 Mack pumper was delivered in February 1943.

(7) **Commercial Car Journal**, Vol. 65, No. 6, (August 1943) p.180.

(8) Vanderveen, **op.cit.**, p.7.

The creation of a standard series of military truck chasses, like the class A and B Liberty trucks of World War I fame, was considered from time to time by the W.P.B. Opponents to the Liberty truck idea cited the retooling job with its huge cost in materials and man hours needed to accomplish the change over.(7) During World War I, the truck building industry was fragmented, with about 200 assemblers, but by 1940, the industry had matured, with less than a half dozen producers turning out nearly all of the light and medium duty trucks. These producers made the lighter duty military trucks needed in largest quantities, and the custom builders of heavy-duty vehicles were able to turn out their product, which was not needed in such large numbers. The result was that no really serious crisis ever developed in the supply and use of the various kinds of vehicles and spare parts needed for the war effort.

Mack built a large variety of military vehicles, the uses of which can best be understood by describing the broad divisions and sub-divisions into which such vehicles fitted. Generally speaking, military vehicles can be divided into two broad types: **Administrative** and **Tactical**.(8)

Administrative vehicles were ordinary commercial types used in routine work, mostly at military bases. Being regular civilian production models, these vehicles were cheaper to acquire and maintenance could be had through regular commercial repair shops, if need be.

Tactical vehicles, on the other hand, were acquired to fulfil some actual combat or close support function, and because of more stringent requirements, many were of highly specialized design. The **Tactical** type can be subdivided into four general groups as follows:

1) **General-purpose Vehicles** These were wheeled vehicles designed for the movement of troops, ammunition, equipment, and general supplies, and which also could be used for pulling trailers or wheeled guns. Having general cargo bodies, for the most part, their use was quite flexible and satisfied the general automotive transport needs of the various branches of the service without further modifications. Most of the Mack military trucks built during World War II fell into this catagory.

2) **Special-equipment Vehicles** These were also wheeled vehicles which had chasses basically identical, with some modification, to the general-purpose vehicles. However, they had mounted on them some kind of special equipment, such as search lights or a mobile repair shop. The Mack model LMSW, heavy breakdown wreckers designed for the British are a good example of this type of military equipment.

3) **Special-purpose Vehicles** The chassis and body of this type of vehicle was designed or adapted for a specific function. Examples would be non-combat half-track and full-track vehicles, although some wheeled vehicles should also be included in this catagory. Mack built a number of experimental vehicles of this type, the largest being the T-8, double end tank transporter, produced in 1945.

4) **Combat Vehicles** These were basically armored vehicles, which were designed for specific fighting functions, such as tanks and half-tracks equipped with howitzers or other large guns. Mack built a number of pilot models of the T1 and T45, 105-mm. howitzer, gun carriages, and was a major supplier of medium tank power train assemblies.

In addition to the development and production of war vehicles and their components, Mack was also assigned by the Navy the job of developing a 400 horsepower, 12 cylinder, V-type, supercharged Diesel.(9) In developing this experimental engine, Mack utilized some of their previous work started during World War I on the welded steel engine, for which they had been assigned a number of basic patents. Mack also built a number of 200 horsepower, supercharged, Mariner Diesel engines for the Navy's smaller landing craft.

Mack received a number of awards for their good record in producing vital war supplies. The War Department, on November 21, 1942, presented the Army-Navy "E" Award for excellence to the Mack Manufacturing Corp. at their Allentown plant.(10) This award was a recognition of high achievement in the production of war materials. It was announced at the Mack annual meeting, in April 1942, that the company was as much as 50% ahead of schedules on important war

(9) **Diesel Progress**, Vol. 14, No. 5 (May 1948) p.210.

(10) **New York Times**, Nov. 22, 1942, p.17.

This T8 Tank Transporter was completed by Mack during 1945, just at the close of World War II, and did not go into regular production.

(11) **Ibid**., April 23, 1942, p.36.

(12) **Fire Engineering**, Vol. 96, No. 12, (Dec. 1943) p.774.

contracts.(11) Mack also received the National Security Award, which was given out by the Office of Civilian Defense to only those plants which had achieved outstanding success in programs for the protection of employees, plants, and production or service operations against fire, explosion, air raid, accident, and other emergencies.(12)

Before the conflict was over, Mack had produced 4,500 five ton, four wheel trucks, and almost 26,000 six wheel trucks for the military forces of the United States and Allied Nations.

Postwar products and problems

Concentration on the production of vehicles for the war effort severely restricted the development of new civilian vehicle designs during the 1942-1944 period. Production of heavy-duty Macks for such home front industries as petroleum and mining, however, did foster some improved civilian models.

The Mack off-highway model LMSW-M was developed in 1944 for the petroleum industry for hauling machinery through the gumbo of the southwestern oil fields. It was designed with an extra long wheel base, but with little chassis overhang to allow for the skid loading and unloading of concentrated and long loads, without harmful effects to the chassis. In addition to the long wheel base oil field chassis, the LMSW-M was also offered as a compact dumper and tractor chassis for the mining industry. There was also a medium wheel base type for the logging industry, and all the LMSW-M series were equipped with power steering.

Continued demand for larger off-highway hauling units for the essential mining industry led Mack to adapt other concepts of truck engineering which eventually classified the new off-highway vehicles as construction equipment, rather than motor trucks. Perfected during 1945-1946, the model LR off-highway dumper had a massive electrically welded, I-beam, alloy steel frame, and the new Mack Plani-drive, a special three-pinion, planetary drive in the rear wheels. The Mack Plani-drive, rear axle unit was designed to provide the greater reduction required in this

To serve the vital extractive industries such as petroleum and mining, Mack developed the LMSW-M off-highway model with off-set cab, during 1944.

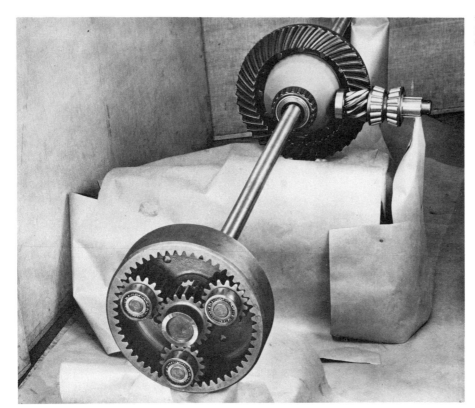

This view shows the gear design in the Mack Planidrive rear axle used first on the model LR off-highway model.

The huge Mack LR off-highway truck had design characteristics, such as welded I-beam frame and planetary rear axle drive, which led to the continuing development of larger Mack models.

type of vehicle without the excessive size of the differential carrier or axles. Power steering as well as air operated Mack clutch were standard equipment, and engines available ranged from 200 to 275 horsepower.

The different operating conditions and state laws found in the western portion of the United States prompted the design of special truck models for this area. Because of local motor vehicle weight laws, these west coast trucks had longer wheel bases than normal and more powerful engines for ascending the long mountain roads of the area. Mack's first west coast model, the trim looking LTSW, was developed in 1946, to meet these requirements. In addition to a longer standard wheel base, the LTSW had a wide choice of engines, ranging from 196 to 306 horsepower, needed to fight the long western hills and pull the full trailers many west coast truck operators favored. The basic design also included Budd

The Mack LTSW was a special West Coast model, put into production shortly after World War II to meet specific conditions affecting truck operation in the western states

disc wheels, manual or air operated radiator shutters, and ten-speed, Mack Duplex transmission.

The Mack Mono-Shift Duplex, ten speed transmission was introduced in 1946 as a single lever shifter with vacuum assist. The new Mono-Shift did away with the extra lever common to all auxiliary two speed gear boxes by substituting a finger control flipper under the gear shift knob. The flipper was set to either Hi or Lo speed and the shift took place either simultaneously with the normal shifting of the main gears or separately with just a kick on the clutch pedal.

Few changes were made to Mack's basic line of E, L, and F series, light to extra heavy-duty trucks during the 1941 to 1946 period. Prewar changes were mostly a simplification of model designations, but included the replacing of the CH and CJ models with the LJU and LMU. The LJU was dropped later, leaving the LMU as the largest Traffic Type Mack to be offered in the early postwar years. A heavier conventional LJ series was engineered for introduction after the war, to take the place of the regular LM highway model. To satisfy some of the New England contractors who operated in states allowing a wider truck than normal, the FN chain-drive model, with 102 inches overall rear width and 35,000 lbs. g.v.w., was introduced in 1940. The FN was replaced in 1941 by the FT, of similar width and capacity, and the FG was phased out during 1942.

The lightest duty models, the ED, DE, and MR delivery truck, were not produced after the war, leaving the EE model as the smallest Mack to be built in the early postwar period. Also, the ST-20 and ST-30 semi-trailers were not produced after the war.

Bus production increased in importance with the continued motorization of street car lines prior to 1942, and with transit lines serving large defense factories having to expand their services. In 1939, Mack had begun to increase their line of

The L series heavy-duty truck line was introduced in 1940 but civilian production of the L models was cut during 1942 until late in 1944, when limited numbers were produced for essential users.

A Mack LF heavy-duty dairy truck delivered in January 1946. Note the chrome work has returned to the hood, but the front hub cap still has the war-time paint scheme.

Fuel oil dealers and other big city distributors of bulk commodities were good customers for the Mack LMU heavy-duty model.

The L-25 Mack was developed in 1939 as a 23 to 25 passenger bus for lighter duty service than the model CW. This L25 Mack was delivered to Grand Forks, North Dakota early in 1940.

A new medium-duty line of Mack buses was represented by this 31 passenger RC model delivered to a New Jersey transportation system in 1941.

Mack school bus chasses based on the E model truck line were produced in five basic sizes by 1941. This large model 43SB demonstrator with a Superior body was built in 1939.

buses by introducing parallel models for light, medium, and heavy-duty service, starting first in the smaller capacity ranges. Operating conditions included the total daily mileage, length of peak loadings and ruggedness of the route covered. The L-25 Mack, 23 to 25 passenger model was produced for operating under conditions less severe than those warranting the use of the heavy-duty model CW. By 1941 a few K, R, and L type buses were introduced, which were designated for light, medium, and heavy-duty service respectively.

Mack also produced five school bus chasses by 1941, which were equivalent to the E series trucks, from the DE to the EH models. In addition, the CB series of six conventional type bus chasses were produced mainly for export to some South American and European countries.

Anxious to get back into bus production again, after the Navy's requisition of their bus plant in 1942, Mack finally received the clearance from the W.P.B. in 1944, and the Defense Plants Corporation started construction on a new bus plant for Mack at Fullerton, Pennsylvania, in March 1945.(13) However, the new factory was not needed, as V-E Day came along two months later, and Mack was able to regain control of their regular bus building facilities at Allentown.

(13) **New York Times**, March 26, 1945, p.27.

During the summer new production lines were set up, patterns for chassis parts fabrication worked out, and by late fall of 1945, 92 buses were under construction. The first of the newly designed C-41 Macks rolled off the assembly line late in December, realizing company plans of being in actual bus production before the end of 1945.(14)

(14) **Ibid**., Dec. 28, 1945, p.22.

The early postwar Mack C series buses were built in two sizes, having 41 and 45 passenger seating arrangements, and represented a standardized design with many new or improved engineering concepts. The new Fortress Frame construction, a product of war-time production techniques, resulted in a very rigid body, making all the postwar Mack buses basically heavy-duty vehicles. Improved heating and ventilation was achieved through ducts concealed in the floors, ceilings, and seat pedestals.

One of the first postwar C41 model Mack buses completed in January 1946.

The early postwar years turned out to be a crazy period. Reconversion to a peace-time economy was uppermost in everyone's mind, but the realities of America's general war mobilization dictated a slow, more painful process of readjustment. Prices and wages had been frozen by the government and controls administered by the Office of Price Administration during the war, with the Price Decontrol Board trying to unravel the controls in an equitable fashion after the war.

Millions of new workers had been hired by defense plants during the war, and fears of the loss of jobs during the reconversion period created a question of seniority rights among some union workers. Also, the fact that wages had been held down for about four years created a demand for sizable wage increases right after the war. To add to the problems facing industry, many basic materials were in short supply, with companies scrambling to get what they could in order to resume peace time production without costly delays.

The labor unrest of the 1945-1946 period was particularly severe with strikes of long duration hitting many industries. Automobile manufacturers lost $45,234,000 during the first half of 1946, due to strikes in supplier plants and shortages of basic materials. The shortages were said, by an automobile trade association official, to have been caused in part by governmental controls over raw materials.(15)

(15) **Ibid.**, August 18, 1946, p.24.

A brief strike hit the Mack plant at New Brunswick, N.J., in June 1945, and quickly spread to the Plainfield and Allentown facilities, and included about 8,500 production employees.(16) At issue were fears that seniority rights would not be observed as layoffs took place after government contracts terminated. This strike was of short duration, lasting about two weeks, but it was symptomatic of unsettled conditions at the time.

(16) **Ibid.**, June 29, 1945, p.17.

The real test of collective bargaining came in the fall of 1945, when the New Jersey and Pennsylvania Mack union locals filed strike vote petitions with the National Labor Relations Board, indicating a 30% raise in wages would be sought.(17) Evidently, labor and management were far apart, for when the strike was actually called, the following May, it lasted for six months. The 195-day Mack strike was an unfortunate occurance in all respects. Not only did the workers and company loose vital earnings, but Mack could not satisfy the demands of truck users, many of whom had been without new models for five years. It was quite a test of loyalty for the regular Mack customers, who desperately needed new vehicles for replacements and additions to their fleets.

(17) **Ibid.**, Sept. 27, 1945, p.16.

Profits from operations were severely restricted during and immediately after World War II. A profit of $3,162,829 on sales of $76,560,265 was recorded in 1941, but while sales jumped to $140,089,858 in 1944, the net profit climbed only to $4,047,701.(18) Net profit margin on sales in 1944 was less than 3%, the result of excess profits taxes and the constant renegotiation of government contracts that saw healthy profit margins whittled away. Operating results for Mack in 1946, the first full peace time year, were, of course, distorted because of the stoppage in production, and the loss of $909,025 on sales of $36,714,696 was not greater due to large tax credits.(19)

(18) Mack Trucks, Inc., **Annual Report**, 1947.

(19) **Ibid**.

Production and domestic truck registration figures were also distorted, due to the heavy defense spending in 1941, the war effort of 1942 to 1945, and finally, the 1946 strike. In 1941 a total of 9,468 new Mack trucks were registered, versus only 4,687 during the strike year of 1946.(20)

(20) **Commercial Car Journal**, Vol. 79, No. 2, (April 1950) p.118.

A major management change was caused by the death of President Fink, on January 1, 1943, after a brief illness. Louis G. Bissell was elected Chairman of the Board and Charles T. Ruhf, President. Mr. Ruhf had been with Mack since 1912, starting as a clerk in the Allentown plant. He had risen to manager of the plant and then Vice-President in charge of all production, before being named President of Mack Trucks, Inc., in 1943. Also, Edwin D. Bransome, President of the Vanadium Corporation of America, was elected to the Board of Directors in 1943.

From 1938 to 1943 a publication was issued called the **Mack Bulldog**, but this was subtitled "Spot News From The Selling Fronts" and concerned itself with illustrating new product sales, with brief articles concerning these. National advertising of Mack products was launched again in 1942 with the commissioning of one of America's outstanding commercial artists, Peter Helck, to do paintings showing Mack trucks doing their part in the war effort. These paintings were reproduced in full page advertisements in **Saturday Evening Post** and **Collier's**, up to 1946. After that period full page advertisements were placed in **Fortune** magazine and other national publications on a more limited basis.

Like other manufacturers of essential war material, Mack's concentration on military orders had increased their mass production knowledge, but, at the same time, restricted their ability to develop many new models for introduction when peace returned. Production of over 15,000 Diesel engines and about 26,000 six wheel trucks gave Mack valuable experience in the design and manufacture of these two products which were just gaining civilian favor prior to the war. Financially, Mack was in sound condition, for although the ratio of net profit to sales had been severely restricted during the war, the steady yearly net profit allowed the company to reduce their debt to a negligible level by the end of the war.

1947 - 1952 9
Delivering the truck message to the public

"National security rides on trucks"

Growth of the American trucking industry in the post-World War II period was almost phenomenal. There were about 4,859,000 privately owned trucks in the United States during 1941, and over 6,521,000 in 1947, for a gain of 1,662,000 over the six year period.(1) During the war years, 1942-1945, production was averaging about 150,000 units per year, but with scrapping and mothballing of trucks, actual truck registrations resulted in a net decline in civilian trucks by 1945. So the huge increase of 1,662,000 trucks in use by 1947 was the result of record production of slightly over two million units, less the scrapping of obsolete vehicles, during the years 1946 and 1947.

Ever since 1917, total truck registrations had increased by about 200,000 a year, except for the early depression and World War II years, when a slight decrease was evidenced. However, the postwar demand for trucks tripled the yearly increase to over 600,000 units, resulting in total registrations of slightly over 7,690,000 trucks by 1949, an increase of over 2,800,000 since 1945. Automobile registrations also increased at a record rate, leading to almost 10,000,000 more motor vehicles on the road in 1949 than in 1941.(2)

With no new roads having been built during the war years, and the few major postwar arteries still under construction in 1949, highway congestion became a serious headache for the nation. It was only logical that trucks, being the largest and sometimes slowest vehicles on the roads, would be singled out for the biggest share of criticism.

The general charges usually heard against the trucking industry were: Trucks were ruining the highways, tying up traffic, and actually benefiting unfairly from the use of publicly owned highways, while railroads had to maintain their own rights of way and also pay local taxes. These were serious charges which went right to the core of the America's national transportation policy, as evidenced in all the federal laws regulating interstate commerce.

In the spring of 1950, a United States Senate subcommittee held public hearings to determine if existing conditions in the industry did conform to the national transportation policy, and to find out the over-all cost effect to the consumer of both public and private spending on transportation charges. Expert witnesses from the American Trucking Associations, Inc., offered rebuttals to

(1) American Trucking Associations, Inc., **Trends**, (Washington, D.C., 1953) p.1.

(2) Automobile Manufacturers Association, Inc., **Automobiles of America**, (Detroit, 1961) p.104.

the charges of railroad witnesses that highway trucks had harmful effects on the nation's roads and had an unfair competitive advantage.(3)

(3) American Trucking Associations, Inc., **The Case For The Trucking Industry**, (Washington, D.C., 1950) Forward.

Evidence submitted by the A.T.A. spokesmen showed how frost damage from improper drainage and many other design and structural problems in road building were very often responsible for most of the deterioration blamed on trucks. It was shown that truckers paid huge sums in federal, state and local taxes which would more than offset the added cost attributed to the slightly heavier road construction needed for most highways used by trucks. As to the charge of unfair competition, it was pointed out that there were 25,000 American communities not directly served by railroads that were completely dependent upon highway transportation,(4) and that many businesses were locating new factories in areas not served by the railroads.

(4) **Ibid.**, p.52.

Regardless of how convincing the A.T.A. testimony appeared at the subcommittee hearing, the public still had to be informed of the trucking industry's vital role in the American way of life so that restrictive motor vehicle laws would lack popular support and might be changed. In essence trucks had become an economic necessity. The railroads had lost traffic because they did not, or could not, provide the efficient services supplied by their competition.

Members of the trucking industry started speaking out in 1950, and Mack joined in this campaign by mapping a broad gauged institutional advertising drive with the world famous public relations consultant, Edward L. Bernays. A nephew of Dr. Sigmund Freud, Mr. Bernays had started in his field as press-agent for Enrico Caruso, but after World War I switched to advising industries in their efforts to draw favorable public attention to their products.(5) The start of the Korean war in June 1950 once again cast trucks in the role of a vital national defense tool, and this fact was brought home in the Mack program to inform the public that "National Security Rides On Trucks."

(5) **Literary Digest**, Vol. 117, No. 22, (June 2, 1934) p.26.

In addition to supplying speakers, Mack set up three information bureaus which had important separate functions, although all were closely connected with meeting the public: 1) The Truck Information Service supplied the press, periodicals and radio with important developments effecting trucking and highways; 2) The Trucking Service Bureau supplied truck owners with various printed aids and speakers needed to get their story across in the areas they served; 3) Better Living Through Increased Highway Transportation was set up to supply information to the nation's important group leaders concerning both news and background information showing the vital role played by American trucking.

In May 1949, C.T. Ruhf had resigned the presidency of Mack Trucks, Inc., along with L.G. Bissell, chairman of the board of directors, and Edwin D. Bransome took over in the dual role of president and chairman of the board after resigning his position as president of the Vanadium Corporation of America. Mr. Bransome started the Mack public relations campaign rolling with several talks in front of trade groups where he emphasized the vital role trucks were playing in national defense. To counter anti-truck propaganda, and to advance the fight for better highways, other Mack executives gave talks to a wide range of audiences in various parts of the country outlining the important place trucks had in the national economy.

Full page advertisements were placed in newspapers and magazines by Mack during 1950 and 1951 to give the trucking industry's side of various events. The 1951 national railroad strike was one example used to show the truck's vital role in keeping essentials moving during national emergencies. Reprints of these ads and other Mack-produced booklets on the importance of trucks were made available on request.

In helping to enlighten public opinion to the importance of trucking to the American way of life, Mack did not ignore the need for informing the industry itself about their own unique line of highway transportation products. To introduce the new Mack END 672 Diesel engine to the trucking industry, and to explain the operation of the automotive type Diesel, Mack set up an exhibit of these engines in a trailer, which then traveled around the country for 7-1/2 months in 1949. A team of specially selected engine experts traveled with the

Mack Diesel Caravan and gave lectures on the Diesel's advantages to fleet owners. Later, Mack service personnel were also instructed in this manner, and finally, in 1950, a formal instruction course for Diesel mechanics was set up and lectures given in many major cities in the nation, with a certificate awarded to those completing the course.

Publication of the **Mack Bulldog** house organ was revived again in the fall of 1947, to constitute a third series. It was similar in size to the first **Mack Bulldog** magazine, published in the 1920's, and contained illustrated reports on Mack trucks, buses, and fire equipment in the hands of users, interlaced with articles on new Mack products and technical advances.

Advertising novelties featuring the famous Bulldog trademark designed by Colonel Masury were made available to customers and the public after World War II. Favorite items were ash trays and cigarette lighters, but even neckties and golf balls were available with the pup's engraved image. About 1950 a series of large, die cast models of Mack trucks was put out by a prominent toy manufacturer, and some of these were used in Mack's promotional work.

Improvements in the Mack product line

With the Mack plants concentrating on production to meet the unprecedented postwar demand for motor trucks, few new models were introduced in 1947 and 1948. Those that were offered were improvements or extensions of existing series.

A companion model to the west coast LTSW introduced in 1947 was the Mack LTLSW, which was first produced in 1950. The LTLSW utilized 140 separate heat-treated aluminum alloy parts to achieve savings of more than a ton in chassis weight over conventional steel construction. Components such as bogie support brackets, some frame cross-members, the hood, wheels and hubs, were all of aluminum alloy. Cummins Diesel engines of 200 to 300 horsepower were offered, and along with the Mack constant mesh five speed transmission and Brown-Lipe 3-speed auxiliary, gave this model exceptional pulling power and speed.

In the off-highway field, the larger LV model was introduced, in 1948, with a capacity of 22-1/2 tons, as a companion model to the LR, which had a capacity of 15 tons. Optional gasoline, Diesel, and butane powered engines, providing a power range up to 306 horsepower, were offered with the Mack LV. Standard

An LTLSW light weight Mack tractor, especially designed for West Coast operators, is shown here with a huge bulk cement trailer, in the early 1950's.

This gigantic LRVSW model pushed the capacities of Mack's growing line of off-highway trucks up to 34 tons by 1952.

A model FT chain-drive chassis with sheet metal configurations developed shortly after World War II.

equipment included the Mack Planidrive rear axle, and Mack Duplex, 4 speed, constant mesh transmission with 2-speed auxiliary box mounted as a unit, providing a total of 8 speeds forward.

Later on, in the early 1950's, an even bigger off-highway dumper, the six-wheel LRVSW, was developed. This model had a carrying capacity of 34 tons and was powered by a huge 12 cylinder Cummins Diesel engine which developed 400 horsepower.

To satisfy the demand from those contractors and building supply companies who still favored chain-drive, Mack reintroduced a few of their F series models during 1947. The model FT was the smallest chain-drive, having a 35,000 g.v.w.,

The FW chain-drive Mack was a companion model to the smaller FT truck, and was built in limited numbers between 1941 and 1949.

and except for a larger engine was basically the same as the prewar model internally. The model FW which had replaced the prewar FK by 1942, was redesigned, and the new version was rated at 50,000 g.v.w. The FW used the large EN707A gasoline engine rated at 196 horsepower. Some of the large FC off-highway models were also manufactured in limited numbers after the war.

The FT and FW models sported cycle type fenders and a modified L series cab that had half-doors with no windows. The F model also had a squared off radiator, and in general had a rugged all-work, no-nonsense look to them. However, very few of the F series trucks were manufactured, and they were phased out of the Mack line by 1950. Two other Macks, the LJX and LMX, dual reduction dump trucks, had similar front end designs and carrying capacities to the FT and FW models.

In 1949 Mack management decided to develop a new series of medium and heavy-duty trucks to replace the E series, the lighter models of which were still powered with Continental engines. The new A series trucks were styled after their big brothers, the L series, with cleaner, heavy-duty look. Along with the new A model trucks, the Magnadyne gasoline engine was introduced in three sizes, 291, 331, and 377 cubic inch displacement, for the A20, A30, and A40, respectively. The Magnadynes had an "L head" valve arrangement, while their larger brothers, the Thermodyne engines used in the L series trucks, had over-head valves.

The A series trucks along with the Magnadyne engines were introduced in mid-1950 to help commemorate Mack's "50 years as a builder of commercial motor vehicles." The new Golden Anniversary A model trucks, as they were fittingly

The LJX dual reduction chassis replaced the chain-drive FT model by 1950. It was used in construction and light mining service.

This LMSWX Mack was fitted out with special oil field equipment for skid loading and unloading of huge drilling equipment, and was built to take the terrific strains that tailgate handling created.

The new A series, introduced in 1950, replaced the E models and in styling were patterned after the larger L line. This A20 was the smallest model in the A series.

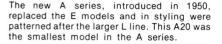

An A30 Mack being used by a large New York City area lumber dealer in 1951.

called, and their E series equivalents were: A20, EF; A30, EG; A40, EH; A50, EQ. The smallest E series truck model, the EE, was dropped without a replacement in the A line. Gross Vehicle Weights for the A20 to A50 ranged from 17,000 to 40,000 lbs. as straight trucks. 1951 and 1952 saw some additions to the A series in the larger capacities.

The growth of the long-haul, over the road truck lines using tractor semi-trailer combinations was quite rapid in the 1946 to 1950 period. To satisfy the demand for an almost unending variety of tractor units for hauling trailers, Mack intro-

The Mack A50 series provided over-the-road operators with a comparatively light weight tractor, having a wide variety of optional engines and transmissions to suit their individual operating requirements.

duced additional A series models in 1951 and 1952. The A51T Diesel and the A54T gasoline powered were comparatively light weight tractor models offered with a variety of optional components for a highly selective market.

Many truck operators had grown accustomed to certain makes of transmissions and power plants found in the non-Macks that they used, and when ordering Macks would very often specify these same components. Although Mack preferred to manufacture all the major components that went into their vehicles, there were also situations where a special component for a small order did not warrant the heavy cost that would be involved in the design and production of that component.

Along with the decision to introduce the new A line of medium and heavy-duty trucks, it was also decided to drop those truck models which had not shown any signs of improved sales by the second half of 1949. The basic aim was to cut costs by simplifying the product line and to improve profitability by concentrating selling efforts on those models that showed the most sales potential.

All the Traffic Type, cab-over-engine E models were dropped, along with the LMU, in 1950. It was only later, in the fall of 1951, that a number of c.o.e. A20 and A52U models, similar to the Traffic Type E series, were made to satisfy a few customers. Chain-drive was also considered passe by 1950, and the F series was dropped about that time.

Mack fire apparatus proved very popular at this time, with many local fire departments ordering the more traditional types of body styles, having open or semi-cabs, and with the enclosed, or sedan type, bodies of the late 1930's being temporarily overlooked. During 1949 Mack designed a new series of 65 and 75 foot aerial ladders for the type 85 fire apparatus chassis. Also in 1949, Mack designed, along with Chief Lockhart of the Minneapolis Fire Department, the largest single pump fire engine of its time, rated at 2,000 gallons per minute.(6) Fire apparatus manufacture was continued at the Long Island City plant until 1951, when operations were gradually transferred back to Allentown.

(6) Mack Trucks, Inc., **Mack Bulldog**, Third Series, Vol. 4, No. 2, (Summer 1950)

Postwar bus production, between 1945 and 1947, was concentrated in the larger capacity C-41 and C-45 models. Air-operated gear shift mechanism, developed prior to the war, was used up to March of 1947. After that a fully automatic torque converter drive was utilized in the Mack buses, eliminating the normal geared transmission and clutch arrangement. Production of the first postwar C-41 and C-45 Mack Diesel buses started in 1947, followed in 1948 with the two smaller C-33 and C-37 bus models. The new END672 Mack Diesel, of the single-lobe combustion chamber, Lanova type, was first used in the larger capacity buses during 1948, before being offered in the heavy-duty Mack truck models.

Mack bus engineers in collaboration with Colonel Sidney H. Bingham, of the City of New York's Board of Transportation, worked out plans for a 50 passenger

The E model Traffic Type Macks were dropped along with the basic E series in 1950. However, this EFU model, pictured here in 1948, was built again during 1951 and 1952 as the A20U.

A type 85 Mack pumper delivered to Riverdale, Maryland and used later as the model for a modern fire engine on a stamp issued in the fall of 1948, honoring 300 years of volunteer fire fighting in America.

In 1949 Mack began offering 65 and 75 foot aerial ladders on the type 85 fire engine chassis. This 75 foot aerial truck was delivered to West Hempstead, New York late in 1950.

The smallest of the postwar bus models was this C33 Mack produced in 1948 for a Grand Rapids, Michigan suburban line.

136

A huge new Mack transit bus with a basic 50 passenger seating capacity was developed during 1948. Over 400 of the C50 buses were eventually delivered to New York, where one is pictures on fashionable Fifth Avenue early in 1953.

This Mack model FCD rail bus was one of nine identical units built in the early 1950's for a railroad which had also purchased Mack rail equipment in the 1920's.

(7) Randolph L. Kulp, Edit., **History of Mack Rail Motor Cars and Locomotives** (Allentown, Pa., Lehigh Valley Chap., Natl. Ry. Hist. Soc., Inc., 1959) pp. 9 & 10.

bus during 1948. The first two pilot models of the new Mack C-50 bus were produced in 1949, one of which was shipped to Stockholm, Sweden. Several unique features were incorporated in the C-50, the most outstanding of which were the ease of maneuvering and the sharp turning radius provided by the power steering.

New York City ordered 400 of the C-50 Macks and these were equipped with special fittings so that they could become giant ambulances without the removal of any seats. This stretcher-bearing feature was a civil defense concept brought on by the limited national emergency during the Korean conflict period. Many of the C-50 buses delivered to New York City in 1950 and 1951 were used to motorize most of the last major street car lines in Brooklyn, such as Flatbush and Nostrand Avenues.

About 30 years after ordering their first Mack rail car, the New York, New Haven and Hartford Railroad worked out plans to purchase another series of such vehicles from Mack. In October 1951, the Allentown bus plant turned out a 21 ton, double end, model FCD prototype rail bus, which was based on the C-50 Diesel bus. After some modifications to the original plans, an additional nine Diesel-electric rail buses were produced, and all ten FCD models built between 1951 and 1954 were delivered to the New Haven Railroad.(7) Unfortunately a change in management of the railroad prompted the demise in 1954 of another effort to put branch line passenger service on a less costly operating basis.

Changes in plant and service facilities

A postwar boom and bust economic cycle, reminiscent of the 1919 to 1922 period, took place during the years 1946 to 1949. Demand for new and replacement commercial vehicles, pent up during the war period, was basically satisfied by the peak production year of 1947, and by the middle of 1948 a buyer's market had definitely set in. Nearly all motor vehicle manufacturers suffered a sharp decline in sales by 1949, and Mack was no exception. And, although export sales held up generally, domestic registrations of new Macks dropped to 6,866 in 1949, as compared with 9,795 in 1948.(8) A loss of $3,995,139 was sustained in 1949 on sales of $78,327,752, versus a profit of $2,328,000 on sales of $109,187,519 in 1948.(9) A restructuring of plant and service facilities was decided on to bring overhead more in line with actual production and sales.

During the summer of 1948 four buildings were added to the main Plainfield, New Jersey, motor factory complex.(10) But with a large operating loss in the first six months of 1949, it was decided to combine most of the New Brunswick plant's operations with those at Plainfield.(11) Mack had virtually eliminated manufacture of steering gears by 1949, and therefore only the fabrication of transmissions and geared units for axles was transferred to the Plainfield plant by the summer of 1950. Several million dollars was expended for new machinery and a new building at Plainfield to house part of the moved operations, but factory overhead showed a satisfactory decrease by the end of 1950.

Operation of the New Brunswick plant had been officially carried on by a Mack subsidiary, International Brunswick Motor Company, and this name was changed to the Brunswick Ordnance Company. Part of the New Brunswick foundry was then leased and other parts of the plant used by the new subsidiary to manufacture special government ordnance material.

Construction of a special building to house the Mack Research Division was started in 1944. This building was finished by 1947 and most of the research personnel from the various Mack plants were centered here to coordinate their activities. The Research Division had chemical, metallurgical, and testing labs for the determination of the basic physical qualities of substances, such as oils and metal alloys. A design department worked out plans for experimental projects and the division's machine shop constructed them. A special electronics laboratory built the electrical test equipment for the entire division, and special heat treating equipment was used to discover better ways of hardening vital Mack component parts to make them last longer.

Another plant to be consolidated into the operations of the other factories was the Long Island City plant in Queens County, New York. The building of the highly customized fire apparatus bodies had been carried out on the third floor of this structure, and nearly all of this operation was transferred back to the Allentown plant by the end of 1951. A manufacturing operation for service parts for some of the discontinued models was located on the second floor, as was the major overhaul and servicing depot for Mack truck and bus operators in the New York City area. The Long Island City plant was sold to C.B.S. - Columbia, Inc., an electronics manufacturing subsidiary of the Columbia Broadcasting System, early in 1952,(12) and a new one-story Mack service branch was established in the nearby Maspeth section of Queens.

Company owned branches were reduced from 67 at the end of June 1949 to 53 by the early part of 1951.(13) Distributers took over the Mack facilities either by purchase or lease and most of the key personnel were retained under the new arrangements. Also, by 1950 it was decided to drop the name International from the title of the main Mack sales organization, and henceforth the Mack Motor Truck Corporation handled the branch operations in the continental United States, except in New England, where the Mack Motor Truck Company operated as before.

To increase the efficiency of Mack's service parts division, in 1951 a new 422,000 square foot warehouse was built in Bridgewater Township, near Somerville, New Jersey, on U.S. Highway 22. Concern for civil defense strategy during the early 1950's prompted government officials to encourage private enterprise to locate new facilities away from established industrial centers which could be the target of an enemy air attack. The new Mack parts facility drew praise from the government's Industrial Dispersion Task Force for its location, which

(8) **Commercial Car Journal**, Vol. 85, No. 2, (April 1953) p.124.

(9) Mack Trucks, Inc., **Annual Report**, 1950

(10) **New York Times**, Aug. 10, 1948, p.37.

(11)**Ibid**., Sept. 10, 1949, p.20.

(12) **Ibid**., Feb. 10, 1952, Sec. VIII, p.1.

(13) Mack Trucks, Inc., **Annual Report**, 1950.

Directly after World War II Mack engineers began work on a new advanced truck series, as this 1945 view of the mockup for the M8 indicates. Note the incorporation of a streamlined version of the old Mack hood design in the M8.

There was also a cab-forward version of the proposed new Mack series, called the M8U, which was developed by 1948.

(14) Mack Trucks, Inc., **Mack Bulldog**, Third Series, Vol. 6, No. 1, (Winter 1952)

was convenient to major highways and not dependent on rail transportation.(14) The old Plainfield service parts plant was then phased out during 1952 as all operations were transferred to the new Bridgewater facility.

Several agreements were reached with other manufacturers to help improve sales and manufacturing efficiency during the early 1950's.

The most outstanding of these agreements was the one worked out with the Palmer Engine Company of Cos Cob, Connecticut, a 50 year old builder of

This 1949 view of the M8 experimental truck gives a good comparison of its advanced design with that of an E model on the left and an L series tractor on the right.

marine gasoline engines. Under the arrangement, Mack made the basic Diesel engine and Palmer adapted it to marine use by adding the necessary reduction and reverse gears and special fittings. The Mack Mariner Diesel was marketed by Palmer under the trade name Palmer Mariner, starting in 1951.(15)

Another agreement was worked out with the Wooldridge Manufacturing Company, with a new plant in Sunnyvale, California, for the assembly of Mack LR and LV off-highway trucks, which had been sold to western customers in 1951 and 1952. Also, Mack trucks were to be assembled in the Middle East by an agreement signed with another concern in 1952.(16)

The early 1950's might be called a turning point for both the trucking industry and Mack. Trucking was finally recognized for the important role it played in the nation's economy, and few new state taxes or motor vehicle laws penalizing trucks were enacted after 1952. In fact, headway was being made by highway user groups to unify the various, and often conflicting, state motor vehicle laws, which tended to impede the free flow of interstate commerce.(17) Truck manufacturers were also working out new models to cope with the length and weight restrictions common in many states.

Production and sales of Mack products picked up in 1950 and 1951, with new domestic registrations reaching 9,794 Mack trucks in 1951.(18) A large government order for five ton military trucks had helped Mack production during 1951 and 1952, but defense business tended to be spotty. Mack had a number of prototypes of new highway and city delivery truck models in their test sheds at Allentown, with which they would greet a resurgent demand for quality built heavy-duty trucks in the mid-1950's.

(15) **Ibid**.

(16) **New York Times**, Feb. 15, 1952, p.28.

(17) National Highway Users Conference, **48 States ... United**, (Washington, D.C., Sept. 1951) pp. 8 & 9.

(18) **Commercial Car Journal**, Vol. 85, No. 2, (April 1953) p.124.

The Bridgewater parts supply warehouse near Somerville, New Jersey which was built in 1951, is shown in this 1971 aerial view after the building of a large addition at the rear.

A new management takes a new approach

Although the vital need for motor trucks had been reaffirmed during the Korean War period of 1950 to 1952, a business slump during the years 1953 and 1954 adversely affected the investment in capital goods by many industries. The purchase of heavy-duty trucks tends to follow a cyclical pattern, much the same as the investment in machine tools, railroad freight cars, and construction equipment, with periods of high demand for such items, often followed by periods of low demand.

The downward trend in demand for heavy-duty trucks during this period proved to be only a temporary phenomenon, not the beginning of a long term trend. But while it lasted it was very distressing for most of the independent manufacturers, who witnessed a steady upward spiral in their production costs; at the same time a buyer's market kept the price of their products to a bare minimum. Domestic registrations of new Mack trucks showed a decline between 1952 and 1954, being 7,138 in the former, and 6,098 in the latter.(1) Sales in 1954 were $120,287,659, resulting in a net profit of $1,345,487, or a return of just a little over 1% on sales.(2)

In order to combat the problem of low prodution and low profitability in the heavy-duty building industry, during the 1950's a number of mergers took place. The White Motor Company, builders of White trucks and buses, was the main merger partner at this time, absorbing Sterling Motors in 1951, the Autocar Company in 1953, and Reo Motors in 1957. A few other truck producers were taken over by companies not in the truck producing field, who wished to diversify.

After the original merger of the manufacturers of the Mack, Saurer, an Hewitt trucks , in 1911 and 1912, forming the International Motor Company, the Mack policy had been to operate as an independent, self-sufficient manufacturer, developing its own products without the need to buy out competitors. However,the reality of the low profitability of Mack operations during the early 1950's helped to spark some profound changes in both management and policies.

During the early 1950's, a group of financial men headed by Christian A. Johnson became interested in Mack Trucks, Inc. Mr. Johnson and his associates had control of the Noma Electric Corporation, which became the Northeast Capital Corporation in 1953,(3) after the transfer or sale of all its manufacturing operations in 1952.(4) Northeast Capital Corporation then purchased a large block of the stock of Mack Trucks, Inc., and in April 1954 four directors of Northeast were elected to the Mack board of directors.(5) Before taking over active management through the board of directors, the Northeast group had indicated an interest in seeing a continuation and expansion of the Mack operations, rather than its liquidation,(6) but talks were still carried out with the White Motor Company during the summer of 1954,(7) before a definite course of expansion and diversification was launched for Mack in 1955.

The first major change in the operating officials of Mack Trucks, Inc. took place early in 1955, with the choice of Peter O. Peterson to be president, with E. D. Bransome remaining as chairman of the board of directors. Mr. Peterson had started in the automobile industry during the First World War, as a 25 cent-an-hour inspector at the Buick Motor Company's Flint, Michigan plant. Through a succession of promotions and a change in employers, he became executive vice president at Studebaker Corporation in 1951, his last position before coming to Mack.(8)

The new management group soon showed the effect of its new policies by the diversification into electronics in 1955, and the acquisition of a truck and a bus manufacturer the following year. With the pick up in heavy-duty motor truck sales finally taking place during 1955, and with the acquisitions adding fuel to the expanded business, the years 1955 to 1958 were quite dynamic for Mack.

(1) Commercial Car Journal, Vol. 97, No. 2, (April 1959) p.210.

(2) Mack Trucks, Inc., Annual Report, 1954.

(3) New York Times, Nov. 6, 1953, p.35.

(4) Ibid., Nov. 8, 1952, p.21.

(5) Ibid., April 29, 1954, p.49.

(6) Ibid., Jan. 26, 1954, p.36.

(7) Ibid., July 24, p.17, and Aug. 26, 1954, p.35.

(8) Ibid., June 19, 1955, Sec. III, p.3.

Mack's merger partners

Another form of merger, besides the joining together of firms with similar products, was the marriage of manufacturers having entirely different types of products. Many companies tried to diversify their product lines, especially those firms who found their regular markets depressed for long periods. Through diversification a manufacturer would not be completely dependent on one basic market, but could take advantage of the upswings of various markets, the cycles of which would, hopefully, not coincide.

Mack's first step in a diversification program came in February 1955, when it was announced that they had acquired two electronics firms. These were the Radio Sonic Corporation and White Industries, Inc., of New York, which were manufacturers of electronic equipment and components for aviation, industrial, and military applications.(9) The two companies were merged as the Mack Electronics Division, and new facilities provided for expanded manufacturing operations in Plainfield, New Jersey.

(9) **Ibid**., Mar. 18, 1955, p.43.

In August 1956 an agreement was signed which eventually led to the acquisition of the Brockway Motor Company, through a form of lease-purchase arrangement. Brockway had been a producer of quality trucks, in Cortland, New York, since 1912, although it had its origins in a carriage and wagon business developed by the Brockway family in Homer, New York, back in the 1870's. And while the Brockway was essentially an assembled truck, its reputation for an honest product was unquestioned, which is attested to by the fact that the company built a healthy regional market with virtually no advertising.

The early Brockway trucks built between 1912 and 1914 used a 3-cylinder air-cooled engine and were built in four basic capacities up to 4,000 pounds.

At the time of the agreement with Mack, the Brockway line of heavy-duty trucks consisted of about 20 basic models, which ranged from 20,000 to 65,000 pounds gross vehicle weight. Standard Brockway components at that time were: Continental engines, Fuller transmissions, Timkin axles, and Ross steering gears. Brockway trucks were conservatively styled, and company engineers worked closely with truck operators to provide the best trouble free designs. Ease of access to the engine on Brockway trucks was achieved by the exclusive swingaway fender design and Brockway built cabs were known for their comfort and safety.

After 1956 Brockway Motor Trucks was operated as an autonomous division of Mack, retaining their same basic personnel and organization. In 1958 the new Huskie line of Brockway trucks was introduced with an advertising campaign in various trade magazines, and although domestic sales of new Brockways tended to hang slightly below 1,000 during the years 1956 to 1958, the operation was very profitable.

Modern engineering and conservative styling have been the keynotes of Brockway design. A model 158W tractor with Continental Diesel power, built in 1955.

(10) **Bus Transportation**, Vol. 35 No. 10, (Oct. 1956) pp. 54 & 55.

(11) **Motor Coach Age**, Vol. 23, No. 1, (Jan. 1971) p.4.

(12) **Fire Engineering**, Vol. 107, No. 1, (Jan. 1954) p.52.

(13) **Ibid**., Vol. 108, No. 9, (Sept. 1955) p.801.

The agreement with Brockway was followed by the purchase of the C.D. Beck Company, of Sidney, Ohio, in September 1956. Beck was basically a producer of custom-built inter-city buses whose production never exceeded a few hundred vehicles a year. The Beck operation also included the manufacture of Ahrens-Fox fire apparatus since 1953, first on contract, later as sole owner and producer.

Mack had gradually dropped out of the inter-city bus market during the 1930's to concentrate on transit buses, of which they had built many thousands by 1956. It was with the expressed desire to re-enter the inter-city bus market that Mack purchased the C.D. Beck Company.(10) The end result though was more advantageous to Mack's line of fire apparatus than to the bus business which they had hoped to expand.

The C.D. Beck Company was the outgrowth of a small auto body firm, the Anderson Body Company, which was reorganized by Mr. Beck and his associates in the motor bus field.(11) From its reorganization as a bus body builder in 1932, the firm gradually increased the size and type of its bodies, until by the late 1930's fully integral inter-city coaches were the main product. After World War II a modern plant was constructed, and regular production lines set up for the new series of custom Beck buses which were to come. Production of a large deck-and-a-half, silver sided, inter-city coach, model 9600, was undertaken by 1955. However, small production runs of their various bus models had prompted Beck to seek another product with which to take advantage of unused plant capacity. This was accomplished through an agreement, in November 1953, with Ahrens-Fox, Incorporated of Cincinnati, Ohio, to build the Ahrens-Fox line of custom fire apparatus on contract. (12)

Ahrens-Fox fire apparatus had acquired a world-wide reputation for quality built piston pumpers, which were distinguished from centrifugal and rotary gear type pumpers by the huge chromium plated ball-like pressure dome on top of the pump, at the front end of the fire truck. As the piston pumper went out of favor with department chiefs, the last one being built in 1951, Ahrens-Fox had switched to other types of pumps, and it was streamlined versions of their apparatus that Beck built under contract for two years. Ahrens-Fox, Inc. had remained in Cincinnati, supplying service and repair parts, and this arrangement evidently continued after Beck acquired the exclusive rights to manufacture all Ahrens-Fox fire apparatus in 1955.(13) Early the following year, just a few months prior to the Mack merger, a new cab-forward line of fire apparatus was introduced by Beck. The merger with Mack marked the end of both the Beck line of buses and Ahrens-Fox custom fire apparatus, although some of the Beck engineering concepts were adapted in new Mack buses and fire apparatus.

The Beck operation, which Mack acquired in 1956, was a builder of moderately priced intercity buses. This group of 1939 Beck Super Steeliners was delivered to an intercity operator based in Charlotte, N.C.

New highway and city delivery trucks

The years 1953 to 1955 saw the introduction of several completely new lines of heavy-duty Mack trucks for highway and city delivery use, and the phasing out of the A and L model Macks of similar capacities. The most outstanding and long lived of the new Mack model lines was the B series, introduced in the spring of 1953, with ratings from 17,000 lbs. g.v.w. for the smaller model B-20, up to 60,000 lbs. g.v.w. for the bigger B-42 tractor. Other larger B models were added to the series as they were developed.

Fully rounded fenders, hood and cab, resulted in an eye catching design for the B series, which caused many a road-weary trucker to take a double look at the new Macks. Safety and accessibility were important features of their functional design, with the Flagship cab being a good example. This new cab, which was standard on all the B model trucks, had improved ventilation, lighting, and a V-type windshield, set at a specific angle to cut harmful glare. Instrumentation was set in a readily demountable panel and all fuses were positioned in a central location for easy access and replacement. Various sheet metal parts at the front of the truck were quickly demountable for ready access to the engine compartment.

The chassis frames of the B series were widened at the front to provide more space for engine servicing and to take larger power plants on the bigger models. A new wider front axle permitted greater cutting of the wheels, which in turn provided for better maneuverability, much needed in city delivery work. Traditional rubber shock insulator cushion connections for the spring ends were highly modified due to the use of the new Vari-rate springs. The installation of Vari-rate springs, which stiffened with heavier loads and softened for light loads, was the basic solution to the extreme variation in the riding quality between a loaded and unloaded truck.

Mack introduced a large variety of tractor models in the new B line between 1953 and 1956, which proved very popular with over-the-road truckers. One of the popular tractor series, which had the Mack Magnadyne gasoline engine as standard equipment, was the model B-42T, produced in four and six wheel versions, with gross ratings of 40,000 to 60,000 pounds. Other larger tractor series were the B50 and B60, which came equipped with either gasoline or Diesel engines, depending on the specific model ordered. A wide range of optional engines and transmissions was availble to help meet the needs of various operators. A specially designed Contour Cab, having a six inch concavity in its back, which helped truckers pull longer trailers and yet keep within the 45 foot overall length restrictions, was introduced in the mid-1950's.

A completely new line of cab-over-engine highway tractors, designated the H-60T and H-61T, having the 170 horsepower Mack Thermodyne gasoline and Diesel engines respectively, were introduced in 1953. Also introduced in 1953 was the W-71S model, as a cab-over-engine, light weight companion to the con-

The new streamlined B series Mack trucks were introduced in the spring of 1953. Note the design similarity of this model B42, six-wheel chassis, with the picture of the 1949 version of the experimental M8 truck. (on page 140)

The medium sized B42 model proved very popular in both straight truck and highway tractor versions; but with the demand for Mack tractors increasing during the 1950's, fewer Mack straight truck models in the lighter capacities were built.

ventional LTLSW, so popular on the west coast. The H models had very high cabs, which were referred to by the truckers as "Cherry Pickers."

The main feature of the H-60T and H-61T was their short bumper to back of cab length, which enabled them to haul 35 foot trailers and yet stay within the 45 foot overall legal limits of many states. The problem of not having full engine accessibility, so common in the larger c.o.e. trucks, was solved through the use of a hand powered mechanical-winch device, which tilted the cab forward, uncovering the engine and all its accessories for servicing. The payload was increased by the extensive use of aluminum alloy in various components of these tractors, and the gross combination weight was rated at between 50,000 and 63,000 pounds. A modification in design in 1954 reduced the overall height by one foot, with two new models, the H-62T and H-63T, still being over 9 feet high.

Designed specifically to meet the axle spacing laws of many of the western states, the Mack W-71S, introduced in 1953, featured a long wheel base, weight

SEAWAY

Speeding operations on the St. Lawrence Seaway, Mack 6-wheel dump trucks come through where other trucks often bog down . . . thanks to the Mack-built Balanced Bogie with Power Divider—the flexible, four-wheel rear-axle drive that transmits power to the wheels with traction.

ORANGE JUICE

Some Macks move mountains; others . . . frozen orange juice. While perhaps not as dramatic as the big off-highway projects, distributing highly perishable foods over long routes also puts to the test a truck's reliability. The frozen foods industry, among many others, makes good use of dependable Macks with their proved ability to make light of the long haul and deliver on time . . . *every* time.

where dependabl

Macks

Next time you see America's important ca goes—products, produce or raw materials moving down the highway . . . look for th Mack bulldog! Next time you see big co struction trucks in action—re-shaping th landscape, carving out craters, moving mou tains . . . look for the Mack bulldog!

You'll start seeing Macks everywhere! B

A typical Mack color advertisement of the mid-1950's which appeared in various national publications; this ad appeared in *Fortune*, June 1957.

hauling counts the most...

HANDLE THE IMPORTANT JOBS!

cause all over the world, more and more truck users are discovering that "Built like a Mack" spells out the ultimate in clockwork schedules under demanding service, in years of trouble-free durability, in long, long vehicle life and in solid earning power.

Why not find out for yourself? Give Macks an inspection in depth. Measure the capabili-

ties of their superbly engineered transmissions, engines, axles and differentials against the toughest hauling jobs you're likely to run into. You'll find out why Macks are more in demand than ever before . . . why Mack sells more diesel-powered trucks, year after year, than any other maker. Mack Trucks, Inc., Plainfield, New Jersey.

DEW LINE

Building America's line of Arctic radar stations called for an unparalleled transport argosy across the howling, roadless roof of the world. Pitting their giant strength and endurance against this incredible terrain . . . driving through bitter blizzards, over icy mountain passes and across the frozen Arctic Ocean . . . standing up to temperatures of 80° below and gales of up to 100 mph . . . huge Mack tractors, each grossing over 164 tons, forged through to deliver the construction materials—perhaps the toughest 1,500 miles ever faced by wheeled vehicles.

IT'S PART OF THE LANGUAGE...BUILT LIKE A

TRUCKS • BUSES • FIRE APPARATUS
AND ELECTRONIC EQUIPMENT

This Mack B50 tractor was powered with a Thermodyne gasoline engine, and is seen here pulling a specially designed manifold trailer for the delivery of compressed oxygen gas in the New England area.

A 1957 Mack B65 tractor having the specially designed Contour Cab, which allowed truckers to pull longer trailers and still keep within the 45-foot-overall-length laws of certain states.

Because of their extremely high cabs the Mack H60 series were popularly referred to as "Cherry Pickers," when first introduced. Here is a model H61T Diesel tractor delivered in 1953.

A lowered version of the Mack H60 cab-over-engine tractor series was introduced in 1954 and built in several models until 1962. Note the array of license plates on this H67 tractor photographed in 1960.

A large and powerful cab-over-engine six wheel truck chassis, designated the W71, was introduced in 1953 specifically for the West Coast market.

saving aluminum alloy components, and a 200 horsepower Cummins Diesel engine. Basically a six-wheel, cab-over-engine, straight truck chassis, the W-71S sported a cab with an overall height of 9 feet. Engine accessibility was achieved through the use of hinged engine hood and readily removable floorboards and seats.

Designated the Great Western Group, a new B series with models such as the B-72, B-73, and B-75 was introduced in 1956 to replace the LTL and LTLSW models. In addition to the usual light weight aluminum alloy components, Great Western models were also available in standard weight versions. A wide range of powerful Mack and Cummins power plants was available, having from 205 to 262 horsepower. In addition to the optional engines, various truck models in the Great Western Group were also available with Mack 5, 10, 15, and 20 speed transmissions.

To round out its line of cab-over-engine trucks, in the spring of 1955 Mack introduced the D series for city delivery service. The new D series was actually a cabforward type, having the engine between the seats, and instead of tilting, the cab lifted vertically to expose all the front chassis parts for servicing. The new Verti-Lift cab came either with manual or optional hydraulic lifting mechanisms, and was quite different in concept to similar delivery trucks having tilting cabs,

The Mack Great Western was introduced in 1956 as a replacement of the LTL and LTLSW models. This B72LST, part of the new light weight series, was delivered to a Portlant, Oregon lumber company in 1956.

which were produced at the time by White, Diamond-T, and International. Mack D series models were offered in sizes from 20,000 to 28,000 lbs. g.v.w., as delivery trucks, and in 40,000 to 53,000 lbs. g.c.w., as tractors. Model designations were similar to the smaller B series, being D-20P, D-30P, D-42P, and D-42T, and had the Magnadyne gasoline engine as standard equipment.

In 1958 a new cab-forward line of Mack trucks, called the N group, replaced the D series. The new N group used a modern looking Budd built tilting cab, which was raised through the use of balanced coil springs. The N-42 through N-61 models had ratings ranging from 28,000 lbs. g.v.w to 65,000 lbs. g.c.w., and a wide range of Mack engines, including Diesel, were available, along with transmissions of 5, 10, 15, and 20 speeds forward.

New components and super-duty trucks

Perhaps the most important fundamental development in the Mack product line during the 1950's was the creation of the new END 673 Thermodyne Diesel engine, introduced in 1953. The new Diesel was of the open-chamber, direct-injection type, which was a departure from the Lanova, pre-combustion, energy cell design, formerly used in all Mack Diesels. This change was the result of certain problems which developed with the END 672 Diesel, having the single-lobe energy cell, and the desire to use another combustion chamber design having a greater horsepower potential.

Use of the open-chamber, direct-injection, combustion system was accomplished through an exchange agreement with the Swedish automotive firm of AB Scania-Vabis. A group of Scania-Vabis engineers had visited the United States in 1949 to find and then recommend a design for an integral bus their firm wished to manufacture.(14) An inspection tour convinced the Swedes that the solid construction of the Mack bus was up to the design standards of other Scania-Vabis products, and a licensing agreement was made soon after. The new Mack Diesels incorporated the applicable improvements which had been previously developed, such as the Mack Synchrovance automatic injector timing control, and the END 673 used the same basic block as the END 672.

A turbocharged version of the END 673 was introduced during 1953, and the basic 170 horsepower was raised to 205. The turbocharger was a turbine-propelled intake blower which used the waste energy of the exhaust cases

(14) **Motor Coach Age**, Vol. 24, No. 2, (Feb. 1972) p.16.

1955 saw the introduction of the Mack D series, city delivery trucks, which had a cab-forward design with the engine between the seats, and a very unique cab-raising device for quick engine servicing.

Complete servicing of the front end of the D series Macks was achieved through the unique design of its Verti-Lift cab, which raised straight up by the use of either a manual or hydraulic lifting mechanism.

A new N series heavy-duty city delivery truck line replaced the D models in 1958. The new N model Macks used the Budd-built tilt cab.

from the engine for its power. In this manner additional air was packed into each power stroke, for a 20% gain in horsepower from the same 672 cubic inch displacement, and at the same engine speed of 2100 r.p.m. The new Mack Diesel models quickly proved their economy of operation, and soon many fleets were using the new power plants in their new Mack trucks and buses.

Also adopted for use on Mack trucks during the mid-1950's was the Diesel exhaust brake, which increased the natural retardation of the engine by 50 per

The Mack END673 Thermodyne Diesel engine had a basic 170 horsepower which was raised to 205 in 1954; the turbocharged version is shown here. The drum-like device in the upper left on the engine is the turbocharger.

cent. Use of the Mack Diesel brake was considered an added safety factor, which also helped to increase the normal service life of the vehicle's regular brakes. The addition of a butterfly valve in the exhaust pipe and the connection of a system of automatic switches allowed the engine's compression to be increased by the build-up of back pressure. An exclusive control design allowed the system to function automatically whenever the brakes were applied, or continuously when coasting. But the automatic control operated the butterfly valve only after fuel injection had ceased, thereby insuring that only air would be trapped in the manifold to create the back pressure, which helped to slow the truck.

Improvements in Mack power trains during the mid-1950's included the introduction of several new transmissions. The Mack Triplex, 15 speed, and Quadruplex, 20 speed transmissions used the Mack designed Tetrapoid gears, for longer life and quieter operation, and also had a positive forced lubrication. There was, in addition, the new Unishift, 10 speed transmission, which used a single lever for the manipulation of both the main and compound gears.

The B-80 series of super-duty trucks for the construction industry and certain off-highway applications was developed during 1955 for general introduction during 1956. Typical features of the B-80 line were: frames of double channel for their full length, Dual Reduction in both four and six wheel models, transmissions of up to 20 speeds forward, and various engines, mostly Diesel, having between 170 and 320 horsepower. There was even a six wheel drive model, using the Mack front drive axle with triple reduction, which was developed for off-highway, dumper, mixer, logging, and carry-all tractor services. The B-80 models, which used the Flagship cab, were distinguished from other B series Macks not only by their size, but by the use of exposed, cast tank radiators, and simplified heavy-duty, square, military type fenders. With capacities in excess of 60,000 pounds gross vehicle weight, the B-80 line was an adequate replacement of the prior LJ and LM off-highway series.

The basic line of huge LV and LR off-highway dump trucks using the Mack Planidrive, planetary wheel hub gears, was continued in production through the 1953 and 1958 period. These Mack monsters, with engines of up to 400 horsepower, ranged in capacity from 15 to 34 tons in the four and six wheel versions,

The Mack LJ and LM models which had been so popular in the construction industry, were replaced in 1956 with the new B80 line. This B80SX is seen on a Montana construction project in 1959.

and could pull up to 100 tons when used as tractors. During 1958 an even larger off-highway model, the LYSW six wheeler, was introduced, which had a capacity of 40 tons and a 450 horsepower Diesel engine.

Defense business took on renewed importance in the three years 1955 to 1957, with Mack receiving several multi-million dollar contracts for both military vehicles and electronic equipment. Mack assembled over 1,600 standard Army 5 ton, 6 x 6, cargo carriers during 1955, at a contract price of over $17,000,000,(15) as well as developing in collaboration with the Army a new 10 ton prime mover. The new prime mover was a 6 x 6, using mostly Mack components. Several contracts were received for these vehicles after initial units passed months of rigorous testing. A 1.6 million dollar contract from the United States Air Force for U.H.F. transmitting equipment was received by Mack during 1957.(16)

(15) **New York Times**, Nov. 1, 1954, p.42.

(16) **Ibid**., May 8, 1957, p.54.

Mack received several large contracts, starting in 1955, to develop and build a large 10-ton prime mover for the Unites States Army. One of the Mack M125 prime movers with general cargo body, photographed in 1958.

Developments in bus and fire apparatus production

Public riding on local urban and inter-city transit lines declined at a rather sharp rate after World War II, with patronage losses of 50% or more common to many systems between the years 1945 and 1955.(17) A number of reasons have been cited for this decline, the chief one being the desire of many people to drive their own cars to work or place of amusement. However, the result of this decline, which has only abated gradually in recent years, has been the general financial insolvency of many local transit companies, and their takeover by publicly owned operating authorities.

During the early 1950's, with most local bus operators finding themselves squeezed between rising costs, declining patronage, and long-delayed fare increases, the market for new buses naturally declined. Few cities still had sizeable street railway systems to motorize, and the replacement bus business tended to wither because of the operator's financial problems and also because many of them found themselves with surplus equipment. A number of major bus builders including ACF-Brill and White decided to call it quits in 1953 and 1954, leaving General Motors, Mack, and a couple of smaller manufacturers to contest for the remaining business.

Major improvements in the Mack bus line were developed during 1953 and 1954, which centered on the larger size models, as few orders had been received for the smaller Mack C-33 and C-37 buses, and these were phased out by 1955. The C-45 model was redesignated the C-47, and a new C-49 bus, about a ton lighter and a foot shorter than the C-50, was introduced to replace the C-50. The END 673 Diesel was standard equipment now on the C-41, C-47, and C-49 models, with the more powerful turbocharged Diesel as optional. Mack Airglide suspension system was introduced in 1955, and used a group of nylon and rubber bellows to provide a smoother, easier ride. A highly sensitive levelling control was built into the new air suspension system which maintained uniform floor height regardless of load, and was used on the C-47 and C-49 buses.

Demand for the improved Mack bus line zoomed in 1955, with a special order for 400 large buses from San Francisco, and other sizable orders coming from various other cities in the United States and Latin America. Encouraged by the revival of their bus business, Mack set out to increase their share of the market with some new approaches. In 1955 Mack hired Alexis de Sakhnoffsky, the famous automotive stylist, to make a thorough study of bus design, both inside and out.(18) The result of his efforts was the Mack "Dream Bus," having large side windows, standee windows which curved into the roof, complete air conditioning, full fluorescent lighting, and many other innovations. A prototype of this bus was displayed at the annual convention of the American Transit Association at St. Louis in the fall of 1956.

In 1956 it was determined to re-enter the inter-city bus field, which Mack had dropped out of during the 1930's when concentrating on the development of new transit type city buses. With the purchase of the C.D. Beck plant at Sidney, Ohio in the fall of 1956, Mack was able to announce, shortly thereafter, plans for several new inter-city and suburban bus models. Expansion of the Sidney plant was then undertaken in 1957, with a tripling in floor space that allowed some of the bus manufacturing to be moved from Allentown, as well as most of the fire apparatus.

Chief model in the new inter-city bus line was the Mack 9700, with a seating capacity of up to 45 passengers. This bus had all major components built by Mack, and could be fitted out as either a regular inter-city coach or sightseeing bus, with glass roof panels. During 1957 a 39 passenger, six-wheeled cross-country luxury bus was developed, and then tested by Greyhound lines in 1958. This ultra-modern coach featured increased height for better scenic viewing and more storage capacity for luggage and express, as well as lounge, lavatory, air-conditioning, and foam rubber, reclining-type seats. However, new bus models, including new styling in the transit types, did not result in increased sales, as the bus market returned to its downward trend during 1957 and 1958.

(17) American Transit Association, '71 - '72 **Transit Fact Book**, (Washington, D.C., 1972) p.7.

(18) **Bus Transportation**, Vol. 34, No. 10, (Oct. 1955) pp. 54 & 57.

In 1955 Mack received an initial order for 400 of the recently designed C49 transit bus from San Francisco. Here we see the first completed bus in this order being loaded at the Allentown plant, October 1955.

The Mack "Dream Bus," or "Bus of Tomorrow" as it was also called, was based on a design created by automotive stylist Alexis deSakhnoffsky, and was first exhibited in the fall of 1956.

The 41 passenger model 97D intercity bus was designed by Mack engineers after the purchase of the Beck bus plant at Sidney, Ohio where this vehicle was built for a Colorado operator.

This ultra modern 39 passenger model MV39 cross-country luxury Mack was developed in 1957 for testing by Greyhound Lines in 1958.

Demand for Mack fire apparatus continued to grow throughout the 1950's, with over 1,000 communities and industrial firms using Mack built fire fighting equipment by 1953. A number of important innovations and improvements were incorporated into Mack fire apparatus which resulted in a continued expansion of this important part of the Mack product line.

Typical of these improved units was a fleet of 25 type 19 Macks with special high pressure pumps delivered in 1954 to the N.Y.C.F.D.. These allowed the city to highly modify its separate high pressure hydrant system located in the old high value area, below 34th Street.(19) The new B line of Mack fire engines, using highly modified B series commercial chasses, was introduced in the fall of 1954. High performance engines of over 200 horsepower were standard equipment, as was a selection of centrifugal pumps of from 500 to 1,250 gallons per minute capacity. The basic Flagship cab was also standard as a coupe type, or semi-open version on certain models. The sedan type cab, which Mack had pioneered in 1935, was also available as optional equipment on some models. The new B line was a great success and Mack fire apparatus sales increased in 1955 by 25 per cent over 1954, and by an even greater 38 per cent during 1956.

The Mack Fire Apparatus Division was transferred to the newly acquired and expanded Sidney, Ohio, plant in 1957. Floor space totaled about 200,000 square feet and a large engineering staff was gathered to work out new designs for both fire apparatus and buses. One of the most important additions to the Mack fire apparatus line at this time was the production of a new cab-forward series, similar in concept to the last Beck built Ahrens-Fox fire engines. The new cab-forward line was designated the C series, and was built with pump sizes of 500 to 1,250 g.p.m. There were also aerial models having extended ladder lengths of 65, 75, 85, and 100 feet.

Mack pioneered the use of automatic transmissions in fire apparatus, with the installation of a torque converter in a Mack unit in 1956, and in 1957 a fully

(19) **Fire Engineering**, Vol. 107, No. 4, (April 1954) p.325.

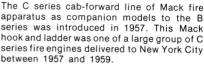

Mack B series fire apparatus, with gasoline engines of over 200 horsepower as standard equipment, was introduced in the fall of 1954. This B95 1,000 g.p.m. pumper was delivered to Cornwall, New York late in 1958.

The C series cab-forward line of Mack fire apparatus as companion models to the B series was introduced in 1957. This Mack hook and ladder was one of a large group of C series fire engines delivered to New York City between 1957 and 1959.

automatic transmission was offered as optional equipment. The automatic transmission, which obviated the need for clutch and shift lever, was considered a help for city driving, as it allowed rapid acceleration and quick stop and go operation without shifting. During 1957 Mack also offered the world famous German Magirus aerial ladder unit, with lengths up to 144 feet, installed on Mack fire apparatus.

The years of progress

Growth in the demand for heavy-duty trucks was made manifest during the years 1955 and 1956 triggered by a general upswing in the economy. In 1955 over-the-road truck fleet operators enjoyed one of their biggest boom years, with a huge surge in highway freight volume which created a record demand for new tractor-trailer equipment. More activity in the heavy construction industry also pushed up sales of heavy-duty dumper and concrete mixer trucks. During the mid-1950's construction started on the multi-billion dollar federally funded 41,000 mile Interstate highway system. In addition to the construction itself, increasing the market for heavy-duty trucks, the new highways would eventually help to decentralize industry and create more communities totally dependent on highway transportation.

Sales of Mack trucks more than doubled between 1954 and 1956, with new domestic registrations of 6,098 in the former, and 13,190 in the latter.(20) Net profit increased even more dramatically to a record $12,103,763 on sales of $254,243,784 in 1956, as compared to a profit of $1,345,487 on sales of $120,287,659 in 1954.(21) A net profit ratio of 4.7% on sales in 1956, the best rate of return since 1947, was due in part to a more efficient use of production facilities and greater interchangeability of some components, such as cabs, among the various truck models. During this period the manufacture of tractors for semi-trailer operation became the dominant part of total Mack truck production.

Company owned sales and service facilities in North America were increased to almost 60, for a net gain of about 10 by 1958. These newly opened branches served areas of new or resurgent growth in the use of Mack products, and were supplemented by over 300 distributors and service stations. An agreement was reached with the Belgian firm of Electro Rail, S.A. in 1955 to manufacture certain Mack products for distribution throughout Europe,(22) and an affiliate, Mack Belgium, S.A., was later set up.(23) National advertising was increased, starting in 1955, with many large two-page color spreads appearing in such magazines as **Newsweek** and **Fortune**. On June 1, 1956, Mack changed the titles of their manufacturing and sales subsidiaries to Mack Trucks, Inc., leaving only Mack Trucks of Canada, Ltd., and Mack Electronics Division, Inc., retaining their old names.(24)

With the heavy-duty truck market remaining on a basically high level, although sales declined somewhat during the slight recession of 1957, Mack's remaining problem was the ever rising cost of production, which cut into profitability in 1957 and 1958. Cash dividends had been resumed during 1957, after being deferred for a number of years as net working capital was built up from earnings. Mack, as with other truck manufacturers, was forced to tie up large amounts of capital in inventories of both original and spare parts, which tended to have a restrictive influence on the growth of the organization.(25)

P.O. Peterson was named chairman of the board in June 1958, succeeding E.D. Bransome, who retired. However, Mr. Peterson resigned at the end of 1958, ostensibly to devote more time to personal business matters.(26) And during the mid-1950's, the general offices were transferred from the Empire State Building to the Plainfield plant.

The lack of increased profitability led to a change in some of the expansionist policies that had been followed since 1955. In December 1958 it was announced that the Sidney Division would be closed and its operations transferred to the Allentown plant complex.(27) The Electronics Division was discontinued in 1958,

(20) **Commercial Car Journal**, Vol. 97, No.2, (April 1959) p.210.

(21) Mack Trucks, Inc., **Annual Report**, 1958.

(22) **New York Times**, March 11, 1955, p.39.

(23) **Ibid**., Jan. 23, 1956, p.35.

(24) **Bus Transportation**, Vol. 35, No. 7, (July 1956) p.47.

(25) **Forbes**, Vol. 77, No. 9, (May 1, 1956) pp. 25 & 26.

(26) **New York Times**, Nov. 19, 1958, p.57.

(27) **Ibid**., Dec. 9, 1958, p.64.

due to its lack of profitability and the generally poor prospects of any increase in volume which might help its situation.(28) Other important changes were in the offing as Christian A. Johnson, president of Central Securities Corporation, took over as chairman of the board of directors and chief executive officer of Mack Trucks, Inc., on January 1, 1959.

(28) Mack Trucks, Inc., **Annual Report**, 1958.

11 | 1959 - 1964 Consolidation and reorganization

Closing the productivity gap

With the announcement of the change in top management late in 1958, little time passed before major changes were announced in Mack's manufacturing facilities and corporate organization. The new chairman of the board and chief executive officier, Christian A. Johnson, whose financial holdings had effectively controlled Mack Trucks, Inc. since 1953, showed that he was determined to increase the truck manufacturer's profitability, which had again showed a downward trend since 1957. Mr. Johnson's battle to increase productivity and to cut manufacturing overhead costs at the various Mack plants resulted in a minor upheaval in the company's operations and organization.

When the market for heavy-duty trucks eased, as it did in 1958, profits seemed to plunge in a manner out of proportion to the decline in sales. But when the market showed renewed strength the following year, profits increased dramatically. A financial comparison of the years 1958, when 11,865 new Mack trucks were registered in the United States, with 1959, when 13,472 were registered,(1) will illustrate this point. Net profit for Mack Trucks, Inc. during 1958 was $7,774,977 on sales of $253,787,924, versus a net profit of $15,786,272 on sales of $297,352,562 in 1959.(2) The doubling of the net profit during 1959, while gratifying, only obscured the root cause of the problem: a basically low productivity at the Mack plants.

(1) **Commercial Car Journal**, Vol. 99, No. 2, (April 1960) p.260.

(2) Mack Trucks, Inc., **Annual Report**, 1959.

If Mack was to remain a viable industrial organization with an adequate net return from its working capital, which would in turn provide the flow of funds needed for developing new products and the buying of efficient new production tools, then a solution to the productivity problem had to be found. Added competition from the big three automobile producers, whose heavy-duty truck models had made their appearance and impact felt during the late 1950's, helped to pinpoint the productivity problem as detrimental to Mack's future growth, if not survival.

The discontinuation of the Mack Electronics Division in 1958 was followed in December of the same year with the announcement of the intended closing of the Sidney Division.(3) A bombshell was dropped with the news in October 1959 that the Plainfield plant would be replaced with a facility to be located in another area. The decision to close Plainfield, after almost fifty years of operation, was made because, it was stated, production efficiency was below comparable standards in the rest of the industry and the present plant site provided only limited possiblities for future expansion.(4) Several alternative locations for a new engine and gear plant were considered, including the possible combining of the Plainfield operation with the main truck assembly plant at Allentown. A site in Hagerstown, Maryland, was finally chosen, and the announcement of the plans for a new multi-million dollar one-story plant was made in June 1960.(5)

(3) **New York Times**, Nov. 19, 1958, p.57.

(4) **Ibid**., Oct. 23, 1959, p.23.

(5) **Ibid**., June 24, 1960, p.24.

A merger with the Northeast Capital Corporation, which had owned 29% of the outstanding Mack stock, was brought about during late 1959. Northeast had sold off its manufacturing subsidiaries prior to the merger, so that the merger was in

A composite view of the Plainfield, New Jersey Mack engine plant and parts warehouse, taken just before World War II. Gear production had been moved here from the New Brunswick plant by 1950, but operations at the Plainfield factory complex were considered too inefficient by the late 1950's.

Mack's plant at Hagerstown, Maryland, to which engine, transmission and differential carrier manufacture was transferred in the fall of 1961.

(6) **Forbes**, Vol. 84, No. 8, (Oct. 15, 1959) p.52.

(7) **New York Times**, May 24, 1960, p.51.

essence an injection of $12 million in cash into Mack's working capital.(6) Central Securities Corporation, having owned 26.7% of Northeast Capital Corporation, continued to excercise effective control of Mack by receiving a substantial block of the new Mack stock issued for the merger. The cash was evidently needed to help pay for at least one of several transactions taking place during 1959 and 1960. The Brockway lease-purchase agreement, entered into in 1956, was wound up in 1959, with Mack paying for Brockway's plant and branches, which had previously been leased.

Another important need for additional capital was for the creation of the Mack Financial Corporation, which was set up to handle all customers' installment credit. The new subsidiary was to begin operations with over $150 million in capital to be obtained from bank loans, long term notes and the sale of both preferred and common stock. A major objective of the new subsidiary was to relieve the parent company, Mack Trucks, Inc., of $110,000,000 of debt, thereby reduce its heavy funded indebtedness and in turn restore its long term borrowing power. The Mack Financial Corporation was formed during the spring of 1960,(7) but transfer of the installment receivables did not take place until April 1961.

End of the line for the Mack bus

The motor bus business of the late 1950's could be described as continuing on a downward trend, with only an occasional hopeful development to add a little light to an otherwise darkening picture. In the face of steadily rising operating costs most local transit operators were forced to seek fare increases which they also knew would help to accelerate the continuing decline in patronage. It was a decline that most businesses suffering from economic obsolescence are faced with, and their basic efforts are simply to survive. With the majority of transit companies restricting the purchase of new equipment, a dwindiling market for new buses was then divided among General Motors, Mack, and a couple of smaller manufacturers.

Even the trend toward public ownership of urban transit lines did not paint a brighter picture for future Mack bus sales. By the mid-1950's many municipally owned transit systems, like those in New York and San Francisco, were in serious economic difficulties. In 1953 San Francisco voters had turned down a multi-million dollar bond issue intended for vitally needed new transit equipment, and in order to obtain the new buses the management had to devise a lease-purchase program and ask for bids. Mack, being the only bidder, was awarded the contract, and supplied a total of 450 C-49 Diesel buses by the time production ended in 1960.(8) However, with most municipal purchases being made strictly on a low bid basis, and with Mack products built up to certain standards and not down to a price, any new business that could be acquired under such circumstances would be of doubtful profitability.

During 1958 plans for a "new look" Mack transit bus were worked out with the Niagara Frontier Transit System of Buffalo, New York. The 60 new buses delivered in 1959 to N.F.T. had wrap-around windshields, dual headlights, and a lower body silhouette. This special new C49 model was offered along with the traditional Mack bus models up to June 1959, when the last Mack bus advertisement appeared.(9) Another late improvement in bus design was the adaptation of the Power Divider as a non-spin differential for use in Mack buses which might encounter icy roads.

Bus sales had shown little real strength during 1958, with intercity models selling only in small unit lots, and few substantial transit bus orders were received during 1959. What had started out as expansion in 1956 turned into contraction in 1959, with the Mack bus being quietly phased out of production by early 1960.

Mack buses had been built from the late 1920's at Allentown's largest single factory unit, plant 5C, and at various times the whole of this building was given over to their manufacture. With the slackening of bus production there was little economic justification for the continued use of these facilities for producing a few hundred vehicles a year, at least not when sales of Mack trucks had gone well over 13,000 in 1959. Plans were also being formulated for changes in work standards at Allentown during 1959, and a general reorganization of the production lines for greater efficiency was also under consideration.

Bus production ended at Allentown early in 1960 when the last units, in an order for 75 for Puerto Rico, rolled off the assembly line. Mack had built over 22,000 buses since they started in the commercial motor vehicle business. The vast majority of these were transit types, and were built after the depression years of the early 1930's. The Mack reputation for building a solid, economical bus had not saved it from extinction when adverse economic forces militated so strongly against the independent bus manufacturer.

(8) **Motor Coach Age**, Vol. 24, No. 11, (Nov. 1972) p.34.

(9) **Mass Transportation**, Vol. 55, No. 6, (June 1959) pp. 4 & 5.

A "new look" bus design was worked out in 1958 and 60 of the new style Mack C49 buses, with wrap around windshields, were delivered to Buffalo, New York early in 1959.

(10) Mack Trucks, Inc., **Annual Report**, 1960.

Nestled among the rolling hills of north-central Maryland, the new Mack Hagerstown plant started taking shape in September 1960, with completion scheduled for the last quarter of 1961. Planned as a one million square-foot, one story structure, the new facility was to have a much larger capacity than that of the old Plainfield plant, with 50% of its machinery purchased new and the balance being transfers of Plainfield equipment acquired in the previous five years.(10) The huge Hagerstown project symbolized the major effort to restructure both the manufacturing processes and management policies of the Mack company into a highly competitive organization.

Guidance and responsibility for implementing the major changes at Mack were vested in Nicholas Dykstra, who was named president and chief executive officier in July 1961. Mr. Johnson continued as chairman of the board of directors. Mr. Dykstra was a 26 year veteran of the Curtiss-Wright Corporation, and came to Mack from a short stint as vice-president of finance of the McDonnell Aircraft Corporation,(11) where he "had reportedly done a good, if at times overexuberant job of cost-cutting."(12)

(11)**New York Times**, July 24, 1961, p.27.

(12)**Forbes**, Vol. 89, No. 3, (Feb. 1, 1962) p.13.

Before the end of 1961 Mack management was undergoing vast changes which took place at the same time that the Plainfield plant was being phased out and the new Hagerstown plant beginning start-up operations. By March 1962 most of the Mack executive officiers were either replaced or reshuffled, and over 30 top executives had departed, many replaced with former Curtiss-Wrighters.(13) The new management structure was explained as providing a group of personnel, including Mack career people, who had a broad experience in a variety of industries which could provide for rapid, flexible movement and decision to serve the ever-changing markets for Mack products.(14)

(13) **Ibid**.

(14) Mack Trucks, Inc., **Annual Report**, 1961.

The job of transferring the Plainfield operations to Hagerstown was a monumental physical task which took several months to complete. The ramifications of the move took a few years to straighten out. The transfer of Plainfield employes to Hagerstown started in August 1961, with only 700 of the 2,700 employes agreeing to go, the bulk of the force declining pay cuts of from 46 to 74 cents in hourly rates at the new location. The reduced pay was attributed to a lower cost of living in Maryland.(15)

(15) **New York Times**, Aug. 17, 1961, p.14.

More than 1,000 van loads of various materials, including work-in-process, were moved over a two month period, as well as 400 loads of production tools and machinery. Before the operations were completely phased out on October 31, the Plainfield plant produced enough Mack components to keep the Allentown factory going until pilot operations at Hagerstown were started by year end.

The cost of the big move to Maryland was high in both human and material values. By the end of 1961, the investment in plant and equipment was stated at $34 million, with another $9 million committed for additional purchases. At the time of the move special separation and early retirement benefits were estimated to cost Mack over $4 million.(16) But start-up costs ran up to at least another $13 million, which were written off over a period of years, creating a continuing drag on net profits.

(16) **Ibid**., Nov. 1, 1961, p.79.

A costly strike ensued at the end of a three year contract with the United Auto Workers, which expired during October 1961. A union official was quoted as saying that the main issue was a union demand that workers get the right to transfer with jobs whenever a plant was moved.(17) The strike, which hit the Allentown, Somerville, and Cortland plants, lasted 44 days, and was ended through the efforts of the Federal Mediation and Conciliation Service, without the terms of the settlement being made public.

(17) **Ibid**., Oct. 21, 1961, p.21.

Job security was a natural concern as evidenced by the 1,800 dislocated Plainfield workers who had signed up for a special skills program sponsored by the New Jersey Department of Labor and Industry. The job program was started a month before the Plainfield plant closed and its main effort was to find openings for skilled workers and retrain those whose skills were not in demand.(18) The most difficult problem facing many of the older workers, besides the age factor

(18) **Ibid**., Jan. 31, 1962, p.16.

itself, was the lack of incentive to start learning a new trade if their own was on the decline. Plainfield too had become affected by time. What used to be thought of as a moderate sized manufacturing city was now a well-to-do residential and shopping area.

1961 had started out to be a comparatively slower year for production, consequently providing a good opportunity for the Hagerstown move and rearrangement of the Allentown production lines. However, just as orders for new trucks picked up in the fall and the move to Hagerstown was being completed, the 44 day strike paralyzed production lines and helped to batter earnings down to their lowest level since 1954. The earnings of $2,956,906 on sales of $226,848,269 in 1961 meant a return of only 1.3% on sales.

A new generation of truck models

The new truck models for highway and city use introduced by Mack during the 1959 to 1964 period were designed with the concept of a short bumper-to-back-of-cab dimension. With the increased liberalization and uniformity in state motor vehicle weight and length laws, new truck models were called for to take full advantage of the changes. In trucking industry parlance these new highway tractors became known as "BBC" models to indicate the accent on their short bumper-to-back-of-cab dimension, and their consequent ability to haul longer semi-trailers, or semi-trailer and full trailer combinations. Also, functional design for ease of operation and maintenance, improved cab accessories providing greater driver comfort, and bigger engines for increased pulling power were features of the new generation of trucks.

First of the new super-short "BBC" type Macks was the G series, introduced in 1959 as a basically light weight over-the-road tractor for West Coast operators. The Mack built cab featured all aluminum construction and an extremely wide flat front with a grill like the improved H models. A standard cab length of only 51 inches, measured from bumper to the back of cab, and 80 inches with an over-sized sleeper compartment, meant the ability to pull longer trailers with additional cargo space. The light weight chassis made possible by various standard and optional aluminum components also made possible additional payloading. In the new G series more than adequate power and gear ratios were provided by standard Mack engines and transmissions. Mack or Cummins Diesel engines were available in both naturally aspirated and turbocharged versions,

Sporting an all aluminum flat front cab, the new Mack G series of West Coast models was introduced in 1959, replacing the model W71 which has been phased out in 1958.

The Mack F series cab-over-engine tractor series provided an extremely short bumper to back of cab dimension and was adaptable to operating conditions in various parts of the country.

Many important safety and driver oriented features were incorporated into the F series models which were introduced in 1962. Note the large two-piece wind shield and rainproof fresh air vents.

with the optional Cummins Diesel reaching 335 horsepower. Accessibility to the engine was provided by a manually actuated, hydraulically lifted tilt cab.

A substantial upswing in demand for trucks during 1962 reversed the two year downward trend in Mack sales, with the company capitalizing on the improved market conditions with a major new c.o.e. highway tractor series. The new F series had a newly designed "BBC" type cab available in three lengths: 50" in the standard version, or 72" and 80" for the regular and deluxe sleeper cabs **163**

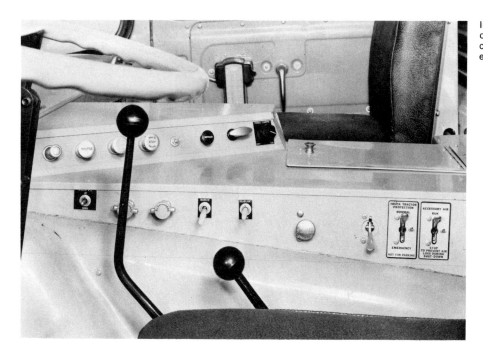

In the F model cab the engine control and other important switches were mounted on convenient panel boards located on the engine tunnel to the driver's right.

respectively. The shortness of these tractor models, and their improved cab design, gave them almost instant popularity with over-the-road truckers.

The F model cabs had an unusually large Solex heat-resistant windshield of two piece construction, giving the driver a safer, clearer view of the road than most competing makes. Other important driver oriented features were: 36,500 B.T.U. climate control heater for zero-weather comfort, large rain-proof fresh air vents, optional air conditioning, adjustable chair-high seats with foam-over-spring cushions, and choice of 22 or 30 inch wide sleeper compartments. The important engine control and other switches were positioned on convenient panel boards mounted on the engine tunnel at the driver's right. For fast servicing of the engine, the cab tilted 42 degrees by a mechanism built on the torsion bar principle, which could be adjusted to provide the exact amount of tilting force needed.

The recently developed END 711 Mack Thermodyne engine, which produced 211 horsepower without turbo-charging, was featured with the F series, but many other power plants having less or greater power were also available. In the six wheel version, the F series had the new Mack built spring-and-beam bogie, which combines light weight with high capacity. For front end suspension, long 54" springs provided an improved ride for these short wheel based tractors. Many light weight components, standard as well as optional, provided a very favorable horsepower to weight ratio, which also explained the quick acceptance of the new F series by the trucking industry.

Several new Mack Thermodyne gasoline engines, having between 160 and 204 horsepower, and a new version of the Magnadyne gasoline engine with 150 horsepower, were introduced during 1960. However, by 1959 about 75% of all Mack trucks were already being produced with Diesels. After 1960 Mack concentrated on developing only new Diesel engines. And after more than five years of developmental work, the Mack END864 V-8 Diesel went into production at the new Hagerstown plant in 1962. Rated at 255 horsepower without turbo-charging, the compact, high torque, V-8 engine was considered powerful enough to haul top legal loads at maximum legal speeds in any part of the nation.

Mack engineering developed new and more rugged transmissions to keep pace with the continued rise in the power of the truck engines. Five improved transmissions incorporating a new "coarse pitch" gear design, providing increased capacity, were introduced during 1960. Further research led to the introduction of the Mack "Durapoid" gear tooth form and another new series of

The END864 V-8 Diesel was developed by Mack engineers over a more than five year period. It was rated at 255 horsepower, without turbocharging, when introduced in 1962.

END864-1162C12509

rugged transmissions for both highway and off-highway trucks during 1963. Following the concept of balanced component design, new axles, bogies, and other Mack made parts were also placed in production during the early 1960's.

Described as combining the best features of both conventional and cab-forward type trucks, the new Mack C series was introduced in 1963. Having a sloping foreshortened hood, of roughly three feet in length, and raised cab of conventional appearance, the C models had a snubnosed look. Also, the use of B series front fenders and the old L series type cab gave them a slightly composite appearance. The 89 inch BBC dimension provided the C model tractors with the ability to haul 40 foot trailers and yet keep within a 50 foot overall length. Tremendous horsepower was supplied by the new END 864, V-8 Diesel engine, and other engines of lesser power were available, as was the usual selection of Mack or vender built transmissions.

To round out the Mack line of highway and city truck models, the MB series of Diesel powered city delivery trucks was also announced in 1963. The new END 475 Diesel Engine, specifically developed for the rigors of stop and go city delivery work and built by the Swedish firm of Scania-Vabis, was standard equipment. Developing 140 brake horsepower, the new Scania Diesel used the same open combustion chamber principle as the Mack built Diesels. For those users desiring gasoline power, Chrysler V-8 engines, developing 189 brake horsepower, were available.

A Mack built cab, featuring a squared-off clean-cut design, was mounted in a low, forward position on the new MB series. A set-back front axle permitted full-sized bodies with shorter wheelbases, and a 45 degree turning angle of the front wheels provided extreme manuverability for city delivery work. The engine was positioned between the two cab seats and was quickly exposed for servicing by the tilting cab, which was raised by powerful spring action.

Mack's popular conventional B series was continued, with some additions, through 1964. A special B-53S, weight-saver, six-wheel, concrete mixer chassis was introduced in 1962, which could accomodate a seven cubic yard mixer body.

The C line was introduced in 1963, basically as a tractor series with a short bumper to back of cab dimension of only 89 inches.

Servicing of the new C series Mack was made easy by the hinged fender design, shown opened for inspection of the powerful Mack V-8 Diesel engine.

in the powerful B73 and B75 highway tractor series, the larger L series cab was made optional equipment for those truckers who wanted more space than provided in the standard Flagship cab. A new B-615 series powered by the END 864 was put into production by 1964. Also, a new H model was developed for use mainly as a 6 x 4 concrete mixer chassis, having a gross vehicle weight of 65,000 to 100,000 pounds.

The postwar trend toward the production of heavier Mack trucks continued at an accelerated pace into the 1960's. By 1964, out of a total of 12,064 new Mack truck registrations, 10,353 were over 33,000 lbs. g.v.w., and 1,432 were in the 26,001 to 33,000 catagory. Only 279 Macks were registered in the upper medium-duty classification of 19,501 to 26,000 lbs. g.v.w., representing the sales of the model B-30 truck.

Brockway Motor Trucks, an autonomous division of Mack Trucks, Inc.,

The Mack N tilting cab series was phased out in 1962, being replaced with a new MB series having a Mack built cab which also tilted for servicing of the power plant.

The B53S concrete mixer chassis, with special weight saving features, was introduced in 1963. Shown here is a tri-axle version available the same year. Mack's own Tri-Axle bogie models have been available since 1967.

During the late 1950's some of the B70 series Mack tractor models became available with the former L series cab. Pictured here is a B773LS being used in 1966 by a Washington logger.

The Brockway Huskie line, introduced in 1958, proved very popular with over-the-road truckers. This model 257 Huskie tractor, delivered in 1960, is pulling a large bulk product trailer.

Brockway introduced a number of short BBC type trucks and tractors between 1959 and 1961. Seen here is the model 158, having a bumper-to-back of cab dimension of 90 inches, introduced in 1961.

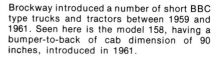

A cab-over-engine Brockway 400 series was introduced in 1963. Power plant options ranged in horsepower from 200 to 265, provided by various specialized engine manufacturers.

continued to expand its popular Huskie line of conventional trucks, first introduced in 1958. A new version of the model 258, with a BBC dimension of 87 inches, and built basically as a tractor, was introduced in 1959. The standard 100 line, with gross vehicle weights starting at 23,000 pounds and reaching 55,000 in gross combinations, was continued through 1964, with a new 158 series added during 1961. The new 158 series featured a functional, compact design having a BBC dimension of 90 inches, and was available as either tractor or straight truck. As trucks their gross vehicle ratings ran from 23,000 to 50,000 pounds, and as tractors, from 45,000 to 60,000 pounds gross combination weight.

Brockway introduced its first real cab-over-engine model in 1963, using a modified Mack F series cab. The new c.o.e. 400 series Brockways offered a choice of Continental gasoline or Cummins and Detroit Diesel engines. Sales of Brockway trucks continued to edge upward with new yearly registrations going over the 1,000 level each year during the 1962 to 1964 period.

Off-highway trucks and fire apparatus

Two pilot models of a new off-highway M series were displayed by Mack at the American Mining Congress show in October 1960. These two giant dumpers were the models M-30X four wheel, and the M-45SX six wheel, having capacities of 30 and 45 tons respectively. The new M line featured a newly designed cab, having reverse slope windshield which reduced dangerous glare, reflection, and accumulations of dust. The offset and slightly forward mounting of the cab gave better vision and allowed for shorter front axle to back-of-cab dimension, with a consequently improved weight distribution on the front axle. Because of the M series' excellence of design, it was selected by the American Society of Industrial Designers to be part of the American exhibit at the International Design Show at the Louvre, Paris, in June 1963. With the introduction of the M models in 1961, the last of the old L series off-highway trucks was phased out the same year.

Other new features of the M series were: tubular front axles, with a 7" diameter, tread of 107" and weighing over one ton; broad semi-elliptic, progressive-rate leaf springs with cam-faced slipped ends and radius rods; improved wide flanged

Mack produced this pilot model of their M45SX six wheel off-highway truck during the summer of 1960. The new M series was a great success with many new models of various capacities added in succeeding years.

This huge 60 ton capacity dumper, the model M60X, was introduced in 1962 and was the largest Mack off-highway truck for only a couple of years until an even larger model was added.

This giant Mack tractor, model M651XT introduced in 1964, had the capability of pulling a 100 to 110 ton capacity bottom dump semi-trailer.

I-beam alloy steel frames; and larger radiators. Also standard equipment were the Mack Planidrive, rear wheel gear reduction, and two-lever, 8-speed, Mack Duplex transmission. Customers had a choice of either Cummins or Detroit Diesel power plants, and the semi-automatic Torqmatic transmission was optional.

In 1962 the M-60X, 60 ton dumper, was introduced at the American Mining Congress show at San Francisco. Encouraged by the steadily increased interest in their off-highway trucks, the Mack line was added to each year, and by 1964 a huge tractor model, the M-651XT was available that could haul 100 tons in a bottom dump, model 112 BDT semi-trailer.

After the Mack Fire Apparatus Division was transferred back to the Allentown plant in 1959, the Sidney Division plant was sold to the Westinghouse Air Brake Company.

By 1959 Mack fire apparatus engineers were convinced that the Mack Diesel engine had been developed to the extent that its power, flexibility, and fuel economy made it suitable for fire department use. A practical demonstration of this theory was provided by an order for three B series pumpers, powered with 230 horsepower turbocharged Thermodynde Diesel engines, which were delivered to Hamilton, Bermuda, in 1960. But by 1962 missionary work still had to be done to prove the Diesel's value in fire service, and so two Mack Diesel fire engine pumpers were sent on a 10,000 mile nation-wide trip to demonstrate their superior features to local fire department officials.

Another Mack fire apparatus development during the early 1960's was the marketing of a new aerial lift platform, mounted on a hydraulically actuated boom. This was followed by the development of a new telescopic aerial lift platform, during 1962 and 1963. The newer aerial platform was called the Mack Aerialscope, and had a three-section, hydraulically operated boom, with a

(19) **Fire Engineering**, Vol. 117, No. 4, (April 1964) pp.260 & 261.

(20) **Ibid**., Vol. 116, No. 7, (July 1963) p.528.

working height, when extended, of 75 feet.(19) But the most dramatic development during the 1960's was the announcement of Mack's involvement with the marine architectural and engineering firm of Cox and Gibbs in developing a "Super Pumper," having a capacity of 4,400 gallons per minute at 700 pounds pressure. This new pumper was considered a "pumping station on wheels" and was being developed for the New York City fire department at an estimated cost of $875,000.(20)

During the 1959 to 1964 period Mack continued their lines of B conventional series, and C cab-forward style fire apparatus, with pump ratings of 500, 750, 1,000 and 1,250 g.p.m. Aerial ladders of 65, 75, 85 and 100 foot lengths were also available in both the B and C series, as straight trucks or tractor and semi-trailer configurations.

Mack at the crossroads

Another corner was turned in the continuing changes in Mack management when, in June 1962, C.A. Johnson stepped down as chairman of the board in favor of C. Rhoades MacBride. Mr. MacBride was a former management consultant whose last job before coming to Mack was as vice president of General Dynamics

Mack deserves major credit for bringing the advantages of modern Diesel power to fire department service. These B series pumpers at Hamilton, Bermuda were the first Mack Diesel fire engines and were delivered in 1960.

The Mack Aerialscope elevating platform was developed during the early 1960's to provide a versatile fire fighting unit which could act as both a manned water tower and highly maneuverable aerial rescue device.

Corporation.(21) In September Mr. MacBride succeeded Nicholas Dykstra as president and chief executive officier, when a disagreement on management philosophy caused Mr. Dykstra to resign.(22) Christian A. Johnson had continued as a member of the board, but died in January 1964. He was succeeded on the board of directors by Arnold R. LaForce, who also became president of Central Securities Corporation. The Mack main office was moved from Plainfield to a newly constructed headquarters building at Montvale, New Jersey, in the spring of 1964.

Since the end of World War II, and the subsequent burgeoning of international trade, all efforts by Mack to set up branch assembly plants in foreign countries seem to have floundered. Following a reorganization of the Mack International Division in 1961, another effort to establish foreign assembling facilities was embarked upon, and late in 1962 Mack Trucks Worldwide, Ltd., was set up to coordinate all overseas marketing. Assembly plants, jointly owned by Mack and local interests, were built in Venezuela and Australia during 1963. Also in 1963, joint ventures with various public and private interests led to the assembly of Mack trucks in Pakistan, with a subsidiary, Mack Trucks of Pakistan, Ltd., later setting up its own plant at Karachi.

The French truck manufacturer, Camions Bernard, S.A., was purchased during 1963 to help increase Mack's penetration of the highly desirable European Common Market, as well as countries in North Africa and the Middle East. However, an extensive reorganization of the Bernard firm followed a rather severe loss on the French operation during 1964.

Mack had for many years planned branch manufacturing operations in Canada, and finally in 1964 small scale production was started at Toronto by a newly created subsidiary, Mack Trucks Manufacturing Company of Canada, Limited. Since the creation of Mack Trucks Worldwide, Ltd., international distribution of Mack trucks had shown great progress, with overseas sales in 1964 being about twice those of 1961.(23)

Sales by Mack to the United States Government became significant again in 1962 with the sale of 2,564 M-54 Diesel engines, to be used in the initial phase of an army program to standardize five ton military trucks with Diesel instead of gasoline power. A special government sales department was established by 1963 and a marketing program planned to serve this very important customer. Government sales continued to be encouraging, with a sale of 61 model MB Diesel tractors to the U.S. Post Office in the fall of 1964.

(21) **Forbes**, Vol. 90, No. 7, (Oct. 1, 1962) p.28.

(22) **New York Times**, Sept. 8, 1962, p.32.

(23) Mack Trucks, Inc., **Annual Report**, 1964.

The French truck building concern of Camions Bernard, S.A. was acquired by Mack in 1963. The French firm had produced specialized chasses for various industries since the 1920's. The company was disbanded in 1966.

Several important new concepts and changes in marketing were tried by Mack to improve and strengthen their sales efforts. The most significant innovation was the leasing of new trucks to customers, and this business grew steadily from a small beginning in the late 1950's. The branch operation was centralized in 1960, with their control directly under the Mack home office, instead of through regional divisions as before. National advertising was stepped up in leading business and trade publications, with the slogan "They've worked their way into the language" used to emphasize Mack's world wide reputation for quality built trucks.

In spite of a resurgent heavy-duty truck market during 1963 and 1964, and a corresponding pickup in Mack truck sales, profitability remained at a discouraging low level. New domestic Mack truck registrations, although significantly above the low of 10,353 in 1962, were flat in 1963 and 1964, being 12,099 and 12,064 respectively.(24) Record Mack sales in 1963 of $305,891,205 resulted in a net profit of $8,764,524, for a net profit ratio on sales of just under 3%. And although sales were still higher in 1964, reaching $306,362,111, net profit declined sharply to only $3,409,681,(25) due mainly to a six week strike in the fourth quarter. The 1964 net profit ratio on sales was just a shade over 1%. The continuing need for additional working capital led to a merger agreement with the Chrysler Corporation in 1964, which was then blocked by a government anti-trust action.

The 1959 to 1964 period of consolidation and reorganization had seen many fundamental changes in the organizational structure of Mack Trucks, Inc., but increased profitability and labor stability were still elusive goals. What Mack seemed to need most of all was a "second effort" spirit that would provide the determination and teamwork for a smooth running and successful organization.

(24) **Commercial Car Journal**, Vol. 109, No. 2, (April 1965) p.116.

(25) Mack Trucks, Inc., **Annual Report**, 1965.

1965 - 1972 | 12
The Bulldog bites back - a Signal success

Progress with profits

A new era dawned for Mack with the start of 1965. The board of directors had finally decided that an experienced executive from the truck manufacturing industry must be brought in to return Mack to an upward course in both sales and profits. In January 1965 announcement was made of the resignation of C. Rhoades MacBride from his posts as chairman of the board and president of Mack Trucks, Inc., and the election of Zenon C.R. Hansen as president.(1)

(1) **New York Times**, Jan. 8, 1965, p.48.

The unfortunate situation at Mack in January 1965 was of massive proportions, with many of the problems being of a chronic nature which seemed to defy the financial men running the organization and their outside consultants. However, such problems are actually challenges to an individual who has the expertise to correctly analyze the over-all situation, and who also has the courage of his own convictions to move forcefully for the proper changes. Such a man was Zenon Hansen, who brought to the Mack organization the sum of 38 successful years in the motor truck industry.

Mr. Hansen's long and busy career in trucks started in 1927 when he began his first job with the International Harvester Company, later serving in various domestic and overseas posts with this firm until the opportunity of a partnership occurred in 1944. The new enterprise was named the Automotive Equipment Company, which took over the Diamond T truck dealership for the Portland, Oregon, area. It was Mr. Hansen's successful connection with the Diamond T organization that eventually propelled him in 1953 to director of sales for the Diamond T Motor Car Company in Chicago, and finally president of that firm in

1956. After the merger of Diamond T with the White Motor Company, in 1958, Mr. Hansen became executive vice president of White, from which position he came to Mack.

Perhaps the most formidable task facing the new Mack president was lifting the low morale caused by the constant changes on the managerial level and the rumors of mergers, or other drastic changes, which kept sweeping the organization. Meetings were quickly called with salaried and hourly workers at which assurances were given of a stable labor relations program, that promotions would be made basically from within, and that the days when waves of outsiders descended upon the firm were over.

An ancillary problem involving the personnel and internal communications was the centrifugal tendency in locating the Mack plants and offices. Moving the Mack headquarters to Montvale, in northern New Jersey, from its location at Plainfield, took the top management further away from the main Allentown, Pennsylvania, assembly plant. Likewise, the moving of the old Plainfield plant to Hagerstown, Maryland, about doubled the distance of the main Mack component plant from Allentown. The most distant management group was Mack Trucks Worldwide, Ltd., which was responsible for most of Mack's international operations, with their office located in Hamilton, Bermuda. Also, some board meetings were still being held in New York City, a convenient location for the chief council and members of the Central Securities Corporation.

By the end of 1965 executive office locations formerly in Montvale, New Jersey, New York City, and Bermuda were relocated near the Allentown plant. Getting it all together paid off, not only in greater managerial efficiency, but in real economic savings, a result of the reduced overhead. Staff meetings could be quickly called and important decisions affecting operations reached and carried out in a shorter time.

To help provide the spirit to keep the unified operations rolling, the corporate symbol, the tenacious Bulldog, was given new importance. No change was made to the Bulldog radiator mascot, but all pictures now showed the Bulldog with a brindle-colored coat. The change in the Bulldog's hair coloring from its previous white was reportedly done to keep the public from confusing this symbol with Mack's rival, the White,(2) but this was really done to make the Mack symbol more life-like.

(2) **Forbes**, Vol. 96, No. 11, (Dec. 1, 1965) p.46.

The use of the Bulldog symbol, which seems to sum up so much of the spirit of the Mack product, has taken on greater meaning since Mr. Zenon C.R. Hansen became the chief executive officer at Mack Trucks, Inc. in 1965. Here we see Mr. Hansen taking orders from his "boss."

The Bulldog has growled forth again in all manner of ways since 1965, with wall pictures for Mack offices, and many new types of Bulldog crested novelties being added to a whole catalog of promotional items available to the public. Perhaps the most novel use of the Bulldog symbol, is in the lapel pin which visitors to Mack's Allentown facilties are invited to wear by one of their charming receptionists.

The establishment of a company airline was considered essential to cut executive travel time between the distant Mack facilities. By the spring of 1965 the Mack aviation department, which is known as Bulldog Airlines, was functioning with two Twin Beech aircraft. The new communications system immediately improved interplant coordination, with the benefits soon extended to both distributors and customers. To increase the service new executive jets and even two jet helicopters were purchased. To mar what was otherwise a highly successful operation, Mack IV Lear-jet dropped into Lake Michigan on an approach to Racine, Wisconsin, on November 6, 1969, taking the lives of five Mack engineers and two pilots, all those aboard.

Bulldog Airlines, the private airline of Mack Trucks, Inc.,created in 1965, includes this Executive Fan Jet, which helps to save management countless hours of travel time and improve interplant coordination.

Revival of the house organ, **The Mack Bulldog**, took place in 1966, marking a fourth series in the career of this publication, under the management of the Advertising and Sales Promotion Dept. **The Mack Bulldog** quickly grew into a regular magazine, which featured important messages from top management as well as illustrated news about personnel and new products. During 1969 the Public Relations Department took control of its publication, and with a change in format, the April-May 1970 issue started a fifth series.

Mack advertising took on a very patriotic theme during 1970, which soon saw several Mack trucks painted in red, white, and blue, stars and stripes. This effort to reverse the publicized decline in patriotism soon brought favorable nation-wide recognition, including awards from the Freedoms Foundation at Valley Forge.

A West Coast assembly plant had been planned a number of times since the First World War period, but aside from the assembling of some off-highway models under contract during the early 1950's, no conventional Macks had been built there. This situation was finally corrected in September 1965 with the purchase of a 100,000 square foot plant at Haywood, California,(3) about 10 miles south of Oakland. While Mack had, for many years, been making special West Coast truck models, the cost of transporting these finished vehicles to their market area tended to give locally built trucks a better sales advantage. The opening of the new Haywood plant, in January 1966, not only helped to increase Mack's share of the West Coast market, but also allowed the Allentown plant to increase its production of the other truck models.

Other sorely needed improvements and additions were made to other Mack facilities. Large storage facilities were built at the Allentown plant to help handle the glut of parts which had to be stock-piled in order to off-set the chronic delivery delays of some vendors. New production machinery was purchased for the

(3) Mack Trucks, Inc., **The Mack Bulldog**, Fifth Series, Vol. 1, No. 11, (March-April 1971) p.3.

Allentown and Hagerstown plants to obtain greater efficiency. By 1966 a 100,000 square foot addition to the Bridgewater parts warehouse was underway, and a computerized parts inventory control system was being installed for use by all Mack branches.

The small scale Canadian assembly operations, started in Toronto during 1964, were so successful that construction of a regular plant was authorized in 1966. The new Canadian factory, located in the Toronto suburb of Oakville, was completed late in 1966, and operated by Mack Trucks Manufacturing Company of Canada, Ltd. The original Toronto plant was then used as a parts warehouse. During 1966 and 1967 Mack products were also being assembled in France, Australia, Venezuela, Guinea, Iran, Pakistan, Belgium and Portugal.(4)

President Hansen's top to bottom reorganization of Mack Trucks, Inc., coupled with a continuing strong heavy-duty truck market, soon showed very favorable results. Record sales were booked for both 1965 and 1966, being $368,388,191 in the former, and $411,830,634 in the latter. A decision to write-off against 1965 income the remaining excess costs on the Hagerstown move, resulted in only a slight rise in net income to $4,303,065.(5) However, the 1966 net profit of $13,736,696 resulted in a slightly over 3% return on sales. New Mack truck registrations increased with the improved production from the revamped facilities, being 13,127 in 1965, and 15,014 in 1966.(6) The successful turn-around of the Mack operation was highlighted in a cover story in **Business Week** late in 1966. In March 1967 Zenon Hansen was elected chairman of the board.

(4) Mack Trucks, Inc., **Annual Report**, 1966.

(5) **Ibid**.

(6) **Commercial Car Journal**, Vol. 113, No. 2, (April 1967) p.223.

A new series of highway trucks and components

Meeting the new surge in demand for heavy-duty trucks, Mack introduced a number of new truck and component lines during 1965 and 1966 which had been under development for several years. Included in these new products were design and engineering innovations which greatly enhanced Mack's prestige and market potential among many classes of truck users. The first of these new products were the R and U model truck lines which were introduced in 1965. However, the popular F series highway tractors and MB city delivery trucks were continued with few changes.

The introduction of the new R series Mack conventional truck line, in 1965, was followed by the phase out of the Mack B series in April 1966. A model R763S being used by a Utah based construction firm in 1966.

The Mack R series was a conventional line of highway trucks which eventually superceded the highly popular B models. A large one-piece fiberglass hood and fender assembly and more prominent cab gave the new R models a clean-cut business-like appearance. Although of the same general width as the former B series Flagship cab, the greater height of the new cab on the R series provided more vertical room, and a larger windshield and rear window resulted in greater visibility, both fore and aft. A fully adjustable chair-height driver's seat gave more comfort, and double-wall, welded sheet metal construction meant longer cab life and added protection to the occupants. The tilting hood and fender unit gave ample walk-in space around the tires for quick servicing. When introduced, the R series was offered with both gas and Diesel engines from 140 to 255 horsepower, in in-line sixes and V-8 types. Gross vehicle weights started with 26,000 pounds for the smaller R-400 models, and went up to all legal limits with the larger R-600 and R-700 models.

Described as an "unconventional conventional-type tractor," the new Mack U series, with offset Commandcab, raised many a passing driver's eyebrows on first and even second sighting. From a direct front view it was obvious that moving the cab 11 inches to the left of a normally centered position placed the driver directly in line with the left front fender, greatly improving his visibility. Also adding to greater visibility was the fact that the cab was raised slightly and moved forward, somewhat in the same position as the close-coupled C series cab, providing a 90 inch BBC dimension, which was comparable to the C model's 89 inch BBC.

The Commandcab with adjustable steering wheel and extra large windshield had many of the other improved features also found in the R series cab. And as on

Building a truck with an offset cab was not new in 1965 when the Mack U series was introduced, as nearly all the off-highway Macks built since World War II employed the offset cab design for greater driver visibility.

177

the R series, a manually tilted, one piece, molded hood and fender unit provided a clean-cut design and ready access to the engine area for servicing. Power plants and gross vehicle weight specifications for the U-400 and U-600 series were, for the most part, similar to those offered with the R models. The U series tractors became a quick success in 1965, and the C series Macks were phased out the same year.

In the spring of 1965 an engineering task force was established at Allentown to develop a new West Coast series of light weight Mack conventional and cab-over-engine trucks. As the project neared completion additional personnel were added to form a nucleus of the operating staff that would move to California and start up the new Hayward plant. The two Mack prototype West Coast models were finished by November 1965, at which time 19 families went to California to help set up Mack Western operations.(7)

During 1966, the first year of production, the Hayward plant turned out over 300 of the new Mack FL-700 series. The FL models, while using the basic F series cab, were offered with a wide range of Mack and vendor supplied components. As with most other special West Coast Mack trucks before it, aluminum was used extensively as a weight saving device in various chassis parts.

In 1967 the RL series, similar in outer design to the conventionally styled R model trucks, was introduced by Mack Western. In addition to the weight saving chassis components, 16 optional engines of from 200 to 380 horsepower were offered in the RL models. Other Mack Western engineering developments were the RS and FS model series, having frames with steel side rails, which were also introduced in 1967.

Designed specifically for the rugged conditions found in the construction industry, the new DM series was named for its main use; Dumper and concrete Mixer service. The DM line was introduced early in 1966, replacing the larger B series, including the B-80 models. All DM models had an offset cab similar to that used on the U series, with the driver conveniences and safety features native to that cab. The unitized fiberglass hood and fender assembly was standard on the DM-400 and DM-600 models, complete with the tilting feature. The larger DM-800 models were equipped with steel butterfly hood and swing-up fenders to provide accessibility to the power plant, and this same arrangement was optional with the smaller DM-400 and 600's. The largest DM-800 models were available with engines of from 195 to 335 horsepower and had a prominently set back front axle for better weight distribution and maneuverability. Gross Vehicle Weights were: DM-400/600, 43,000 to 66,000 lbs.; DM-600SX, 66,000 to 76,000 lbs.; and DM-800, 66,000 to 100,000 lbs. By 1967 the DM line included, in addition to the regular 6 x 4 rear drive models, a 6 x 6 all-wheel-drive and an 8 x 6 model having the Mack tri-axle bogie, with drive to all three axles.

(7) Mack Trucks, Inc., **The Mack Bulldog**, Fifth Series, Vol. 1, No. 11, (March-April 1971) p.3.

The Mack FL series was the first result, in 1966, of a special task force being created to design and then build a line of light weight West Coast models at a newly acquired plant at Hayward, California.

New RL Mack models quickly followed the FL series into production at the Hayward Plant in 1967. The special West Coast Mack models used many aluminum alloy parts to save weight wherever practical.

A special line of heavy-duty construction trucks, called the DM line, was placed in production late in 1965. This view shows a DM600 model with the sheet metal hood assembly optional with the 400 and 600 series.

A large Mack DM800 model used to deliver building bricks in Atlanta, Georgia. Note the set back front axle for better weight distribution, which is a characteristic of the DM800 series.

Mack engineering established an important break-through in Diesel power plant design with the announcement in late 1966, after seven years of experimentation, of a relatively "constant horsepower" truck engine. Described simply, the new Maxidyne Mack Diesel engine developed its maximum horsepower over a longer range of revolutions per minute, from 1,200 to its top governed speed of 2,100 r.p.m., instead of at a shorter, but higher peak of over 2,000 r.p.m. in standard automotive Diesel engines.(8) Mack engineers accomplished this new engine performance by matching both the turbocharger's maximum air input and the fuel available from the injector at below 1,500 r.p.m. A special attachment to the governor section of the injection pump limits the fuel injected as r.p.m. increase, with the result that the turbocharger does not receive the additional exhaust thrust to force relatively more air into the cylinders at the higher engine speed. The result is a leveling of the horsepower curve with a great reduction in the need for a driver to shift gears to save the engine from lugging when ascending long grades. It was determined then that a transmission having five speeds, instead of ten or more, would surface with the Maxidyne in most over-the-road applications.

(8) **Commercial Car Journal**, Vol. 112, No. 4, (Dec. 1966) p.130.

The maximizing of the horsepower at the lower engine speeds had a number of other beneficial results, the chief being substantial fuel savings. The new ENDT 675, although having the same 672 cubic inch displacement as the previous ENDT 673 engine, was actually an entirely new design, built of much heavier parts to stand up under the longer range of sustained horsepower. The Maxidyne was rated at 237 horsepower at 1,700 r.p.m., while the ENDT 673 provided 225 horsepower at 2,100 r.p.m.

A uniquely designed five-speed transmission was also developed to match the horsepower characteristics of the Maxidyne engine. This new transmission was called the Maxitorque and was engineered with a triple countershaft, which enabled the overall length to be shortened by a third. Also, the new Maxitorque was lighter than comparable transmissions, which increased its appeal to weight conscious truckers.

In 1970 Mack introduced a 325 horsepower Maxidyne V-8 Diesel, and a new series of Maxitorque transmissions for both over-the-road and dumper-mixer service. A new U-795 tractor model was offered with the new V-8 Maxidyne engine and appropriate Maxitorque transmission. Also offered at this time, with the new ENDT 865 V-8 Diesel, was a simplified engine-compression brake system named the Mack Dynatard. The reliability of the Dynatard brake has resulted in 50% of the Mack V-8 engines being ordered with this option. The success of the original

The Mack DM series includes a number of special models, like this six-wheel drive concrete mixer unit, which are tailored to meet the needs of specific operating conditions.

After seven years of continuous experimentation, the outstanding Maxidyne engine, Model ENDT675, was introduced in 1966. The relatively "constant horsepower" feature of the Maxidyne ushered in a new concept in Diesel engine design.

six cylinder Maxidyne was marked on August 22, 1972, when the Allentown plant turned out its 50,000th chassis to be equipped with the Maxidyne engine.

The MB city delivery truck received a new Diesel engine in 1969, the Turbo Mack Scania ENDT 475 of 190 horsepower. A newly improved cab for the F series, providing better maintenance, safety, and driver comfort features, was introduced in 1971. This improved F series cab, called the Interstater, has the RCCC, Regular Common Carriers Conference, recommended instrument and control panels, which should eventually be standard equipment on most over-the-road tractors. An enlarged R series cab with the standardized RCCC panels and other improvements was introduced in 1972.

New fire apparatus and off-highway models

One of the most spectacular developments in modern fire fighting history was the acceptance by the New York Fire Department of the giant Mack Super Pumper System in 1965. A Mack engineering team had been working on this special project since 1963, when the N.Y.F.D. indicated the desire to have a mobile pumping station which could supply tremendous amounts of water at, or near, the scene of a major conflagration.

At the heart of the new fire fighting system was the huge Super Pumper, which consisted of a trailer mounted Napier-Deltic, 18 cylinder, 2 cycle, turbo-blown Diesel engine, rated at 2,400 brake horsepower, which in turn was directly connected to a DeLaval centrifugal pump.(9) The pump was a 6-stage unit which could deliver 8,800 g.p.m. at 350 p.s.i.g. in parallel, or 4,400 g.p.m. at 700 p.s.i.g., when in series operation. The trailered pumping unit was pulled by a Mack F-715ST model tractor, powered by a Mack END 864, V-8 Diesel.

The second part of the Super Pumper System was the Super Tender which was also a trailerized unit pulled by a Mack F series tractor. The Super Tender was designed to haul 2,000 feet of 4-1/2 inch hose in the trailer, and had a water cannon rated at 10,000 g.p.m. mounted behind the tractor's cab. To round out the

(9) **Fire Engineering**, Vol. 118, No. 10, (Oct. 1965) p.117.

181

A new concept of fire fighting was the Mack Super Pumper System, which is best described as a mobile pumping station. At the heart of the new system, delivered to New York City in 1965, is the 2,400 horsepower trailerized pumper shown in the upper picture. The lower view shows the Super Tender unit which carries 2,000 feet of hose, and on which is mounted a giant water cannon rated at 10,000 gallons per minute.

The CF line of cab-forward fire apparatus, with Mack built cabs, replaced the C series in 1967. This CF685F model, with radio controlled pump, was displayed at the Cleveland convention of the International Association of Fire Chiefs in 1972.

system, there were three Mack C model satellite tenders, each having bodies holding 2,000 feet of 4-1/2 inch hose, and a water cannon rated at 4,000 g.p.m.

The regular B and C lines of Mack fire apparatus were phased out with the introduction of the new R series in 1966, and CF series in 1967. Both the R and CF lines were basically heavy-duty pumpers, being offered with engines of between 237 and 375 horsepower, and pumping capacities of 750, 1,000, 1,250, and 1,500 g.p.m. The R series was an adaptation for fire service of the conventional Mack R line of commercial trucks, and replaced the B series fire apparatus. The new CF cab-forward line replaced the C series and used a newly designed cab adapted in part from the F model Mack. Many safety features were built into the CF cab, and power steering, for ease of handling in heavy city traffic, was standard equipment. The low position of the CF cab made this model especially suited for

A Mack Aerialscope purchased for the San Francisco International Airport in 1971. Outriggers and supporting jacks stablize the truck while the Aerialscope is in use.

(10) **Ibid**., Vol. 118, No. 12, (Dec. 1965) p.54.

(11) **Ibid**., Vol. 122, No. 3, (March 1969) p.76.

the back mounting of an aerial ladder, which then could extend over the top of the cab when in the lowered position, making for a highly compact design.

The results of Mack's developmental missionary work in the fire apparatus field during the 1950's had become manifest in the 1960's and early 1970's. In 1965 a Mack engineering team received an award from **Product Engineering** magazine for their work in developing the Mack Aerialscope.(10) Automatic transmissions, which Mack had introduced to fire service in 1956, were being offered as standard or optional equipment by nearly every other fire apparatus manufacturer by 1972. Diesel power, which was almost unheard of in fire apparatus prior to a Mack installation in 1959, grew very rapidly in popularity, and constituted 64% of the total fire engine sales during 1968.(11)

The good acceptance received by the Mack M series off-highway dumpers, first introduced in 1960, encouraged the company to offer more models in an expanded line. By 1970 the basic Mack off-highway line constituted about a dozen models in 5 ton increments covering a span of 15 to 75 ton capacities, with some special tractor-trailer combinations of higher capacity built to order.

New models added during the mid to late 1960's used the basic frame, Planidrive, and offset cab design common to the earlier M series, but with improved suspension and lowered body heights, in proportion to the higher tonnage ratings, for increased stability and easier loading.

A model M70SX being loaded at Port Newark, New Jersey for shipment to Gloucester, England early in 1967. This 70-ton capacity truck is fitted with a 44 cubic yard capacity body and weighs 50 tons empty.

After test runs of the new off-highway hauling units, a technique called PhotoStress Analysis was used to detect any unusual stresses which chassis parts had been subjected to. Customers were thereby protected from possible sudden failures of the huge welded alloy steel frames, and improved designs in chassis construction were more quickly determined.

A notable addition to the M series was introduced in 1965, the M70SX, 70 ton payload capacity six wheeler. The Mack six wheeler had what was described as a self-steering bogie axle, which allowed the axle centers to move together or apart on turns, thus eliminating chafing of the huge tires on the four rear wheels. Besides increased tire life, better traction was also claimed for the six wheel design, which used a Mack bogie having solid walking beam suspension with rubber insulators. A Cummins 700 horsepower Diesel engine was offered as standard equipment, with a Detroit Diesel of similar horsepower being optional. In 1970, the model M-75SX, of similar general design, but having a capacity of 75 tons, was introduced to constitute Mack's largest regular production off-highway model.

By 1969 the Mack off-highway line had six models of four wheel design, the latest of which was the M-35X introduced the same year. The M-35X used semi-elleptic vari-rate springs for both front and rear suspensions. However, the larger four wheel model M-50AX, introduced in 1968, used a combination of leaf springs and rubber blocks in the front end, and semi-elleptic constant frequency springs in the rear. The even larger M-65AX, introduced in 1967, used stacked rubber discs in steel cylinders for both its basic front and rear suspensions.

Brockway and Hayes trucks

Brockway Motor Trucks, continued as an autonomous division of Mack Trucks, Inc., introducing a major new model series in 1965, and increasing its sales through 1972.

The first models in the new 300 series were the 358 and 359, which were designed with three basic important features: short BBC dimension of 90 inches, engine accessibility, and continuity of design for parts interchangeability. An 8

A Brockway model 358TL tractor pulling a "double bottom" semi and full trailer combination on the New York State Thruway in 1968.

Brockway General Manager and Mack Vice President R. J. Matthews, on right, discusses new Huskidrive installation in a model 361 truck, with Editor-in-chief of *Fleet Owner* magazine, C.W. Boyce in 1968.

inch high substructure under the standard Brockway built cab gave the model 359 almost the same height as the cab-over-engine 400 model, and allowed the 359 to take a larger engine than the 358. Walk-in access to the engine and front end area was made possible by Brockway's swing away fender design. The mounting of the radiator shutter behind the radiator was considered the ideal solution to better temperature control, and actually resulted in a savings in fuel and even prolonged engine and shutter service life.

To round out the 300 series, two conventional models, the 360, with forward located front axle, and the 361, with setback front axle, were introduced at the 1967 A.T.A. convention. Except for conventional hood length and cab height, the new 360 series contained all the basic features of the Uni-Matched design of the 300 line.

In 1968 the new Huskidrive combination of two-speed rear axle, five speed transmission, and high-torque-rise Diesel engine was introduced. The rear axle shift was controlled by a dash mounted switch which allowed the driver to start in

The model 527 Huskiteer cab-forward model was introduced by Brockway in 1971, as a versatile heavy-duty truck for either city or highway operation where the advantages of shortened length are an important factor.

Power and then switch to Cruise position after shifting through only five gears. Finally, in 1971 a new low-profile tilt-cab model 527, also called the Huskiteer, was introduced for both city and over-the-road delivery work.

With its wide variety of power train options and its reputation for quality engineering and workmanship, the Brockway line has continued to increase in popularity. Distribution has been extended into some southern and mid-western states in recent years, with production and profitability reaching new highs.

During 1969 Mack Trucks, Inc., purchased a two-thirds interest in the Hayes Manufacturing Co., Ltd., a Canadian heavy-duty truck producer based in Vancouver, British Columbia. Founded in the 1920's, the Hayes operation had specialized to a certain extent in the production of huge off-highway trucks for the logging industry that is native to the British Columbia region. Over the years Hayes also produced fire trucks, buses, rail cars, and a variety of industrial equipment for a basically local trade. In 1971 the corporate name was changed to Hayes Trucks, Ltd.

Current Hayes production includes the off-highway HDX series, first introduced about 1950, and other H model conventional trucks used in both highway and off-highway service. Late in 1970, a new Clipper 100 cab-over-engine highway truck, similar in design to the West Coast F series Macks, was introduced. Since the connection with Mack, Hayes has embarked upon an aggressive expansion program which will eventually see Hayes trucks distributed in most parts of Canada and some foreign countries as well.

A Signal success

The chronic shortage of working capital which had plagued Mack and caused the board of directors to defer cash dividends and issue only stock dividends

The huge Hayes HDX1000 series, produced by Hayes Trucks, Ltd., has been the standard off-highway logging truck in Canada's western lumber regions for many years.

Hayes also makes special logging trailers which are used as a unit with the Hayes HDX 1000 series trucks.

since 1964, was the only basic problem still facing the company by 1967. The relative prosperity of the reorganized operation was in itself a major cause for the continuing tightness of ready funds. The more trucks Mack built the more money had to be tied up in spare parts and enlarged facilities for the service of these vehicles. Also, a greater number of trucks were now being financed through Mack Financial Corporation, which in turn could obtain funds at rates only slightly below those it could charge the Mack customers - a rather tight financial situation, and one which would obviously hamper the proper growth of the company until an adequate source of low cost ready funds could be obtained.

During the month of March 1967, White Consolidated Industries, Inc., a Cleveland based conglomerate, which was an outgrowth of the old White Sewing Machine Company, actively sought a merger with Mack.(12) However, with White Consolidated's earnings being similar to Mack's, although on a lower sales volume, and because of other factors standing in the way, the Mack board of directors turned down the bid. With the Mack interest in a beneficial merger being no secret in the financial community, a number of other companies were reported to be seeking ties with the truck producer by the spring of 1967.(13)

Finally, after a series of fruitless talks with various firms, a company representing the right situation was contacted, and a merger agreement quickly drawn up. Mack's merger partner turned out to be the Signal Oil and Gas Company, a Los Angeles based petroleum company which had combined sales of over $1 billion in 1966.(14) According to the merger agreement, which still had to be ratified by the stockholders of both firms, Mack would retain complete

(12) **Wall Street Journal**, March 6, 1967, p.26.

(13) **New York Times**, April 30, 1967, Sec. III, p.3.

(14) **Wall Street Journal**, May 5, 1967, p.28.

autonomy and no other truck producer would be taken into the combine. Mack officials were now satisfied that their search was successfully concluded and after stockholders voted their approval, on August 18, 1967, Mack Trucks, Inc., officially became a member of a growing industrial family.

Like Mack, the Signal organization was the result of close teamwork by a family which struggled against great odds to forge a new concept into a successful industrial enterprise. The Mack Brothers were pioneer builders of commercial motor vehicles, while the father and son team of Henry M. Mosher and Samuel B. Mosher started a petroleum company founded on a process to extract gasoline from a form of natural gas.

In January 1922, Samuel B. Mosher was a struggling young agriculturist trying to raise citrus fruits on 17 acres of land in the shadow of Southern California's oil rich Signal Hill. A sudden freeze had wiped out his citrus crop and in desperation he decided to risk whatever funds he could obtain on a process for extracting natural gasoline from the wet gas that was being wasted in the air by the oil drillers on nearby Signal Hill. After setting up a makeshift processing plant, which went on stream in May 1922, Sam's father, Henry M. Mosher, invested $10,000 in the struggling young enterprise. Encouraged by the progress being made, incorporation papers were soon filed by the Moshers, and the Signal Gasoline Company was formed with stock being sold publicly.[15] There was no sure road to success for the young enterprise, but a steadily rising demand for gasoline in a car-driving nation provided a strong market, and by the late 1920's the Signal Gasoline Company had become the Signal Oil and Gas Company, after the firm began drilling its own wells.

(15) Signal Oil and Gas Co., **The Blender**, Vol. 6, No. 2, (June 1, 1967) p.2.

Because of its unique position in the petroleum industry as a bulk producer of gas and oil mainly for wholesale to other oil companies, Signal has faced many vicissitudes since its founding. Retail marketing was entered in 1931, during the depths of the depression, when a contract to supply gasoline to a major oil company was not renewed, and Signal had to look elsewhere for its sale. Since the boom period of the 1950's, Signal has completely restructured its marketing, refining, and overseas exploration operations a number of times to keep ahead of conditions which might adversely affect its basic growth. In the face of external

In order to cover the 1968 Winter Olympics at Grenoble, France one New York television station sent several of their Mack F series tractors with trailerized equipment right to the base of the ski slopes.

This special Mack powered road train operates in Australia's Northern Territory, where dependability is a must for the transportation of cattle over the long distances of this sparsely settled area.

pressures which had caused these extensive realignments of the company's operations ever since the early 1930's, Signal has continued to show an overall growth pattern.

Perhaps as a hedge against the fluctuations in their own business field, Signal management decided to invest in other industries, and an initial investment in American President Lines in 1952 eventually led to a 48% stock holding in that steamship company. Acquisitions by Signal were made only after careful consideration of a company's management and potential. In 1963, Signal invested in the then dynamic aerospace industry with the purchase of the technically oriented Garrett Corporation, a West Coast based producer of

A 10-ton military truck being tested on the Allentown special test incline. Mack built several hundred of these tractors during 1968 and 1969.

gas-turbine engines and other aircraft related equipment, having sales of $226 million in 1963.(16) After the merger with Mack in 1968, and two other firms in diverse fields in 1967, a new holding company, The Signal Companies, Inc., was named. The larger expansion and realignment programs planned by Mack between 1965 and 1967, which had not been finished before the merger, were completed with the backing of the Signal organization.

A frame assembly plant to have 171,000 square feet of floor space was started in 1968, along the south side of plant 5C in Allentown. This would give Mack stricter control over its own frame manufacture, which it had discontinued in 1963.(17)

Work on the multi-million dollar Mack World Headquarters at 2100 Mack Boulevard in Allentown, started in 1967, was finally finished toward the end of 1969. Employees started to move into the structure early in February, with the official opening taking place on April 28, 1970.

Activity continued to strengthen the Mack International Operations Division, consisting of Mack Trucks Worldwide, Ltd., Mack Trucks Western Hemisphere Trading Corp., and the Export Division of Mack Trucks, Inc. Since 1967 the foreign operations had shown strong profitability and by early 1972 Mack products were being distributed in 67 foreign countries, with seven of these having local Mack assembly plants.

The autonomous operation by Mack Trucks, Inc., as one of the Signal Companies has proved to be years of sustained progress. Demand for heavy-duty trucks and Macks in particular increased again after a momentary dip in 1967 duced combined sales of Mack to $358 million.(18.)

Coming back fast after the 1967 dip, Mack sales rose to new records of $439 million in 1968, and $533 million in 1969, resulting in pre-tax profits of $36.1 and $52.7 million respectively.(19) For comparison with prior years net earnings, an estimated after-tax income of $19 and $28 millions can be obtained for the years 1968 and 1969 respectively by using the 48% standard corporate tax rate, before taking into account any unusual gains or losses. Therefore, the ratio of estimated net profit to actual sales would then be slightly over 4% in 1968, and slightly more than 5% in 1969. New Mack truck registrations during 1968 were 14,932, and 15,655 in 1969.(20) And although restricted consumer credit and a weakness in the economy put a squeeze on profits in 1970 and 1971, combined Mack sales again reached new highs in both years.

1972 turned out to be a record year in truck production with Mack sales going well over $700 million, on a combined production of over 27,000 units. Mack profits also hit a new record level with a pre-tax profit figure more than double that of 1971. Lower profit margins among the aerospace and petroleum branches of the Signal family highlighted Mack Trucks, Inc. as the major income contributor to the Signal Companies.

(16) **Forbes**, Vol. 95, No. 12. (June 15, 1965) p.48.

(17) Mack Trucks, Inc., **The Mack Bulldog**, Fourth Series, Vol. 3, No. 6. (Nov.-Dec. 1968) p.13.

(18) The Signal Companies, Inc., **Annual Report**, 1967.

(19) **Ibid**., 1969.

(20) **Commercial Car Journal**, Vol. 119, No. 2, (April 1970) p.192.

The Mack World Headquarters building near the main assembly plant at Allentown, Pennsylvania which was officially opened in the spring of 1970.

Mack tackles the energy crisis

(1) **Commercial Car Journal**, Vol. 124, No. 6, (Feb. 1973) p. 7.

What seemed to be the first signs of an impending shortage of diesel fuel appeared in certain parts of the country during a rather severe cold spell in January 1973. Some carriers in the East, Midwest, and South found themselves temporarily without fuel, or on a strict allocation by their regular suppliers.(1) However, most industry people seemed to pass over the situation as being only of a local or temporary nature. It took the Arab Oil Boycott of late 1973 to bring the truck industry face to face with a very serious problem, as well as shake American industry out of its complacency.

By December 1973 both gasoline and diesel fuel were in such short supply, following the ramifications of the recent Arab-Israeli War, that lines were appearing at filling stations in many parts of the country. The sharp rise in diesel fuel prices was particularly harmful to the small owner-operator truckers, who worked under fixed contracts. Faced with a severe drain on their finances with the pro-

Mack's advertising's patriotic theme, started in 1970, was reflected in the paint scheme on this FS700 series truck with roll-off container.

Frustrated truckers protesting the shortage of diesel fuel and its sharp price rise are confronted by riot-equipped state highway police. This action took place at a road block set up by the drivers on the Ohio Turnpike on December 6, 1973, near Elyria, Ohio.

spect of having to default on their equipment payments, the independent truckers soon massed in an unprecedented strike action. Interstate highways were blocked by hundreds of trucks at some key junctions across the country, and several deaths resulted from the anarchy early in 1974.(2) However, like Pearl Harbor 32 years earlier, public attention was being forced to focus on a national emergency.

(2) **Ibid.**, Vol. 127, No. 1, (March 1974) p. 118.

Unfortunately for the nation as a whole, and the truck industry in particular, there were no quick answers for the sudden escalation of foreign oil prices. Practical substitutes for gasoline and diesel fuel were out of the question in the short-run, and stringent conservation was advocated from the White House on down as the best way to ease the shortage. Mack product development has had a long history of concern for maximizing horsepower while minimizing fuel consumption. The energy crunch of the mid-1970's had emphasized the vital need for the efficiency of design found in basic Mack components.

To substantiate the fuel economy of the new Maxidyne 300 series with 5-speed Maxitorque transmission, introduced in 1973, an engine was tested along with two competitive power plants of similar horsepower by an independent test laboratory. Three Mack F model tractors, each with a different make engine, operated for a total of 10,000 miles; with 3,300 miles at a speed limited to 65 mph, 3,300 miles at a top speed of 55 mph, and 3,300 miles at a maximum of 50 mph. Test results indicated a 12.8% to 20.5% savings in fuel for the new Maxidyne over the two competitive engines at speeds in the 50 to 55 mph range. Projections of the fuel savings over a 100,000 mile span totaled between $1,004 and $1,440.(3)

(3) Mack Trucks, Inc., **The Mack Bulldog**, Fifth Series, Vol. 4, No. 2, (Mar.-Apr. 1974) pp. 6 & 7.

In order to understand the advantage of the new Maxidyne 300 series engines, the functions of its basic features should be outlined. As with the basic Maxidyne engine, the new series retained the highly successful "constant horsepower" concept. However, with a turbocharger packing a greater amount of air into each charge in the power stroke than in naturally aspirated engines, the temperature of the compressed air rises in proportion to the ratio of its compression, and thereby increasingly resists further compression as it heats up. The addition of the air-to-air aftercooler, between the turbocharger and intake manifold reduces the temperature of the initially compressed air and the resultant back pressure, thus allowing an even greater air charge to be delivered to the engine by the turbocharger.

192

The Maxidyne 300 series engine, rated at 285 hp., entered full production on June 1, 1973. Also designated Model ENDT676, it is distinguished by the large intercooler located on top of the engine head.

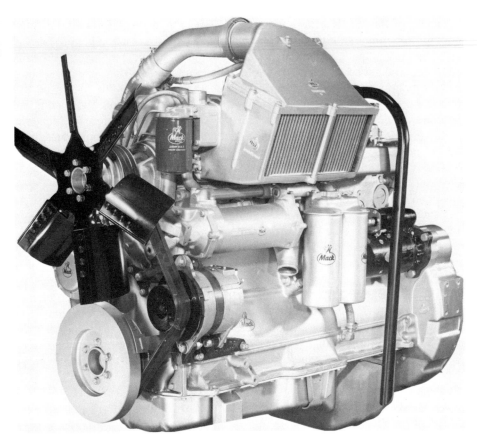

The Maxidyne 300 series with turbocharger and aftercooler, also called an "intercooler," is rated at 285 horsepower and shares the same 6-cylinder block with the 237 horsepower Maxidyne engine. The air-to-air aftercooler unit was developed and manufactured by AiResearch Manufacturing Company of Los Angeles, a subsidiary of the Garrett Corporation. Full production of a 300 series Maxidyne, having the model designation ENDT676, started on June 1, 1973.

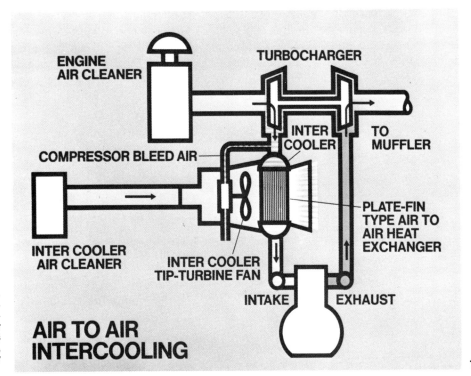

Schematic diagram of Mack's air-to-air intercooling system shows its basic simplicity. Ambient air is drawn into air cleaner at the extreme left, and pushed through the intercooler at the center. Air for the combustion system is drawn into a separate air cleaner at the top left, and pushed down through the intercooler by the turbocharger on the top right.

Easing of the fuel shortage by mid-1974 led to a renewed interest in higher horsepower engines for the more efficient moving of heavy loads in both on- and off-highway applications. A new fuel-efficient high horsepower diesel, called the 300-Plus, was added to the Mack engine line late in 1975. While using the same basic block as the 6-cylinder Maxidyne 300 engine, the 300-Plus achieved 315 brake horsepower at 1,900 r.p.m. with a modification of the "constant horsepower" characteristic of the standard Maxidyne. Although having comparatively conventional torque and power curves, a 7.8% fuel savings was achieved in comparison to competitive fuel-economical engines. The Mack 300-Plus engine was designated as Model ETAZ673A, and considered applicable to those operators needing the additional horsepower as well as preferring to use a 10-speed transmission.(4)

Several other high-horsepower engine concepts have been under active study by Mack engineers on a long-term basis. An experimental ENDT-1000 series V-8 diesel, with a power output in the 360 to 500 horsepower range, was reported to be undergoing field testing during 1973. Mack engineers were also taking a close look at the gas-turbine engine, which promised a very favorable horsepower-to-weight ratio. During 1973 Mack Trucks, Inc., and the Garrett Corporation joined forces with the German firm of Klockner-Humboldt-Deutz AG, to form Industrial Turbines International and develop a turbine engine in the 450 to 650 horsepower range. Initially, the Swedish firm of AB Volvo also joined, but dropped out later. Early in 1977 I.T.I. announced the successful completion of tests on the prototype GT601 engine, which was built at Garrett's AiResearch facilities in Phoenix, Arizona.(5)

Ever mindful of the need to help the nation's trucking industry fight the onslaught of steadily rising operating costs, Mack has helped introduce various energy saving devices. After extensive testing, a new type of dual speed governor, called the Maxi-Miser, was introduced early in 1976. Its basic concept is to limit engine speed of the Maxidyne diesel to 1,800 r.p.m. when the Maxitorque transmission is shifted into fifth gear, as well as in 4th, 5th, 6th, and 7th gears in the 7-speed version of the transmission. This combination coincides with the area of optimum power for the fuel consumed at a road speed of between 55 and 60 mph. Also, lower parasitic losses are evidenced at 1,800 r.p.m. than at 2,100 r.p.m. Of course, rear axle gear ratios and tire sizes must be taken into account when determining the Maxi-Miser's precise application.

Another device which has been found useful in reducing some parasitic power loss is the variable-speed fan. This engine fan has its drive controlled by a thermal unit which varies the fan speed according to the engine's basic operating temperature. A constant-drive steel flex-blade fan can draw as much as nine

(4) **Ibid.**, Vol. 5, No. 4, (4th Quar. 1975) pp. 10 & 11.

(5) **Ibid.**, Vol. 7, No. 2, (2nd Quar. 1977) p. 28.

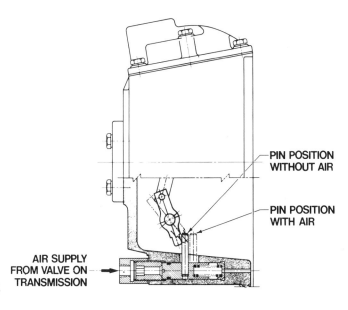

PIN POSITION
WITHOUT AIR

PIN POSITION
WITH AIR

AIR SUPPLY
FROM VALVE ON
TRANSMISSION

The Maxi-Miser dual speed governor was introduced early in 1976. It is one of several fuel saving devices introduced by Mack to fight the energy crisis of the 1970's.

A Mack 300 series Maxidyne, with energy efficient variable-speed fan, travels down the engine grooming line at Allentown. The variable-speed fan was made a standard feature on all Mack-engined highway trucks and optional on construction models in 1976.

(6) **Ibid.**, Vol. 6, No.2, (2nd Quar. 1976) p. 5.

horsepower from a 6-cylinder diesel, and therefore it was decided to make the variable-speed fan available on all Mack engines in 1976.(6)

Other areas of increased efficiency on Mack highway vehicles include new extended service intervals and expanded engine and transmission warranty periods. At the end of 1976 Mack announced that all highway trucks powered by its 6-cylinder diesels could now be operated for 25,000 miles between oil changes. Also, that chassis lube jobs for Mack components in these vehicles were now recommended at 50,000 miles. Then on November 1, 1977, an expanded warranty program went into effect on all Mack highway vehicles, that covered certain key engine and transmission parts up to 36 months, or 300,000 miles, whichever came first.

By early 1973 Mack was using "fiber optics" to illuminate, from a single light source, all the instruments and switches on its vehicle dashboards. Mack engineers are also working on various "space age" devices to help increase truck operating efficiency. However, the complexity of any new components, along with the possible increased servicing costs, must be carefully weighed against any advantage obtained in their ultimate usage.

New trends in truck design

The importance of fuel-efficient engine and vehicle construction is just one of many areas that Mack engineers must concentrate on during their design studies. Great pressure has been put on the automotive industry all during the 1970's to steadily reduce the level of toxic emissions from gasoline and diesel engines. This is a laudatory goal, as it is meant to improve the quality of the atmosphere people breath, especially in places like Southern California which has had a very serious smog condition in recent years. However, much of the anti-pollution changes made to gasoline engines have lowered their fuel milage to a great extent, although diesels have fared somewhat better in this regard due to the inherent efficiency of their combustion systems.

Noise suppression has also become a major cause for Federal, state, and local regulatory agencies during the 1970's. Federal noise regulations issued by the Environmental Protection Agency in mid-1976 were thought to mean an increase in new truck prices of up to three percent to cover the manufacturers' costs involved with compliance.(7) Mack must work with equipment suppliers to achieve lower exterior noise standards, as certain components, such as tires, must be redesigned to lower their noise levels.

A third Federal edict which had almost disastrous effects on the truck building industry was the Department of Transportation's brake standard MVSS 121, which mandated highly sophisticated automatic anti-skid brake installations on all new heavy-duty highway trucks by March 1, 1975. The computerized anti-skid systems helped increase the need for heavier front axles and brakes, as well as a redesign of some suspension and steering setups, all in addition to the system's own exotic valves, piping, and sensing devices. These new components would easily add $1,000 to $2,000 to the sales price of heavy-duty trucks, which already had seen many price increases due to the inflationary spiral that followed in the wake of the energy crisis of 1973 and 1974.

The surge in truck building for several months prior to the MVSS 121 deadline left most truck manufacturers with large stocks of heavy-duty units to work off during the summer and fall of 1975.(8) Many truck plants, therefore, shut down or curtailed operations for extended periods, and some independent producers showed severe losses for 1975. Another one of the unfortunate results of the Federal brake standard, and other mandated changes, is that compliance is greatly inflating the cost of highway trucks and trailers without a concomitant increase in the productivity of that equipment.

Designing new trucks and their related components to properly fit the exacting requirements of many specialized trucking firms is an extremely challenging job for the engineers, especially in light of all the governmental regulations that stifle the use of less complicated concepts in vehicle construction. However, Mack has met the continuing need for divergent types of efficient heavy-duty trucks with the introduction of a wide variety of new models in the 1970's.

Early in 1973 the Mack RM series for road maintenance and heavy snow plow work was introduced. The RM features full-time all-wheel drive and is built in both 4 x 4 and 6 x 6 configurations. A new heavy-duty transfer case proportions torque between front and rear wheels according to basic axle load, and has a driver-controlled differential lock to help alleviate excessive wheel-spin. Extended frame and setback front axle facilitate the attachment and use of many types of snow removal equipment. The center-mounted cab with slanted butterfly steel hood assembly, and short fenders, provides good left- and right-hand shoulder visibility.

(7) **Commercial Car Journal**, Vol. 131, No. 4, (June 1976) p. 58.

(8) **Ibid.**, Vol. 129, No. 2, (April 1975) p. 7.

Introduced early in 1973, the Model RM was designed as an all-wheel drive unit for heavy snow plow and road maintenance work. The steel butterfly hood, center-mounted R-series cab, and extended front frame are basic design features.

The RD series features center-mounted cab and heavy-duty components best suited for the severe service requirements of the construction industry. This RD685SX has the optional steel butterfly hood and fender assembly.

The Model RD is another heavy service Mack with center-mounted cab that has proved popular for both road maintenance and construction work. Extra frame reinforcements, heavy-duty components, and unitized fiberglass hood and fender assembly are standard, with the steel butterfly hood and fenders optional. First introduced in 1970 as a companion to the DM series, the RD has found extensive use in dump truck service and as a tractor to haul heavy-duty trailers.

Legal restrictions on axle loadings in various sections of the United States and Canada have been a major challenge to the construction industry in the 1970's. In order to help promote the use of high-capacity mixer units, the Model DMM all-wheel-drive chassis was developed during 1972. Characteristics of the DMM are front axle positioned under the back of the engine, a modified DM cab, but with basic DM frame construction, and various axle and drive configurations. The

The Mack DMM-EX was specifically developed for the Canadian construction industry during 1972, and has proven the economy of the high capacity hauling unit in urban contracting work. Single front axle DMM units also gained market acceptance in the U.S. by the mid-1970's.

The Mack-Pack, introduced in 1974, presented a new concept in off-highway material haulage. Designed for use with front-end loaders, the Mack-Pack has a 40-ton capacity and is powered by a rear-mounted 475 horsepower engine.

DMM-EX units with tandem front axles have proved quite popular in the Canadian construction industry, where they have been employed in both dumper and mixer service since 1972.

A highly specialized vehicle for the construction industry, the Model HMM Mack was designed specifically as a front-discharge mixer chassis. Introduced late in 1973, the HMM is characterized by a half-cab which provides excellent visibility, a triple-axle tandem rear suspension, with drive to the two rear-most axles as well as to the single front axle. The one-man cab can be tilted hydraulically to the left 45 degrees for access to the engine. Drivers have a comparatively easy job of maneuvering the unit to the exact location, without the need of an extra ground spotter, and can also control the complete pour from the cab.

In the off-highway field a new type of articulated bottom-dump hauler, called the Mack-Pack, was presented to the heavy construction and mining industries late in May 1974. The Mack-Pack was designed for use with front-end loaders and has a 40-ton capacity. A huge rear-mounted 475 horsepower, 12-cylinder, Detroit Diesel engine powers all four wheels through Mack Planidrive front and rear drive axles.

The push for higher horsepower in highway trucks, despite the increase in fuel costs, is leading to a new generation of commercial vehicles. Much larger radiators are a necessity with the new super powerplants, but all the recent restrictive motor vehicle legislation must also be taken into consideration by the engineers when working out compatible designs. Since the early postwar years Western truck operators have fostered the development of higher horsepower vehicles, due mainly to the mountainous terrain and long runs found in their service areas. Because of this tradition, it followed that the first of Mack's new generation of cab-over-engine and conventional models would be introduced for the Western market and built at the Hayward Plant.

First of the new Mack highway trucks was the cab-over-engine Cruise-Liner, which was previewed at Dallas for the trucking industry in November 1974. Also designated as the W series, the Cruise-Liner drew many favorable comments from the editors at the preview for its superior features. The many creative concepts reflected in the Cruise-Liner can be described best by going over the high points **198** of the chassis and cab construction separately.

The backbone of the WL series is made up of heat-treated aluminum alloy side rails, while the WS models have frame rails made of heat-treated manganese steel. Frames on both the WL and WS series have a special drop-front section to accommodate the larger radiators required for 400 to 500 horsepower engines. Power ratings of the standard Maxidyne and optional Cummins, Detroit Diesel, and Caterpillar engines, range from 237 to 440 horsepower. A unique axle-mounted steering gear provides better wheel cutting angles and lessens the transmittal of road shocks to the steering wheel. Taper leaf front spring suspension provides a much lighter construction and, along with shock absorbers, a smoother ride.

Functional styling which combines the factors of safety, light-weight, efficient controls, and driver comforts, are the essence of the Cruise-Liner's cab. Aluminum body panels are neatly riveted over box shaped extrusions to form a sturdy, but light weight cab, which tilts to a full 90 degrees for engine servicing. Outstanding visibility is provided by a windshield of 2,648 square inches of tinted safety glass. Special pantograph-type wiper arms clear a larger portion of the windshield than regular single-arm wipers. In addition to the regular right-hand rear view mirror, a special convex mirror, mounted over the right-hand door, provides a good view of the road area adjacent to the cab.

A proper interior environment and efficient controls have been provided in the Cruise-Liner cab to contribute to the driver's well-being and productivity. Noise and vibration normally transmitted through cab walls are greatly reduced through the use of insulating foam sandwiched between the cab's double wall construction. In order to obtain a better seal of the cab, a separate shifting lever tower is attached to the cab floor, with a ball-joint linkage to the chassis gear shifting mechanism. Fully padded interiors in pleasing brown and beige vinyls add to the cab's sound proofing.

Controls for operating the Cruise-Liner include an adjustable steering wheel and column, which allows the driver to adjust both the height and angle of the steering wheel. Full console RCCC approved instrument grouping has hinged panels and removable clusters for quick servicing. An all-season climate control unit provides a huge volume of air for the heater/defroster system, and openings under the entire width of the windshield and in front corner posts clear fogged windshield and door glass in record time. Optional equipment includes "Combo"

An all new Western cab-over-engine series, named the Cruise-Liner, was introduced to the trucking industry in the fall of 1974. Many new features are included in Mack's light-weight Model RL/RS highway hauling units, which are designed to meet the challenges of the 1980's.

heater-air conditioning units, and both AM and AM/FM radios and stereo tape decks.

Full production of the Cruise-Liner started at the Hayward Plant early in 1975, by which time the Western FL/FS series had been phased out. However, the regular F series Macks, including the Interstater, were continued in production at Allentown, although it was predicted that should demand warrant it the Cruise-Liner would be built at both plants.(9)

Announcement of the new conventionally styled Super-Liner, RW series, to replace the Mack RL/RS 700 models, was made at another special presentation in October 1977. The Super-Liner employs the same basic drop-front section frame used in the Cruise-Liner chassis, in order to accept larger radiators and engines of up to 500 horsepower. The Super-Liner also has the taper leaf front spring suspension and axle-mounted steering gear features of the WL/WS series.

An impressively styled front end has been achieved in a new one-piece fiberglass hood and fender assembly. The assembly tilts forward to a full 90 degrees for engine servicing, and has a bright-finish aluminum shell and grill work to highlight its massive appearance. A look-alike grill of fin and tube construction is used as a condenser for the optional air conditioning system. And a Donaldson air cleaner, available in two different sizes, is mounted under the hood, being supplied by a special intake duct mounted behind the front of the grill.

The basic R series steel cab, with spot-welded construction, was adopted for use on the Super-Liner. Cab modifications included a rust inhibiting primer specially bonded to the metal and polyurethane foam insulation inside the double-wall construction. The RCCC approved instrument panel and a 43,000 BTU heater/defroster unit are standard equipment. Other standard cab features include a two-way roof vent for intake or exhaust, and the adjustable steering wheel and column. Several deluxe interior trim packages have been made available.

A wide variety of standard and optional power train components was approved for the Super-Liner. While the Mack ET673 6-cylinder turbocharged diesel with 260

(9) **Ibid.**, Vol. 128, No. 5, (Jan. 1975) p. 96.

The conventionally styled Western series, called the Super-Liner, was announced in October 1977. Featuring an impressive wide-front radiator grille, this Super-Liner, Model RWL-766LST, has a sleeper box and chromed accessory package.

Driver's eye view of a basic Mack R-series cab shows the efficient cockpit-style instrument console. Gauges and controls are grouped according to RCCC-SAE recommendations, with space available to accommodate most optional instruments including the recording-type tachagraph.

hp. is standard, other Mack and vendor supplied engines available range from 237 to 450 hp. Transmissions approved besides Mack include those built by Fuller, Spicer, and Allison. Rear axles include a full line of Rockwell units, each available with various types of Hendrickson, Neway, and Reyco suspensions. A "severe service package" for on/off-highway service, to include special chassis protection fittings and various extra heavy-duty components, was expected.(10)

Regular R-700 models were continued in production at Allentown, mainly for the East Coast market. Also, Hayward continued to build the RL/RS 400 and 600 models for customers who did not need the heavier-duty RW units.

(10) Mack Trucks, Inc., **The Mack Bulldog**, Fifth Series, Vol. 7, No. 4, (4th Quar. 1977) p. 21.

New facilities and new management

The five year plan developed by Mack management early in 1972 was the start of a huge capital expenditure program to provide both product and facilities to keep Mack ahead of market requirements. Management also terminated certain subsidiary operations in an apparent move to concentrate all efforts on the Mack-built product line. The retirement of Zenon Hansen resulted in several changes in top management, and basic changes in the structure of the parent Signal Companies have proved very beneficial.

The year 1975 was a banner one for the expansion of Mack facilities in the Allentown area, with three important structures completed that year. Opened in the spring of 1975 was the smallest, the Product Review Center, located near World Headquarters. Basic function of the building, which has a conference room with large picture window facing the inspection bay, is to provide an efficient place to review the pilot units in fleet orders.

The official opening of the Engineering Development and Test Center, located on a 62-acre tract in the Queen City Industrial Park about one mile from the World Headquarters, took place on August 20, 1975. The Center, completed at a cost of $10 million, is a far cry from the old Test Shed concept and also from the former Product Development Center, that was set up in a leased building in 1966.

The Engineering Development and Test Center carries on various functions in separate wings connected to a central core, which has vital support facilities for the other operations.(11) The core area has machine and sheet metal fabrication shops, tool crib, receiving and storage areas, as well as a five-bay shop for constructing prototype vehicles. The wing to the right of the main entrance contains the Styling & Drafting Section where new concepts in cab design flow from the **201**

(11) **Ibid.**, Vol. 5, No. 3, (3rd Quar. 1975) p. 5.

A key factor in Mack's facilities expansion program initiated in 1972, was the concept of the ultra-modern Engineering Development and Test Center. Located at Allentown, the Center handles all advanced engineering as well as the building and testing of prototype vehicles.

drawing boards to the mock-up stage. Directly behind the central core is the Chassis Modification Wing where changes are made to test vehicles and general maintenance is performed on them.

The area to the left of the entrance contains the Vehicle and Component Test Wing, and consists of huge rooms where specific tests are conducted under laboratory conditions. A main test chamber contains a controlled environment capability, wherein a chassis can be subjected to head winds up to 60 mph. and extremes of hot or cold, while running at a road speed of up to 80 mph. on a chassis dynamometer. Another huge chamber contains the "quiet room" where special acoustic walls produce no echoes, so that accurate levels and locations of nearly all engine produced truck noises can be determined. A road simulator can produce almost any road conditions for general chassis stress evaluations, and a special bump machine tests the durability of cabs along with their mountings.

An oval track encircles the Engineering Development and Test Center on which vehicles can be tested in all areas of operation, including grades of up to 20%. A section of the outdoor area contains a special skid pad over 1,000 feet long, made up of three basic road surfaces, and on which vehicle braking systems can be evaluated. The Center has many other testing capabilities and is charged with the basic job of maintaining Mack's long tradition of leadership in product design.

Technicians at the Test Center watch carefully as a Mack F-series tractor is subjected to a 60 mph headwind while running on the chassis dynamometer. This particular test chamber has a controlled environment capability, and vehicles can be run at speeds of up to 80 mph on the dynamometer.

Another key facility in Mack's expansion to meet the needs of the 1980's is the huge Macungie Plant, which was dedicated on December 8, 1975. With over 23 acres under roof, the Macungie Division was selected to produce all fire apparatus, c.o.e. models, and off-highway units.

(12) **Ibid.**, Vol. 5, No. 4, (4th Quar. 1975) p. 5.

Another keystone in the expansion program is the huge plant built in Lower Macungie Township, about nine miles from the established Mack facilities in Allentown. Ground breaking for the $25 million Macungie Plant occurred on May 31, 1974, with actual construction taking less than a year to complete. After a successful three-month phase-in period, Macungie was dedicated on December 8, 1975, with Mack officials describing all the ramifications of the new facilities at a press conference.(12)

The Macungie Plant was carefully planned by Mack engineers to provide flexible facilities for the efficient production of custom-built vehicles. Over 23 acres under roof can be effectively allocated among warehousing, component grooming, sub-assembly work, painting, and final chassis assembly functions. Some engineering and the final testing of production units are also carried on at the plant. Concentrating on the lower production models, Macungie went on full-stream with the transfer of all of Allentown's c.o.e. models, as well as its fire apparatus and off-highway units.

(13) The Signal Companies, **1977 Annual Report**, p. 33.

Several other important facilities were opened during the 1973 to 1977 period as part of the estimated $137 million expansion program.(13) Additions to the basic Allentown operations started during 1973 were the expansion of the CKD Building at Plant 5C, where Mack vehicles in knocked-down form are boxed for export; and the new chassis Dynamometer Building located just west of the 5C complex. During 1977 a $5.6 million painting facility, combining the most efficient paint application, emissions control, and energy conserving systems became fully operational at Plant 5C.

Important additions to the vital Hagerstown engine and gear train plant were made in 1973 and 1974. Chief among these additions was the Engineering Test and Development Center, which was needed not just to develop new Mack drive components, but to make sure they pass the rigid governmental emissions certification tests. The ground breaking for this $4.5 million facility took place during the summer of 1972. Early in 1974 a huge automated storage and retrieval system serving the Hagerstown Plant became fully operational. The new warehousing facility employs a one-man operated computer and has conveyors that stack palletized materials in racks 62 feet high, handling as many as 150 ''ins'' and ''outs'' in one hour.(14)

(14) Mack Trucks, Inc., **The Mack Bulldog**, Fifth Series, Vol. 4, No. 1, (Jan.-Feb. 1974) p. 2.

The Mack Western operation at Hayward, California, opened a modern office complex on the northeast portion of it 43 acre property. Ground breaking took **203** place in the spring of 1974 for the new headquarters building completed in the fall of 1975.

Early in 1975 Mack's first Engine Rebuild Center went into production at New Cumberland, Pennsylvania, just south of Harrisburg. This was the start of an engine rebuilding business tied in with the overall service operation, and having the basic objective of reducing vehicle down-time and "...to insure traditional Mack quality and durability."(15)

Four regional parts centers were opened up to 1976, and several modern sales and service facilities were also occupied by both the branch and dealer organizations. Approximately 500 service/parts dealers were available to help Mack customers all across the country, with the central parts warehouse at Bridgewater, New Jersey, extending its order entry and processing capability to 24 hours per day on weekdays to speed deliveries.(16)

North of the border, Mack Trucks Canada, Ltd., sustained a tremendous growth during the 1973 to 1977 period in production facilities, sales and service outlets, and in both models offered and total units produced. A $4 million expansion of the Oakville Plant, near Toronto, from 65,000 to 272,000 square feet, completed in 1973, was followed in 1975 with a special addition for off-highway trucks. The first off-highway units approved for production were the M35AX, M50AX, and M65AX. Also, the first two prototypes of the Canadian Logger, Model CL350ST, were built at Macungie in 1976 and put into production at Oakville the same year.

The 10,000th Canadian-built Mack rolled off the Production line on March 8, 1974, followed on February 14, 1977, by the 25,000th. The Oakville Plant has been on-stream since November 1966, and local content has risen greatly in Canadian-Mack units, especially since a weakness in the Canadian dollar had a severe impact on the cost of imported parts during 1976 and 1977.(17) However, a reciprocal trade agreement between the United States and Canada has fostered a flexibility in facilities use that has seen many Mack units go to customers on opposite sides of the border from where they were produced.

(15) **Ibid.**, Vol. 5, No. 3, (3rd Quar. 1975) p. 9.

(16) **Ibid.**, Vol. 8, No. 1, (1st Quar. 1978) p. 3.

(17) Mack Trucks Canada, Ltd., **The Mack Bulldog** (Canada), Vol. 77, No. 2, (2nd Half 1977) p. 4.

In 1976 the Canadian Logger, Model CL350ST, joined the expanding line of off-highway units being turned out at Mack Canada's plant at Oakville, Ontario. All-time Canadian production of all types of Mack trucks reached a 25,000 unit total on February 14, 1977.

(18) **Bus & Truck Transport** (Canada), Vol. 50, No. 3, (March 1974) p. 39.

Also on the Canadian front, Mack Trucks, Inc., quietly sold its two-thirds interest in Hayes Trucks, Ltd., early in 1974. The purchaser was Gearmatic Company, Ltd., a subsidiary of Pacific Car and Foundry (Paccar) of Bellevue, Washington, also corporate parent of Kenworth and Peterbilt trucks.(18) However, during the fall of 1975 the Hayes operation was completely closed down, unfortunately ending the firm's over half-century career in the production of high-quality transportation equipment. The specific reason for closing the Hayes operation has not been publicized, but no doubt the economic setback starting in 1975 played an important part, as it had a severe impact on most heavy-duty truck builders on both sides of the border. During 1975 the independent Diamond Reo operation in Lansing, Michigan, was liquidated, and Mack's Brockway subsidiary in Cortland, New York, followed in 1977.

The liquidation of Brockway Motor Trucks took place after an aborted sale of the division in May 1977. According to a feature story in the June 1977 **Commercial Car Journal**, Brockway's problems started about 1973 with a shortage of engines, and escalated drastically when the MVSS 121 brake standard played hob with the production line. Apparently the Brockway operation lost substantial sums of money for two consecutive years, and by the time labor contract talks started in the summer of 1976 Mack management had discussed its sale with several interested parties.

With labor talks apparently stalled during the fall, a wild cat strike erupted early in 1977 which utterly complicated an orderly sale or shutdown of the Brockway operation. The strike was finally terminated on April 29th, only after a New York City attorney had a purchase agreement almost concluded with Mack management. However, on May 2nd a Mack spokesman announced that the sale had not taken place and that therefore Brockway would be liquidated. A service parts warehousing operation was quickly set up in Pennsylvania, and another custom truck builder came to the end of the road.

Growth of Mack International, especially during the years 1974 and 1975, was almost phenomenal. Helping to fuel this growth was the industrial expansion of such oil producing countries as Iran and Venezuela, where local assembly operations are fed by Allentown's greatly expanded CKD operation. During the 1970's other assembly operations have been active in such widely located places as Australia, Belgium, France, Ghana, Greece, Ireland, Israel, South Africa, and Trinidad. Mack achieved record overseas deliveries of about 12,000 units during 1975. While foreign sales of American-built heavy-duty diesel trucks have slumped since 1976, Mack has maintained a better than 60% share of this market. Mack trucks are sold in at least 55 countries, and management is actively seeking local partners for new assembly operations in developing nations.(19)

(19) Mack Trucks, Inc., **The Mack Bulldog**, Fifth Series, Vol. 7, No. 4, (4th Quar. 1977) pp. 16 & 17.

This Model 758TL Brockway, with Mack R-series cab, was one of five new 700 series models introduced late in 1973. During the spring of 1977 Brockway Motor Trucks was liquidated after the Mack subsidiary was operated at a loss for several years.

Managerial changes during the 1973 to 1977 period, due to retirements and realignments of operating divisions, were rather extensive. After 9-1/2 years as chief executive officer of Mack Trucks, Inc., Zenon C. R. Hansen retired on July 31, 1974. In reviewing the successful growth of the Mack organization since 1965, Mr. Hansen cited the following key points: damn hard work, improved quality control, reduced dependence on vendors, better production scheduling, and accurate forecasting. A sixth factor, perhaps the most important, involved the human element: "Mack's great success is directly proportional to the efforts of its Management Team."(20)

Prior to Mr. Hansen's retirement, Henry J. Nave was made president of Mack Trucks, Inc. Mr. Nave received the Mack post on January 21, 1972, after a long career in the sales and service areas of the automotive industry. Starting with his first job in sales for the Firestone Tire and Rubber Company in 1936, Mr. Nave switched to the truck industry in 1950 when he joined the White Motor Company as service sales manager. A successful career with that organization led to his being elected president and chief operating officer in 1970 of the White Motor Corporation. Following Mr. Hansen's retirement in the summer of 1974, Mr. Nave was elected chief executive officer of Mack Trucks, Inc., and also chairman of the board of directors. Mr. Nave had been elected to the board of the parent Signal Companies in May 1974.

During the August 1974 Mack board meeting, Roger W. Mullin, Jr. was elected vice chairman of the board and empowered to act as chief executive officer should the need arise. A lawyer by profession, Mr. Mullin joined the Mack organization in 1961 as executive assistant to the president, but was soon made the vice president, general counsel, and secretary. In September 1967 he was elected executive vice president and soon after also elected to the Mack board of directors.

On January 1, 1976 Alfred W. Pelletier became president and chief operating officer of Mack Trucks, Inc., and in March he was also elected to the post of chief executive officer. Mr. Pelletier started a life-long career in the transportation field in 1939 after graduation from Danforth Technical School in Canada. A job as mechanic with the Toronto Transportation Commission was interrupted by five years naval duty during World War II, and after his return he was later promoted to shop foreman. In 1952 Mr. Pelletier joined the Toronto Branch of Mack Trucks Canada, Ltd. as shop foreman, and two years later was named service manager. His managerial talents recognized, Mr. Pelletier rose steadily through the ranks,

(20) **Ibid.**, Special Edition (August 1972) p. 9.

In August 1976, Roger W. Mullin, Jr. was elected to the office of Chairman of the Board of Mack Trucks, Inc. A lawyer by profession, Mr. Mullin joined Mack in 1961 and was soon handling the firm's legal matters as general counsel.

A thorough knowledge of heavy transportation equipment is just one facet of the background of Mack's President, Alfred W. Pelletier. Mr. Pelletier rose through the ranks of Mack Canada after his employment at its Toronto Branch in 1952, becoming President of the Canadian operation in 1974, and then President of Mack Trucks, Inc., early in 1976.

(21) **Ibid.**, Vol. 6, No. 1, (1st Quar. 1976) p. 2.

(22) The Signal Companies, **1973 Annual Report**, p. 13.

being elected president of the Canadian Mack organization in February 1974.(21)

Announcement was made after the August 1976 board meeting that Roger W. Mullin, Jr. had succeeded Henry J. Nave as chairman of Mack's board of directors. Mr. Nave resigned as chairman and accepted a special advisory post to the president. Mr. Mullin's duties included overall responsibility for Mack's internal administration as well as formulating long term policy planning.

Profound changes in the make up of the Signal Companies took place during 1974 and 1975. In January 1974 the Signal Oil and Gas Company subsidiary was sold to the American subsidiary of Britain's Burmah Oil Limited, for a net consideration of $420 million.(22) Included in the deal were valuable drilling rights in the North Sea, which Signal management felt required capital commitments beyond the prudent scope of the organization as it was then constituted. Debt was thereby reduced by part of the proceeds of the sale, and the ground work prepared for future expansion of the Signal Companies.

In May 1975 Signal acquired a 50.5% interest in Universal Oil Products, a high technology company in petroleum refinery processes, design and construction, as well as several related fields. The upswing in business activity, especially in the investment in capital goods, had boosted the Signal Companies combined sales and earnings to record levels in 1977.

As a conventionally-styled companion to the popular Mack CF fire apparatus, the R series was introduced in 1966. This R685F unit was built in 1972.

The MB fire apparatus series features two- or five-man tilt cabs, and pumps with capacities of 750 to 1,500 gallons per minute. With its comparatively short wheelbase and high degree of maneuverability, the MB is considered an excellent first-run or attack pumper.

Mack Trucks, Inc., although adversely effected by the "stag-flation" of the mid-1970's, has remained financially healthy and well in control of its basic market. In 1974 combined sales reached $995.7 million, with an after-tax net profit of $39 million, for a net profit ratio on sales of about 4%. Mack and affiliates produced 36,080 trucks, an increase of at least 27% over 1972.(23) While Mack sales reached the $1 billion level in 1975, profits were cut by over half due to the inflationary price spiral and a generally demoralized market for heavy-duty trucks following in the wake of imposition of the Federally mandated MVSS 121 brake standard.

Favorable economic conditions in 1977 found total Mack chassis deliveries world-wide reach 33,136 units, and a total sales volume of $1.3 billion. Net profit of $37 million would have been higher except for $13.8 million in special one-time adjustments to after-tax profits.(24) Income from parts sales and customer financing made new records in 1977, with every indication that record sales and earnings will also be achieved in 1978. To keep pace with the favorable business demand, Mack management has again approved a major expansion of the Hagerstown power train plant as well as Mack Western facilities. Mack is still on the grow-II!

(23) **Ibid.**, 1972, p. 9, and 1974, p. 6.

(24) **Ibid.**, 1977, pp. 10 & 13.

During the 1970's Mack products were actively sold in at least 55 countries and built in a dozen. This view shows a basic assembly operation in Venezuela, South America.

A completed Mack unit leaves the plant of Mack de Venezuela in Caracas. This operation is owned equally by local interests and Mack Trucks, Inc., and was founded in 1963.

It might be said that the sun never sets on the Mack truck! This Australian-built Model A8-FT785RS, with 5,000 gallon tank body, hauls fuel to a copper mine from the main port facility on Bougainville in the Solomon Islands.

While future Mack models are a competitive secret, this artist's rendering suggests a possible short BBC tractor with roof-mounted auxiliary radiator to help cool a power plant with extra-high horsepower.

The stars and stripes paint scheme, introduced
during 1970, is shown here on two Mack DM
models owned by a Maryland based operator.

Appendix

MODEL	PRODUCTION	TOTAL
Early Trucks		
S	1913-1917	98
T	1913-1913	1
1 ton	1909-1915	426
1½ ton	1905-1915	378
2 ton	1908-1916	557
2 ton H.T.	1905-1911	85
3 ton	1906-1916	661
4 ton	1907-1916	169
5 ton	1905-1915	344
6 ton	1910-1916	37
7½ ton	1909-1916	74
Winch	1911-1915	39
1½ ton dump	1912-1912	1
2 ton dump	1912-1913	5
3 ton dump	1908-1915	50
4 ton dump	1911-1916	9
5 ton dump	1908-1916	105
6 ton dump	1911-1916	10
7½ ton dump	1911-1916	84
Other Makes		
Hewitt	1907-1914	352
Saurer 5 ton	1912-1917	1,952
Saurer 6½ t.	1914-1918	112
Mack. Jr.	1936-1937	4,974
Prewar Trucks		
AB	1914-1936	51,613
AC	1916-1938	40,299
AD	1919-1919	1
AF	1920-1920	1
AK	1927-1936	2,819
AL	1927-1929	57
AP	1926-1938	285
BB	1928-1932	700
BC	1929-1933	1,513
BF	1931-1939	1,179
BG	1929-1937	2,904
BJ	1927-1933	1,862
BL	1929-1936	502
BM	1932-1941	3,030
BQ	1932-1937	327
BX	1932-1940	3,032
CH	1934-1941	478
CJ	1933-1941	799
QA	1939-1939	1
Early Buses		
Built in N.Y.	pre-1905	15
Various	1905-1914	142
Prewar Buses		
AB	1925-1934	3,813
AL	1926-1929	578
BC	1929-1937	411
BG	1931-1937	183
BK	1929-1934	544
BT	1931-1934	87
CD	1940-1940	1
CG	1933-1937	76
CL	1932-1937	441
CM	1939-1942	1,877
CO	1939-1942	165
CP	1942-1942	1
CQ	1934-1941	886
CT	1935-1942	574
CW	1935-1941	1,310
CX	1935-1938	50
CY	1937-1941	329
KB	1941-1942	14
L-25	1939-1941	350
LC	1940-1943	503
LD	1941-1943	371
RB	1941-1942	172
RC	1940-1942	190
Trolley Buses		
CR	1934-1943	275
FR	1937-1942	15
School Bus Chassis		
EH	1936-1939	53
EJ	1937-1938	38
Various	1938-1941	535

SD	1941-1942	10
SE	1941-1942	39
SF	1941-1942	47
SG	1941-1942	31
SH	1941-1941	3
Rail Cars		
Various	1905-1937	8
AB	1920-1931	30
ACR	1921-1923	12
ACX	1922-1925	10
AH	1923-1923	1
ACP	1925-1925	3
AS	1928-1930	4
AQ	1928-1930	9
AR	1928-1929	6
FCD	1951-1954	10
Locomotives		
AC-type	1921-1921	1
BR-SPL	1928-1928	1
12 ton	1929-1930	2
15 ton	1929-1930	8
30 ton	1929-1930	4
45 ton	1929-1929	2
60 ton	1929-1930	2
Military Vehicles		
EXBX	1940-1940	260
HT	1941-1943	3
NB	1940-1940	368
ND	1940-1940	1
NH	1940-1941	4
NJU	1941-1941	700
NM	1940-1945	7,236
NN	1942-1942	3
NO	1940-1945	2,053
NQ	1942-1942	3
NR	1940-1945	16,548
T8-T54	1945-1951	5
Various	1952-1969	8,782
Trailers		
Various	1927-1944	2,601
Fire Apparatus		
Types 19-125	1937-1955	3,240
HP	1936-1936	21
B-types	1954-1966	908
C-types	1959-1969	1,046
N-types	1960-1963	5
F-types	1965-1965	2
Later Trucks		
DE	1939-1942	2,164
EB	1936-1941	134
EC	1936-1941	123
ED	1938-1944	2,686
EE	1938-1950	9,719
EF	1938-1951	13,783
EG	1938-1950	7,349
EH	1936-1950	31,539
EJ	1937-1938	762
EM	1937-1943	1,584
EQ	1937-1950	10,661
ER	1936-1941	359
ES	1938-1940	75
ETX	1950-1950	50
FC	1936-1947	273
FG	1938-1942	162
FH	1937-1941	265
FJ	1938-1943	322
FK	1938-1941	123
FN	1940-1941	150
FP	1940-1942	365
FT	1941-1950	241
FW	1941-1949	63
LF	1940-1953	12,453
LH	1940-1953	822
LJ	1940-1956	13,931
LM	1940-1956	2,391
LP	1941-1942	55
LR	1943-1964	1,275
LT	1947-1956	2,009
LV	1948-1961	515
LW	1947-1947	1
LY	1958-1962	65
MR	1940-1942	290
NW	1941-1941	16
A20	1950-1954	2,158
A30	1950-1953	3,356
A31	1953-1953	25
A40	1950-1953	7,666

A50	1950-1953	3,319
A51	1950-1953	2,575
A52	1951-1953	100
A54	1952-1953	864
A55	1952-1953	494
Later Buses		
C-33	1948-1948	59
C-37	1948-1953	252
C-41	1945-1957	2,300
C-45	1947-1954	1,980
C-47	1953-1960	519
C-49	1954-1960	1,409
C-50	1950-1955	576
97D	1958-1958	26
ADS	1956-1956	1
MV260D	1958-1958	1
Bus Chassis		
B30	1955-1962	33
B33	1965-1965	10
B34	1953-1961	376
B35	1954-1954	10
B43	1959-1965	171
CB-Series	1941-1950	1,685
FC13	1964-1965	108
FC23	1964-1965	102
FC33	1963-1966	16
FC607B	1968-1971	118
FCR607B	1974-1974	40
FCR685B	1970-	C
FC685R	1976-	C
B-Series Trucks		
B13	1964-1965	124
B20	1953-1960	1,113
B23	1963-1965	131
B30	1953-1965	4,115
B31	1953-1960	177
B33	1955-1965	437
B37	1962-1962	1
B331	1963-1964	113
B332	1963-1963	1
B334	1963-1964	5
B41	1953-1954	220
B42	1953-1965	19,729
B43	1954-1965	1,841
B44	1955-1958	76
B45	1964-1965	142
B46	1958-1965	473
B47	1964-1965	437
B421	1954-1965	2,144
B422	1960-1965	923
B4226	1961-1964	14
B424	1961-1965	14
B426	1958-1966	221
B428	1961-1962	10
B462	1960-1965	110
B4626	1960-1960	1
B473	1956-1962	128
B50	1953-1955	233
B53	1962-1966	2,625
B57	1964-1966	281
B576	1965-1966	26
B60	1953-1963	6,357
B61	1953-1966	47,459
B62	1954-1958	1,463
B63	1954-1958	2,028
B64	1955-1958	119
B65	1955-1958	1,623
B66	1958-1965	177
B67	1957-1965	8,780
B68	1960-1966	1,503
B613	1955-1966	4,810
B615	1962-1966	575
B633	1956-1958	486
B653	1955-1958	93
B655	1955-1955	10
B673	1958-1966	176
B70	1953-1966	1,073
B71	1953-1958	522
B72	1956-1965	98
B73	1955-1966	2,520
B75	1955-1966	1,619
B77	1958-1964	113
B79	1961-1961	10
B733	1955-1966	720
B753	1955-1966	1,825
B755	1963-1966	456
B773	1957-1966	264

B80	1956-1965	368
B81	1955-1966	2,626
B83	1956-1966	1,164
B85	1956-1964	77
B86	1957-1959	5
B87	1956-1964	75
B813	1956-1966	969
B815	1963-1966	220
B833	1956-1966	216
B853	1956-1965	29
B873	1956-1966	167
B8136	1957-1966	85

Miscellaneous Trucks

C607	1963-1965	301
C609	1963-1965	1,064
C611	1963-1965	16
C615	1963-1965	208
D20	1955-1957	124
D30	1955-1958	67
D42	1955-1958	601
D44	1955-1957	40
G72	1961-1961	2
G73	1959-1962	1,116
G75	1959-1962	319
G77	1960-1962	24
G733	1959-1962	177
G753	1959-1962	502
G773	1959-1962	41
H60	1953-1954	81
H61	1952-1957	484
H62	1954-1958	64
H63	1954-1958	4,091
H64	1955-1959	16
H65	1955-1958	63
H67	1957-1962	5,954
H68	1961-1962	13
H69	1958-1962	378
H613	1956-1956	3
H628	1955-1955	2
H633	1956-1958	408
H653	1956-1957	52
H673	1958-1962	550
H693	1958-1962	55
H81	1964-1966	36
H813	1961-1964	36
H6-8WC(G.M.)	1956-1956	10
N42	1957-1962	726
N44	1958-1961	91
N60	1958-1959	83
N61	1958-1962	896
N68	1960-1961	47
N613	1957-1960	67
N422	1960-1961	32
N442	1961-1961	3
PK5RP	1967-1967	156
W71	1953-1958	215

DM-Series

DM401	1967-1973	37
DM403	1966-1969	249
DM410	1966-1970	59
DM477	1966-1971	404
DM487	1968-	C
DM491	1970-1973	73
DM492	1975-	C
DM607	1965-	C
DM6076	1966-1967	59
DM609	1966-1975	2,012
DM6096	1967-1968	18
DM611	1966-	C
DM6116	1967-1973	636
DM6118	1967-1971	26
DM612	1976-	C
DM615	1966-1971	205
DM640	1966-1967	23
DM685	1967-	C
DM6856	1967-1973	158
DM6858	1972-1972	6
DM686	1973-	C
DM807	1966-1971	172
DM809	1966-1972	527
DM811	1966-	C
DM812	1976-	C
DM815	1965-1971	478
DM819	1967-1972	75
DM823	1967-1967	4
DM831	1966-1973	157
DM833	1974-1974	1

DM837	1966-1973	182
DM845	1966-1971	65
DM847	1973-1973	2
DM861	1971-1971	1
DM863	1966-1974	543
DM865	1967-1973	25
DM866	1975-1976	9
DM867	1971-	C
DM885	1967-	C
DM886	1974-	C
DM895	1970-	C
DM897	1971-	C
DML811	1974-1976	7
DML886	1975-	C
DML895	1973-	C
DML867	1975-	C
DML897	1975-1975	2
DMM4876	1975-1975	1
DMM6116	1972-	C
DMM685	1974-	C
DMM6856	1972-	C
DMM6858	1973-1976	8
DMM686	1975-	C
DMM6866	1973-	C
HMM685	1976-	C
HMM6856	1973-	C

F-Series

F607	1962-1967	2,435
F607R	1963-1963	43
F609	1962-1967	8,692
F609R	1964-1967	20
F611	1962-1967	1,746
F611R	1967-1967	20
F615	1962-1962	14
F685	1966-1967	854
F685R	1967-1967	2
F700	1973-1973	1
F707	1968-1973	131
F709	1968-1974	94
F709R	1968-1969	17
F711	1968-	C
F711R	1968-1970	26
F712	1976-	C
F715	1962-1971	2,616
F715R	1964-1968	36
F719	1963-1970	145
F719R	1967-1967	3
F723	1965-1967	5
F726	1977-	C
F731	1962-1971	154
F733	1971-1974	141
F735	1973-	C
F737	1962-1973	1,541
F737R	1970-1970	16
F739	1968-1970	14
F741	1963-1965	8
F743	1963-1964	13
F745	1962-1964	83
F747	1972-	C
F749	1962-1964	4
F759	1963-	1
F761	1970-1974	634
F763	1963-1973	859
F763R	1970-1970	3
F765	1964-1975	51
F767	1972-	C
F769	1973-1974	23
F773	1968-	C
F785	1968-	C
F785R	1968-	C
F786	1973-	C
F786R	1975-	C
F795	1969-	C
F795R	1971-	C
F7954	1976-1976	3
F797	1971-	C
F819	1970-1970	1
F885	1973-1973	1
F8856	1971-1971	1
F8956	1973-1974	44
F897	1973-1974	5
F985	1973-1973	45
F995	1971-1973	5
F9956	1972-1976	15
F997	1973-1973	3
F9976	1973-1973	4
FM786	1977-	C

MB-Series

MB401	1963-1975	3558
MB402	1966-1967	26
MB403	1964-1968	907
MB410	1963-1970	325
MB477	1967-1971	681
MB483	1971-1974	79
MB487	1968-	C
MB491	1971-1974	365
MB492	1975-	C
MB605	1964-1966	369
MB607	1966-	C
MB609	1964-1974	705
MB611	1968-	C
MB685	1969-	C

R-Series

R401	1965-1975	990
R402	1966-1968	219
R403	1965-1969	1,376
R403R	1965-1968	95
R410	1965-1970	450
R477	1967-1970	112
R487	1968-	C
R487R	1971-	C
R489	1969-	C
R489R	1972-1972	7
R491	1971-1974	18
R492	1975-	C
R492R	1976-	C
R607	1965-	C
R607R	1968-	C
R609	1965-1976	8,039
R609R	1965-1972	429
R611	1965-	C
R611R	1966-	C
R612	1975-	C
R612R	1975-	C
R615	1965-1971	1,381
R615R	1965-1967	25
R640	1965-1967	97
R685	1967-	C
R685R	1967-	C
R686	1973-	C
R686R	1974-	C
R709	1966-1967	42
R711	1966-	C
R711R	1970-1970	30
R715	1965-1970	123
R715R	1970-1970	5
R719	1965-1970	262
R723	1967-1967	4
R731	1966-1973	112
R733	1972-1974	17
R735	1977-	C
R737	1965-1973	563
R739	1969-1971	15
R747	1972-	C
R761	1970-1974	92
R763	1965-1974	629
R767	1972-	C
R769	1975-1975	13
R770	1977-	C
R773	1967-	C
R785	1969-1972	44
R785R	1970-1970	60
R795	1970-	C
R795R	1970-	C
R797	1971-	C
R797R	1972-	C
R863R	1968-1968	4
RD487	1971-	C
RD492	1975-	C
RD607	1971-	C
RD611	1971-	C
RD612	1976-	C
RD685	1971-	C
RD686	1973-	C
RD733	1972-1972	3
RD747	1975-1975	1
RD767	1975-1976	2
RD769	1974-1975	12
RD773	1971-1974	12
RD795	1970-	C
RD797	1972-	C
RM4874	1973-	C
RM4876	1973-1975	3
RM6074	1973-1974	4

Model	Years	Units
RM6076	1975-1975	4
RM6114	1974-1974	1
RM6116	1975-1975	5
RM6126	1976-1976	1
RM685	1977-	C
RM686	1977-	C
RM685R	1975-	C
RM6854	1972-	C
RM6856	1972-	C
RM6856R	1975-	C
RM6864	1975-	C
RM6866	1974-	C
RM6866R	1976-	C
U-Series		
U401	1964-1972	138
U403	1965-1967	124
U410	1964-1969	7
U487	1973-1976	45
U492	1975-1976	2
U607	1964-	C
U609	1964-1973	2,624
U611	1965-1976	869
U612	1976-	C
U615	1964-1971	729
U626	1977-	C

Model	Years	Units
U640	1966-1966	1
U661	1970-1973	65
U685	1966-	C
U686	1973-	C
U773	1976-	C
U795	1970-1976	91
U797	1972-	C
Fire Apparatus		
CF608F	1967-1973	173
CF611F	1968-	C
CF612F	1977-	C
CF685F	1968-	C
CF686F	1973-	C
CF719F	1967-1972	14
CF795F	1971-	C
CF797F	1974-	C
MB487F	1972-	C
MB492F	1975-1976	4
MB611F	1973-	C
MB685F	1973-	C
R487F	1972-	C
R608F	1966-1973	61
R611F	1966-	C
R685F	1967-	C
R686F	1974-	C

Model	Years	Units
Off-Highway		
M15	1962-	C
M18	1961-1963	31
M20	1963-	C
M25	1961-	C
M30	1960-1969	386
M32	1963-	C
M35	1969-	C
M40	1960-1970	2
M45	1963-	C
M50	1964-	C
M60	1962-1963	2
M65	1962-	C
M70	1965-1971	21
M75	1971-	C
M100	1967-1968	3
MP404X	1976-	C
CL350ST	1976-	C
Hayward Models		
FL/FS	1965-1974	10,628
RL/RS	1967-	C
WL/WS	1975-	C

This is a composite table of domestic mack vehicle production/sales by model through 1977, based on information supplied by Mack Trucks, Inc.

'C' in the total units column denotes current models.

Credits

Permissions

The author wishes to express his appreciation for permission to quote from the following books: **Those Were The Days**, by Edward Ringwood Hewitt, copyright 1943. Reprinted by permission of Hawthorn Books, Inc. **The Way of a Transgressor**, by Negley Farson, copyright 1936. Reprinted by permission of the Estate of Negley Farson.

Photo Credits

The following individuals and organizations are thanked for providing graphic materials to help illustrate this history:

Mr. Henry Bender, San Jose, Ca.
Mr. Peter Helck, Boston Corner, N.Y.
Mr. John M. Peckham, Troy, N.Y.
Mr. Winton Pelizzoni, Allentown, Pa.
Mr. Thomas F. Schweitzer, Queens Village, N.Y.
Brockway Motor Trucks, Cortland, N.Y.
Bus & Truck Transport, Toronto, Ont., Canada
Hayes Trucks, Inc., Vancouver, B.C., Canada
Long Island Automotive Museum, Southampton, N.Y.
Mack Canada Inc., Islington, Ont., Canada
Mack Trucks, Inc., Allentown, Pa.
Rotocopy, Inc., (Photo-finishing) New York, N.Y.
Adolph Saurer, Ltd., Arbon, Switzerland
United Press International, New York, N.Y.

Index

Mack Vehicle Registry

Those people owning or knowing of a Mack vehicle (bus, fire apparatus, rail car, etc.) are asked to send the type, model and serial number to the Mack Vehicle Registry. This will help in compiling a list of many of the older Macks, and current, their where-abouts and condition for those wishing to restore and preserve this great marque.

Mack Vehicle Registry
P O Box 50046
Tucson, AZ 85703

AZTEX Corporation—Research Information

This book is part of a continuing research project. Please advise us of any additions or corrections which you come across in reading this volume. Any information, no matter how obscure or seemingly unimportant, is welcomed. In sending information, please make reference to the title and author and mail to:
Editor, AZTEX Corporation, P O Box 50046, Tucson, AZ 85703